STRANGE COVENANT

May and I had declared each other blood sisters. I turned up at her place early and went into her room to wake her. I approached May's bed but there was something else underneath the covers. A lump under the blankets moved. I reached out and flicked back the covers and a huge black crow was looking at me. I shrieked and it spread its wings. I covered my face and when I looked, the crow had taken off out the window. That was the day May disappeared.

SENSATIONAL PRAISE FOR
THE AUTUMN CASTLE

Please turn to the bac
Kim Wilkins's upcor

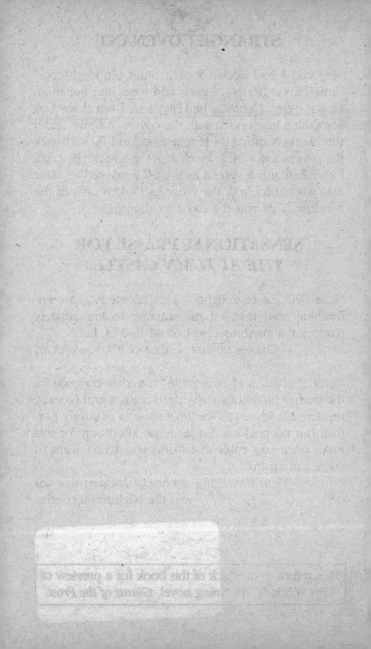

The
Autumn
Castle

KIM WILKINS

ASPECT®

NEW YORK   BOSTON

Copyright © 2003 by Kim Wilkins
Excerpt from *Giants of the Frost* copyright © 2004 by Kim Wilkins
All rights reserved. No part of this book may be reproduced in any form or by any electronic or mechanical means, including information storage and retrieval systems, without permission in writing from the publisher, except by a reviewer who may quote brief passages in a review.

The Aspect name and logo are registered trademarks of Warner Books.

Published in arrangement with HarperCollins Publishers, Australia, 25 Ryde Road, Pymble, Sydney, NSW 2073, Australia.

Cover design by Don Puckey
Cover illustration by Shasti O'Leary Soudant

Warner Books

Time Warner Book Group
1271 Avenue of the Americas, New York, NY 10020
Visit our Web site at www.twbookmark.com

Printed in the United States of America

First Paperback Printing by Warner Books: March 2005

10 9 8 7 6 5 4 3 2 1

Mirko
Alles Liebe, So Weit Der Himmel Himmel Ist

The
Autumn
Castle

PROLOGUE

— from the Memoirs of Mandy Z.

Once upon a time, a Miraculous Child was born. That night was the last of April—Walpurgis Night—on the summit of the Brocken in the Harz Mountains. It has long been thought that the devil holds court on the Brocken on such a night, but I am not a devil (for that Miraculous Child, dear reader, was me); I am the only son of the thirteenth generation of a special family. In the dim, distant past, my ancestors bred with faeries, bringing our family line infinite good fortune, but making a terrible mess of our gene pool.

My name is Immanuel Zweigler, but I am known as Mandy Z. I am an artist, renowned; I am wealthy beyond your wildest dreams, and always have been, for my family has money in obscure bank accounts in sinister places the world over. I am color-blind, truly color-blind. I see only black and white and gray, but if you wore a particularly vibrant color, perhaps a little of its warmth would seep into my field of vision and be rendered the palest sepia. But I have an extraordinary sense of smell, and an extraordinary sense of touch. That is why I like to sculpt.

You may wonder why someone so miraculous has waited

until the age of forty-eight to commence his memoir. Simply, it had never occurred to me to do so, but then the British journalist came to interview me. He was a genial man. We had a good conversation and then I left him with the view from my west windows while I went upstairs to fetch a photograph— I always insist on providing my own photographs to be published with interviews. I was rummaging in the drawer of my desk in my sculpture room, a room I prefer to keep private, when I heard the British journalist clear his throat behind me.

"You should not have followed me in here," I said.

"This is extraordinary," he replied, advancing toward my latest sculpture.

Ah, the beautiful thing, so white and gleaming with gorgeous curves and ghastly crevices.

"It's called the Bone Wife," I told him as he ran his fingers over her hips (she only exists below the waist at present). I was amused because he didn't know what he was touching.

"Are you going to finish her?" he asked, gesturing to where her face would be.

"Oh yes. Though some would say she is the perfect woman just as she is."

He didn't laugh at my joke. "What medium are you using?"

"Bones."

His fingers jumped off as though scalded. "Not human bones?"

I smiled and shook my head. "Of course not."

So he returned to his examination, confident that these were the bones of unfortunate sheep and pigs, and then I gave him his photos and asked him to leave. I sat for a long time looking at my Bone Wife, and mused about my continued disappointment in how I am represented by the world's media, and about how so much of what I do can never be made public. I wanted to read about a version of myself that I recognized, even if I had to write it with my own pen; and that's when I decided upon a memoir. I decided to celebrate me. Miraculous me.

Not human bones?

No. The thought is as repulsive to me as it was to the British journalist. As is the thought of animal bones; I bear no grudge against our four-legged companions. Not human bones, not animal bones. A rarer medium: faery bones. The bones of faeries I have killed.

Because, you see, I have a measureless loathing for faeries. And I am the Faery Hunter.

PART ONE

There is nobody at home. Autumn fills the rooms;
Moonbright sonata
And the awakening at the edge of the twilit forest.
                        "Hohenburg," *Georg Trakl*

The water started to boil, and the flesh fell away
from the bones, so he took the bones out and put
them on the slab; he knew not, however, in which
order they should go, and arranged everything in
a big muddle.
            "Brother Lustig," *Jacob and Wilhelm Grimm*

CHAPTER ONE

Please don't make me remember, please don't make me remember. Inevitable, however. Christine had known from the moment the man had glanced at her business card, his eyebrows shooting up.

"Starlight. That's an unusual surname."

"Mm-hm."

"You're not any relation to Alfa and Finn Starlight? The seventies pop stars?"

Pop stars! Her parents had considered themselves musicians, poets, artists. "Yeah, I'm their daughter." Amazingly, her voice came out smooth, almost casual. She didn't need this today; she was already feeling unaccountably melancholy.

"Oh. Oh, I'm so . . ."

"Sorry?"

"Yes. Yes, I'm very sorry."

Because he knew, as most people did, that Alfa and Finn Starlight had died in a horrific car accident from which their teenage daughter had been the only survivor. Suddenly there was no point in resisting anymore: she was back there. The English Bookshop on Ludwigkirchplatz, its long shelves and neat carpet squares, spun down to nothing in her perception; it was all blood and metal and ground glass and every horror that those evil, stubborn thirty-five seconds of consciousness had forced her to witness.

"I'm sorry too," she said. Her lower back twinged in sympathy with the remembrance. She wouldn't meet the man's gaze, trying to discourage him. He was pale and clean-shaven, had a South African accent, and was clearly battling with his impulses. On the one hand, he was aware it was rude—maybe even distressing for her—to keep asking about the accident; on the other hand, he was talking with a real-life survivor of a famous and tragic legend. Christine was used to this four seconds of struggle: enthusiasm versus compassion. Compassion never won.

"When was that again? 1988?" he asked.

"1989," Christine replied. "November."

"Yes, of course. My sister cried for days. She'd always had a crush on Finn."

"I think a lot of women did."

"He was a good-looking man, and your mother was beautiful too."

Christine smiled in spite of herself, wondering if the man was now pondering how such stunning parents had managed to produce such an ordinary-looking child.

"One thing I've always wanted to know," he said, leaning forward.

Christine braced herself. Why couldn't she ever tell these people to leave her alone? Why had she never developed that self-preserving streak of aggression that would shut down his questions, lock up her memories. "Yes?"

"You were in a coma for eight weeks after the accident."

"Yes."

"The kid who ran you off the road didn't stop."

"No."

"And there were no witnesses."

"That's right."

"Then how did they find him and convict him?"

Yes, her back was definitely twinging now, a horrid legacy of the accident, the reason November 1989 was never really consigned to the past, to that cold night and that long tunnel. Her doctor back home would tell her that these twinges were psychosomatic, triggered by the memory. She had no idea what the word for "psychosomatic" was in German, and the doctor she had seen twice since her arrival in Berlin two months ago was happy to prescribe painkillers without too much strained bilingual conversation.

"I was conscious for about half a minute directly after the accident," she explained. "The kid who hit us stopped a second, then took off. I got his license plate, I wrote it on the dash."

"Really?" He was excited now, privy to some new juicy fact about the thirteen-year-old story. Many details had been withheld from the press because the driver of the other car was a juvenile. The law had protected him from the barrage of media scrutiny, while Christine had suffered the full weight of the world's glare.

"I'm surprised you could collect yourself to find a pen, under the circumstances," he continued. "It must have been traumatic."

Oh, yes. Her father crushed to death; her mother decapitated. Christine smiled a tight smile; time to finish this conversation. "If you phone at the end of the week, we should be able to give you an estimated due date for that book. It's a rare import, so it could take a number of months."

He hesitated. Clearly, he had a lot of other questions. Chief among them might be why the heir to the Starlight fortune was working as a shop assistant in an English-language bookshop in Berlin.

"All right, then," the man said. "I'll see you when I come to pick it up."

Christine nodded, silently vowing to make sure she was out back checking invoices when he returned.

He headed for the door, his footsteps light and carefree, and not weighed down with thirteen years of chronic pain, thirteen years of nightmares about tunnels and blood, thirteen years of resigned suffering. A brittle anger rose on her lips.

"By the way," she called.

He turned.

"I didn't have a pen," she said.

"Pardon?"

Had he forgotten already? Was that how much her misery meant to anybody else? "In the car, after the accident," she said. "You were right, I was too traumatized to find a pen."

His face took on a puzzled aspect. "Then how . . . ?"

Christine held up her right index finger. "My mother's blood," she said. "Have a nice day."

❧

Gray. Black. Brown. No matter which way Christine surveyed it, this painting of Jude's looked like every other painting he had ever done. "It's beautiful, darling."

He lifted her hair and kissed the back of her neck. She pondered the colors, Jude's colors of choice as long as she'd known him. She often wondered if his preferences bore any relation to the reasons he was attracted to her. Jude was alternative art's pinup boy, with a wicked smile, a tangle of blond hair, and sparkling dark eyes. Christine, by contrast, knew she was profoundly forgettable. She was thin but not sleek, pale but not luminous, her brown hair was thick but not shiny; and with her button eyes, flat cheeks, and snub nose she possessed not even the distinction of ugliness.

No matter how hard she tried to be good-natured and generous and kind, Christine knew that she was cursed with invisibility.

"What's it called?" she asked him.

"*Urban Autumn,*" he said, dropping her hair. "You really like it?"

"Of course."

Jude stood back and smiled at the painting. "Today's the first day of fall," he said. "It's kind of a tribute."

"First day of fall?"

"On the pagan calendar, according to Gerda. Except she calls it autumn."

"Perhaps that explains why I'm feeling so odd. Summer's gone, winter's on its way."

He turned to her, concern crossing his face. "What's the matter? You sound kind of melancholy."

She sighed. "I am melancholy. Don't know why."

"Is your back giving you trouble?" His hand dropped to the small of her back and pressed it gently. This was the locus of the chronic pain that—unbelievably—she was still not used to after so many years.

"No more than usual." She thought about the twinges she'd felt while talking about her parents' accident.

"Nothing else bothering you?"

There was, but she could barely articulate it. Fuzzy memories of her childhood, a recurring half-remembrance about a crow she had seen once, a fluttering buzzing anxiety lacing everything, a breath caught perpetually in her throat. "I don't think so. I guess being back here reminds me of . . . happier times."

He smiled and folded her into his arms and she tried to take solace in his beating heart—

He doesn't love you as much as you love him.

—and to put aside all her irrational feelings.

"Hey, love pigeons!"

Jude released Christine and she turned to the door of the studio. Gerda stood there, shaking her head so her blond dreadlocks bounced around her shoulders. "You guys are always smooching."

"Can't help ourselves," Jude said, shrugging.

"We're on our way out," Gerda said. "Coming?"

"Who's 'we'?" Christine asked.

"All of us. Me, Pete, Fabiyan. Shall we make it a Hotel Mandy-Z outing?"

"Yeah, cool," Jude said, "just don't ask Mandy."

Gerda giggled; nobody genuinely liked their wealthy benefactor. "If we run into him downstairs in the gallery we won't have much of a chance of losing him. Coming now?"

"No, give me a half-hour to get cleaned up." Jude indicated his shirt, which was splattered with brown paint.

"We'll be at Super Jazz on Chausseestrasse. It's just been voted the smokiest club in Europe."

"I'll bring my gas mask," Christine joked.

"Yeah, yeah, I'll convert you yet, Miss Starlight," Gerda said. "You can't be the only person in the hotel who doesn't smoke." With a cheery wave she disappeared. Jude had turned back to his painting.

"I want to give it another fifteen minutes," he said, picking up his brush. His eyes were taking on a distracted gaze.

"I'll wait upstairs." She'd lost him; until he came back from wherever it was in his head he went when he was painting, he was no longer hers. She glanced at him as she left the studio: his right shoulder was flexed, his hair fell over his eye as he touched the brush delicately, carefully to the canvas. As long as he was happy, his painting was a mistress Christine was prepared to tolerate.

Two hours had passed before they arrived at Super Jazz, and by then the others were all drunk. Mandy was not with them, to Christine's relief. She found Immanuel Zweigler the most loathsome being she had ever met. He was a tall, corpulent man with pinkish skin and pale watery eyes. He dyed his hair black, but ginger roots peeked through, conspiring with his ginger eyebrows to give him away. He usually smelled of the heavy incense he burned in his upstairs rooms, where he also wandered around naked and didn't care who came to the door; Gerda had already reported popping in to borrow coffee and getting an eyeful she'd never forget. But it was none of these things—his appearance or his habits—that Christine despised. It was some other ineffable malignancy that washed off him, some calculating miserliness or inhuman detachment, that made her lean away whenever he spoke to her.

"Drink for you?" This was Fabiyan, the Belarusian sculptor who lived across the hall from them. He had to yell over the band playing loud Miles Davis in the corner. Jude slid onto the sofa next to Gerda, and Christine took the seat opposite.

"Beck's," Christine said.

"Beck's!" Gerda exclaimed as Fabiyan went to the bar. "You're so predictable."

"I'm living in the capital of Germany," Christine responded. "It's only right I should drink German beer."

"Berlin's not the capital of Germany," Gerda said, waving her cigarette effusively, "it's the capital of the world."

Every year in summer, four new artists took up residence at Hotel Mandy-Z for their twelve-month Zweigler Fellowships. This year they were Jude Honeychurch, New York's hottest young thing with a paintbrush, fresh from an immensely successful West Chelsea exhibition; Gerda Ekman, an ebullient Swede who worked in metal and stone; Pete Searles, a nineteen-year-old Australian who put together bizarre video and multimedia installations that required warnings about epilepsy; and Fabiyan Maranovich, first time out of Belarus where he had spent his life working as an electrician. Christine had a soft spot for Fabiyan especially. He had conscientiously learned German before taking up his fellowship, only to find that English was the linguistic currency at Hotel Mandy-Z. He was picking it up quickly, but sometimes Christine had to translate for him into German. Not that her German was faultless, but she had lived here briefly in the seventies with her parents and a refresher course taken over the spring left her with a better grasp than the rest.

"So," Gerda said to Jude, snaking her arm around his shoulders, "I like your painting. Nearly finished, is it?"

"Nearly."

"You must be so proud of him, Christine," Gerda said, smiling her Cheshire-cat smile.

"Yes, I am."

Fabiyan leaned down and handed Christine a beer. She sipped it gratefully, then rested it on the scarred table. If she were to be totally honest, she didn't think much of anybody's art in the hotel. All those abstract, impenetrable shapes and images. It baffled her far more than it delighted her. But she was perfectly willing to admit she wasn't an expert and she hadn't the faintest idea about what artists felt or intended, even after four years with Jude.

Pete, who sat next to her, pointed at her beer and said, "Did you know that Germans drink around 127 liters of beer per person per year?"

"No, I did not know that." Christine smiled. She was discovering that Pete had an endless store of facts and figures. He had been lauded as a genius since he was twelve, and perhaps that meant he had never outgrown some of his adolescent obsessions.

"It's topped only by the Czechs, who drink 160 liters."

"What's that in pints, Pete?" Jude asked.

Pete looked skyward briefly, did the math, then returned with, "About 336."

Jude doubled over with laughter, deep lines arrowing out from his eyes. She loved his smile, the gorgeous changeability of his expression. His face settled smooth again as he got serious about the business of lighting a cigarette.

"I don't know how many liters they piss every day though," Pete added in a solemn tone.

Gerda, as she did so often, looked at Pete with an expression bordering on alarm. She hadn't caught the rhythms of his humor yet. Jude glanced across at Christine and winked; she felt herself smile and blush like a teenager. She downed more beer and began to shed the day's despondency.

The first band finished and the second came on—Duke Ellington in thick German accents. Christine grew drunk but Gerda was always drunker. Sometime around two A.M., while Pete, Jude, and Fabiyan were making enthusiastic conversation with Sparky, the club owner, Gerda pulled Christine down next to her on the sofa.

"Here, here," she said, trying to shove a lit cigarette in Christine's mouth.

"No, really. I'll be sick."

"You're the luckiest girl in the world," Gerda said, reaching for her drink and missing by at least six inches. "Oops."

"Yeah, I know." Christine and Gerda had had this conversation before. Gerda had a big crush on Jude, but then, Gerda had a big crush on every second man she met.

"He's so beautiful. Why couldn't he turn up on my doorstep?" Then Gerda laughed, because that was exactly how Christine had met Jude. He had been sitting on the stairs in front of her West Twenty-third Street home, trying to read a badly drawn map directing him to a gallery party.

"Don't despair. You and Garth might work things out," Christine said.

Garth was Gerda's husband back in Stockholm. He had refused to come with her to Berlin. Gerda was shaking her head. "No, never. You just keep your eye on Jude, Miss Starlight. I'll steal him the first opportunity I get."

"You'd better not. I don't know where I'd find another one just like him."

Gerda waved her hand dismissively. "Impossible, of course. He'd never look at another woman."

Christine knew this was true. Her silly jealousies had so often been directed at a paintbrush, never at a person. But it was nice to hear someone else say it. "Do you think so?"

"Darling, he's always got his hands all over you. He never lets you out of his sight. It's damn frustrating. Look at my tits, they're wonderful—not like your tiny little things—but he's never looked at them once."

Christine laughed loudly, then said, "Well, thank you for being so reassuring. You know, he's so gorgeous, and with the age difference and all . . ."

Gerda scoffed. "Three years? It's nothing. He's twenty-eight, not eighteen. But don't worry . . . if I ever see another woman making a move on him, I'll do everything in my power to keep her away. Lie, cheat, steal, whatever."

"That's very sweet," Christine said, giving her a squeeze.

Gerda lit another cigarette. "So, what's up with you lately, Miss Starlight? You seem a bit blue. It's not just the pain in your back, is it?"

Christine shook her head, her eyes darting off to locate Jude. He was on the other side of the room, a cigarette jammed between his lips, drawing a shape in the air with his hands for Sparky, who laughed enormously.

"What's it all about? Not Jude?"

"No, not Jude." Christine shrugged. "Autumn, I guess. Gray skies, winter coming."

"Bullshit. It's more than that."

She tore her eyes away from Jude and met Gerda's gaze. "It's weird, Gerda. Just the last few days I've been feeling on edge. Like something's about to happen. And I keep having these flashes of old memories, things I haven't thought about in years."

"Like what? Stuff to do with your parents?"

"No, actually. You know we lived here in the seventies, but not here, not in the East. Berlin was still divided. We had a big house out at Zehlendorf. My best friend was the English girl who lived next door. A cute little redhead. I keep thinking about her, and then the memory gets all caught up with something else which I can't put my finger on. Something to do with a crow I saw once . . ." She trailed off, realizing what she said made no sense.

"A crow?"

"Yeah, I know it sounds nuts."

"No, not at all. What was her name? The little girl?"

"Miranda. Her father was an English soldier, Colonel Frith. But nobody ever called her Miranda; we always called her Little May."

"What else?" Gerda prompted. "Just these memories, this feeling of anxiety?"

Christine reached for her near-empty beer bottle, and swished the contents around halfheartedly. "She was murdered," she said.

"Really?"

"Abducted from her bedroom one night. God knows what awful things she . . . They never found her."

"That's sad."

"Yeah."

"So it's no wonder it gives you a bad feeling to think of her."

"I guess so." She drained her glass. "Only, it's not just an ordinary bad feeling. It's dread, and it's half-remembrance, and it's a weird foreboding about that bird and trying to remember where I saw it."

Gerda snapped her fingers, her eyes round and bright. "A ghost!" she said. "Christine, maybe Little May is haunting you."

"Huh?" Christine adjusted her frame of reference quickly. Gerda had a strong interest in spirits and crystals and psychic powers, and conversations with her often took this turn.

"Yes, it makes sense. She died all those years ago, when you were here as a child. Maybe she's been wandering on the earthly plane all this time, and now you're back she's attached herself to you."

"I don't know, Gerda. I'm more likely to think it's a change-of-seasons melancholy."

Gerda shrugged. "Believe what you like. Do you want another drink?"

Christine looked at her empty beer, then nodded. "Yeah, a big one."

She watched Gerda go to the bar. The band was still playing, Jude was still talking in the corner, the air was blue and thick with smoke and conversation. But she felt lonely and isolated and strangely afraid, and it had something to do with a twenty-five-year-old blurred memory of black wings.

CHAPTER TWO

from the Memoirs of Mandy Z.

I first conceived of the Bone Wife as a child of eight in Bremen. My mother had taken me to a traveling exhibit of puppets, dolls, and automatons in the town square. I had always been, and continue to be, overly interested in contraptions, inventions, gadgets with wheels and cogs. The exhibit was set up in the shadow of the Dom—its dark spires pointing toward the broad sky—on a summer afternoon that stretched on for miles. I wandered between the exhibits, clutching my mother's fingers in one hand, and a sticky ice cream in the other. Such an array of painted faces: some plain with round black eyes and pointed noses, some so garishly colorful that even I could sense their brightness; clown faces, girl faces, boy faces, cat faces, elephant faces; spindly legs, silk feet, straw-stuffed arms, antique lace, and stiff linen. I was swept away by the sea of ghastly wooden smiles and laughing fur eyebrows. One doll in particular caught my eye as it was the exact image of my mother, but without her stern hairstyle and clothes. This little doll had perfect ringlets and a pretty frilled dress. Oh, I cried for that doll!

"Mama," I said (in German, of course, as it is my native language), "if you do not buy that doll for me I shall die."

"Nonsense," she replied, dragging me farther into the exhibit.

She did not understand that I needed to possess it, to have a version of my mother with pretty curls and a frilly dress. I hated her for dragging me away from it. We stopped in front of a display of an automaton, which from the front looked like an ordinary doll but from the back was a mass of whirring wheels and gears. The doll's owner—a hefty, mustachioed man dressed like a nineteenth-century traveling salesman—wound it, and the doll began to bounce up and down, its arms scissoring through the air and its head bobbing, its mouth articulating silent words. Then the mustachioed man placed a peanut on the table in front of it, and the doll bent down to pick it up. It was the most amazing thing I had ever seen and all the way home to our farmhouse at Niederbüren I pictured that automaton over and over, and in my mind the face of the mother-doll became imposed over it, for it was often that I had seen my mother pick up the objects that my father and I left behind us when we had tired of them.

I secluded myself in my bedroom that evening, drawing plans for a mother-doll. A life-size automaton shaped like a woman, who could pick up my toys and could not speak. That, I thought, would be the perfect wife for me. I was not interested in women then, and I'm not now. Don't make the mistake of thinking that I am interested in men either. I have never experienced the faintest twinge of the sexual urges with which the rest of the world is obsessed. I believe it to be a legacy of the genetic damage suffered by our family, and I have never envied the passions of others, as they too often lead to vulnerability.

I shelved my plans for a mother-doll or a wife-doll, partly

because I was a mere boy with no idea how to build an automaton, but also because soon after this occasion I saw my first faery, and it had such a profound effect upon me that most childish thoughts were permanently driven from my mind.

My parents had told me about faeries, and about the special connection our family had with them. I had taken for granted that one day I would meet one, and perhaps thank him or her for our good fortune. I imagined they would look like the faeries in the books in my bedroom: tiny people with little wings and sparkly eyes. I didn't know then, as I do now, about the many different breeds of faeries and how vastly they differ from one another; the complexities of their bodies that I now understand so intimately.

On this day, on the day I saw a faery for the first time, I was playing with my toy boat in a puddle on the banks of the Weser. It was the first fine day in a week, and the grass and trees were clean, washed. I was concentrating hard on the boat in front of me. In my imagination, I was making an Atlantic crossing. A shadow fell across me and I looked up to see a man smiling at me.

"Hello," he said, "that's a nice boat."

My body had never before performed such a complex reaction to the mere sight and voice of another being. My eyes dilated, my skin grew warm, my body felt stiff, and a fist of nausea pushed up inside me. I opened my mouth to scream, and only a low groan came out.

"What's the matter?" he asked. "Don't be afraid." And then he knelt down across the puddle from me and reached out to touch my boat. I could smell him then, I could smell his bones deep under his skin, and such a thrill of revulsion shuddered through me that I felt I might actually lose control of my body, that I might explode or die. Instead, I took a deep breath and called at the top of my lungs, "Mama!"

The stranger stood immediately and took two steps back. "I didn't mean to frighten you," he said.

"Mama!"

But it was my father who heard my calls and emerged from the house, peering across the narrow road at me. "Immanuel?"

"Immanuel," the stranger said. "That's a fine name."

I sprang to my feet and ran to my father, locked his right leg between my arms and buried my face in his soft stomach. "Papa, that man is strange," I managed to say. Then I heard the stranger's voice. He had followed me.

"I didn't mean to frighten him," he said in a soft, tender voice.

Then my father's voice, rumbling deep in his stomach. "Oh, you're a faery. That's why he's frightened. He's never met one before."

Now I looked around, glared up at the stranger. So this was what a faery looked like. I was disappointed and disgusted. While he was near me, I felt as though my skin might be sick.

"How do you know?" the stranger said.

"My family knew faeries. In 1570 the first child of that union was born."

The faery's eyebrows arched upward, and I marveled that such a revolting being could look and move so much like a normal human. "Really?"

"So you see, Immanuel," Papa said, "there's nothing to be afraid of."

The faery reached out to me, and I spat on his hand. "Don't you touch me, you foul creature."

My father gave me a hard smack on the side of the head and apologized to the faery.

"I should leave," the faery said. "I don't want to distress the child further."

He walked off, and I tried not to think about the obscene bones and joints that moved under that skin.

"What was all the fuss?" said my father.

"I could smell his bones."

"The faeries are our friends."

"I feel sick. I hate the faeries, they make me sick."

"Their bones gleam like silver. I'm sure they don't smell bad."

Gleam like silver! I wanted to open up the faery and see such a bone. Carve away the layers of flesh and muscle and discover the grand secret inside. It made me quiet, and Papa thought that his reprimand had touched me. He fetched my boat and brought me inside.

Despite the sunny days that followed, I spent all my time in the corner of my room with my drawing pad. I drew dozens upon dozens of pictures. Pictures of the faery, whose eyes were dead crosses, with flaps of his skin peeled back to reveal shining bones. Pictures of the bones with tiny sparks drawn around to indicate the gleam of precious metal. Pictures of the bones emerging, as if spontaneously, from the faery's mutilated body. Pictures of body parts, half-stripped to reveal the surprise within, like the silver coin in a plum pudding. Drawing the pictures provided me with an addictive sensation of relief. Such an ache would well up inside me just thinking about the faery and the odd smell of his bones that the only way to feel relaxed and peaceful again was to imagine him divested of those bones.

When my mother found these pictures, I was pulled by the ear to appear before my father and my grandfather and answer for my sins. She waved the sheaf of drawings in front of them, and their mouths became little circles of shock.

One by one, in the white sterility of the room, their faces loomed in front of me.

"Immanuel, no," Papa said, "you are not to think such things about the faeries."

Opa, who was a terrifyingly large man with a white beard and gleaming eyes, grabbed my upper arms in his strong hands and shook me. "You rotten little scoundrel! You evil boy! Why do you think we have so much money? Why do you think you live in a giant farmhouse with every toy you could ever want? It's because of the faeries."

"You must put every one of these ideas out of your head," Papa said, brandishing the drawings.

"You must respect the faeries."

"We have our good fortune because of them," Mama said. "You owe them gratitude and love."

But no matter how long they nagged and bullied me, no matter how many clips around the head and bruising shakings they gave me, I knew the opposite was true.

I owed the faeries only contempt. I owed them only my sincerest hatred.

The afternoon air bit cold as Christine walked home from Friedrichstrasse Station, vainly pulling her cardigan tighter. Of course, she could have taken the U-bahn down to Oranienburger Tor, which was much closer, but underground travel was something she avoided at all times. Thirteen years of bad dreams about tunnels meant an obsessive frostiness stole over her skin every time she approached an underground space.

Her back ached in hot buzzes. It had been a bad day. Busy and tiring, and the continual stress of those half-forgotten memories haunting her as though they were desperately important. As she crossed Weidendammer Bridge, she scratched at her left thumb. It had become irritated around lunchtime and now an itchy red blotch had spread across its tip. She paused, leaning on the bridge railing above the pale gray Spree, and examined her thumb. An old memory fought back toward her and she shook her head in wonder. This was too weird. May Frith had disappeared nearly twenty-five years ago, but her memory was alive in Christine's body. At seven, after reading a cowboy story together (May was a precocious reader), they had decided to become blood sisters. They had each pricked their thumbs, then smeared the tiny drops of blood together. Christine touched the spot now, and it prickled gently. Surely coincidence. Surely she had received a tiny paper cut during the day, and it had grown inflamed. She put the tip of her thumb in her mouth and sucked it delicately; thought she could faintly taste blood.

"I'm going nuts from the pain," she muttered to herself, turning and heading home.

Hotel Mandy-Z was a gently crumbling, late nineteenth-century apartment building on Vogelwald-Allee, a dead-end street that dipped into an enormous storm drain and a square of green behind Friedrichstrasse. It had once been the head office of an Asian travel agency, but the Reisebüro sign had been painted over in gray (she could still see the letters faintly underneath) and "Hotel Mandy-Z" had been added in gold by one of 1998's Zweigler Fellows. She let herself into the tiny lobby, checked the mail, dashed past the gallery door so Mandy wouldn't see her, then proceeded upstairs. The gallery was situated on the lower floor with the studios, Gerda and Pete lived across the hall from each other on the first floor, and Jude and Fabiyan on the second. The third, fourth, and attic were Mandy's.

Christine unlocked the apartment door and called out, "Jude?"

"In here."

Christine looked around as she closed the door behind

her. Jude had cleaned the entire apartment. The kitchen gleamed, the ashtrays were empty, the tables were free of the usual piles of books and papers. Jude had clearly had a bad day too. When he couldn't paint, he cleaned. Obsessively.

She followed his voice to the main bedroom, where he was smoothing the covers over.

"I washed the sheets," he said.

"Bad painting day?"

He stood up and sighed. "Awful. Didn't feel like I was painting at all, just putting marks on the canvas."

She reached down to help him with the corner of the duvet, pulled a muscle in her back and winced.

"Christine?" he said, approaching her.

"Bad-back day too," she said, lowering herself onto the bed. "Maybe I'll just stay here."

"Can I get you anything?"

"Sit down a minute."

He sat next to her; she held up her thumb. "Can you see that spot?"

He peered closely. "Yeah. What is it? An insect bite?"

"I don't know. It itches really badly." She sighed and lay back on the bed. Jude leaned over her and kissed her forehead.

"Jude, I think I'm going crazy."

He smoothed her hair. "No, you're not. You're just adjusting to a new city."

"It's not new for me." She held up her thumb again. "When I was seven, out at Zehlendorf, I pricked this thumb—right where that red spot is—and became blood sisters with the girl next door."

He smiled. "That's a long incubation period for an infection." His teeth were slightly crooked. That was something she loved about him. A lot of her friends back home were getting their teeth bleached and capped, giving them all the sterile, homogeneous look of movie stars.

She gently punched his arm. "Don't make fun."

"I'd never make fun."

"The thing is, Jude, I can't stop thinking about her. It's like an obsession. It's like my mind keeps throwing her name back at me . . . her face."

"Maybe you should try to find her."

Christine shook her head. "She was kidnapped. It was one of the reasons my parents left Berlin. She was taken right from her bed, from her house." And there was some connection with a crow . . .

"Did they ever find her?"

"No. She was probably raped and tortured and killed. Poor little kid."

"Maybe you never got to process that trauma because you left Berlin behind. Maybe being back here is stirring it all up again." He patted her shoulder. "You'll be fine. It'll pass in a few weeks."

"I hope so."

"Want me to bring you a couple of painkillers?"

She propped herself up on her elbows. "Yeah, and a notebook and a pen."

Jude kissed her again. "You wait right here."

A few minutes later he returned. She dutifully swallowed the two tablets he held out for her, and took the notebook and pen.

"What are you writing?" he asked.

"I'm trying to solve a mystery."

"A mystery? About the little girl?"

"No. About a crow."

He shook his head. "I'll leave you to it. I might go wait in the studio with a paintbrush in my hand, see if the Muse drops by." He backed out of the room and closed the door. A couple of moments later, she heard the apartment door shut behind him.

Christine rested the notebook on her knees and wrote, "May Frith."

Then underneath she listed as many things as she could remember about the little girl: her hair and eye color, her father's name, her mother's name, the colors of her bedroom, her favorite toy. And then it started to emerge—ever, ever faintly—the memory of the black wings and the window and . . . No, it was gone again.

"Crow," she wrote, and circled it. The painkillers were starting to do their work, and she grew heavy-limbed and sleepy. She put the notebook aside and closed her eyes, trying to force her mind down long-locked corridors of memory. As she drifted to sleep, a flash dashed through her mind and disappeared: wings beating, a little girl shrieking, the wide world outside a window.

🐦

Christine woke in the dark. But not completely dark. The blinds were still open, and the light of a nearby street lamp cast a pale glow on the bed. She was disoriented: still in her work clothes, not under the covers, blinds not drawn. Then she remembered taking the painkillers. Her watch said it was eleven o'clock. Jude was not asleep next to her. She rolled over and eased herself out of bed.

"Jude?" she called, opening the bedroom door a crack and peering out. Not there. Probably in the studio still, finally painting something.

Her back felt marginally better. She stretched up, felt a twinge. She carefully put one foot in front of the other and made it to the kitchen, where she poured a glass of water to drink by the light of the open fridge.

Starving. She hadn't eaten since lunchtime. She crouched

to inspect the contents of the fridge and found some leftover spaghetti. Jude probably hadn't eaten either. Perhaps she could make them both some dinner and take it down to the studio. She grabbed the bowl and backed up.

Bang!

Jude, in his housecleaning frenzy, had moved the table. Its corner struck the small of Christine's back, sending a shooting barb of pain deep inside her spine. The bowl jumped out of her hands and crashed to the floor. Her fingers went to her back, searching vainly for the place to switch off the awful pain. A hot gush of white noise swept past her ears, making her head spin. Oh, no, she was going to black out. Her body wasn't able to process the pain, was choosing oblivion instead. She felt for the table, tried to hold herself up, heard a twisted groan that she barely recognized as her own. A whoosh of fluttering wings battered her head. The world went white; then gray; then, finally, black.

CHAPTER THREE

*R*elief. *Instant, marvelous, floating relief.*
   I must be dead.

Because never, in the past thirteen years, had she been completely without the pain. She savored it, the loose drifting freedom in her back. Relief, glorious relief. It was overwhelming and intoxicating and—

Wait a minute. Where the hell am I?

Christine opened her eyes and was dazzled by golden slanted sunshine. A canopy of trees stretched above her, their leaves stained with the tawny streaks of autumn. She lay on a bed of leaves; the world smelled damp and earthy.

This must be a dream: she had blacked out and slipped into a dream. But could that be right? She had been unconscious a number of times in her life and had never dreamed, not even in her long coma. Unless she had dreamed and hadn't remembered on waking. The thought struck her heart sadly: to know such pleasure yet not remember was tragic.

She sat up, determined to memorize everything. But the forest yielded more details than she could commit to memory. This dream landscape was perfectly realistic. For a startled moment, Christine wondered if she had somehow strayed down to a remote corner of the Tiergarten in her stupor, and fallen asleep among the leaves. But no, the trees were too vast and the air was too quiet.

A flutter in the branches behind her caught her attention. She peered into the dark, but could see nothing. An instant later, the fluttering approached from her left. She cried out as a shining black crow swooped down and plucked at her scalp. Cowering under her hands, she waited for it to return. But it settled on a branch nearby, gazing at her, one of her long brown hairs in its beak. Christine rubbed her head. Why did that hurt, when her back didn't? The bird spread its wings and took off. This was the most vivid dream she had ever experienced.

She rose, reveling in the easy movement. The trees thinned out a few hundred feet in the distance so she headed in that direction, walking a few paces and then running, a laugh on her lips. The trees parted and she emerged in a rocky ravine, bathed in golden light. Across the slope was a path, leading her eye up to . . .

A crooked little castle.

"My God!" she exclaimed, laughing. Its slender twisted turrets, long, fluttering flags, and curved stone walls hovered in the distant golden mist of setting sun. What an imagination she had. If Jude had dreams like this, he'd never have painter's block again. Then she smiled to herself. Jude could dream this and still he would paint monochrome abstracts.

She picked her way over the slope toward the path. It was difficult; she was still wearing the black dress she had worn to work that day, and her feet were bare. A pair of dream-shoes and dream-jeans and a more level dream-ground would have been useful. A rancid smell wafted toward her. She turned her head but saw nothing behind her. She walked on. She was nearly at the path when she glanced up and saw that she was about to drop a bare foot into a stinking mess of rotted flesh.

She shrieked and scrambled back, falling onto her buttocks. A pig, it was just a pig. Dead, eyeless, its stinking flesh black and the ground beneath it stained.

A light *click-click* sounded behind her. She turned. The crow again. A shudder moved through her body as she imagined it plucking out the dead pig's eyes. She got to her feet, shaking and confused. She had fallen down and felt no irritation of her old injury, so she must be dreaming. But everything seemed so real and fluid, not at all like the surreal and disjointed images she was used to in dreams. A thread of panic wormed into her stomach.

Just be calm. Maybe unconscious people dream differently than sleeping people.

The crow cricked its head to gaze at her, its golden eyes wary. She headed off toward the path, trying not to look at the dead pig. It would be really good to wake up now, to be back in the apartment with the broken spaghetti bowl.

But she banished the thought as soon as it occurred to her. A return to the apartment was a return to the pain and, oh, it was going to be excruciating after that bruising she'd taken against the corner of the table. No, she would stay a while in this pain-free world; enjoy the relief if not the scenery.

She checked on the crow and was startled to see a wolf sitting where the bird had been. She swallowed a shriek.

"Okay . . ." she said to the large gray creature. "I know this is just a dream, and it's my dream, so you can just get lost. I don't want you in my dream."

And then it spoke to her: opened its mouth and said something. Not English and not German—or, at least, not any version of German she recognized—and she took comfort in that. Dream gibberish, at last.

"Yeah, whatever, Mr. Wolf. Just stay away."

She wished she hadn't left the forest. Everything had been fine in the forest. She warily glanced at the path, and saw two figures with a cart and horse. The wolf wasn't following her. She picked her way toward them.

"*Vienc si!*" This was the wolf, calling out behind her.

Christine turned. "I don't understand," she said.

"*Vienc si!*" he said, but she realized he wasn't talking to her at all. He was calling to the men with the cart.

She whirled around to see them running toward her. They wore plain brown tunics, belted in the middle, and peculiar woolen hats. Christine put up her hands and said, "Now, just wait a second. I don't mean anybody any harm."

One of the men was upon her an instant later. She struggled with him briefly, but then the second man was there, throwing a sack over her head and bundling her over his shoulder.

"Hey. Hey, this is my dream! Stop it! Put me down."

She heard muffled voices, but couldn't make them out. The men carried her for a few moments and then dumped her, she presumed in the back of the cart. She kicked, but they had tied off the sack. "Let me go!" she shouted. The sack stank like animal sweat and urine and she held her breath for as long as she could.

"Jesus," she said. "Jesus, that stinks."

They bumped up the path. She hoped the wolf was gone at least. Next time she got the opportunity to talk to someone, she would have to try German.

She twisted around, trying to make herself comfortable. A tiny pinpoint of light came through the sack up near her forehead. She pushed her finger through the hole to make it bigger, and peered out. They were crossing into the castle grounds, under a raised iron gate whose spikes pointed toward the earth. The walls rose above—pale gray, but stained with sunset colors—then disappeared behind her. The cart rolled across a courtyard toward a dark front entrance, a heavy wooden door set back in a lichen-covered recess, and an inscription in the stone above them. She read it, and groaned.

MAYFRIDH

So, first the crow, and now her childhood best friend, May Frith. Every recent obsession was making its way into this dream. She half-expected to find her headless mother waiting inside the castle. This wasn't fun anymore; too fine a thread separated dreams from nightmares.

More muffled voices. The cart stopped. Christine shrank back into the sack, bracing herself for what twisted scene her dreaming consciousness might conjure up next.

Rough hands grabbed her legs and shoulders and she was lifted out of the cart and carried away. A few moments later, she was dumped on a hard floor. A woman's voice barked orders, and the sack was opened. Christine was released and roughly pulled to her feet.

She found herself in a dank stone room, with dark vaulted ceilings, woven bronze and amber tapestries, and high narrow windows. Tree branches obscured any light from outside. The air smelled damp and yeasty. Was this a movie set she had seen once? If so, why was she dreaming of it? A pity she'd had to leave her therapist back in New York—he would have reveled in all this cryptic symbolism.

In front of her, a round dais rose from five stairs, and in the middle, sitting on an elaborate golden chair under a hanging wooden wheel of candles, was the most beautiful woman Christine had ever seen. The woman was addressing her in an angry voice.

Christine still couldn't make out the language, but some of it sounded German, so she said, "Ich verstehe nicht"—*I don't understand*—all the time gazing at the woman. She wore a soft brown dress, gathered by tight ribbons criss-crossed around the waist, and long trailing sleeves embroidered in gold. A golden belt with seven keys on it hung low on her hips. Her hair was a rich coppery red, and hung in a thick, waist-length plait over her shoulder. Her face was as pale and soft as a small child's, her mouth a plump rosebud, her cheeks flushed red, and her dark blue eyes fixed on Christine with an expression mixed of anger and curiosity. The wolf sat faithfully at the beautiful woman's feet.

Christine realized she was surrounded by the two men from the cart, three other men, and a woman, all of whom eyed her apprehensively.

"Ich verstehe nicht," Christine said again, slowly in case her pronunciation was bad.

"Aha," the woman said, nodding to indicate that Christine's point was understood. Then the woman rose from her throne—a throne, that must make her the queen—barked orders at the assembly, and descended the stairs to take Christine's hand.

"*Kom.*" It was close enough to "come" in any language she knew, so Christine allowed herself to be led, several people and the wolf following her, around the back of the dais to a wooden doorway. The queen stepped forward and threw the doors open, admitting a shaft of golden light into the cavernous room. She led them into an overgrown garden of trailing vines and wild hedges, all spattered with the first yellow streaks of autumn. Beyond the garden they reached a slope that led to a crumbling stone wall and an iron gate. The queen ushered Christine ahead of her into dense trees.

Christine hesitated. Was she going to be taken back to the place where she had first arrived? Was she being sent back to her own world, where a week of painkiller-induced half-existence was waiting for her? For a moment she couldn't decide which was worse—dreams or reality—but it appeared the choice was out of her hands anyway.

"*Kom,*" the queen said again, pulling Christine's hand gently.

"Okay, okay," she muttered, and the queen looked at her sharply, but didn't pause, leading her deeper into the forest. The sun had now almost disappeared over the horizon, but its flaming golden fingers bathed the scene. Christine could hear the noises of little animals at work in the forest, and the skitter of lonely leaves dropping to the ground, early casualties of the season. Finally, they came to a clearing surrounding a crooked stone well. The woman released Christine's hand and leaned over the well.

"*Hechse!*" she called. "*Hechse!*"

It sounded like the German word for "witch," and Christine steeled herself for what ghastly thing might emerge from the well.

A stream of words Christine didn't understand was directed down into the dark. Then slowly, as if by magic, the reel began to creak and roll upward. Christine watched as, squeak-clunk-squeak-clunk, something heaved itself out of the well. A black shape appeared, an ancient rusty cage. It drew slowly above the stones, then stopped with a lurch. Hunched over inside it, dressed in smeared rags of an indeterminate color, was a white-haired hag with a wispy beard.

The queen seized Christine and forced her forward.

"Hey," Christine cried in protest. Four other pairs of hands were on her, and she was forced to her knees in front of the well, her head held down on the cold stone.

The queen directed more commands at the witch and, without warning, the hag's bony gray hands shot out and clapped Christine deafeningly around the ears.

"Ouch!" Christine cried, then heard somebody say, "Don't complain, we do you a favor." Only, she didn't really hear it. She heard something completely different—a sentence in that garbled half-German they all spoke—and yet when it entered her ears and slid into her mind, it turned into words she understood completely. She raised her head, gasping.

"Give Hexebart your tongue," the queen said.

Christine flinched away, tried to get to her feet, but more hands forced her down.

"Your tongue, foolish girl," one of the queen's assembly said. "You must speak as well as hear."

The thought of the hag touching her tongue repulsed her, but she was afraid these dream-characters were about to get violent, so she gingerly poked out her tongue. Once more Hexebart's fingers stole out from behind the bars of her cage. The witch grabbed her tongue, yanked it, and then released it.

"Jesus! That really hurt." But even though these were the words she said, they came out sounding completely different to the collected assembly. Hexebart cackled at Christine's bewildered expression. The queen pressed a dainty hand to her mouth to hide her smile, then collected her queenly demeanor.

"Hexebart," she said, turning to the hag. "Begone!"

"Gladly, you preening pig, you buttered turd, you sugared sow." Hexebart released the rope and slid back down the well.

The queen turned her attention to Christine and tried a smile. "I shall receive you in the south turret in twenty minutes."

"Okay. Fine." The odd echo of her words in a foreign tongue shivered in her ears.

"Hilda, take her and feed her. She's far too thin."

"Yes, your Majesty," a portly woman said, stepping forward to seize Christine's arm. "Come, girl."

Christine was led back into the dim castle, hoping that she would stay in the dream for the next twenty minutes so she could hear what this dream-queen was going to say. Perhaps she knew all the secrets of the universe: the truth about God, the reason evil exists, life after death. . . .

Christine's skin froze. Perhaps this wasn't a dream at all; perhaps it was a near-death experience. What if she had been hurt so seriously in her fall in Jude's apartment that she was even now lying on a hospital bed, a drip in her arm and a monitor blithely blipping out the beats of her heart? What if these visions were the result of horrific brain trauma, trauma that grew worse every second she was unconscious? Was Jude there by her bedside, crying and praying for her to live? A panicked grief gripped her, and she seized Hilda's hand and said, "You must help me. I have to get home."

Hilda laughed. "You have to meet with the queen first." She was leading Christine down a paneled hallway lined with closed doors.

"Then take me to her now."

"She's not expecting you for twenty minutes, girl."

"You don't understand," Christine said, stopping and taking Hilda by the shoulders. "I might die if I don't get back."

"You look alive and well to me."

"But I'm not from this world. I belong somewhere else."

Hilda detached herself from Christine's pleading hands and propelled her firmly forward. "You will do as the queen says. You are not sick and you will not die if you wait a mere twenty minutes."

"But—"

Hilda unlocked a door, bumped it open with her hip, and pulled Christine through. A mullioned window was pushed open to reveal the autumnal landscape beyond, with the dying sunset beams diffused through it. A table was laid with a wooden plate and a hunk of rough bread, and a tarnished silver cup.

"I'm really not hungry."

"I don't care. You will stay here, and you will eat, and I will return to fetch you when the queen tells me to." Hilda slammed out of the room, and the lock clicked into place. Christine took deep breaths, trying to calm herself. *You don't even know if you believe in near-death experiences, so just get a grip.* This was merely a wild dream, wilder than usual because she had fainted. She lowered herself to the floor, curled her arms around her knees, and screwed her eyes tight. "I want to wake up, I want to wake up," she said, over and over, but nothing happened. Tears began to prick at her eyes and her skin twitched. Pain or no pain, she just wanted to be back home with Jude.

For a long time she lay curled up on the floor, willing and willing herself to wake up from this dream—preferably at home and not in a hospital—without any success. Finally, footsteps approached and Hilda unlocked the door. She saw that Christine hadn't touched the food and sniffed disapprovingly.

"I said I wasn't hungry," Christine said, springing to her feet.

She followed Hilda dutifully along the hall and into a steep spiral staircase; it wound unevenly up and up in a windowed stone turret saturated with dusty twilight colors. At the top of the stairs, Hilda thrust Christine ahead of her into a cool stone room. The round walls were hewn smooth and covered in lavish tapestries. The floor was spread with thick rugs of dirty sheepskins that overlapped each other. Three hard wooden chairs were arranged around a low wooden chest, topped with dripping candlesticks and a large brass bear. The last rays of sunlight filtered in through windows made of dozens of tiny diamond-shaped panes.

The queen, her hair loose around her shoulders, knelt on the floor next to the wolf in the dim light, feeding him treats. She glanced up as Christine entered the room.

"Thank you, Hilda," she said. "You may leave us."

Hilda nodded and closed the door behind her.

Christine didn't wait for the queen to speak. "Listen, you have to help me. I need to get back to my own world because I'm really worried that I'm dying all the time I'm here."

The queen stood, a puzzled expression on her face. "What you say makes little sense."

"I'm not from here. This is a . . . a dream, or a vision, or something. I need to be conscious again." She sounded helpless and needy.

The queen extended a hand. "I shall endeavor to understand you better, stranger. My name is Mayfridh."

Christine grasped her hand distractedly. "Of course it is. You're named after a little girl I once knew."

Mayfridh shook her head, dropping Christine's hand. "No, I'm sure the little girl was named after me. I'm the queen, after all. Children are often named in my honor. What's your name?"

"Christine Starlight," Christine replied. "Please, you've got to—"

"Christine Starlight?" Mayfridh said sharply. "Truly?"

"Queen Mayfridh?" the wolf said, uncurling himself and standing. "You seem surprised."

Mayfridh ignored him and moved closer to Christine to examine her. "Of course it's Christine. You'll forgive me for not recognizing you. It has been a long time."

Christine flinched away from her inspection. "What are you talking about?"

Mayfridh smiled at her and, in perfect crisp English, said, "Christine, don't you remember me?"

Christine was momentarily disoriented. She had only just grown used to the odd word-echo-word-echo of their language. To hear her own language, and spoken like a British public school graduate, startled her.

"We were friends in our youth," Mayfridh continued. "You lived next door to me. Oh, we have so much to catch up on." Mayfridh stepped back and settled in one of the heavy wooden chairs. She patted her knee and slipped back into her own language. "Eisengrimm, come." The wolf approached her, resting his head between her knees to gaze up at her adoringly. "Fox," Mayfridh said, and Christine was astonished at what happened next. In an instant, the wolfish features had reduced and contracted, the gray fur had burnished over with red, and Eisengrimm jumped into Mayfridh's lap, a perfect, gleaming fox. Mayfridh caressed his head and looked at Christine expectantly.

"I'm tired of this dream," Christine said. The light in the room was changing. Although Christine had been certain a moment past that the sun had just set, it seemed a glimmer of dim morning light reflected in the windows.

"Dream? You think this is a dream?"

"Yes . . . no . . . I'm scared that I'm lying nearly dead on some hospital bed, and the longer I stay here the closer I get to dying."

Mayfridh shook her head. "You should never name the very thing of which you're most afraid. It's dangerous." Then she held up her thumb. "It's because of this, you know. It's because we mixed blood as children. Why, I'd forgotten until just now. You and I are blood sisters. Do you remember?"

"I remember. I've been remembering for two weeks, and that's why I'm dreaming about you."

"We made a bond, and somehow we've been drawn back

together." She pulled gently at the fox's ears. "Do you have any idea how that happened, Eisengrimm?"

The fox looked up. "No, Queen Mayfridh. Though I will think upon it." Eisengrimm's voice stayed the same whichever form he took: a rich mellow tone that made Christine think of oak and honey.

"Eisengrimm is very wise," Mayfridh said to Christine. "He'll find the answer. I've never had a human visit me here before."

"You mean you're not human?"

"Not after all these years, no. I'm a faery. Everyone you've met here is a faery."

At this, Christine felt a huge laugh bubbling up inside her. "Of course. Yeah. I'm in faeryland, right?"

Mayfridh frowned. "Our land is called Ewigkreis. Why do you laugh?"

"And this is a faery castle?"

"It's called the Autumn Castle. Why do you laugh?"

"And that thing on your lap is some kind of a faery pet?"

"His name is Eisengrimm and he's my most trusted counselor. Christine, *why* do you laugh? It's very rude."

"Because this is the stupidest dream I've ever had, and I want to go home."

A strange shuddering began to move under her feet.

Mayfridh gazed at her forlornly. "But I don't want you to go. I've been so lonely."

A finger of pain crept into Christine's back. She stiffened, placed her hand there.

"What's the matter, Christine?" Eisengrimm asked.

"The pain," she said, then the turret room, and Mayfridh and Eisengrimm, all started to shimmer and pale and she knew she was waking up. She screwed her eyes tight. Reality pressed in on her. The next time she opened her eyes she was in the kitchen in Jude's apartment, on the floor, in the dark. And the pain was a heavy juddering pressure on her spine.

Christine groaned. She flailed her right hand out to find something to help pull her up. She grasped the table leg, heaved, felt a shot of agony spreading up from the curve of her back toward her neck, and down toward her tailbone. It felt like someone had lit a blowtorch inside her spine. Tears and sobs and moans flowed out of her spontaneously and uncontrollably. To come back to this, after the wonderful dreaming respite, was almost more than she could endure.

She tried once more to stand, without success. She lay back, managed to get her watch in front of her eyes. As far as she could deduce, she'd been out for only three minutes. She flopped her arm back down and looked up at the ceiling in the dark, trying to breathe through the pain, setting her jaw against it, wriggling slightly in hopes of easing it. Then the jingle of keys outside the door. Jude returning from the studio. The light went on.

"Oh, my God. Christine!"

"I can't get up, Jude."

In an instant he was kneeling in the spilled spaghetti, his hair wild and his shirt splattered with paint. "What happened?"

"I backed into the corner of the table. I blacked out."

"The corner of the . . . oh, God, that's my fault. I moved it today. I'm so sorry. Christine, I'm so sorry."

"It's okay, just . . . can you help me into bed?"

Slowly and gently, he eased her to her feet. With infinite care he led her, one agonizing step at a time, back to the bedroom.

She gratefully stretched out on the soft bed. The pain was still and sharp, but at least the hard floor wasn't adding to her discomfort. "Jude, I'm going to need the blue tablets."

The blue tablets. How she hated taking them. They were

the strongest painkillers she had, but they also made her tongue heavy and her mind cloudy. They would knock her out swiftly, but she would wake in a weary fog.

"I'll get them," Jude said.

She listened to him in the kitchen—finding a glass, opening the bottle of pills—and contemplated the dream. It wasn't growing hazy like dreams did. It was staying fresh and clear like a memory. A moment later, Jude was there with a glass of water and two of the tablets in his palm, and the material demands of pain dispelled her reflections.

"Second time this evening, huh?" Christine said, smiling. "You're such a brave girl to smile."

"I had the weirdest dream while I was out. Remind me to tell you about it some time." She swallowed the tablets and settled back; tears welled up and she was unable to hold them in.

"Christine, I'm so sorry," Jude said, his fingers frantically smoothing her hair. "This is all my fault. I would give anything not to see you in pain. Everything is my fault."

"God, Jude. It hurts. It hurts so much." And she found herself wishing she were back in faeryland with her childhood best friend, a shape-shifting wolf, and a witch who lived in a well.

🐾

Where did she go?" Mayfridh sprang from her seat, sending Eisengrimm scrambling to the floor. "Eisengrimm, where is she?"

Eisengrimm sniffed the place where Christine had stood.

"Well?" Mayfridh demanded. "How could she leave?" It had been so long since Mayfridh had spent time with a real friend.

"She must have been pulled back into her own world, Majesty."

Mayfridh returned to her seat, pouting. "It was very rude of her to leave like that."

"I don't think she had any control over it."

"Oh, Eisengrimm, I *remember* Christine. We played together as children in the Real World. I loved her so much. And yet I had forgotten her for so long."

"It's the way in our world, you know that. Seasons change—"

"Yes, and memories bury themselves too deep for us to find them. But now I remember it all."

"A sympathy of time and blood, Mayfridh. Our world and hers have aligned. Their season must be the same as ours, she is nearby, and her blood in your veins attracted her."

Mayfridh sighed, leaning her head on the side of the chair and idly running her fingers over the carvings in the wood. "You're so wise, Eisengrimm." She held out her hand and beckoned him forward, rubbed his smooth ears. "Do you think she'll come back?"

"I don't know," he said, "but with Hexebart's help I believe I could learn more."

"Hexebart! That wizened old grape. She becomes more and more willful. It's not fair, Eisengrimm. It's *my* magic."

"Hexebart is selfish and stubborn."

"I should cut off her feet," Mayfridh muttered. "I should slice off her nose." Then remembering what Eisengrimm had suggested, she said, "Why do you speak of Hexebart helping you?"

"I stole a hair from Christine's head when first I saw her in the forest. Hexebart could weave a spell with it, and we could learn all about her world."

"Do you think we could bring her back?"

Eisengrimm transformed into Crow and fluttered to the

window. "I doubt she'd be willing to return," he said, "but there may be another way to see Christine."

"What do you mean? Where are you going?"

"I'm going back to the forest to find the hair, and then I'll pay Hexebart a visit." He cocked his head and fixed Mayfridh with a golden eye. "Then, Queen Mayfridh, we can send you through."

"To the Real World?" Mayfridh's chest tightened with fear. Her parents had made a passage to the Real World and never returned. Although many faeries made the passage on the rare occasions when the worlds aligned, Mayfridh had developed a terrible anxiety at the merest suggestion that she do so. Despite this, Eisengrimm persisted in encouraging her to go if she had the opportunity. He believed it would expand her horizons, make her a better queen and a more accomplished ruler.

"Consider it an adventure, Mayfridh," he said.

"I won't go," she said.

"We shall see," Eisengrimm replied, spreading his wings and flying away.

"I won't go, I will not go," Mayfridh called after him. But her stomach lurched and her heart sped. This time she might; this time she just might.

Hexebart is tired of this old well, yes she is. She's tired of the cold and the cage and the damp and the ugly frogs. Hexebart is tired of spinning and weaving spells for the nasty little changeling princess.

> *Spin, spin, spin and weave,*
> *Hexebart can never leave.*
> *Oh, oh! Oh, oh!*

Beastly Queen Mayfridh. Not the real queen, no. Just a cuckoo in the nest. When Hexebart sees the dead body of the real queen, then Hexebart will believe. Until then, all the magic stays here in the well. Hexebart sits in the cage and spins until her fingers dribble blood, and Hexebart dreams of eating the horrid little queen with a knife and a spoon. And Hexebart saves all the magic for herself.

> *Mine, mine, mine,*
> *Until the end of time.*

Hexebart is good at saving things. When the bossy wolf asks for special spells and gives her special stuffs, she rubs them between her scabby fingers and if she likes them she keeps a little. Hexebart has many stuffs. See . . . she has buttons and a silver clasp; she has a scrap of swaddling and a rusty thimble; and here inside this pea shell . . . here, Hexebart has half of a strand of long brown hair. It's human hair.

> *Human hair, human hair,*
> *Humans all live Over There,*
> *And when her time in here is through,*
> *Hexebart will go There too.*

Hexebart clicks her tongue and keeps spinning and weaving. Spinning through the night, spinning through time, saving a little something for herself.

CHAPTER FOUR

*H**ey, the cripple walks. It's a miracle,"* Pete exclaimed.
Gerda shot him an irritated glance. "Glad you could
make it, Miss Starlight. We saved you a seat."

Christine laughed. "I don't mind being called a miracle,
Gerda. On Tuesday I thought I might have to spend the rest
of my life on my back." Fabiyan pulled out a chair for her
and she eased into it, Jude hovering around in concern. They
were at a bent table outside a cheap Tex-Mex cantina on
Georgenstrasse, right under the train line out of Friedrichstrasse Station. "But now I'm recovered, I need beer."

"Get the girl a beer," Gerda said to Pete.

"I'll get everyone a beer," he said. "With a bit of luck
Mandy will foot the bill." He shot out of his chair and
headed for the bar.

"Mandy?" Jude asked.

"He's coming," Gerda replied. "Sorry. He caught us at
the front door and asked where we were going."

Jude reached for Christine's hand and squeezed it affec-
tionately. "I guess we can't keep avoiding him."

Christine shifted in her chair, trying to make herself more
comfortable. The truth was that her back was still throbbing

and pulling, but she had been flat out in bed for four days and needed to get out. Not just out of bed, but out of her own claustrophobic head.

"Why, thank you, Gerda," Mandy said, horrifying Christine by pulling up a chair next to hers. "Tell the waitress to bring out a tray of dips and so on. Dinner will be on me tonight."

Pete cheered and joined Gerda in finding a waitress. Mandy smiled at Christine, baring an uneven row of small yellowed teeth. "I see you are up and about. Jude told me you hurt yourself."

Christine shrank back an inch. "Yes, I'm feeling better."

He clicked his tongue. "A nasty business, falling in the kitchen. You know most accidental deaths occur at home."

"Is that right?"

"Yes, it is. You may worry more about flying, or driving, or swimming. But you're far more likely to meet your death by slipping in the bath." He smiled.

"How . . . interesting."

"What's your fear, Christine?"

"I beg your pardon?"

"What accident do you fear most of all?"

Jude leaned forward and curled a protective arm around Christine. "Mandy, Christine lost her parents in a car accident."

"I am so sorry," Mandy said, smiling and nodding. "I hadn't meant to upset you."

"It's fine," Christine muttered, reaching for her beer. She noticed Mandy watching her hands move, and his nostrils flared slightly. She barely controlled a shudder. He glanced up at her quickly, a puzzled look crossing his face.

"What's the matter?" she asked, dreading the answer.

"Nothing. You reminded me of . . . something."

"Something nice, I hope?"

He didn't answer. Instead, he stood up, said, "I should mingle," without any trace of humor, and plonked himself down at the other end of the table between Pete and Gerda.

"You okay?" Jude asked, his breath soft against her ear.

"Yeah. It's good to be out."

He gently kissed her cheek.

"I love you, Jude."

"I love you too."

There, he said it, it must be true. Cling to it. Too late. Already a part of her heart reminded her that he never said it first; that his love was reactive, not spontaneous, so she must love him more than he loved her. Then she got sick of herself, sick of her weird abandonment issues. So she'd lost her parents when she was eighteen; it didn't excuse all this babyish fretting at the age of thirty-one. If he didn't love her, then he deserved an Oscar for the previous four years' performance. She put it out of her mind, determined to enjoy herself for at least a couple of hours.

The food was good, the beer was better, and around ten o'clock Mandy paid the bill and departed, telling them all he was an early riser. The remaining five pulled the chairs closer around the table, a circle of cigarettes was lit, and Gerda said, "I cannot stand him. I simply cannot stand him."

"He's creepy," Christine agreed. "The way he looks at people."

"The way he looks at you," Pete said. "I'd never noticed it before tonight."

Christine shivered. "Gross. Don't mess with my head."

"What do you hate most about him, Jude?" Gerda said, blowing out a long stream of cigarette smoke.

"The way he looks at Christine," Jude said, laughing. "Truly, Christine, didn't you see? He sat up there and kept sneaking glances at you all night. I think you've won his heart."

"Don't," Christine protested. "I mean it, Jude, he gives me the creeps."

"How about you, Fabiyan?" Gerda said, speaking slowly. "Do you hate Mandy?"

"He come to me on the Wednesday," Fabiyan said. "I think he will ask me about my new sculpture. No. He ask me to make him a point."

"A point?" Pete asked.

Fabiyan mimed plugging an electrical cord into a wall. "Yes, for electricity."

"He asked you to install an outlet?" Christine asked. "Are you kidding?"

Fabiyan shook his head.

"That's so disrespectful. You're an artist," Gerda said, enthusiastically stubbing her cigarette on the side of the table. Fabiyan looked puzzled so Christine translated into German for him.

"Did you do it?" Jude asked.

Fabiyan nodded. "I feel I must say yes to him."

"I hate him because he listens to the worst music in the universe," Pete said. "New Age Pan flute music, and classical symphonies with a pop backbeat. Sometimes he puts it on in the gallery when I'm trying to work in the studio and it's counter-inspirational."

"I'm with you on that one," Jude said.

"And there's something weird about the way he moves," Pete added. "He's this big, lumbering fat guy, and yet he has this uncanny speed and accuracy. I've seen him catch a fly in mid-flight."

"No way!" Jude exclaimed.

"Yeah. He let it out a window. For a horrible moment I thought he was going to eat it."

They all laughed, then Gerda tapped out a cascade of ash

and said, "I wish I had a good reason to hate him, but I think I just hate him because he's hateable."

"Unbelievably hateable," Christine agreed.

"Irrationally hateable," Gerda continued, "because he's generous, he loves art, he's devoted his life to the development of artists from all over the world, and he never interferes creatively with any of us."

"There's just something about him," Pete said.

Christine drained her beer. "I'm glad to hear someone else say that. It's true, there's just something about him."

"Poor guy," Jude said. "Imagine going through life being irrationally hateable."

"There are worse fates," Gerda said, indicating Christine's empty bottle. "More beer?"

"More beer," Christine said, gazing off down the long dark street. The giant TV tower at Alexanderplatz blinked against the night sky in the distance. Jude was right, now she thought back on it. Mandy had been staring at her tonight. But that was strange, because at first it had seemed as if he wanted to get away from her. He had said she reminded him of something and then moved to the other end of the table.

"Where are you?" Jude said quietly in her ear.

"Excuse me?"

"You're a million miles away."

"Just thinking about something," she said with a smile, and decided not to think any more about Immanuel Zweigler.

Jude's body was one of the undiscovered wonders of the world. His skin was hot and smooth, his lips and his hands were agile and passionate and gentle. Late that night, the best way he knew how, he managed to take Christine's mind off the pain.

"You're a god," Christine gasped as he slid back to his side of the bed.

He smiled at her in the dark. "The pleasure's all mine, I promise."

"Why do you love me?" she asked.

"Because you remind me so much of Christine Starlight, who I've always had a big crush on."

She laughed. "Idiot."

"Hey, you asked the stupid question."

"It's not stupid."

"Yes, it is. Anyone who ever loves anyone truly loves them because of their indefinable essence, not because they conform to some checklist."

"A checklist would be nice though," Christine said, rolling carefully onto her side. "Sometimes girls like compliments."

"All right then. You're beautiful and clever and kind."

"No, it's no good giving me a compliment when I asked for it."

"Why not?"

"Because I asked for it. Because it's not sincere. You have to give me one when I'm not expecting it."

"But you'll still know you asked for it, won't you?"

"Not if you leave it long enough between this conversation and the compliment."

"But if I leave it too long, you'll remind me again and then we'll be back where we started."

Christine giggled. "Nobody said love was easy."

He pinned her down and kissed her again, and her senses flared with passion. This bodily response was the only physical thing that could match her pain for intensity. He let her go and she sighed.

"You know," she said, "I had the strangest dream when I blacked out the other day. I was in a place where I felt no pain at all."

"Yeah? What happened?"

"In the dream? Not much. Just silly dream stuff." Telling him would be too much like acknowledging its power.

"Was it nice? To be without the pain?"

"It was incredible, Jude. Absolute freedom." She locked her fingers with his under the covers and thought about how pain had become a default setting in her life. Everything was geared around it. How she walked, how she moved, how long she could stay in a conversation without distraction, how she slept, showered, ate, drank. "Do you think someone can go mad from pain?" she asked.

"I don't know. But you're strong, you'll be okay."

"Maybe it wasn't a dream," she said carefully. "Maybe it was a hallucination. Maybe I'm going nuts."

"Hey, don't worry yourself about silly things like that," he said. "You're perfectly sane."

"But the dream was so—"

"Shh, you're getting worked up over nothing," Jude said, stroking her hair. "Don't be afraid of shadows. A dream is only ever just a dream."

❧

"Eisengrimm!" Mayfridh swept up the corridor, setting the autumn-colored tapestries dancing in her wake. "Eisengrimm, where are you?"

She poked her head into the dim, low-ceilinged kitchen. "Has anyone seen Eisengrimm?"

A flurry of fumbling curtsies and slack mouths and shaking heads greeted her. Idiots. She backed out and kept walking. Why did people have to turn all silent and fearful in her presence? She was not a cruel queen. Nobody ever spoke to her with their hearts, only with their heads—ever mindful of their careers, or their reputations, or their fortunes. Her own heart was aching under the unexpressed weight of this truth. Eisengrimm was the only one she could tell her woes and insecurities to, and he was a good listener and a good counselor. But he was a wolf. She couldn't marry him or adopt him as a brother; he could never be of her kind.

She threw open the door to the garden and called, "Eisengrimm!"

The garden was strewn with fallen leaves. She knew she had until the last leaf of autumn fell to find Christine, because then it would be time to move to the Winter Castle and away from this favorable alignment of their worlds. Mayfridh couldn't explain, even to herself, why she had become so desperate to find Christine again. The faery world worked on the memory in strange ways. She had forgotten so much about her previous existence, about Christine and her own Real World parents, but now it was swirling back to her in gentle waves. All those warm memories, filling her with an unutterable longing for a simpler, happier time.

Mayfridh lowered herself to the ground and stretched out on her back among the leaves. The sky was pale above her and she breathed deeply. Every breath brought her closer to agreeing to make passage to the Real World. She reexamined all those nasty fears about the disappearance of the king and queen before her—her faery parents. Perhaps they had not been murdered or killed in an accident, but had good reasons of their own for disappearing. They would have known that, after the six-week period decreed for their people to wait for their return, the throne would pass to their daughter. Perhaps they even had reasons for wanting her to take the throne at nine years of age, though she couldn't imagine what those reasons might be. A nine-year-old girl is a poor ruler, a fifteen-year-old one even worse. She shuddered as she remembered some of her mistakes.

A leaf descended and brushed her shoulder. Footsteps alerted her to Eisengrimm's presence.

"So there you are," she said, turning her head to see him nearby, his jaw wrapped tight around a glowing object. "What do you have for me?"

He loped over and stood above her. She could see now that his mouth was full of spells. He released them so that they bounced over her. She sat up and gathered them.

"Sorry," he said, "you know I can't talk and carry at the same time."

Three spells. She nursed them in her lap, tiny glowing balls of woven magic from the well. Two were the usual general-purpose spells that Mayfridh could use as she wished. The third had a strand of brown hair threaded through it. "What's this one?" she said, holding it up.

"I had Hexebart weave a special introduction to Christine's world. To prepare yourself."

"I need not prepare myself. I remember it."

"Things change quickly in the Real World. It's not like here, where things don't change at all. Twenty-five years is a long time."

"I see."

"The other two are to use as you wish. To conjure the passage, to contact me back here, to protect yourself against emergencies."

Emergencies? Her heart jumped. "So you think I'll go?"

"I know not, Mayfridh. Do you think you'll go?"

She fiddled with the spells in her lap. They were smooth and warm, feather-light. "Perhaps."

"Perhaps, my Queen?"

Mayfridh narrowed her eyes. "Are you laughing at me?"

"You know wolves can neither laugh nor cry."

"But if you could laugh, would you be laughing now?"

Eisengrimm nudged one of the spells with his nose. "Go on, Mayfridh. Try it."

She collected the spells in her left hand and stood. "Fine, then. We shall go to the spell chamber, and I shall reacquaint myself with the Real World."

The Autumn Castle's spell chamber was under the ground, above the crypt and the dungeons. No light permeated the gloom except for the brass lantern Mayfridh brought with her, and the soft daylight from a tiny high window that opened onto the grass outside. The room was cold, the rough-hewn stone bare of tapestries or hangings or anything else that might absorb magic. Laid out around the chamber were mirrors and bowls and burners and ladles and mortars and pestles and bottles. Once, before her faery parents had departed for the Real World, all magic in the realm had been spun and woven in here, rather than in Hexebart's well. Mayfridh always looked around the room with a sense of sadness. Its ghostly emptiness was a reminder of her inadequacies as a ruler.

"One day, Eisengrimm—" she started.

"Be kind to yourself, my Queen. You are still young, and if you are patient and strong, this difficulty with Hexebart will be overcome."

Mayfridh had brought wine from the kitchen. She slumped on an unsteady stool in front of the long wooden table that ran almost the length of the room and stood the bottle in front of her. Eisengrimm transformed to Crow and joined her. He used his beak to uncork the bottle.

"I wish you would be Bear and use your hands. Why do you never change to Bear?" she asked him.

"You know it hurts my joints. Bear is so heavy. I'm bruised for weeks afterwards."

"I don't like you as Crow. I know you eat the eyes of dead squirrels in the forest."

"As Crow, I can think of nothing tastier." He clicked his beak on the table. "Come, Mayfridh. Pour yourself a cup of wine."

Mayfridh reached for a cup and filled it with wine. Eisengrimm plucked out the spell that had Christine's hair woven through it, hopped across the table, and dropped it into the cup.

"What will it do?" Mayfridh asked as she waited for it to sizzle and shimmer into the wine.

"It will introduce you to the feel and pace of her world. As it is only hair, it will give you no insight into her personal circumstances. If I could have snatched one of her eyes, I might have been able to furnish you with memories, dreams, visions. . . ."

"I prefer her with two eyes in her head, as I'm sure she does." She swirled the cup and looked into it. The spell had vanished, and the wine was now golden. "Well, then, I'll drink it."

"Go on."

Mayfridh raised the cup to her lips and took a cautious sip. At once, unfamiliar sensations began to wash over her and she closed her eyes. In a rush, with a sound like a great breath being expelled, she experienced—*refrigerator noise, demolition sites, antihistamines, newspaper ink, cheap plastic toys, techno-pop, eyelash curlers, Internet porn, central heating, the* Love Parade, *roller coasters, roadworks, bookshops, building cranes, cigarettes, lawn mowers, airplanes, fluorocarbons, chlorine, shampoo, traffic, Coke, Shrek, smog, bombs, PVC, FTP, DVD—*

Mayfridh opened her eyes and caught her breath.

"My Queen?"

She closed her eyes again, and more sensations charged

at her, slipped past her, and left their traces on her. "When will it stop?" she shouted over the barrage of images, sounds, smells.

"Be patient, it should slow down soon."

She took big breaths, tried to relax through the assault of impressions. Finally, as Eisengrimm had said, they began to slow, to fade, to grow still. But she didn't open her eyes. She didn't want Eisengrimm to see the disappointed tears that pricked at them, because now she was terrified, now she doubted she had enough courage to make passage to such a world.

"It's awful," she said, trying to keep her voice even.

"Awful?"

"And wonderful," she added. "So full of wonders."

"You will see it firsthand, the first of the royal family in over a dozen years to—"

Her eyes flicked open and she held up a finger to caution him. "I will not do anything I don't want to do. I am the queen."

"But Little May," he said—he always called her by this pet name when she reminded him of her status—"what about Christine? You want to see her again, do you not?"

"Yes, but . . . I know nothing about her. She may be a murderer."

"A murderer?" He cawed a laugh.

"She may be a villain of some sort. Just because she was a sweet child does not mean she has grown into a kind woman." Eisengrimm stared at her, his bland crow face unreadable. "Change out of Crow. I can't stand it when you look at me like that."

He transformed to Fox—her favorite—and approached, ducking his head for an ear rub. "You are making an excuse, and a poor one," he said.

"What if I am? I can do whatever I want—"

"Yes, yes, I know. You're the queen." He sat back and sniffed at the potion in the cup. "How could I convince you that Christine is not a villain, that you will be safe if you make a passage to see her?"

"I know not."

"What if I go ahead of you, watch her for a few days? I'll see where she lives, what she does, and who she knows."

Mayfridh felt her resolve shift again. "Would you?"

"Of course I would."

"But I could still make up my mind afterwards? I could still decide not to go?"

"Of course." He met her gaze steadily. "But, Mayfridh, don't leave it too long. You only have until the end of the season."

"I know."

With his nose, Eisengrimm tipped over the cup so it spilled out on the table. Mayfridh watched as he lapped up the spell, then lay forward on his paws with his eyes shut. His tail twitched a few times, but then he opened his eyes. "I am ready."

"How will you go?"

"As Crow."

"Open your wings."

He transformed and spread his shining wings. Mayfridh carefully picked up the two remaining spells, and tucked one under each wing. The golden light disappeared among the black feathers.

"Be safe, my friend," she said, and the memory of the last time she had seen her faery parents came back to her. *We're going to the opera. We'll be back before midnight.* "Please be very safe, Eisengrimm."

"Mayfridh, the Real World is not so dangerous as you think it is."

"I trust that you are right." She touched his feathered head gently. "Return to me soon."

[decorative ornament]

Christine saw the crow as soon as she emerged from the front entrance of the bookshop. It was perched on the hood of a silver Opel parked nearby. When she approached, the bird took to the sky. She paused and watched it for a moment. *It's just a crow.* A breeze swept up the street, making red-stained maple leaves swirl around her and then settle on windshields and in gutters. Her heart beat an intense rhythm. Just a crow. It disappeared out of sight over the top of the shops opposite.

She started walking toward Zoo Station. At the entrance to Uhlandstrasse U-bahn, she hesitated, and considered going underground. At least there would be no crows down there. Then she reminded herself that crows were common city birds, that they had nothing to do with her stupid dream, and that four steps down toward the platform her nerves would all be singing out of tune.

Among the crowds of people near Zoo Station she felt safe. She checked up and around her. A few pigeons; no crows. She found the platform and a half-second later, her train slid into the station.

She watched out the window. A flash of black at Tiergarten could have been anything, not necessarily wings. Nothing at Bellevue. Really, this was ridiculous, to get so concerned about a crow. She had probably seen a hundred of them since she arrived in Berlin, and just hadn't noticed before. Buskers got on at Lehrter Stadtbahnhof and played an enthusiastic rendition of "She Loves You." Everyone ignored them, and they disembarked before her at Friedrichstrasse. Christine realized her eyes were darting everywhere, looking for the bird. But there were no birds. There were buildings and bridges and banks and brisk autumn breezes, but nothing else beginning with "b." She turned into Vogelwald-Allee, looked up, and saw a crow sitting on the turret of Hotel Mandy-Z.

"Leave me alone," she called out to it, fumbling for her key.

At that moment, the front door opened and Mandy stepped out. "Good evening, Christine."

"Hi, Mandy."

"Did I hear you talking to somebody?"

The crow fluttered down and came to rest on a first-floor windowsill. Mandy must have seen Christine flinch, because he asked, "Were you talking to the crow?"

"Yeah," she said, trying to laugh at herself. "I'd swear he's followed me home."

Mandy eyed the crow. "From Charlottenburg? No, I'm sure he hasn't. Perhaps you saw his twin earlier. They all look the same, you know."

"Yeah, I know."

"Although they can probably tell each other apart." He turned his attention to Christine again. "I've been meaning to ask you. Have you been out of the city at all since you arrived? A day trip? A weekend in the country?"

She shook her head, wondering where this line of questioning was heading. "No."

"Really?"

"Why do you ask?" An indistinct sensation of uneasiness crept up her spine. She had been on a day trip all right; all the way to faeryland and back. Had he overheard her talking to Jude? But no, she'd barely told Jude anything about the dream.

"The other night at dinner you seemed remarkably . . . refreshed."

"Probably had something to do with lying flat on my

back for nearly a week." Crows, faeryland, Mandy. She just wanted to get inside, take a warm shower, and crash in front of the television all night. "Do I still seem 'refreshed' now?"

"No. Sorry for my bluntness. You now seem just as you were when first I met you." He smiled, revealing those tiny teeth, not much bigger than milk teeth. "You must think me odd, Christine."

Hell, yes. "No. I'm used to artists. Four years with Jude, you know."

He patted her shoulder. "I'll leave you to go inside out of the cold. Look, your crow has decided you're home safely and you no longer need his guardianship." He pointed up at the sky, and Christine saw the black outline of the bird against the gray clouds. A sudden twinge of memory snapped into her mind.

"Oh," she gasped.

"Christine?"

"Nothing," she said, forcing a smile. "Good night."

He buttoned his coat and trudged down the street. She watched the crow as it disappeared into the distance, and finally she remembered why those black wings had been plaguing her memory for weeks—and why they horrified her so much.

Mayfridh sat in the spell chamber, a bowl of water resting on the table in front of her. She tried to breathe very softly so the water would remain undisturbed. In the bowl, she could see what Eisengrimm could see as he darted around Christine's corner of the Real World. She had seen busy streets and shiny cars, shops and building sites, and Christine's home on a leafy street. She had even seen the man she assumed was Christine's beloved, a large black-haired fellow who had touched her shoulder very gently and carefully.

He was rather an ugly man, but Christine was a plain little thing and couldn't expect much better.

Mayfridh sighed and leaned forward, sending ripples swelling out across the surface of the water. Plain little Christine had a lover and Mayfridh didn't and never had. She had not yet met a man whom she could imagine spending more than a few minutes with, let alone a lifetime. Eisengrimm had caused a number of men—handsome, powerful, strong—to be brought to the castle for her review, but none of them had appealed to her. Love was such a complicated function. How was it possible that anyone ever found love when it was dependent on so many mutual perfections?

Oh, but she was lonely.

She closed her eyes and let herself imagine visiting with Christine in the Real World. They would reminisce about their shared childhood, they would talk about love; perhaps Christine would introduce her to her other friends and the black-haired man. Leaves were falling every moment and the Autumn Castle would have to be left behind, and then she would forget Christine again. She would be friendless and alone once more.

"I will go, then," she whispered, watching her breath dance on the water. "Come what may, I will go."

CHAPTER FIVE

I thought you had a morning off."

"I do." Christine turned from the dresser and smiled at Jude, who had just woken up.

"Then stay in bed. Sleep in, with me." He patted the mattress.

She turned and resumed dressing. "No. I'm going out to Zehlendorf."

"What's at Zehlendorf?" Then before she could answer, he said, "Oh, your old house."

"That's right."

"Do you want me to come?"

She buttoned up her blouse. "If you like. I'm going on the bus though. There are tunnels on the train line."

"Would you prefer me to be there with you?"

She shrugged. "It might be nice."

"You're not going to knock on the door or anything?"

She sat on the edge of the bed and pulled on her jeans. "No, I don't know the new owners."

"Then why—?"

"I just want to see it again. I want to collect my thoughts

and put the past behind me." *Where it belonged, instead of turning up in wild hallucinations.*

"Okay then, I'll come."

"Then hurry. I'm catching the ten o'clock bus from Zoo."

The sky was dark and heavy outside and Jude muttered about forgetting his umbrella. The bus dropped them off on a busy suburban street lined with bakeries and parks. Christine looked around for remembered landmarks.

"That church was there," she said. "My street is behind it."

"It's pretty here," Jude said, following her.

"Yeah, it always was." She took him down a narrow side street. The road was cobbled and the gutters filled with leaves. "We were only here for just over a year. From '77 to '78." She smiled at him. "David Bowie came over once. I sat on his lap."

"Was he a friend of your parents?"

"Um . . . yeah. They kind of knew everyone." She paused on the corner. A dark blue Mercedes swept past. "This is the street."

"Come on then. What are we waiting for?"

"Good question." What was she afraid of? The whole point of coming here was to sort out the memory of the crow once and for all. "Jude, do you believe that some things are so disturbing that you can bury them under deep layers and forget them?"

"Of course. Psychiatrists make their living out of stuff like that. Why, is there something really disturbing on this street?"

She shook her head. "Not really. I mean . . . I was six . . . seven. Some things get into your imagination and run wild."

"Tell me."

"Come on," she said, grabbing his hand and leading him across the road. "I'll show you."

Christine recognized all the houses. Their high-peaked

roofs and painted shutters had barely changed in twenty-five years. There were more trees than she remembered, more traffic noise in the distance, and lots of cars parked in the street. "That one was my house," she said, pointing out a painted white house with a cobbled path and tidy gardens. "That one was the Friths'." This house was the worse for wear, with an overgrown garden and peeling shutters. "And that window up there . . ." She pointed to the window directly under the gable, and found she couldn't finish the sentence.

"What is it?" Jude asked. A drizzle had started to descend.

"That's where it happened."

"What happened?"

Christine found it hard to begin. Now she had remembered everything, she was experiencing all the childish fear and sadness again. "May and I had declared each other blood sisters the day before. My thumb was still hurting when I turned up at her place early the next morning. I crashed in as I always did and Mrs. Frith said that May wasn't awake yet, but that I could go up and wake her. It was a Saturday. I raced up the stairs, I had a new book to show her I think . . . or a record to play her. My parents were always bringing home records, strange experimental music, but May and I didn't care what it sounded like. We just loved new records, poring over the covers and the inside sleeves and . . . Sorry, I'm rambling."

"It's okay, babe."

"So, I knocked gently on her bedroom door and called out to her, then went into her room. She had a fabulous room. She was really spoiled and her mother had spent so much time painting her bedroom all these wild colors and with scenes from faery tales on the ceiling and . . . anyway,

I went in and approached May's bed. But May wasn't in the bed. There was something else underneath the covers."

"What was it?"

"I called out for May, and I stepped closer to the bed, peering at it. A lump under the blankets moved, too small to be May. I must have held my breath a full minute, staring at it, wondering if I'd imagined it moving. Then it stirred again. I reached out and flicked back the covers, and a huge, black crow was sitting there looking at me. I shrieked and stumbled back. The crow spread its wings and cawed, that awful noise they make . . . I swear it pierced my eardrums. Then it darted up, into my face, like it wanted to steal my eyes. I screamed again, covering my face. When I looked, the crow had taken off out the window. That's when I noticed it was open. May never slept with the window open. Her mother had a weird phobia about it.

"Her parents burst in then, all panicked and angry with me for screaming. Then her mother said, 'Where's May?' and I said I didn't know, but there had been a crow in her bed."

"That was the day she disappeared?" Jude asked.

Christine nodded. "Yep. The police arrived, like, nine minutes later. I'd been sent home, but the police came to speak to me. Dad had to translate everything for me, I was too upset to remember any German except 'krähe'—crow."

"Did they figure out what the crow was doing there?"

Christine gazed up at the window. It was firmly shut against the October drizzle. "No," she said, "because they didn't believe me. I was too little, I wasn't a reliable witness. Everybody thought I'd made it up. At least, everybody except Mrs. Frith." She pointed at the Friths' house. "She turned up one day, about two weeks after May had gone missing. My parents were reluctant to let me talk to her. The poor woman was nearly insane with grief and anxiety. She smelled terrible, like she hadn't bathed since it happened. She kept demanding to know . . ." She trailed off into a long silence.

"What?"

"It's crazy, Jude."

"Go on."

"She kept demanding to know what the crow had said to me. It was terrifying and it sowed a seed in some dark corner of my mind."

"What it *said* to you?"

"Yeah. Oh, Jude. If you knew what a relief it is to me to remember all this. It's all been barricaded back there in my head, making me feel weird feelings and dream strange dreams. You know, I got spooked when I saw a crow the other day. I thought it had followed me home." Finally she could laugh at herself. "God, I even told Mandy that it had followed me home."

Jude slipped an arm around her and gave her an affectionate squeeze. "Ah, don't worry, nobody's crazier than Mandy."

Christine sighed, gazing at her childhood home. "You know, I'd hardly even thought about Little May all this time."

"You've been on the other side of the world, you've been living your life. Being here in Berlin has made you remember things, that's all."

"I guess you're right. There are lots of memories for me here." She imagined knocking on the door of her old home, and finding her parents inside, safe and happy and enjoying their retirement. The impossible thought brought fresh tears to her eyes. It was so damn unfair. She sank into Jude's side and he pressed her against him.

"What's wrong, Christine?"

"I miss them."

"I know."

"Sorry for being all emotional."

"It's okay." He stroked her hair. "It's okay, you're allowed to be emotional."

"You're all I've got, Jude. Without you, I'd have nothing."

She felt his chest stiffen momentarily, as though he were clutching his breath against some burden, and then relax. "What's wrong?" she asked, standing back.

"Nothing's wrong," he said, looking puzzled. "Why do you ask?"

"I thought . . ." Maybe she'd imagined that moment of caught breath, and everything it might have signified.

"Look, we're getting wet," Jude said gently. "Do you mind if we go find a cafe somewhere?"

"Sure. Okay, sure." They headed back the way they had come through the misting drizzle. And even though her fingers were growing cold in the autumn chill, Christine tried not to clutch Jude's hand too tightly.

Mayfridh couldn't remember being more frightened in her life. "You there, pack my warm cloak. And you, find that gold pin I wore on my birthday." She heard her own voice shake as she ordered three servants about—she had forgotten their names, she always forgot their names—while they packed a trunk for her to take with her.

"Could I advise, Queen Mayfridh, that you don't take such a big trunk with you?" This was Eisengrimm, as Wolf, lying amongst the rumpled white bedcovers with his face resting on his front paws.

"What do you mean?" she demanded. Eisengrimm could be infuriatingly calm in the most hectic of circumstances.

"You can come back for clothes. You can make the passage back at any time. And besides, you know that your clothes don't look like Real World clothes. You'll want to go shopping as soon as you get there."

Ah yes, that word. "Shopping." It was one of the Real World concepts that appealed to her the most. Vast buildings full of beautiful dresses in ingenious colors and textures, and all to be had by showing a colored square—a credit card.

"Come, leave all these things behind. You need only take yourself and a bag full of spells."

"If Hexebart will comply," she muttered darkly.

"Hexebart *must* comply, and she knows that. She may not believe you are the true queen, but she knows you are Queen Liesebet and King Jasper's daughter, and she must give you whatever magic you ask for."

"After threats and curses."

"She likes to see you angry. You shouldn't give her the satisfaction."

Mayfridh marched over to one of the servants and snatched a yellow dress out of her hands. "That will do," she said. "All of you, you are dismissed. I need nothing further."

With bows and nervous murmurs they backed out of the room. She slammed the door shut and flung herself onto the bed next to Eisengrimm, flat on her back with her hair spread out around her, gazing up at the white canopy.

"I'm frightened, Eisengrimm. I'm so frightened." The fear was like a big, inescapable bubble welling up inside her, making her tap her fingers, and twitch her legs, and hold back a fragment of every breath.

"I know you are, Little May. But look at me, I came back. I was gone but a few hours, and then I came back."

She turned on her stomach and met his gaze. "Eisengrimm, what do you think happened to my mother and father?"

"I know not."

"Make a guess then."

"I have no way of guessing."

"Perhaps they were murdered," Mayfridh said. The dark fear spun down on her. "Oh, I don't want to be murdered."

"The risk is very low in the Real World. Murder accounts for very few deaths. They may have met with an accident."

"But Eisengrimm, we sent a dozen men through to find them. Nobody had heard of them or seen them, nobody found them or their bodies. They simply disappeared. A murderer would hide them, would he not? To avoid capture."

"It would be best not to think of it, Mayfridh." He stood and stretched, and jumped from the bed. "Come, we shall pay Hexebart a visit."

Mayfridh sat up, her legs hanging over the side of the bed. "Eisengrimm," she said mournfully, "what if they didn't *want* to be found? What if they liked the Real World so much, they wanted to stay? What if they didn't really love me?"

Eisengrimm gripped the sleeve of her dress between his teeth and pulled her to her feet.

"Yes, yes, I'm coming," she said, following him with heavy footsteps.

❦

The early morning was very cool, and a golden autumn glow hung misty over the wild hedges in the garden and the trees in the wood. The aspen had already turned bright yellow, and the beech was stained with golden-red. A chance breeze shook leaves loose and they spun and dived toward the ground. Mayfridh pulled her pale bronze cloak around her against the morning chill as they approached the well.

"Hexebart!" Eisengrimm called.

"What do you want, dog-chops?" was the response.

"Witch, come here!" Mayfridh shouted. The anger

jumped in her chest. How she hated Hexebart, the thief of the royal magic.

"And why should I, you nasty little changeling?"

"Because I am the queen and I command it!"

The rope squeaked and began to hoist itself upward. In the end, the witch always complied. Hexebart had once been the most trusted and skilled sorceress of Mayfridh's faery parents, Queen Liesebet and King Jasper. She had pride of place in the spell chamber where she spun and wove the royal magic. It was customary, if the queen and king left the realm together, to store their magic with a guardian. The night that Mayfridh's parents had disappeared, Hexebart was chosen as that guardian. But they had failed to return and Hexebart had never accepted Queen Liesebet was dead, or that Mayfridh was the rightful heir, because she was a human child. Mayfridh had cast her down the well as punishment twenty years ago, but still the witch refused to hand the magic over. Yes, she performed any spells that were demanded of her—she had to, she was bound by a magical oath. But she swore that until she saw the dead bodies of the king and queen, she would believe they simply hadn't returned yet, and would protect their magic as she had been asked.

Hexebart appeared over the rim of the well, her bony gray fingers gripping the rusty bars of her cage. At her feet was a pile of glowing spells.

"What?" she demanded.

"I need spells," Mayfridh said.

"What for?"

"I don't have to tell you what for, just give them to me." Mayfridh held out the woven bag she carried spells in.

"Tell me what for."

"Just give me the spells."

"What will you do if I don't?"

Mayfridh's hands shook with anger. "I'll sew you in a sack and throw you in the lake; I'll put you in a barrel of nails and roll you down the hill; I'll tie you to four oxen and send them off in different directions."

"Ha," Hexebart cried, "you wouldn't dare."

"Give me the spells." Mayfridh was close to tears. "It's my magic, give it to me."

"It's not *yours*," Hexebart said, snatching up a handful of spells, "it's Queen Liesebet's."

"She's dead."

"How do I know you're not lying? You've probably locked her up in a dungeon somewhere."

"How can you suggest such a thing?"

Hexebart began pitching the spells out of the cage, aiming for Mayfridh's head. "Here, piglet; here, dog breath."

"Ow, stop that!" Mayfridh cried.

"Here, princess toadling; here, mongrel." The spells bounced off Mayfridh and to the ground. "Here are your spells, may you accidentally poison yourself with them." When the cage was empty, Hexebart released the rope and descended into the well with a crash.

Mayfridh leaned over the edge of the well and screamed, "I hate you!"

There was a sharp cackle in response and then silence. Mayfridh turned to see Eisengrimm collecting the spells, nudging them with his nose until they gathered at her feet.

"Come, Little May, forget about her."

"How can you be so reasonable?"

"You must be calm for the passage."

She kneeled and began to pick up the spells and slip them into her woven bag. "You are cruel to me, Eisengrimm. I am a poor orphan who is lonely and afraid."

He stifled a chuckle. "You shall be lonely no longer, Mayfridh. An old friend awaits you." He sat on his hind legs, and watched as she collected the last of the spells, a patient statue in the midst of her agitation.

"So," she said, climbing to her feet, her knees shaking beneath her, "I suppose it is time."

"Yes, my Queen. Let me lead you into the autumn forest."

Mayfridh followed him through the misty golden dawn into the woods. The trees were close and dark, shading out the pale light. Dead leaves crackled at their feet, and the constant scuff and skitter of soft falling made it seem as though the woods were whispering farewell and farewell, farther and farther into the gloom.

"There is a forest in the center of her city. Do you remember it from the spell we drank?"

"Yes, the Tiergarten."

"The passage is safest taken there. Fewer witnesses, no traffic. It is a short walk from there to Christine's home. If you become lost, use one of the spells as a map."

"I will."

"Good luck."

Mayfridh bent to kiss the top of Eisengrimm's head, then tried to force a breath down into her panic-squeezed lungs. She pulled one of the spells from the bag and let it rest on her upturned palm.

"Passage," she whispered into it, then blew gently. The spell began to dissolve, and in front of her a long oval shape began to flicker.

"You can return whenever you like," Eisengrimm said.

"Promise me I'll be safe."

"I promise you."

The oval shape resolved itself into a watery picture of the Real World. A dark wood, not unlike the one she stood in. But already she could hear the distant traffic, smell the odd sharp-sour smells.

"Farewell, Eisengrimm."

"Farewell, Little May."

She took a breath, stepped forward into the murky half-light between the worlds, and then through to the other side.

⚊ *from the Memoirs of Mandy Z.*

W riting this memoir is affecting my imagination in odd ways. Just the other night, I started to believe that I had a faery living in my own building. One of the girls, the skinny little thing that hangs on Jude Honeychurch's arm, had a most revolting faery odor clinging to her. I was sitting next to her, and she reached her arm toward me and I could smell it faintly. Like somebody who has stepped in something rotten and can't detect it himself, she was bewildered when I shot out of my chair and moved. How could I have eaten with that smell in my nostrils? And yet, a day or two later (after many hours pondering how I could kill her and bone her without Jude knowing), I ran into her again on the front step. No smell at all. Of course, I should have known she wasn't a faery. They are usually confident and glamorous, and this girl is not. She has an air of hungry-dog desperation about her, like she expects to be kicked at any moment. So what was it? A momentary glitch in my sense of smell? Or was it simply that I have spent so many hours thinking about my own faery stories to assess their suitability for my memoir—the triumphs and failures of my past—that I'm smelling faeries where there are only humans?

At least it relieves me of the problem of killing her. But I must be very certain next time I hunt a faery, because if my senses can lead me astray in such a manner, I could end up murdering an innocent human.

All this talk of killing faeries fills me with such a warm satisfaction, like it's Boxing Day and the clutter of torn wrapping paper is consigned to the rubbish bin, and there are just shiny new things waiting to be played with. My memories of happy moments. I have hunted many faeries in my time, but none were so satisfying as my first kill. I was fourteen and it was Christmastime.

The disagreement with my parents over the faery had never truly been resolved. They grew, I am almost certain, to hate me for my instincts. We fought a great deal, even after I pretended I no longer bore any ill will toward our faery relatives in an attempt to win back their love. They looked at me as if they didn't know me, with a sick despair that drove them eventually to consign me to a boarding school. Not for my own good or for the possibility of re- form, but simply because it became too painful for them to look upon me. I grew into a strong, if somewhat plump, young man and in the sanctuary of their blind spot I returned to my deepest fantasies about faeries. While the other boys were comparing their wispy new facial growth, or sharing their sex dreams about Elke Sommer, or forming sports teams to fill the emptiness of being banished from home, or hefting each other's musky ball sacks under the rough blan- kets at night, I cultivated a zealous solitariness and drew my pictures. By the time I was fourteen, I had nearly an entire suitcase full.

I was back in Bremen with my parents that Christmas, and they took me shopping to a large department store. I smelled him immediately.

Sitting on a pedestal, dressed as the Christmas Man, chil- dren climbing all over his lap.

A faery.

I had to play it cool, of course. My parents hadn't noticed him, so I steered them away from him and allowed the afternoon to pass as if nothing had happened.

But I planned, as soon as I could, to return.

I had an unbearable, sleepless night. I knew I should do something about that awful aberration, but I didn't know what. I couldn't let a faery wander around unchecked in my own city. I fantasized in great detail about killing the faery, but didn't know if I could. I was riddled with self-doubts.

I awoke and demanded that my mother take me to my aunt Marta's house. Aunt Marta lived within walking distance of the department store and Aunt Marta had a toolshed in the back garden, where my uncle Walt had gone to escape her incessant chatter in the years before he died. Mother must have been surprised by my sudden desire to see Aunt Marta—I had never before shown a particular fondness for her—but my parents were always eager to be apart from me. I packed my bags and installed myself at Aunt Marta's until Christmas.

Aunt Marta was a stupid old woman who could not stop gossiping. Every morning she made me breakfast and subjected me to an hour of chatter, made me morning tea and talked some more, made me lunch and so on. But every afternoon at four she went caroling with the small choir she belonged to, leaving me alone for three blissful hours.

Uncle Walt's toolshed hadn't been opened in the two years since he died. I crept out there as soon as Marta was gone, and slipped inside. Snow had fallen the night before, and the air was very quiet and chilled. I knew by now that it was my destiny to kill the faery, but I was too innocent to know where to start. It was necessarily going to be a crude and primitive exercise. As I looked around me, discovering tools that I thought might help—a mallet, a saw, a long screwdriver—I wished for streamlined equipment like daggers and guns. Every time I thought about what I intended to do that evening, such a warm liquid rush of excitement would flood my body that I had trouble remaining on my feet. While weighing the mallet in my hands and imagining bringing it crashing down on the Santa hat, I actually wet my pants. I left my soiled clothes for Aunt Marta to clean up, took the tools in a sack, and returned to the department store to seek out Santa.

Oh, I could smell him; his reeking bones under his skin called to me. I hovered nearby at a shelf filled with toys and watched him. Children climbed in and out of his lap, telling him their Christmas wishes. At one stage he caught sight of me, and patted his lap invitingly. He probably thought I was too embarrassed to volunteer my dearest Christmas wish to him, on account of being such a large boy. I shook my head and sank back between the shelves, savoring the knowledge that my Christmas wish would be granted soon.

I watched him all afternoon, then when the store closed, I hid beneath a rack of winter coats near the toy section and waited to see where he went and what he did. He disappeared from my view and I thought I had lost him. I saw the lights dim, I heard voices calling good night to each other, and I cursed myself for not thinking more clearly about what to do with him. But then luck intervened. After the store was quiet and I was considering how to leave now all the doors were locked, I saw him move back into my line of vision. He still wore his Santa suit and went from shelf to shelf in the toy section, from toy to toy, touching them with his fingers. I chanced slipping out from behind the coats and creeping closer to watch him. As he touched each toy, a glimmer of pale light would briefly envelop it, then fade. He was covering all the toys with faery blessings.

I've since learned much about faeries. Blessing objects, especially for children, is very characteristic of Dutch faeries. I had no idea then that he was from the Netherlands, but when I did realize, years later, that my first kill was Dutch, I took a certain satisfaction in it as I have never liked anybody from that country.

I watched him, horrified that he was putting his foul touch on all those toys. When he had finished two or three shelves, he tired. I followed him silently as he found a back exit from the department store and slipped out into an alley. I was two seconds after him, and he looked up and saw me.

"Hello," he said smiling, "didn't I see you earlier today?"

I glared at him without speaking. If he was unnerved by the fat boy stalking him, he gave no indication.

"Merry Christmas," he said, and turned away.

You may be surprised to hear that my first kill, with those primitive instruments, was so effective and satisfying that I have never actually upgraded to the sleek equipment I fantasized about earlier that day. I still have Uncle Walt's tools, and I still use them from time to time for the sake of nostalgia as much as for the way the grooves sit familiar in my hand. I followed the Dutch faery, I bludgeoned him to death in the alley, and I returned to Aunt Marta's. It was as wonderful as I had anticipated, if a little messy.

But before I left, I took out the saw and I sawed off one of the faery's fingers, wrapping it carefully in his Santa hat. In the privacy of my bedroom back home in Niederbüren on Christmas Eve, I unwrapped my cherished prize to inspect it. With patience, remarkable for such a young man, I stripped away the flesh, careful not to scrape the bone, until I revealed the shining treasure beneath.

Not silver. Although I am color-blind, it was apparent that this bone was not precious metal as I had been told. Rather, it was whiter than anything in my field of vision, and it glowed softly, catching the light and radiating it at pretty angles. I scrubbed it to remove the repulsive faery smell, and from that moment on could barely take my eyes off it. That night, after all the lights in the house had been switched off, I pulled out my old night-light, and by its soft glow placed the bone on my desk. I reached for the sharp knife I used on my model planes and I began to scratch and scrape, carving a crooked face upon the bone. Hours passed, and I was deeply immersed in that wonderful thrill of promise and labor known to all artists. I have yet to experience a Christmas as splendid as that one.

I still have that carving today. It sits in a special silver bracket above the window in my sculpture room. That carving, crude and childish as it is, is unutterably important to me. It represents the finest season of my childhood, a turning point in my identity, the moment when I knew I had found my life's work.

Mayfridh hesitated just outside the building where Christine lived. She had come this far—across worlds, through traffic—but now she wondered if visiting Christine was an ill-considered scheme. Her old friend had not been happy to be in Ewigkreis; maybe her unhappiness was something to do with Mayfridh herself? Maybe Christine didn't like her?

She glanced around her. It was late afternoon, but not yet dark. The Real World was nowhere near as scary as she had anticipated. Mayfridh reminded herself that she was a native of this world, whatever she had become later, and its rhythms and impressions were almost familiar. She remembered traffic lights and train lines and cigarette smoke and electricity. Those memories, added to the spell she had drunk, made her feel almost at home in this land so distant from her own.

Once more she turned her attention to the intercom at the front door. No point in agonizing about it. If Christine didn't want to see her, that would be that. But Mayfridh had to give her the opportunity to say as much.

With a deep breath, she approached the door. Eisengrimm had told her which button to push. It was the one marked "Honeychurch." She wondered why Christine had called her home such a delicious name.

"Hello?" A man's voice came out of the intercom—that painstakingly faked magic they called technology—and Mayfridh was too surprised to speak. Had Eisengrimm got the number wrong? Did Christine live in the unappealingly named "Zweigler" or "Ekman" instead?

"Hello?" The voice again. Mayfridh realized she should say something.

"Er . . . hello. I had hoped to see Christine Starlight."

"She's not back from work yet. Do you want to come up and wait for her?"

Mayfridh realized the voice must belong to the man she had seen Christine with. "Yes, yes I would," she said.

"We're in number three."

The door buzzed and then there was silence. She pressed the button again.

"Hello?" He was impatient, and Mayfridh's heart hiccupped. She wanted Christine's lover to like her.

"I'm sorry, but can I come in?" she asked, warily.

The voice laughed, a soft warm laugh, releasing the impatience. "You have to push the door open when I buzz it. Okay?"

"Sorry." Why hadn't that important detail made it into the spell? She supposed Christine had never had to ring her own doorbell.

The door buzzed again and she pushed it open, and headed up the stairs. This lover of Christine's sounded very friendly. She liked him already, which surprised her. He had seemed like such an ugly stocky fellow when Eisengrimm saw him. She found a door with a "3" marked on it, and knocked.

The door opened. "Hi," he said with a smile. It wasn't the dark, fat man.

Mayfridh stood, stunned into silence. He was beautiful, unspeakably beautiful. His hair was the color of straw, tousled and curling into his neck. His eyes were dark and gleaming under a broad, noble forehead. He smelled of exotic spices and warm clean skin. And he smiled as though he knew the most intimate secrets of all the lovers in the history of the universe.

"Do you want to come in?"

"Who are you?" she asked.

His smile dwindled around the corners, and his face took on a puzzled look. Mayfridh was enchanted by the way his expression moved, his feelings shifting like fluid across his forehead and eyes and mouth.

"I'm Jude," he said, slowly now as though talking to a madwoman.

Mayfridh gathered herself. "I'm Miranda," she said, superstitiously reverting to her old human name. A name was a dangerous thing to reveal to the wrong person. "I'm an old friend of Christine's."

He held open the door and indicated the sofa. "Look, go on in and wait for her. I'm going down to the studio."

"The studio?"

"I'm a painter."

Christine had her own painter? Even Mayfridh didn't have a dedicated painter living with her. But maybe she'd misunderstood the situation. "How interesting," she said, stepping inside. His body was so close her arm brushed his sleeve and she felt a sudden hot shiver.

"Okay, I'll just be downstairs. Christine should be home any minute."

"I'll wait right here."

"Nice to meet you," he said, closing the door behind him.

Mayfridh went obediently to the sofa and sat down. All the details of Christine's life that Mayfridh had been so eager to witness—the objects with which she filled her home, the sights and smells with which she surrounded herself—were suddenly vastly and ever-dwindlingly unimportant.

Jude was a painter. Mayfridh turned the thought over and over in her head, savoring the pleasure that it gave her. A spinning, falling feeling of promise pulled at her heart. With a bubble of joy caught in her throat, she realized she had just fallen in love.

CHAPTER SIX

*C*hristine shut out the windy street and ran directly into Gerda.

"Hi, how was work?" Gerda asked, unhooking her coat from the rack beside the front door.

"Same as always. Boring and unrewarding," Christine replied.

Gerda narrowed her eyes slightly. Christine knew what she was thinking: *But you don't need to work, Christine, you're a millionaire.* It had been the topic of one of the first conversations the two women had shared. Gerda had made it clear that Christine's reason for sitting on her inheritance—her discomfort about benefiting so greatly from the death of her parents—was sweet, but misplaced. Nobody except Jude ever understood. Christine maintained that the right time to crack open the account and make guilt-free use of it would be when she was married and planning children of her own.

"I'm going out for a coffee," Gerda said. "Want to come?"

"Maybe another time," Christine said.

Gerda pulled open the door to the gray afternoon. "Jude's in the studio if you're looking for him."

"Thanks."

Christine shrugged out of her light coat and hung it up, then ducked around the side of the staircase and into the gallery.

The Immanuel K. Zweigler Collection was officially open from one P.M. until eight P.M. Mondays to Thursdays. The walls were painted stark white, and the floor was made of the same broad planks of unpolished wood as every other floor in Hotel Mandy-Z. The gallery was cluttered and over-full: a row of paintings around the walls, and sculptures and installations jammed into every corner. Pete's latest—video footage of eight cats roaming in a fast-food restaurant after hours, while eerie Japanese music played—had a dedicated area marked off with plastic chain. It was Friday, so the gallery was closed. Mandy was nowhere in sight, and the lights in the ceiling were dark. The Japanese music had been left on, hissing and shadowy like a radio tuned just off the station. A corridor opened off the gallery, four doors lined it: one for each of the artists' cramped but warm studios. She pushed open the door to number three.

"Hi," she said.

Jude turned, semidistracted, his mouth pressed into a downward curve of consideration. "Oh, hi."

"Sorry for interrupting."

"It's fine," he said, putting down his paintbrush, then immediately picking it up again. On the canvas in front of him, a gray curve. The blue sofa behind him was covered in rags and paint tubes and canvases. "I'm not sure what I'm doing here."

"Painting a picture?"

He didn't smile; probably hadn't even heard her. "I'm so

sick of the shapes of my own brushstrokes. I'm tired of Jude Honeychurch."

She backed off. Jude got like this periodically, and was best left alone. "I'll leave you to it then."

"Okay, I'll be up for dinner." Then, remembering something, he turned to her and said, "There's someone waiting upstairs for you. Can't remember her name, sorry."

"Who is it?" Christine didn't know anybody in Berlin who Jude didn't also know.

"She says she's an old friend of yours. Her name started with 'M.' "

Christine felt a sharp flutter of cold in her stomach. "What?"

"Miranda, that's it. She's wearing weird clothes, like she's dressed for a medieval costume party or something."

Christine stood rooted to the spot for a moment as Jude started loading up his brush with paint. "What does she look like?"

"Pretty, long red hair. Why don't you go up and see her? She's just waiting in the lounge room." Jude sounded so unaffected, as if it were the most ordinary thing in the world. "Go on, I can't concentrate with you here."

She turned and left, closing the door behind her, grabbing a breath in the corridor before heading for the stairs—

Miranda

—There would be a logical explanation—

like she's dressed for a medieval costume party

—There had to be a logical explanation and the quicker she got upstairs—

pretty, long red hair

—the quicker she would know that explanation and be able to laugh at the blundering panic that now thumbed its way up her ribs.

Her hand shook as she reached for the door and pushed it

open. She took one step inside and saw the faery queen from her dream, sitting on her sofa.

Christine yelped and jumped back.

Mayfridh rose and came toward her. "Christine, what's the matter?"

Christine pressed her hands to her head and screwed her eyes shut. "Get out, get out, get out," she said, willing the vision to go away. But Jude had seen her too. Jude had spoken to her. How could that be?

"You want me to go already?" Mayfridh sounded irritated, even petulant. "You haven't even asked why I'm here."

Christine dropped her hands and stared. Mayfridh looked real, flesh and blood, and Jude had seen her and . . . A surge of dread and nausea and white spangles whooshed up through her lungs. She fought for breath. This was it, she was finally succumbing to insanity. "You're not real," Christine managed to say. "Get out of my head."

"I'm not . . ." Mayfridh paused, considering. "Oh, I see. It's not because you don't like me that you want me to leave, it's because I'm frightening you." And then, before Christine could understand what was happening, Mayfridh had reached into her hessian bag and pulled out a glowing translucent ball.

"Believe," Mayfridh said, blowing gently on the ball. It dissolved on her palm, and a sheer curtain of fresh, clear light washed through Christine's mind.

"What the . . . ?" Suddenly, Christine's dread was gone. She wasn't crazy. Mayfridh really was here, really was the queen of the faeries. Her dream had always been a real experience, and none of these facts threatened to undo her or overwhelm her. "What did you do to me?" Christine said, pressing her fingers into her temple.

"I stopped you from being frightened." Mayfridh beamed, pleased with herself.

"You put a spell on me?" The words should have been so ridiculous, but weren't.

"A little spell." Mayfridh held her thumb and forefinger a half-inch apart. "You needed it."

Christine was annoyed. "Isn't there some code of ethics about putting spells on people? What if I didn't want you to put a spell on me?"

"I was trying to help you."

Christine stared at her. "What the hell are you doing here?"

"Looking for you."

"But what . . ." Christine turned and pushed the door shut with her toe. "But what could you possibly want with me?"

"To talk to you. I'd forgotten all about you until you came, and then I remembered how much fun we'd had as children and I thought you might want to renew our friendship." Although Mayfridh's noble posture and dignified voice matched her status, her dark blue eyes betrayed a childlike vulnerability, a longing.

Christine sighed. "This is just too weird."

"Do you want another spell?"

"No, no more spells. Just give me a minute here. It's not every day the queen of the faeries turns up on my sofa." Christine took a deep breath. "What happened to you, May?"

"My name's Mayfridh now."

"Where did you go that morning?"

"Two faeries came in the night and took me, adopted me. Queen Liesebet and King Jasper. I forgot the Real World soon after."

"There was a crow in your bed."

"Probably Eisengrimm."

"And this . . . faery world of yours. Where is it?"

"It's just Over There." She gestured vaguely around her with both hands. "I think."

"That's not very specific."

This annoyed Mayfridh. "You explain where your world is then," she said.

"It's . . ." Christine paused. "It's somewhere in the universe," she finished.

"So is Ewigkreis."

"And why is it all old-fashioned? I mean, if it exists now like this world exists now, why does it look so . . . medieval?"

"Most faerylands are simple and rural; but thanks to Oma Edelheid, my great-grandmother, ours is particularly antiquated. She was approaching her four-hundredth birthday and wanted time to stop. So it did, in 1487. But she died shortly afterwards, taking the words of the spell with her. Ewigkreis is stuck there, cycling through seasons and starting all over again."

"How did she die?"

"Edelheid? Old age, of course."

Christine raised her eyebrows. "Of course."

"Look, all this is very boring for me. I'll have Eisengrimm explain it all to you sometime," Mayfridh said, flicking her long wavy hair over her shoulder. "I want you to be my friend and I want to get to know about the Real World—it's my native land, after all—and I had rather hoped you would be as eager as me."

Christine shook her head. It was too much, with or without the *believe* spell. She needed some time and space to breathe. "I'm finding it very hard to cope with all this. Can you maybe come back tomorrow? Give me time to sleep on it?"

Mayfridh puffed up with indignation. "But—"

Christine found herself growing amused. "First lesson about the Real World, Mayfridh," she said gently, "you're not the queen here."

Mayfridh smiled sheepishly. "I suppose I'm not."

"You always were kind of bossy," Christine said. "Remember?"

"And you always sulked," Mayfridh said, laughing.

As she laughed, Christine could see in her features the little girl who had once been her dearest friend. "Come back tomorrow," Christine said. "We can have coffee and a long talk, and I'll take you for a walk or something."

"Will Jude be here?"

"Jude?" Christine was perplexed. What did Mayfridh care about Jude?

"Jude, your painter."

Christine laughed. "Jude's not my painter."

"But he said—"

"He's a painter, yes. But he's my boyfriend."

"Oh." Mayfridh's eyes flicked downward, and a wariness stole into Christine's heart. Could a faery with *believe* spells also perform *love me* spells?

"No, he won't be around," Christine said. She would make sure of that.

"I see. I shall return to my home, then. But tomorrow, I'll come back." She hesitated, her eyes darting over her shoulder. "Can I use your bathroom?"

The idea that faeries needed to pee seemed so out of kilter, Christine almost laughed. "Sure."

Christine waited, hoping that Jude wouldn't return. How was she going to explain this to anyone? It wasn't like she had a *believe* spell to hand out with her explanation. Jude would finally agree that she was going nuts if she tried to tell him the truth about Mayfridh.

Mayfridh emerged from the bathroom checking her hessian bag, and moved toward the door.

"Don't you just disappear into thin air?" Christine asked.

"No, I have to return to the passage. It's in the Tiergarten."

"Do you know the way? Do you want me to come?"

"No, no, I can manage," Mayfridh replied.

"I'll see you tomorrow, then."

"I can't wait." Mayfridh gave Christine a spontaneous hug and then, embarrassed, hurried off. Christine winced. The faery was determined to be her friend, and she was even higher maintenance than Gerda. She collapsed onto the sofa and let her head fall back, closing her eyes. Her back twinged and her shoulders felt stiff.

A glowing fissure of understanding had opened up in her universe. Until twenty minutes ago, she hadn't even believed in ghosts. *Not even ghosts.* But now, an alternative realm full of magic and faeries and shape-shifters had become real for her, thanks to Mayfridh's spell. She didn't know whether to sob uncontrollably or laugh hysterically. What wonders, what unknown joys and horrors, had been there all along as she lived her gray life, pole to dreary pole, smugly thinking she knew the limits of reality?

Faeries. Good God, faeries.

And then she opened her eyes, realization feathering into her consciousness like pale clouds at sunset. *No pain.* A place genuinely existed where she experienced *no pain.*

"Oh, God," she breathed, "it's *real.*"

❦

Mayfridh? I had not expected you back so soon."

Mayfridh slammed the door to her bedchamber behind her and flung herself on the bed. "She sent me home!"

"What? Why?"

Mayfridh flipped over and her gaze was drawn to the yellowed leaves in the hazy sunset falling from the massive beech outside her window. Something about their hesitant descent made her feel melancholy. "She said she needed time to think. She wants me to go back, though."

Eisengrimm leapt from the wool rug and joined Mayfridh among the soft white covers. She propped herself on her side, one of her hands idly tangling in the fur over the wolf's ribs.

"That is good, is it not?" Eisengrimm said. "If she wants you to go back."

"Tomorrow." Even though her visit had gone well, even though she was home safe and sound and Christine had invited her to return, Mayfridh felt a gloomy sense of destiny mislaid, of her fingertips grasping for something wonderful only for it to spin past without her.

"What is wrong, Mayfridh?" Eisengrimm asked. She could feel his deep voice rumbling under his rib cage.

"She has a lover. His name is Jude."

"And you are jealous of this lover? You wish for her only to be your friend and nobody else's?"

Mayfridh shook her head and turned to face Eisengrimm. "I'm jealous, yes. But not of him. I'm jealous of her."

"You mean . . . ?"

She sighed, sinking into the bed. "He is so very beautiful, Eisengrimm. For ten wonderful minutes I had convinced myself he would be mine. And then . . . then Christine came and he wasn't."

Eisengrimm's golden eyes narrowed, and the ghost of a sneer creased his muzzle. "Is it not for the best, Little May? Human men are treacherous."

"Eisengrimm, I felt so bound to him. My heart pounded. It never has before."

"But you know nothing of his heart or soul, only his face and body."

"I know his soul, Eisengrimm. I felt it. It touched my own. There was a jolt of recognition, connectedness. I know he felt it too."

"Could it not be your imagination?"

"No, it was real." She sat up. "Eisengrimm, what if he's my soul mate? What if he's the only man I can ever love? Would it be so wrong to fall in love with him if the whole of destiny has decided we should be together?"

"Mayfridh," Eisengrimm replied, a warning note in his voice, "do not think to interfere with Christine's life."

"But—"

"The last leaf will fall, and it will be time to go to the Winter Castle, and you will forget Jude soon enough. He is Christine's lover. Do not destroy her happiness."

"You give good counsel, Eisengrimm," she said through gritted teeth, "though I sometimes despise you for it."

"One day you may thank me for it. Enjoy your time with Christine, remembering always that it will pass." He stretched his legs and leapt from the bed, padding toward the door. "Tomorrow I shall accompany you into the autumn forest again."

She watched him leave. When she was sure he was gone, she searched in her hessian bag for the spell, the special one she had cast and then recovered in Christine's bathroom— Jude's bathroom—in front of the shining mirror.

"Here it is," she said, cradling it in her palm. Yes, it was stealing, but he may never notice it gone. She peered closely, looking for Jude's reflection.

❧

A long way away, that's where she was. The loud jazz music, the smoke-filled air, the taste of the beer, the hot itchiness of heating set too high, all registered on Christine's body, but still she felt a long way away. She looked around. Gerda was involved in some kind of drinking game with Fabiyan, and Pete regaled Jude with statistics about roadkill per square mile on Australian roads; the swirl of people dressed in dark clothes, and the glow of cigarettes being lit and smoked from one end of the bar to the other; everything was flat and staged as if she were watching it in a movie.

I can't tell anyone.

The sooner Mayfridh returned, got her visit over with, and went back to faeryland forever—even though Christine was looking forward to reminiscing with her—the sooner she would be able to feel normal again. Or would she ever completely recover from this shock? How many more things in the world were there to be feared than she had ever imagined? If faeries existed, why not ghosts, aliens, witches, sea monsters? She looked at Jude—one eyebrow cocked, peering at the end of his cigarette to see if it were properly lit— and felt a surge of . . . something. Maybe not love, as it wasn't entirely a pleasant feeling. Yearning and fear as much as desire. One day, perhaps, she would tell him about Mayfridh. In the distant future, when they had left Berlin behind and life had resumed its reassuringly ordinary dimensions.

"So what's with you today, Miss Starlight?" Gerda asked, breaking into her bubble.

"I'm tired, that's all," Christine answered.

"An old friend of Christine's came by today," Jude said. "An English girl."

"I didn't know you knew anyone in Berlin," Gerda said, stubbing out her cigarette.

"What was her name, Christine?" Jude asked. "Miranda?"

"Yes, Miranda," Christine said, wondering again why the

faery queen had given Jude her human name. It was convenient, because she had spoken at length to Jude about a certain May Frith, and he would surely have noticed the similarities in the names and asked too many unanswerable questions.

Gerda had tilted her head, was watching Christine curiously.

"An old friend from when you used to live here?" Pete asked.

This was getting tricky. "I used to know her family," she said, rising from her seat. "Anyone want anything from the bar?"

"I'll come," Gerda said, springing from her chair.

They fought their way through the crowd to the bar. While they waited, Gerda turned to Christine and said, "Miranda, the English girl . . . ?"

"Not a girl," Christine said, wondering where Gerda was heading with these comments. "A woman. My age."

"An old family friend?"

"What is it, Gerda?"

"How did she find you?"

"She . . . ah . . ."

"Christine, you've forgotten. You told me about Miranda—Little May—the daughter of the English colonel. The dead girl."

The bartender arrived, saving Christine from having to respond immediately. They took their drinks, and Gerda dragged Christine away from Jude and the others toward a dark corner near the back of the room.

"Tell me everything," Gerda said. "Is this why you look so pale? Seen a ghost?"

"No, really, it's all just coincidental. . . ." Christine trailed off, realizing this would convince nobody. "Gerda, I just . . . I don't know what . . ."

"Tell me. I'll believe you. Jude saw her too, right? But he doesn't know she's a ghost."

"She's not a ghost. She didn't die. We all just assumed she was dead, but . . . God, I don't even know how to start explaining this."

"Just give it a try."

Christine opened her mouth, about to spill the whole story to Gerda. But she couldn't. As much as Gerda was always on about ghosts and psychics and magic, this was just too far-fetched for anyone to believe. Unless they had been put under a spell. "I can't tell you, Gerda."

"What do you mean?"

"I was wrong; she wasn't murdered. She was . . . it's private. Family stuff. Not for me to say."

Gerda looked skeptical. "How did she find you?"

"Through a customer at the bookshop. Starlight's an unusual surname." Rather than feeling relieved that she had thought up a plausible explanation, Christine felt heavy and sad, her chance to share some of the burden evaporating.

"So she's not a ghost?"

Christine shook her head. "Definitely not. I promise you she's not a ghost. Sorry, are you disappointed?"

Gerda smiled half a smile. "Not really. To tell the truth, I'm afraid of ghosts."

"Look," Christine said, "don't tell Jude about Miranda. He doesn't know, he doesn't need to know."

"I won't tell."

"Thanks. It's all too complex," Christine said, "and anyway, after tomorrow I doubt I'll ever see her again."

❧

Jude slid into bed beside her, his skin cool and his hair damp from the shower. "I drank too much," he groaned.

"You always drink too much at Super Jazz."

"I've got to start taking care of myself. I hate everything I paint at the moment, and I'm sure it's because of all the junk I put in my body."

Christine ran her fingers over his chest. "Your body feels pretty good to me."

"And as for my head . . . God, I must be so drunk," he muttered, pushing her hand away.

"What's the matter?"

"I could have sworn I saw . . ." He didn't finish, and Christine felt her skin prickle.

"What did you see?"

Jude laughed. "Oooh, boy, I drank too much tonight. Christine, it's what I *didn't* see that's the problem."

"I don't get it."

"I looked in the bathroom mirror, and I wasn't there," he said. "Jesus, it sounds even crazier out loud."

"What do you mean you weren't there?"

"I wasn't there. Like a vampire or something. And I leaned close to look and a moment later I *was* there. Vodka-induced hallucination."

Christine forced a laugh. This had to have something to do with Mayfridh, of course. "I guess so."

"Wasn't it just last week you were worried that you were going crazy?"

"Yeah."

"Looks like it's contagious." He kissed the top of her head. "No more alcohol. Not if it's making us crazy."

"I think we're both perfectly sane," Christine said. "In fact, I'm sure of it."

After the first hour, Mayfridh's incantation made no sense anymore. It bounced past her ears like abstract background noise. Perspiration soaked the front of her dress, her hair dripped and clung to her face, and her eyes stung. Mayfridh kept her gaze fixed on the large square mirror in front of her, the reflection of Jude captured and still within it.

This kind of magic was the hardest. To penetrate another's thoughts and feelings was nearly impossible to do with the little magic meted out to her by Hexebart, and required clear focus and unwavering attention. The deep complexities of being always obscured clear pathways to knowledge; to read a person was akin to trying to distill the Bible into one sentence. Still, she persisted. If she couldn't have Jude, she could at least attempt to know what she was denied.

With her eyes fixed on his, she found that glimmers of understanding were starting to form. Jude loved to paint. It was the only time he felt truly disconnected from the petty sorrows of reality. She breathed and focused, trying to explore more deeply. Jude sometimes despaired about the future. She tried to follow that thread farther. Was his despair to do with Christine? But the thread ran out, sent her colliding with another. Jude was filled with compassion, almost to a fault. He cared too deeply about the suffering of others, which made him vulnerable and helpless at times.

"But does he love Christine?" she said, dropping the incantation for a moment to try to direct her exploration.

Oh, yes, he loved Christine, but there was something half-empty about this love. He felt sadness for her, and hope for . . . something. What was it? She pushed further, resumed the incantation. Did he love Christine?

Clunk.

Like a window dropping into its frame. Mayfridh found herself shut out, reeling back along the threads she had explored and out of her trance. Jude's image dissolved and disappeared, leaving her staring at her own reflection, pale and wild-eyed and bathed in sweat.

A thrill of hope and mystery seized her. An obstruction of that magnitude, one that could undo her spell and propel her backward so fast, meant only one thing.

Jude had a secret.

CHAPTER SEVEN

— from the Memoirs of Mandy Z.

This morning, I experimented with my Wife. I was visited by insomnia: my brain was too full and too heavy on the pillow. I arose in the black before dawn, crept up the stairs to my sculpture room, and sat gazing at her in the gently lifting dark for a long time.

My intention has always been that the Bone Wife will be more than a sculpture. When she is finished, she will be able to wash my clothes, and make my bed, and clean my shoes, and so on. I have no magical ability myself, but I have a secret, tucked away amongst the bones, which has imbued the whole sculpture with enchantment. At my command, the bones will move. But it's not as simple as it sounds. Yes, they shake. Yes, they jump. Yes, they twitch. It's up to me to make them shake and jump and twitch in harmony.

My Bone Wife has the finest ankles and the most exquisite knees. I refine them constantly, making the joints more agile and flexible. This morning, as the first weak rays of sunlight crept into my room, I worked some more on the joints of her toes. Then I stood back and told her to walk.

She shook. She jumped. She twitched. The bones clacked and clattered on the floor.

"Walk!" I said.

Clack. Clatter.

"Walk!"

Her right knee jerked up, opened out. Her foot came back down, her weight settling onto it. Then her left knee. Up, out, down, settle. Then her right knee again and I started to laugh, but I laughed too soon, for then she pitched forward and clacked and clattered to the ground. A shining chip of bone sailed through the air and scratched my cheek. A fraction higher and it might have cut my eye. Perhaps my Bone Wife doesn't like being told to walk. It wouldn't surprise me if faeries were as cantankerous dead as they are alive.

Now, to continue with my memoir.

After I had finished school, my parents tried to send me to university. I refused to go. I knew that I wanted to spend my life drawing and sculpting and seeking out faeries to kill and bone. I told my father that I wanted to travel and see great works of art. They agreed that I could do this for two years, but then I must study at university—something useful, like law or business—or they would cut me out of my inheritance. So I packed my bags and my books, and I strung my carved faery bone around my neck for luck, and took off into the wide world.

I wanted to go to the place where I would find the most faeries, so I chose Ireland. I know now that, although Ireland is famous for its faeries, it is not because they boast the highest population. It is simply because Irish faeries are irritatingly conspicuous egomaniacs. They groundlessly believe their race—the Sidhe—to be the supreme race of all faeries. They love to read stories of themselves in the books that humans produce, and often come to the Real World to perform activities they hope will make them famous. Despite this, their Shadowland grows less and less populous every year. They are a dying race. You may be surprised to know that the largest population of faeries is in the United States of America. The faeries there prefer the Real World to their own world, and run about in it without ever giving away the truth about who they are. In fact, I suspect a number of famous actors and performers are faeries; rather too high profile for me to hunt them safely (though you can credit me with a couple of unsolved hitchhiker disappearances in that great nation).

However, as a young man I thought Ireland was the place to be, and so that is where I went.

I found myself in a village on the Antrim coast, passing the hours working with marble. I have always preferred the discovery and drawing-out involved in carving and chiseling sculpture, rather than the molding and shaping used with clay or other soft substances. I like to force my will on stone and bone. I began to produce small sculptures—models of the birds and animals I saw daily—reveling in the challenges of creating something that looked soft and pliable from something so hard and rigid. I grew adept very quickly, and by summer I was selling my sculptures as souvenirs at a local bookshop. Still, months had passed and I had seen no faeries. I began to wonder if my two earlier experiences were the kind of rare luck that is never repeated, and whether I would live the rest of my life, traveling as far as the sky was sky, never to see another faery. While the thought disappointed me, I took great consolation in my art. I could truly be happy while sculpting.

And then, a story began to circulate around the pubs and shops, a story in which I took great interest.

Sorcha O'Faolain, youngest daughter of the O'Faolains who ran the Merry Myrtle, was seventeen and very pregnant. Her boyfriend, Conla, had run off to Dublin and abandoned her. Over the past few months, I had watched the poor girl serving me my dinner and drinks every night in the pub. As she grew bigger and bigger, her face grew sadder and sadder. I saw her parents exercise their sharp tongues on her. I saw her wandering alone and friendless in the village, her shoulders falling lower each day under the burden of the rest of her life.

The story goes that one day she woke up with a desire to walk, to walk fast and far, just to *move*. A rush of energy had gripped her and to sit still was to feel as though she might explode. So she walked. She walked down the path and out the gate, and up the road, and over the fields of ragged grass, and to the cliffs, and right to the water's edge, and up the stony beach for miles, one foot in front of the other, feeling her heart and her lungs and her muscles move.

Then the first wave of pain hit. Starting in her back, spreading up under her like a giant crooked hand. The child was coming.

She took herself back up the cliff path, but just a few steps onto the grass she knew she could go no farther. A biting sea wind had risen, and she took shelter in the roofless remains of an empty stone cottage nearby. She lay down on the old floor and cried and cried for her poor child, and her poor self.

"I will take care of you, Sorcha."

She looked up and saw a beautiful woman, with sharp features and long pale hair, standing over her.

"Who are you?" Sorcha asked.

"I am Duana of the Sidhe. I will take care of you."

And right there, under the wide sky and rotted roof beams, the faery helped deliver Sorcha's baby, administering faery medicine and faery magic in equal measure, and wrapping the child in a strip torn from her glowing faery dress. Then she disappeared, and Sorcha walked back to the village with her babe—a little girl she named Duana—in her arms.

The next morning when she went to look for the scrap of faery fabric, to show her friends, it had disappeared.

Now, this story spread quickly through the village, and Sorcha O'Faolain was considered by some to be one of the chosen few with a faery guardian, and by some to be a barefaced liar. Only I knew the truth: Sorcha O'Faolain was simply in the right place at the right time to take advantage of an Irish faery's narcissism. Duana of the Sidhe knew such an act would make her famous. All I had to do was visit the same place and take the same advantage.

I called in on Sorcha, asked her as many questions as I could without arousing suspicion, then packed my rucksack with weapons and tools and headed out of the village.

Of course, I could hardly pretend that I was a heavily pregnant woman. I had to feign some terrible distress. I found my way to the ruined cottage, taking photographs like a tourist. When I was inside and away from the sun and the eyes of others, I pretended to trip. I cried out, thumped the ground hard, pricked my palm on my knife and smeared the blood over my forehead. Then I lay, very still, and waited.

One's senses grow curiously sharp when one is waiting. I heard every sound around me: the scurryings and skitterings of seagulls in the roof, the crackle and breath of the most fragile breeze, the faraway beat and suck of the sea. And I heard her coming. I heard a gathering of air that hadn't been there before, a ringing underlying everything else, white and hot and strange. I knew she was nearby.

I moaned. "Help me," I said.

"I will take care of you, Immanuel," she said.

She approached, her footsteps delicate on the moss and stone. Her toes came into my view, dainty and pale and ringed with jewels. I must have twitched, the excitement overcoming me, because the toes paused, hesitant, then began to pull back.

I had no time to lose. In a flash I grabbed her by the toe. She screamed and tried to pull away. I seized her ankle with an iron grip. Still she screamed. By now I was on my knees, the faery caught in my right hand. She was small and fragile, as Irish faeries are, with sharp eyes and nose and mouth. Oh, I could smell her, the foul smell of the foulest of all races, and my other hand shot out and pulled her down, pinned her by her throat and her knees, and her scream gurgled and died but I didn't let go, because faeries are tricksters and her head would have to be detached from her body before I'd really believe she was dead.

When I had killed her, I took her down to the stony sea to bone her. It was very messy, much messier than I had anticipated, but I let the sea wash the blood and flesh away, and I returned home many hours later with a sack full of faery bones and an idea to start a grand sculpture.

You must understand: my Bone Wife does not look like a skeleton. I cut the bones and shave the bones and glue the bones together. I make a solid block of gleaming material, and then I begin to carve, saving my offcuts to be glued and polished and used later. It is a remarkable material to work with and one of the rarest, which explains in part why I am still only halfway finished with that sculpture nearly thirty years later. I do not consider myself unlucky though. The secret, diffused through all the bones and making them enchanted, was my greatest stroke of luck. Only one material bears such enchantment.

Royal faery bones.

❧

Mayfridh decided that she liked traffic. She liked the rhythms of its currents, liked the ponderous metal dance of its turns and the hectic weaving of its flow. She even liked the noise. Sometimes Ewigkreis was so silent that she could believe herself completely alone in the universe, but here, in a big city in the Real World, she felt a sense of belonging, of never-alone-ness. She was so busy watching the traffic that she almost walked out in front of it. At the crossing of Unter-den-Linden and Friedrichstrasse, a young woman grabbed her by the shoulder just as she was about to step in front of a van.

"Oh!" Mayfridh cried.

The young woman said something to her in German, but Mayfridh didn't notice. She was staring at the woman's hair. It was brilliant blue.

"Your hair is beautiful," Mayfridh breathed.

The young woman smiled and shrugged, and Mayfridh realized that just because Christine spoke English didn't mean everybody else in Berlin did. She struggled for her childhood German, came up with a clunking sentence that translated to, "Where is your hair from?"

"DC's," the woman answered, and indicated the other end of Friedrichstrasse. "Galeries Lafayette."

Mayfridh turned in the direction she pointed, then turned back to see the young woman crossing the road away from her. She wore a shiny black bodice and skirt, and a long red coat. Mayfridh felt a pang of jealousy for how she looked, striding along in her beautiful colors. In her own world, Mayfridh was a queen, considered the most beautiful, catching the eye of everyone who passed her. Here, she was an unknown woman in a pale brown dress. Perhaps it was time to try this *shopping*.

She walked up to Galeries Lafayette, a shiny gallery of stores, and went in search of DC's. Down the escalator and she found it. She tortured her mind for the German word for color and entered the salon. A deeply tanned hairdresser looked up from his appointment book and asked her a question in German.

"Hello . . . um . . ." Mayfridh tugged her hair and said, "Farbe?"

"Of course," the hairdresser replied in heavily accented English. He reached behind him and pulled out a book, bristling with hair samples in every color of the rainbow.

Mayfridh caught her breath.

The hairdresser smiled. "Which one?"

❧

By seven o'clock that evening, Christine found herself pacing. Jude was in the studio, but would almost certainly be upstairs shortly looking for his dinner. She didn't want Jude and Mayfridh to cross paths ever again. She had expected Mayfridh hours ago, assuming she would arrive at the same time as yesterday. But Ewigkreis's time probably didn't accord with time here in Berlin. Christine's visit there had taken place in the space of three minutes.

Christine didn't know what she would do with Mayfridh once she was here, except get her out of the apartment quickly. Maybe take her to a cafe, satisfy her curiosity, and send her home for good. That was the plan.

Voices on the stairs. Christine ran to the door and threw it open. No, that was Gerda's voice. But who was with her?

"You should come," Gerda was saying, "you'd love it."

"Will Christine be there?"

It was Mayfridh. Gerda must have let her in downstairs and now they were chatting and, oh no, it sounded like Gerda had invited her out somewhere.

"I'm sure she will be, why don't we ask her?"

They appeared on the landing below. Gerda smiled up at her and waved. "Hi, Christine, I met Miranda outside."

And then Mayfridh came into view, only she looked totally different. Gone were the medieval clothes and in their place was a dress of layered black lace and velvet, lace-up chunky-heeled boots, and a long purple and gold brocade coat. Her beautiful face and fine skin were unchanged, but somebody had given her a loving makeover. Her eyelids were painted with glitter and dark kohl, her lips outlined and filled in sheer ruby. Her hair had been cut to her shoulders where it curled in loose ringlets, the coppery red now dyed deep crimson, with fine fuchsia streaks.

"Do you like my new look?" Mayfridh said, bounding up the stairs and grabbing Christine by the hand. "I've been *shopping*."

"Wow. You certainly have."

Gerda joined them. "I've invited Miranda out to Super Jazz tonight. Is that okay?"

"I guess so." It was anything but okay. How was she supposed to keep Jude away from Mayfridh now?

"Great. I'll see you there."

Gerda turned and headed back down the stairs. Christine pulled Mayfridh inside.

"I love all these colors," Mayfridh said, considering a curl between her fingers.

"It's stunning. In every sense of the word," Christine said as she fetched her shoulder bag and checked for her keys. "Come on."

"Come where?"

"Let's go for a coffee."

"Now? I thought we'd stay here a while. Where's Jude?"

Christine already had the door open. "He's working. Ever drink espresso?"

"I don't know. It sounds wonderful."

"It is. Come on."

Mayfridh looked around reluctantly, then followed Christine to the door.

As they walked down to Georgenstrasse, Christine felt like a pale dull shadow next to Mayfridh, who drew glances from everywhere. She pushed her hair behind her ears and tried to walk very erect, and not hunched into her coat like she always was. She led Mayfridh to Cafe Sofie, under the train line near Friedrichstrasse Station. The decor was old and scuzzy, but they made better coffee than so many of the brightly lit, stainless-steel places. Christine ordered two coffees and sat down in a back corner with Mayfridh.

"Okay," she said, leaning forward, "did you put some kind of spell on Jude, or on our bathroom mirror?"

"What do you mean?" Mayfridh asked, her innocence so obviously feigned that Christine felt a pang of pity for her. How was she going to function in this world if she couldn't lie effectively?

"I know you did, Mayfridh. I just want you to tell me why."

"It was the mirror," Mayfridh blurted. "I wanted to see you when I wasn't there. That's all."

Christine was touched by Mayfridh's childlike vulnerability, and tempered the anger in her voice. "Don't do it again, okay? Jude couldn't see himself. He thought he was going crazy."

"I'm so sorry. I won't do it again. Did you tell Jude I'm the queen of the faeries?"

"No, of course not. I didn't tell anyone, and you won't tell anyone either."

"But—"

Christine spoke gently but firmly. "If you want to be my friend, you have to respect my wishes. You'll go back home to faeryland and then I want things here to return to normal. I'm determined."

Mayfridh's eyebrows lowered in annoyance, but she said

nothing. The coffees arrived and Mayfridh sipped hers and then pulled a face. "Ick."

"It's an acquired taste. Stick with it," Christine said. "Do you want something to eat?"

Mayfridh shook her head. "Maybe later. I could have dinner with you and Jude."

Christine hid a smile and watched Mayfridh for a few moments. "How come you didn't tell Jude and Gerda your real name?" she asked.

Mayfridh glanced up over her coffee cup. "Superstition. Some faeries swear it's bad luck to tell your real name. It can be stolen from you by witches, your identity with it."

"So witches are real?"

"In Ewigkreis they are. Hexebart's a witch, remember?"

Christine winced, remembering the experience she had tried to convince herself was a dream. "Mayfridh," she said, "why did I feel no pain in your world?"

"What do you mean?"

Christine realized that Mayfridh didn't know about her accident or about her ongoing pain. It had all happened well after their childhood years together. She felt tears spring to her eyes, but blinked them back. "I should explain. My mother and father—"

"Finn and Alfa? I *loved* them."

"They both died. In a car accident."

Mayfridh pressed her fingers against her bottom lip, her eyes welling with tears. "Oh, oh. That's so sad."

"I was with them. I injured my back and it aches; pretty much all the time. Sometimes real bad. But in your world I didn't feel it."

"Oh, that's simple. The injury is in your bones?"

"In my spine, yes."

"Your bones change. That's how you become a faery."

"I'm not following."

"That's why I'm a faery now, though I was born a human girl. The essence of the world in Ewigkreis is different. It affects the body. Eyes and bones and skin. Say you had been blind, in Ewigkreis you would have seen. It's miraculous."

"So, in the short time I was there—?"

"Your body had already started to change."

"But when I woke up back here, nothing was different."

"You weren't there long enough. After a few years the changes would be more lasting."

"Permanent?"

Mayfridh shook her head. "Not permanent if you come back here. The Real World eventually turns faeries into humans. If I stayed here now, I would become human again. Of course I never would stay, as much as I like it here. I'd lose about three centuries of life. We faeries live for four hundred years and don't age for the first two hundred."

Christine wasn't really listening. She was thinking about the land of painlessness. "Can I go back there?" she asked quietly.

Mayfridh smiled. "Of course, of course. I can take you back with me, we'll have a lovely time, we'll—"

Christine put her hands up. "No, no. Let me think about it. Coming back to the Real World after being there . . . it's hard. Especially if I have to knock myself out like last time to get there."

"But you wouldn't. I could give you a spell."

Movement near the door of the cafe. Christine's eyes flicked up. Jude, Gerda, Pete, and Fabiyan. "Okay, Mayfridh," Christine said quietly, "all my friends are here now, so no more faery talk."

"Whatever you say," Mayfridh whispered, then turned to the door, beaming widely.

"Knew I'd find you here," Gerda said, beckoning from the door. "Come on, we're all going out to dinner."

Mayfridh shot out of her chair and joined them while Christine paid the bill. Mayfridh was already slipping in next to Jude, touching his elbow and asking about his painting. As sweet as Mayfridh was, Christine was going to have to keep a close eye on her new friend.

⬩⬩⬩

Mayfridh coughed for ten minutes upon entering Super Jazz.

"Are you okay?" This was Gerda, the friendly blond woman.

"I'm not used to the smoke," Mayfridh said. "Where I come from, the air is very clear."

"Where *do* you come from?" Gerda asked.

Mayfridh saw Christine shoot her a warning glance. "A village with lots of trees," Mayfridh said, casting her eyes around for Jude. He was at the bar buying drinks. Oh, he was beautiful. He wore dark pants and a white shirt buttoned down the front. The skin on his throat looked very warm. "The music is loud."

"It gets louder as the night goes on," Christine said. "Are you sure you don't want to go home?"

Gerda elbowed Christine. "Come on, Miss Starlight, it's not that bad. Miranda's going to have a great time. She's certainly dressed to kill."

Mayfridh felt herself glow proudly. She loved her new clothes so much, and the color of her hair was beautiful. She pulled a curl in front of her face to admire it. How could Jude fail to fall in love with her? She checked herself. Eisengrimm would no doubt have stern words for her if he knew how fast her imagination was galloping. Jude returned and sat opposite her. She stole glances at him while she talked to Gerda. Christine had disappeared with Fabiyan, perhaps translating for him over by the bar. Mayfridh smiled at Jude.

His lips twitched, but he didn't smile back. He looked away, started talking to Pete. Mayfridh leaned forward, trying to listen to their conversation. She caught the tail end of a joke, didn't understand it but laughed anyway. She inched her hand close to Jude's on the tabletop, trying to feel some of the reflected heat of his body. He withdrew his fingers, searching instead for a cigarette.

Gerda leaned over and spoke very close to her ear. "Give up, Miranda."

Mayfridh turned puzzled eyes on her. "What do you mean?"

Gerda stubbed out her cigarette and grabbed Mayfridh by the wrist. "Come on, we need a girl talk."

"But I'm—"

"Trust me."

Mayfridh could hardly bear to turn her eyes away from Jude, but Gerda had gently pulled her up and was walking her toward the toilets. Inside, surrounded by grimy tiles and a flickering light, Gerda leaned back against the basins, shaking her head.

"What is it?" Mayfridh asked.

"Okay, two things. Number one, you've got to learn to hide it better."

"Hide what?"

"Your interest in Jude."

"I'm not—"

"Miranda, the only thing that's missing from your expression when you look at him is your tongue hanging out." Gerda hung her own tongue out and made a panting noise.

Mayfridh felt embarrassment creeping through her limbs. "Oh no, am I so obvious?"

"Yes. Very, very obvious."

"Then what's number two?"

"You'll never get him."

Mayfridh narrowed her eyes. Was Gerda suggesting she wasn't beautiful enough for Jude? "How do you know?"

"Because he and Christine are inseparable." Gerda shook her head. "I know what you're thinking. You're thinking how beautiful and glamorous you are, and how plain Christine is. I thought that too. I thought that because I'm an artist and she's not, Jude was bound to like me better. I went through exactly what you're going through right now. And I got nowhere. If you try to make eye contact, he'll look away. If you throw your arm around him, pretending to be friendly, trying to get a feel of his body, he'll smile at you coolly and shrug you off quickly. He holds it all back. He's got nothing for girls like you and me. It's all for Christine."

Mayfridh felt her heart slide. "Then he really loves her?" she asked. "Jude really loves Christine?"

Gerda smiled, a wicked twinkle in her eye. "Now I didn't say that."

"Then why? Why won't he look anywhere else unless he loves her?"

"You don't know then?"

"No. Do you?" Mayfridh was thinking about Jude's secret. Did Gerda know it?

"I think I do."

"Then tell me."

Gerda dropped her voice to a whisper. "What's the one thing that a struggling artist never really has, but *always* needs?"

Mayfridh shook her head. "I don't know. What?"

Gerda rubbed her forefinger and thumb together, smiling. "Money," she said, "lots and lots of money."

CHAPTER EIGHT

*B*y *the following morning, Christine found she had* started to relax around Mayfridh. It was clear her friend was happy playing the part of Miranda, was deft at sidestepping Gerda's questions, and had stopped ogling Jude at every opportunity. When they had left Super Jazz, Mayfridh had asked to sleep over in Gerda's apartment rather than Christine's, taking her out of Jude's way. In fact, she found Mayfridh's manner amusing and sweet as the faery queen determinedly attempted to adjust to a social setting where she wasn't in charge: biting her lip when a drunk spilled beer on her, putting up with Pete's constant stream of trivia, and good-naturedly trying every toxic substance Gerda offered her. Jude himself was profoundly unaffected by the gorgeous new interloper, and that was comforting if not unexpected. He'd never betrayed her, not even when Gerda had turned all her charms on him in their first few weeks at Hotel Mandy-Z.

Christine fetched Mayfridh from Gerda's place in the morning, and the two of them went walking in the Tiergarten.

"Did you have fun last night?" Christine asked as they passed under the Brandenburg Gate.

"Yes, though I couldn't really get used to the smoke and the loud music." Mayfridh was wearing a much more sober outfit this morning, a dark blue pullover and black velvet skirt. Her hair glistened in the morning sunshine.

"Gerda took a shine to you."

"Yes," Mayfridh said guardedly, "though I don't know yet if I trust her."

"No, no, Gerda's harmless, believe me. Deep down she has a generous spirit. Just don't tell her anything she might use against you later." They entered the park now. A deep drift of fallen leaves swirled at their feet. In the distance, church bells rang from two directions, eerily out of tune with each other. "Ah, I love the sound of bells."

"Let's sit here," Mayfridh said, indicating a bench under a red-gold canopy of leaves.

"Okay." Christine sat beside her, eyes closed, listening to the bells.

"I remember you always loved the bells on that church near where we lived," Mayfridh said.

Christine opened her eyes on the shady wood. "Yes, that's right. I'd wake up Sunday morning and just lie in bed listening to them."

"You were such a strange little girl."

"I was?"

"Oh, yes. I always thought so, that's why I liked you. I'm sure it was Alfa and Finn's intention to bring you up as the weirdest child on the planet."

"You're probably right," Christine said, smiling. "Do you remember that pinafore my mother made for me?"

"Yes. The paisley one with the tiny stuffed animals hanging off the hem."

"God, what was she thinking!"

"As I recall, you loved that dress."

"Yeah, I was six. I didn't know better."

"She offered my mother to make me a matching one—"

"—and your mother looked horrified! I remember. You were always so beautifully dressed. Your mother really doted on you. She spoiled you."

"Do you think so?" Mayfridh asked.

"Yeah, of course. Remember that fresco she painted on your ceiling? Moon and stars and clouds and colored balloons?"

"I loved that. But I always loved your house better. It was chaotic and warm and smelled like peaches and cinnamon."

"Probably my mom's incense," Christine said. Mayfridh was right; her parents had always been as chaotic as they were compassionate. For the first time in many years, she was sharing memories of her parents with someone who had actually known them. She felt a fond flush of feeling for Mayfridh.

Mayfridh was watching her. "You know, Christine, you're almost beautiful when you smile."

"Um, thanks."

Mayfridh shook her head. "I'm sorry, that was rude."

"Yeah." Christine laughed. "Yeah, it was."

"I'm used to being able to say whatever I want, and do whatever I want."

"It's okay, I know it's true. I'm not beautiful."

"Jude must think you are."

Christine shrugged. "I guess so, I don't know. He says he does."

"Before I came, I sent Eisengrimm to watch you a while. I saw you with another man, a dark-haired fellow, rather large."

Christine felt herself shudder. "Ooh, Mandy."

"Mandy?"

"Immanuel Zweigler. He owns the building. He runs the gallery."

"And you don't like him?"

"He's kind of revolting. Avoid him at all costs. There's about a three-foot gap between the foyer and the stairs where he can spot you from the gallery. Always run past it. He's weird and he asks strange questions and he gives me the creeps."

"I'll take your word for it and avoid him as best I can." They settled into silence for a few minutes. Two joggers ran past, and a woman pushed a pram up the leaf-strewn path.

Mayfridh turned to Christine and patted her hand. "I want to give you a present."

"A present?"

"You make me happy, Christine. You make me feel less lonely. I want to take away some of your pain too." She reached in her bag and pulled out one of her spells.

"Ah, I'd rather you didn't cast any more spells on me," Christine said.

"No, no. I'll give you something you can use whenever you want." Mayfridh closed her hands over the spell, muttered a word Christine couldn't hear—it sounded like "twice" or "wine"—and then opened her hands again. The spell was gone, and in its place was a ball of golden thread.

"What is it?" Christine asked, gingerly reaching out to touch it.

"It's enchanted twine." Mayfridh pressed the ball into Christine's hands. "If you come here to the Tiergarten, to the passage, hold one end and cast it away from you, then follow the thread, it will lead you into the autumn forest."

"You mean . . . ?"

"The place where you feel no pain. Collect the twine and walk around to the gate of the castle. If you call out, Eisengrimm will hear you and come to get you."

Christine studied the ball of golden twine in her hands. Relief, instant relief. She became acutely aware of the humming and pressing in her back. In a second it could be gone.

"All I ask is that you keep it safe," Mayfridh said, "and keep it near you. Don't leave it where someone else could find it."

"Of course I'll keep it safe," Christine answered, her fingers testing the texture of the twine.

"Do you want to go now?"

"Will you come?"

"I'll go back to the hotel. I'll spend the day with Gerda. I'm having too much fun to go home just yet."

Christine considered the offer: although she was unsure whether to trust Mayfridh around Jude, she knew that Gerda would keep an eye on her. "Maybe," she said.

"If Jude asks I'll tell him—"

"He won't ask. He'll be in the studio all day." Jude was working hard on a new painting, torturing himself over it. He would be too busy to concern himself with Mayfridh. "Don't disturb him."

"I wouldn't."

"Maybe I'll just go for a couple of hours."

Mayfridh touched Christine on the wrist. "Keep an eye on your watch. Time doesn't run the same in Ewigkreis."

"No? Faster, slower?"

"Both. Neither. It's just *different.*"

Wonderful relief was calling her. Just a couple of hours. Nothing bad could happen. Christine checked her watch. It was seven minutes to eleven. "Okay, I'm going. I'll be back at one o'clock. I'll come to Gerda's to look for you."

"I'll be waiting. Come on, let me show you where the passage is."

Mayfridh led her deeper into the park, away from the road. They approached a dark elm, its leaves spattered with yellow. "Quickly," Mayfridh said, "while there's nobody to see."

Christine crouched and rolled the ball of twine away from her, holding the loose end between her fingers. It glimmered as though lit from within, and a soft sighing noise accompanied it. She thought the twine would completely unravel in about ten feet but the ball just kept rolling away.

"Go on," Mayfridh said, "follow it."

Christine stood, hand over hand following the twine that ran on ahead of her. "When will it stop?" she asked. Mayfridh didn't answer. Christine checked over her shoulder. Mayfridh was gone; the Tiergarten was gone. She stood amongst the diving golden leaves and slanted sunbeams of the autumn forest.

Mayfridh watched Christine disappear and turned toward the road. It was good to know that Jude would be in the studio today, rather than in his apartment. Mayfridh needed to get in there and collect a few of his personal possessions— ones he wouldn't necessarily miss—and make Hexebart weave a good strong mind-reading spell. What Gerda had said to her the previous night played on her thoughts. Christine was a millionaire, and had vowed not to touch a cent until she was married. Jude was a penniless artist who had lived his adult life so far on scholarships and grants. After his Zweigler Fellowship ran out he would be faced with teaching art to ungrateful amateurs if he were lucky, measuring fat businessmen for suits in a department store if he were unlucky. Christine not only provided him with a great address, having inherited her parents' West Chelsea home, if he stuck around for long enough he would never have to worry about money again.

"You watch," Gerda had said, "he will have proposed to her before the end of his fellowship."

Mayfridh wandered up Unter-den-Linden, past sausage vendors and coffee carts. She didn't want to believe it, not of Jude. Surely Jude must possess the most beautiful spirit that had ever found its way into a human body. Also, she didn't want to believe it for Christine's sake. Then some other instinct engaged, one she wasn't proud of. Surely Christine's millions must pale in comparison to Mayfridh's entire faery kingdom? If Jude sought riches, then . . . She chastised herself for wanting anything to do with a man who could be so deceitful.

If he was deceitful. If Gerda was right.

So was it a protective instinct for Christine, or a need to prove to herself that Jude was good, that drove her this morning? Jude had a secret and she *had to know it;* even more now than before, with Gerda poisoning her ears with stories. If she found out through the mind-reading spell that Jude really was in love with Christine, then she would let him go. She would stop turning on her faery glamour whenever he was around, and she certainly wouldn't be so cruel as to steal Christine's happiness.

Or at least she would try her very best not to.

❧

Eisengrimm!" Christine stood at the gate to the castle wall, which spanned away gleaming in the golden light. She couldn't imagine that Eisengrimm would be able to hear her through all the stone and at such a distance, so she stretched herself out on the ground and enjoyed the liberation of her back.

"Ahh," she sighed, releasing a deep breath. She checked her watch. The hands hadn't moved. She closed her eyes, felt a leaf skitter over her legs. A soft breeze blew, and in the distance were the faint, earthy smells of harvest. This was bliss; this was paradise.

A flapping of wings. She looked up. A crow perched on top of the gate.

"Eisengrimm?"

He fluttered to the ground and, as his feet touched the grass, transformed to Wolf. "Christine?"

She stood, reveling in the freedom. "Hello. Mayfridh gave me this." Her native words were echoed in the strange Old German of the castle. She held out the ball of twine for his inspection.

"Ah, enchanted twine. You wish to visit us regularly then?"

"Yes, I like it here."

"And is my queen in good health?" No expression marked his face, but from his voice she could tell he had concerns.

"Yeah, in good health, in good company, and in great clothes. She said you would . . . you know . . . show me around."

"Certainly. Follow me." He led her through the gate and around the side of the castle. The sunlight was dappled here, and the stone was covered in lichen and moss. Ahead, they reached the grassy edge of a precipice. Christine hung back, but Eisengrimm walked all the way to the edge and lifted his snout to the breeze.

"Come closer," he said, "it's quite safe."

Christine moved forward, testing the ground in front of her with her toes. A deep, rocky slope fell away beneath them.

Eisengrimm tilted his ears. "Behold," he said, "this is Ewigkreis."

A rural village spread out far below them. Two wide dirt roads converged on a large stone well, other narrow streets sprouting left and right and tapering off into forests and farms. The streets were lined with half-timbered buildings and stone cottages with flowering window boxes. Around the well was a bustling marketplace with stalls, vendors pushing carts, and villagers dressed in colorful clothes. Others worked in broad, flat fields, their movements seeming exaggerated and slow at this distance. Puffs of smoke from chimneys drifted lazy and gilded in the late sunshine.

"How many people live here?"

"Three hundred in the village, eleven in the castle with Mayfridh."

That explained the emptied, hollow feeling of the castle. "Ewigkreis is small," she said.

"All the faeries in what you would call Germany live here. We are one of the smallest races of faeries."

Christine cast her eyes into the far distance peering into the afternoon haze to see past the forests, and the river that ran lazy and glittering off to the east. The cliffs, water, and trees dissolved into the misty golden horizon. "What's beyond it?"

"We know not."

Christine was surprised by this answer. "Has no one tried to travel into those forests?"

"Yes. I have traveled in the Eternal Woods myself. For many days I moved forward, through dark woods with no clear paths. Then the woods began to thin, a road spread out in front of me. I thought I was approaching a new village, but I wasn't. I was back in the same forest you first found."

"It goes around in a circle?"

"I cannot answer that, for I do not know. It is one of the mysteries of our world, and of every other faery world. No map can describe them. It is a Real World phenomenon to understand land in terms of definitive space."

Christine tried to comprehend this, couldn't, gave up. "And Mayfridh is the queen of the whole land?"

"Yes."

"Unelected, right? It's like a monarchy."

"That's right."

"The villagers don't mind?"

"They are not humans. They are faeries, and care about more important things than politics and titles. They care about the harvest, the swing of seasons, the magical essence of the air." Eisengrimm turned and began to walk away from the precipice. "Come," he said, "I will show you the castle."

Christine once again glanced at her watch. Although it felt as though twenty minutes had passed, the hands had moved only one minute. She calculated, figured three minutes must pass for every hour, and decided she had plenty of time. Relax, enjoy.

Eisengrimm led her through the back gate and the wild garden, then into the cavernous stone room where she had first met Mayfridh.

"This is our great hall. There is Mayfridh's throne."

"Who are the eleven people living in the castle?" Christine asked, looking around at the tapestries and brass decorations.

"Cooks, servants, and me."

"No guards? Soldiers?"

"We have no real need for them. There is a royal guard, but its role is official rather than martial."

"And you're Mayfridh's only adviser?"

Eisengrimm sat on his hind legs and tipped his head back to look up. Christine followed his gaze up past the long tapestries to the tiny windows at the top of the room. On pedestals carved into the dark stone sat three crooked gargoyles, their mouths stretched open, their snouts crinkled into sneers, their eyes hideous spheres on stalks.

"Mayfridh was only nine when she took the throne. Wolfram, Reinmar, and Sivridh were the counselors appointed to her. I blush for the partiality she showed me, simply because I could turn into a fox and be toted around under her arm. They were good counselors at first, sound politicians. But when she was fifteen—"

"That's them?" Christine asked, astonished.

"They disagreed with her over something petty. They forced their will on her, greedy now of the power, and told her she was just a stupid child. But she wasn't a child anymore.

"It happened that a visitor from the icy north lands was staying in the castle at the time. He was the court magician in his own realm, and a very powerful sorcerer. Sorcery is unknown in Ewigkreis; we use magic for peaceful purposes. In secret, Mayfridh offered him all of Liesebet's jewelry in exchange for a spell of sorcery. Then, in the heat of an argument, she turned the spell on Wolfram, Reinmar, and Sivridh."

"She turned them into gargoyles?"

"Yes. So now they watch the affairs of Ewigkreis from a different vantage point."

"Can they ever . . . I mean . . . are they stuck like that forever?"

"She tries from time to time to turn the spell back, but she did it in such a fit of anger—the anger of a fifteen-year-old girl—that the wrath became part of the spell. She cannot find an equivalent amount of forgiveness for a reversal spell, especially as, I suspect, she is still angry with them for calling her a stupid child."

"Will they die?"

"Who knows? Perhaps."

She was surprised by the lightness of his tone. "Is life very cruel here?"

"We are mostly peaceful folk. No one need fear cruelty if they work for the smooth turning of the seasons and pay their dues to Mayfridh."

"Are the villagers loyal to her?"

"Oh yes, because all faery magic is royal magic. It descends only from the queen." He nudged her hand. "Come, Christine, I will show you the rest of the Autumn Castle."

He tried to lead her downstairs to a windowless area of chambers and dungeons, but she refused, so instead he led her up the long narrow corridor, showing her each room in turn—a bewildering array of dusty libraries, empty drawing rooms, cramped state rooms, and a dark kitchen. Then they ascended the north turret—crooked and narrow—to the royal chambers. Eisengrimm led her to Mayfridh's bedchamber, which was decorated in filmy white curtains and layers of white cloth.

"You may lie down if you are tired," Eisengrimm said, jumping onto the bed and making himself comfortable.

Christine lay down, sinking into the deep covers with a warm weariness stretching through her bones. She considered the ceiling in the half-light for a while, trying to process all she had seen and heard. Did it really matter if it was all too ridiculous ever to be uttered to another human being? Here she felt no pain; here she was the Christine she might have been were it not for the accident. She found the castle's emptiness and gloominess soothing, addictive.

She turned on her side to watch Eisengrimm. His head rested on his paws and his yellow eyes gazed at her serenely. Christine felt an unusual sense of peace around him, despite his size and his strong jaws. His warm voice was friendly and his manner was patient, and he possessed a magical tranquillity she had never sensed in anyone else. "Eisengrimm, can I ask you something?"

"Please do. I'll try to answer all your questions."

"Can Mayfridh cast a love spell?"

"A love spell?"

"You know, to make somebody fall in love with her?" She hated the quiver of her voice, but the question had to be asked.

To her relief, Eisengrimm did not probe further, nor did he jump to defend his queen of any veiled accusations. "No, Christine, she cannot. The hearts of men are not to be bound by the desires of others. It was ever so, it will ever be."

"That's comforting." She smiled, then ventured, "Why do I feel so peaceful around you? Is that magic?"

"I'm flattered. It's not magic."

"Are there many shape-shifters like you in Ewigkreis?"

"No, I am the only one."

"Can you be anything else but a wolf, a fox, and a crow?"

"I can be a bear. But I rarely take on that form. It causes great stress to my joints and organs."

"Can you be a man?"

His voice was suddenly charged with emotion. "I am not a . . ." he started.

A long silence beat out, and Christine rose up on her elbows. "I'm sorry, did I say something wrong?"

"No, no. It is complicated." He pulled himself up and then paused on the end of the bed, as though he were deciding whether to leave, his gray shoulders hunched against the burden of the decision.

Christine was curious now. "Were you once a man? Is that why you're upset?"

He slumped forward. "Now you have asked, so I must answer you."

"You don't have to. I don't mean to be nosy or anything."

"I do have to. It's a burden on my heart that I have yet to express." He turned and sagged down on the bed next to her again. "You are the only person, in over seventy years, who has asked me if I were once a man."

"Really?"

"Shape-shifters exist in faerylands. There is no reason for anyone to suspect I am anything more. Just as you would never ask a bird if she were once a fish, so nobody here has ever asked if I am anything other than I appear. But you, you are from Over There." He muttered, almost to himself, "You have different questions."

"Tell me, then. You were once a man?"

"Yes. A faery man, not a human man. My name was not Eisengrimm. I was being groomed to be one of Queen Liesebet's counselors, but I was young and I longed to travel. I had a yearning spirit. I burned and bubbled with imaginings of places and adventures, and the exotic unknown-ness of other folk. I ran away from the royal court, leaving it all behind me, but intending to return one day in the far time. Just as we can make passage between our world and the Real World, we can also make passage between this world and other worlds of faery. I traveled many places. None of them satisfied my desire because, I have since learned, desire does not exist to be satisfied, only to move men. I moved, I kept moving, and it was in the Slavic faerylands that I met Zosia."

Shadows deepened in the room and dust motes hung in the air. Christine felt herself grow very still as Eisengrimm spoke.

"She was a faery witch; not a hideous hag like Hexebart, but a fair-skinned, silken-haired beauty. I was walking through a tall-treed forest near the faery village. She was gathering herbs for a spell, the sunlight shone on her hair, and I was entranced. When she asked me my name, I told her. Something a traveler should never do.

"We became lovers. I stayed with her for many weeks in her warm stone cottage near the river. Every morning we would wake to the bright sunshine in the window, then she would spend her day in making her spells and potions. I would spend mine admiring her and dreaming about forever with her. And when night fell there were warm fires and spiced wines and tender kisses enough to keep me from noticing what I should have noticed. All was not well with Zosia.

"Slowly, it became clear that Zosia's great beauty in appearance was not matched by a great beauty of spirit. She thought nothing of torturing woodland creatures to steal their essence for spells, and her magic was always directed at acquiring new treasures and supplementing her beauty. The first time I pointed out to her that I despised to hear a linnet screaming as she pulled it to pieces, she laughed at me.

"'You are too fragile,' she said. 'Where is your bravery and strength when such a small creature can soften your man's heart?' From then on, she reveled in taunting me about my delicate manner. I tried to take the mockery in good heart, I loved her still. But the brutality and the vanity did not abate, and I braced myself every morning for her next act of selfish cruelty.

"The very worst came soon after. You see, from time to time, bewildered humans from the Real World wander into faerylands by accident. So it was that a Real World traveler crossed into Zosia's woods. While I was not home—I had gone to the village to collect milk and flour—he stopped at her house to ask for help. Poor fool. Zosia was no doubt delighted to see him. My heart trembles to think of his last moments. By the time I returned, she had chopped him into pieces.

"When I saw the blood upon the hearth, I felt a terrible sickening hatred growing inside me. 'What have you done, Zosia? Have you sunk to murder?'

" 'He was just a human, no worse nor better than the squirrels and foxes who have given up their essence for my magic.'

"I found myself backing away from her instinctively, my hand reaching for the door behind me.

" 'Where are you going?' she demanded, her eyes narrow and flinty.

" 'How can I continue to love you when you are so brutal and vain?' I said.

" 'You will continue to love me as you always have,' she said, practical as ever. 'I see no reason why it should be otherwise.'

"Her confidence angered me, partly because it was true. I had been a slave to my desire for her. 'Perhaps I never loved you, Zosia. Perhaps I was bewitched by your beauty. I can no longer stay here with you. You are heartless.' "

Eisengrimm stopped and sighed, his head sagging forward on his paws and his eyes fluttering closed. "Zosia became enraged. As I turned to the door to leave, I felt a magnetic net of magic envelop me and pull me back into the room. Zosia fixed me with a glare, and with her free hand reached into the pocket of her bloodied apron and pulled out a spell.

" 'Zosia, no. Let me go,' I said. Like anyone faced with a sudden horror, I could not believe that it was truly happening, that she would truly hurt me. I was wrong."

"She put you under an enchantment?"

"My body ran with a peculiar, fluid sensation, as though my skin were milk and my bones were toffee. 'You shall be changed,' she said in a low voice. 'Of the first four creatures you see you may take your choice, and you shall be that creature until you are foolish enough to love again.' "

Eisengrimm opened his eyes. "I felt my heart charge. If I could get to the village without seeing four other creatures,

I could see a man, remain a man. But the woods were deep and too treacherous to close my eyes. As soon as I burst out the door of the cottage, I saw a crow sitting on a branch peering down on me. I thought, not a crow, their voices are so ugly. I ran on. Next I saw a bear napping in a clearing. I thought, not a bear, their bodies are so cumbersome. I ran on. Next I saw a fox running through the grass. I thought, not a fox, they are hunted for sport. I ran on, hoping to make it to the village before seeing another animal. But it was not to be.

"I saw a wolf, and my body began to burst its seams. Bones and organs crushed against one another, my skin ran with tingles and trembles. I heard Zosia from far away, her wild voice dark on the wind, calling, 'Choose your new form.' But I could not. I wanted to be none of those beasts. I thought perhaps if I did not choose, I would die, and maybe that would be better.

"I collapsed to the ground and closed my eyes, waiting for death. I did not die. When I arose, I was in the shape you see now."

Christine reached out and touched a large gray paw, fascinated. "A wolf."

"Yes, and I can be any of the other animals as I choose. The only thing I cannot be is a man; the only thing I cannot be is my true self."

"But the enchantment can be broken?"

"Zosia made it all but impossible. I returned to her immediately to rail at her, to beg her, to threaten her with my teeth. She was intractable.

"'The enchantment will only be broken when you are foolish enough to fall in love again,' she said. 'The woman you love will have to utter your true name.'"

"What is your true name?"

"I cannot tell you. To utter my own name would mean

that the enchantment remains permanent. My love would have to travel to Zosia's woods and find it there, with great danger to herself. Nor can I tell anyone who has not asked directly that I was once a man. As I have said, you are the first person in over seventy years who has asked."

"But when you fall in love can't you—"

"I am already in love, Christine."

"And she's never asked about you? About your past? About why you are as you are?"

"You assume she loves me in return. You assume that she is not too grand and not too proud to care about the heart of a wolf. You know her, Christine, you know what she is like."

Christine was puzzled a moment, then gasped. "Mayfridh. You're in love with Mayfridh?"

"And so you understand, she will never ask me. She has only ever known me as I am. Besides, she is too . . . self-involved to concern herself deeply in the fates of others."

"Can I tell her?"

"No. Any direct efforts by me or by somebody acting for me are bound to make the enchantment stay forever."

Christine bit her lip, not sure what to say. "Could you try to fall in love with somebody with more potential for helping you?"

"You know that hearts do not behave rationally. At least, mine does not."

Christine sat back, staring at him. "I'm so sorry. How can you stand being around her all the time?"

"I endure it, Christine, as best I can. I feel love, but none of a man's desire, which is a small blessing. And I haven't given up hope altogether. I may live another three hundred years. Luck may yet be with me."

Christine turned to the window and was surprised to see the sky brightening outside. "That's weird. I thought it was afternoon when I arrived."

"It was."

"But the sun's coming up. It must be morning."

"It is."

Christine shook her head. "But what happened to night?"

"The Autumn Castle is morning or afternoon. Always either, never neither."

She checked her watch. Ten hours had passed. "Oh, my God."

"What's wrong?"

She hurried to her feet. "I thought time must pass slower there."

"Time here has no relation to time in the Real World."

"I'll have to get back home. Jude will be worried."

Eisengrimm leapt from the bed and moved to the door, all dutiful counselor again. "Of course," he said. "I will lead you back to the woods."

🐾

Hotel Mandy-Z was quiet when she arrived. She hoped Jude would still be working and hadn't missed her. She pushed open the door to his studio but he wasn't there. The room was in darkness, but she could make out the shape of a large canvas on the easel, and it appeared to have paint on it. So Jude had overcome his latest block. She switched the light on to look at it.

Gray. Black. Brown. And in the corner, at the bottom, on the right, a splash of mingled crimson and fuchsia.

She stared at it for long moments, then switched the light off and went upstairs, trying to get used to being back in her own bones, aching and pulling. No light under the door from Gerda's apartment. Maybe she had taken Mayfridh out drinking. No light under the door from Jude's apartment. Maybe he was with them, and hadn't even missed her. She closed the door behind her and went to the bedroom.

He was there, sound asleep, his hair tangled and disarrayed against the pillow, one warm, smooth shoulder exposed above the covers. She sat lightly on the edge of the bed, still in her coat and boots, and reached out to smooth his hair. He stirred, but then settled back to sleep.

"Please don't fall in love with her, Jude," she whispered in the dark. And then realized she had named the very thing of which she was most afraid.

CHAPTER NINE

*M*ayfridh *stepped into the long shadows of afternoon in the autumn forest, hoping she was in time.* It was Eisengrimm's birthday, and she had given orders for a banquet. It had slipped her mind completely—the Real World was so intoxicatingly charming—but luckily Christine had reminded her with something she said.

"How well do you know Eisengrimm?" Christine had asked.

And the light had flickered in Mayfridh's head. Eisengrimm. The birthday banquet. As much as she would have loved to stay and explore the Real World more—shopping with Gerda was more exciting than she could give words to—Eisengrimm's banquet was important. He was her most trusted friend.

She hurried up through the castle gate and into the overgrown garden—where the leaves grew weary and the thorns grew conspicuous—skidding to a halt near the great hall. Relax. Hilda had taken care of everything. The long table had been erected, the musicians from the village were tuning their instruments, branches of evergreen decorated the walls.

"It's all ready then?" she asked as Hilda bustled by.

Hilda paused, startled momentarily by Mayfridh's appearance, then said, "Yes, yes, Queen Mayfridh. Eisengrimm is in your chambers. I have just sent one of the cooks to fetch him. Take your seat, Majesty. You're just in time."

There was no time to change out of her Real World clothes, so she sat at the head of the long table in her red velvet minidress and lace-up boots while others gathered around the sides of the room.

The pipes struck up a solemn tune and Eisengrimm slunk in, his head darting around to take in the scene.

"Oh, a banquet!" he exclaimed.

"Dear friend," Mayfridh said, rising from her seat to greet him. "Happy birthday."

"What have you done to your hair?"

"Sit down," she said, holding a chair out to him.

He jumped into it. The other guests were seated and Mayfridh took her place at the head of the table while the village musicians played.

"I don't like it," Eisengrimm said over the music.

"You don't like what?" Mayfridh responded irritably.

"Your hair. It was such a beautiful color before."

"But now it's even more beautiful, do you not see?" She held a strand out. "Real World colors."

Eisengrimm harrumphed and put a paw on the table to draw his trencher closer. "Not everything in the Real World is better than our world."

"Oh, Eisengrimm, be not so gruff. Of course I do not prefer the Real World. I just like its colors and its noises and its smells."

A servant came by and loaded their plates with hunks of roast meat. The musicians changed to a lively tune and voices in the room grew loud, the roar of the fire grew hot. Mayfridh sipped her wine and for a moment compared this room to the crowded jazz club her new friends frequented. Now it was hard to choose. She had always loved her own world so much, but there was a sparkling edge to the Real World that was missing in this rural place; a sense of knowing and presence that was as smooth and as toxic and as addictive as the cigarettes Gerda had introduced her to.

And, of course, there was Jude.

"Tell me of the Real World," Eisengrimm said, licking gravy from his chops. "What have you done with your time?"

"I have met all of Christine's friends, and I spend my time talking and drinking and shopping with them. They are all artists and Jude paints the most wonderful pictures. They capture the very essence of the Real World."

"Have you put aside any silly fancies towards him?"

Mayfridh thought about the collection of Jude's possessions—a tarnished cuff link, an old T-shirt, and a wad of chewed gum—wrapped safely in the bottom of her bag. "Of course."

Eisengrimm fixed her with a yellow stare. "Really?"

"Why do you ask?"

"Christine wanted to know if you could perform love spells. I presume she suspects your interest."

Mayfridh felt herself blush, Gerda's words of admonishment still stinging. *You've got to learn to hide it better.* "I have since learned to control my interest, as I have no intention of acting upon it."

"Good," Eisengrimm said, "good."

"But, Eisengrimm, I suspect Jude does not truly love Christine."

"And why do you suspect that?"

"Because he . . . he has a secret."

Eisengrimm's snout creased into a sneer. "A secret?"

"Gerda said so, Christine's friend. Gerda said that he doesn't really love Christine and that he has a secret."

"Gossip in the Real World is the same as gossip in our world. It should never be listened to, let alone repeated."

She rolled her eyes. Sometimes Eisengrimm was so righteous.

"I do not find it surprising that Jude loves Christine," Eisengrimm continued. "She is gentle and rare and always sees the best in people. It is on Christine that you should be focusing your attention."

Mayfridh smiled. "Oh, Eisengrimm . . . but there is someone else in the Real World I wish to make contact with."

"Who?"

"My parents."

"Your parents are dead."

"My *real* parents. My human parents." For so many years she had forgotten about them, but now, running around in Berlin with her old friend, memories of her Real World mother and father had begun to impress themselves upon her. "I miss them."

"I would not advise it, Little May."

"Why not? You advise against everything. Are you jealous of my enjoyment?" The music paused just as she raised her voice, and Mayfridh realized a hundred pairs of eyes had turned to her.

"Oh, go about your business," she said with a dismissive wave of the hand.

The music started again and the conversation bubbled once more. Mayfridh sank down in her seat. "I'm sorry, old friend."

"I advise you for your own good, Mayfridh, not to spoil your fun. Time ticks on. The leaves are falling." He indicated the giant birch outside the mullioned window in the deep sunset. "When the last leaf falls from that tree, you will have to leave your Real World parents behind, perhaps forever. It could be centuries before these worlds align again. You will forget them. They will not forget you. Your mother and father have suffered enough. Do not make them lose you twice."

"So I am not allowed to love in the Real World?" she muttered. "Is that it?"

"Love is so permanent a thing, Mayfridh," Eisengrimm sighed, "and your ability to journey there is so very temporary. I only want to save you, and those you would love, the pain."

"Good counsel, Eisengrimm," she conceded, her eyes going to the window. In the dark, in the few brief minutes between the longest shadows of sunset and the pale bath of sunrise, she would go to Hexebart. If she wasn't to love, so be it. But Eisengrimm had not forbidden her from hunting for secrets.

Look at Hexebart's new stuffs. Oh, they are pretty. Here is a . . . a . . . silver thing. And here is a . . . a . . . cloth thing. And here is a . . . a . . . sticky thing. The nasty little queen wants them back, but Hexebart will take her time, yes she will. Hexebart will not be hurried, not for the sulky sow. Hexebart will save a little bit of the stuffs for herself. Hmm, hmm. Scrape and tear and pull. Hmm, hmm.

But, oh, there's a strange thing. Remember the pea shell. The pea shell? Where is the pea shell? Here, here, close by, under the dead frog. Why does the pea shell want to meet the new stuffs? Hexebart opens it and finds a hair. This hair belongs with these new things; they know each other. Hexebart stores her new stuffs in the pea shell and shakes it once.

Now to work. The sulky sow wants a mind-reading spell. Ha! Ha! She'll get nothing from these things. Hexebart breaks a corner off the silver thing and weaves it into the spell. Hexebart pulls a thread from the cloth and weaves it into the spell. Hexebart snaps a blob of the sticky thing and weaves it into the spell. But the queen will be sorely disappointed. Ha! This man, to whom these things belong, is shut up tight, locked down hard. Hexebart laughs, thinking about how the queen will cry and cry when the spell doesn't work.

Sulky, sulky little sow,
Who is strong and clever now?
Ha, ha! Ha, ha!

Hexebart finishes the spell and sucks the line of blood from her fingers where the magic thread has pulled through calluses. Ouch! The pea shell catches her eyes. Oh, it's a pretty pea shell, full of wonderful things. She shakes it again.

And suddenly, knows.

The mixture of stuffs in the pea shell is the spell the queen really wants, yes. Together, the stuffs can make the spell. But the queen didn't ask for that spell, she asked for the other, the one Hexebart has already made and cut her fingers on. Hee, hee. Hexebart will give the queen the spell she was asked for, and make another for herself. And then Hexebart will know what the queen wants to know and that will vex the sow for centuries.

Weave, weave, weave, and spin,
What's the secret, what's the sin?

Hexebart's fingers bleed again but she doesn't care. She makes the spell, she takes the spell, she sees into the corner. The very darkest corner inside a human heart.

Oh, it's a nasty business. Oh, it's a cruel thing.

Oh, oh! Hexebart fills up with singing joy; her heart dances and her fingers play invisible music.

Ha, ha, hee, hee! Hexebart has a secret.

— from the Memoirs of Mandy Z.

I barely slept a wink last night, though I can't put a finger on what it was that disturbed me so much. My thoughts were calm, as they always are. My bed was warm, as it always is. My room was silent and dark. And yet I felt all night as though there were some vague irritation in my muscles and bones, an itch unable to be reached, a sore unable to be soothed. I dreamed strange dreams where a bright foreign object was lodged in my back, but no matter how strenuously I tried, I couldn't see it to pull it free. I tossed and turned all night and half-expected, on waking, to see that I was black and blue all over. Perhaps later this morning, after a pot of hot coffee and a good German breakfast, I will try to sleep again. If not, I can always work further on the Bone Wife. She is able to walk six paces now without falling. She improves every day.

I wrote last time about royal faery magic. It has become a science of mine to understand as much about faery anatomy and faery magic as I can. All faeries are, to some degree, magic, but that magic always proceeds from the queen or king of their particular race. In other words, all faery magic is embodied in the royal family, in their very bones. Within the bones, the magic constantly replicates itself, like the cells in a human body. What I have discovered is that the magic will also replicate into the bones near it.

You see, faery bones are never really dead. They don't

rot, they don't lose their perfect brightness, and they knit together after a while. Although all the bones in my sculpture are glued tight, they have also started to knit to each other, and the magic is spreading through them. I have killed two royal faeries: king and queen. The king was full of magic, the queen was not. I believe she may have stored her magic back in her homeland for safekeeping before coming through to our world. Very prudent, very clever. Not clever enough in the end though, was she? Her ribs made a fine set of ankles.

After Ireland, I traveled the world in search of the raw materials for my project, always aware that these two years would pass and that I would have to return to my family, to university and a respectable job. For me, it was as though a tunnel were growing smaller in front of me as my possibilities closed down and my marvelous, luscious world of art and magic was doomed to its final limit, just hours and days and weeks away. Months and months flew by when I neither saw nor heard of any faeries. Before I returned home, I killed only two more, both in America—one in the deserts of California, one near the Great Lakes in Wisconsin—and so my collection of bones on my return was nowhere as grand as I had hoped it would be. My fate loomed, my art began to slide away. I returned to Germany, enrolled in an economics degree program in Munich, and prepared to live the life my parents wanted me to. Oh, I could have struck out on my own, gone to art school, traveled farther, but what would I have done for money? I was the sole heir to a great fortune, and I am essentially a practical man. It wasn't in me to endanger my inheritance.

So I took courses in my own time in art history and Germanic linguistics (my memory for languages is almost photographic, perhaps another legacy of my ancestry), but for the most part behaved like a serious and committed

economics student. By 1979, I was working for an invest-
ment bank in Vienna, and I hadn't killed a faery in five years.

Man cannot be separated from his love for long, and so it
was that I began to sculpt again; with marble, as my block
of faery bone was little more than a foot high, and I was hesitant to begin carving it. I sculpted for the sheer joy of it, and
I'm sure that's why my skill developed so fast. Perhaps at an
art school, where I would have had to produce works on
deadlines and for assessment, I might have stunted that
spark within me. But I sculpted simply because I could, simply because nothing felt so wonderful to me as to impose the
contours of my pleasure on such a rigid surface. I worked
hard at the bank during the day, and then indulged my love
for art in the evenings and weekends. I entered my sculptures in a number of amateur competitions. It soon became
embarrassingly obvious that my work was far superior to all
others, and I won so many competitions that modesty for-
bade me from entering any more. Within a year—*only a
year*—I had caught the eye of the international art commu-
nity, and sold two of my sculptures to major galleries. In
those early successes were the glimmerings of what would
eventually be a grand and illustrious career.

Faeries still eluded me, until one evening in the middle of
that decade, on my way home from work (for I still maintained my job in the bank as my parents desired), I paused as
I often did to read the program pinned outside the Vienna
State Opera. I didn't like opera then, and I still don't, but I was
a young, wealthy man and mindful of the pursuits that were
expected of me. *La Traviata.* I thought about buying a ticket,
decided not to, then turned and saw an attractive couple approaching. My nostrils itched. I grew excited. Could it be?

I waited for them to draw closer, pretending to examine
the program. They were now just behind me, just over my
right shoulder. I could *smell* them, both of them faeries. I

sneaked a glance. They were stunning, beautiful: tall and perfectly formed. I started to suspect nobility. The female smiled at me.

"Hello, are you going tonight to the opera?" Her German was studied, overly precise, clearly a second language.

"Yes, I think so. Shicoff is singing Alfredo."

"We don't know their names," the male said. He was gruff, suspicious.

"He's wonderful," I replied. "An American tenor."

"We're certainly going," the female said, "aren't we, Jasper?"

He mumbled something inaudible and moved her inside to buy a ticket. I was directly behind them. I didn't speak to them again, but when it came my turn at the ticket window, I waited until they were out of earshot and asked for the seat next to theirs. Then I went home to prepare myself.

That evening, I was waiting in my seat when they arrived. Polite conversation ensued. Isn't it a coincidence we're seated together? Do you come here often? Where do you live? The female—she introduced herself as Liesebet—was very warm; the male, Jasper, was not, but he became less guarded when I spoke of my art. It seems he had seen one of my sculptures in a gallery just that afternoon, and was very impressed with it.

I must express to you how difficult it was to sit and talk to them casually until the curtain went up. Imagine yourself seated next to the very villain who had tortured your child to death, and having to deal with him rationally and even in a friendly manner. That is how hard it was for me to hide my revulsion, the smell was so truly awful. But I was determined to lure them into my trap.

"Perhaps after the performance you would care to come to my home and see my latest sculpture in progress?" I asked. "I live nearby."

Liesebet didn't blink. "Yes."

Jasper blinked, but said, "Yes," all the same. Faeries are curious by nature.

I was well out of my depth trying to kill two faeries at once. I rightly made Jasper my first priority, but the female screamed and screamed, and I thought for certain somebody would hear it. When I had them both dead and in the bath, I covered them with water and left them for a time. I was too exhausted to begin the boning immediately, and I had an early start at the bank in the morning. I washed myself off, then crept downstairs to see if Liesebet's screams had disturbed anybody. I was living in an apartment on Wahlfischstrasse at the time, with a septuagenarian recluse downstairs and a dressmaking and mending studio above. All in the hallway was quiet, my activities had gone undetected.

I was too proud of myself.

I boned them on the weekend, but had nowhere to put the other remains. I packed them in bags and stored them in the deep freezer, supposing I would find a chance in the next few weeks to drive them out into the woods and feed them to the wildlife. I finished work late and collapsed directly into bed, only to be woken the next morning, Sunday, by loud knocking.

I rose, put on my robe, and went to the door. On the other side was Ernst Hoffmann, my direct supervisor at the bank, a small hairy man with long gray eyebrows.

"Herr Hoffmann?" I said, surprised.

"Morning, Zweigler. I need the Leadbetter reports. He's flying in from London this morning."

The Leadbetter reports. I had brought them home to work on the day I met the royal faeries, and forgotten about them since.

"Of course, of course. Come in. I'll find them immediately." I spotted the folder sitting on top of my bookshelf and grabbed it. "I'm sorry, Herr Hoffmann, but I haven't finished recalculating the projected dividends yet."

His left eyebrow shot up. "That's not like you, Zweigler."

"I've been . . . unwell."

"Let's do it now, together. They must be finished before I meet him at the airport."

So I put on a pot of coffee and changed my clothes, and we sat together at my dining table and worked on the reports. After a few hours, Herr Hoffmann asked me to direct him to the bathroom and I gestured through to the hallway, too immersed in the figures in front of me to remember that I hadn't been in the bathroom since I'd finished cleaning it the night before. He was in there a long time.

When Herr Hoffmann emerged, his face was pale.

"Are you ill?" I asked.

"Here, here, give me these reports," he muttered. "I'll take them with me. It's not right for me to intrude on your day off."

As he gathered the papers I felt a sudden chill of fear. I had cleaned the bathroom top to bottom the previous night, but had I left some trace—some blotch of blood, some skerrick of skin—for him to see?

"Certainly, Herr Hoffmann," I said, trying to remain cool. "I will see you tomorrow at the office."

He disappeared quickly. As soon as the door closed behind him, I dashed to the bathroom, eyes searching everywhere. No, the bath was clean and white. No, the handbasin was empty. No, the floor was spotless. I sighed in relief. Herr Hoffmann's disappearance probably had more to do with gastric troubles than with suspecting me of murder. I sat heavily on the lid of the toilet and rested my hands on my knees.

That's when I saw it. Visible at the angle only the toilet seat provided, under the handbasin; a stray, bloodied finger.

I scooped it up. It must have flown off before I'd even started the boning. What did Herr Hoffmann think? More importantly, what was he going to do?

I told myself not to panic. There could be no murder case where there were no murder victims. Nobody would report Liesebet and Jasper missing because they didn't really exist in this world. But I had a freezer full of skin and hair and organs to dispose of, and nothing was stopping Hoffmann from alerting the police immediately.

So I fled.

I packed up all I had of value—my sculptures and materials—and loaded them in my car along with the bags full of frozen tissue, and I left Vienna behind. I drove into the woods and dumped the bags and I kept driving and found myself in Berlin. I withdrew what I could from my bank account and rented a tiny apartment, and lay low for two years.

As I have said, I am a practical man. When I knew my parents had not heard from me in two years, I began to grow concerned about my inheritance. I had watched the newspapers and the television reports for all the long months in between, and had never seen my name mentioned as a murder suspect. Herr Hoffmann, it seems, had decided that as long as I was nowhere near him, he had no compulsion to report me for having an errant finger in my bathroom. (Or maybe it was a gastric problem after all.)

Finally, I made tentative contact with my parents. I told them I had been very sick—mental illness runs in our family and even though I am perfectly sane, I knew they would believe this—and gradually I won back their . . . "affection" is too strong a word. I won back their grudging decision to name me their heir, as long as I worked once again in finance and gave up my dreams of being a sculptor.

I did one but not the other. I found Berlin to be the city of my dreams as far as art was concerned, and soon my celebrated sculptures were outearning my financier's salary fivefold. I met no more faeries, and I longed to travel again, to take off in my van and drive through Europe and hunt and kill and sculpt, but still, I did not let my parents down. I had over a billion reasons not to, in U.S. dollars alone.

Then, at the end of 1989, two wonderful, wonderful things happened. First, the Berlin Wall fell. Second, my parents died. My opa, who had long been senile and sat rocking like a fool in the corner of my mother's overdecorated lounge room, took up a gun on Christmas Eve and shot them both and then himself. The money was all mine.

I was quick to buy real estate in the East and lease it out to businesses. I moved into the top two floors and attic of this building and began to plan my future. No more close calls with screaming faeries—I had a special room soundproofed. And no more messy bonings. I began to draw up my designs for a poisonous boiling acid bath.

My faery-boning vat.

He had painted it out.

Christine stared at the painting. It was the following evening. Jude was cleaning his brushes, whistling to himself. She had come down with the intention of pretending she was seeing it for the first time, of asking him if that blotch of color had anything to do with Mayfridh. But he had painted it out. A black oval covered it. She was gone.

"Do you like it?" he said, slipping an arm around her waist.

"Yeah, I do."

"I feel so good about it. I feel like I'm finally getting there, like I'm finally painting the feeling."

"That's great." She was gone. That was a good thing, right? It meant he had momentarily been interested, and then decided that it was wrong. He had covered her up with black.

But was she still under there?

"Okay," he said, organizing his paintbrushes and wiping his hands on a cloth, "I'll get changed quickly and we'll head out for dinner."

He left the room, leaving her standing in front of the painting. There was no need to be jealous. Mayfridh was beautiful and colorful, and of course she would have caught Jude's eye. She caught everybody's eye. But no trace of her color was left in the painting, and that meant it was all okay, right? Right?

Christine sighed. Jude had been so attentive today. A back massage at six in the morning when she woke with a twinge, a cup of tea in bed, kisses and cuddles. How could she doubt him? Was this that old feeling of inadequacy, returning in a different form? Damn all these stupid insecurities, damn her frightened heart.

Jude was at the door. "You like it that much?"

She turned. He had changed into fresh jeans and a buttoned shirt. "Sorry, lost in thought."

"Come on, I'm starving," he said, reaching for her hand.

"Jude, do you love me?"

He pulled her close to him and kissed her forehead. "You know I do, babe."

"You don't love anyone else but me?"

"I've only got room in my heart for Christine Starlight." He gave her a quick squeeze and stood back to smile at her. "Really, Christine, I'm *starving*."

They met Pete and Fabiyan in the gallery, just on their way out for doner kebabs at the local Imbiss. She pulled her coat on at the door. The Friday night streets were full. Jude and Christine lined up at the Imbiss in the autumn chill, while Pete and Fabiyan went in search of hot glühwein to wash their dinner down. The foursome found a semiclean table next to a cabal of punks.

"You know, we should have invited Gerda," Christine said, carefully unpeeling her kebab.

"We did," Pete said. "She said she was tired. She said she wanted to save her energy for tomorrow night." He had a chunk of lettuce and tahini stuck to his chin.

"What's tomorrow night?"

"The gallery party," Jude said.

"Had your head under a rock?" Pete said good-naturedly.

"Yeah, a real big one. I thought it was next week."

Fabiyan pointed down the street. "There's Gerda. And Christine's friend."

Christine turned to see Gerda and Mayfridh approaching. Mayfridh waved happily. "So she's back."

"Back?" Fabiyan said. "Back from where?"

"Back from . . . I thought she'd gone home for a while." Of course, the gallery party. Mayfridh had expressed an interest in going. Christine shot Jude a sidelong glance. He was concentrating on his kebab; he wasn't looking at Mayfridh.

"Hi, everyone," Gerda said as she approached. "You started without us."

"You said you weren't coming," Pete replied.

"Yeah, and then Miss Miranda shows up looking for Christine. How could I say no to her?"

Mayfridh squeezed in next to Christine and gave her a kiss on the cheek. "I missed you," she said with a shy smile. Despite her jealousy, Christine felt a wash of tender feeling. Mayfridh's affection was so artless, her warm breath as sweet as a child's.

"You weren't gone long."

"It was Eisengrimm's birthday," Mayfridh whispered in her ear. "He was one hundred and nine."

"Hey, don't keep secrets, you two," Gerda said, poaching Pete's glühwein. "Miranda, do you need food?"

"I'll have whatever you're having," Mayfridh said.

Christine watched her, and watched Jude, and saw nothing pass between them that didn't pass between any other two people there. She forced her fluttering emotions to still. She had been paranoid about Jude's affection for too long; she didn't want to project that paranoia onto Mayfridh. For the last three months Gerda had flirted with Jude shamelessly and nothing had come of that. *Relax, relax.*

Dinner finished, they bought four bottles of wine and headed back to Gerda's apartment for what Pete called "a piss-up." By midnight, everybody was roaring drunk and things were getting rowdy. A knock on the door calmed the room to urgent whispers.

"Shit, shit," Gerda said, "that'll be Mandy, for sure."

Pete turned the stereo down and Gerda went to the door. It was, indeed, Mandy.

"Sorry, sorry," Gerda said, "we didn't realize how late it was."

"It's fine," he said, putting his hands out, palms up. "I'm not angry, but I am tired and tomorrow is a big night."

"Of course," Gerda said. "We'll shut up. God, I'm so sorry."

Mandy's eyes swept the room and lighted on Mayfridh. Christine felt herself grow uncomfortable. He focused on her with a gaze that was somewhere between desiring and predatory.

"I don't believe we've met," he said, walking into the room, hand extended.

"Miranda," she said, standing up and taking his hand. "I'm an old friend of Christine's."

He kissed her hand and backed away quickly, apologizing with a laugh for spoiling their fun, and closing the door behind him.

"We'd better get to bed too," Jude was saying.

"And me," Fabiyan agreed.

Christine kept watching the door that Mandy had just disappeared through. So very creepy. She glanced at Mayfridh, who offered her a grimace and a theatrical shudder of repulsion. So she had noticed it too.

In the moment before Mandy had kissed Mayfridh's hand, he had bent to her wrist and sniffed her.

CHAPTER TEN

Christine found herself nursing a hangover the next morning, a cup of black coffee pressed between her hands, as Jude—remarkably refreshed—left for a morning's work in the studio.

"I can't tell you how much I love my new painting," he said with a self-satisfied grin as he disappeared out the door.

She smiled. *Good.* When Jude enjoyed what he was doing, she felt the glow of his reflected happiness. Christine sipped her coffee and rolled her neck, trying to clear away the cobwebs. She was going to have to go sober to tonight's party.

There was a knock on the door. "Come in, it's not locked," she called. It had to be someone from inside the hotel or they would have buzzed downstairs. She braced herself, hoping it wasn't Mandy.

Mayfridh, beautiful without makeup, wearing one of Gerda's outsize T-shirts and a pair of her denim overalls.

"Hi. You want a coffee? I just brewed it."

"Yes, please," Mayfridh replied, "black with no sugar."

Christine smiled as she poured the coffee. "Hell, you

went hard-core real quick. Wasn't it like a week ago I could barely get you to drink this stuff?"

"Everything in the Real World is so intoxicating. Especially the toxic things." Mayfridh took the cup gratefully and sipped from it. "You look tired."

"I am. And I'm supposed to work this afternoon. My boss has a wedding to go to." She shook her head. "I'm going to be a real live wire at the party tonight."

Mayfridh was glancing around her. "Your apartment's nicer than Gerda's. Why is that?"

"I think she just doesn't clean up after herself." She swept her hand around. "Jude, however, is a neat freak, especially when he's got painter's block."

"Would you let me see the rest?"

"Sure." Christine led her to the short hallway. "Okay, there's the bathroom; you've already seen that. This is the spare bedroom." She opened the door on four empty suitcases and a billion dust motes. "As you can see, we don't use it. And this is our bedroom."

Mayfridh entered ahead of her. "It's nice."

The bed wasn't yet made and the curtains were still closed against the weak morning sun. "We can't really get used to these German pillows. Jude keeps telling me to go buy some regular ones, but I always forget." Christine sank down in the chair next to the dresser, and Mayfridh sat on the end of the bed. "I think he's getting a bit annoyed with me."

"Do you and Jude fight much?" Mayfridh asked.

Christine shook her head. "Hardly at all. He's very patient."

"Are you going to get married?"

Christine perched her coffee cup on the dresser. "Maybe. One day. I'd like to, anyway."

"Have you talked about it with Jude?"

"Oh yeah, of course. It's complicated. You see, I get a big inheritance when I get married, and I think Jude is wary of what people might think if he asks me to marry him. He told me he wants to wait until he's financially stable in his own right. I accept that." And she tried really hard to believe it, because it was better than suspecting he didn't want to marry her because he didn't really love her.

Mayfridh was frowning, her head tilted to the side.

"What's the matter?" Christine asked.

"Does Gerda know all that?"

Christine knew where this was going. "Ah, Gerda. Don't listen to a thing she says about me or Jude or my money. Gerda just makes up her own version of events and doesn't care about the truth."

"You don't like Gerda?"

"I like her a lot. She's a lot of fun, but she's really gossipy."

Mayfridh sank back on the bed. "Humans are something of a mystery to me."

"You mean you don't have gossip in Ewigkreis?" Christine finished the last of her coffee.

"I suppose we do, though it's less complicated. Come and sit by me, I want to ask your opinion on something."

Christine eased herself out of the chair and moved to the bed.

"Is your back sore?" Mayfridh asked, moving over to make space.

"A little. It's always worse if I'm tired or sick."

"Lie on your stomach. I can make it better."

"How?"

"I'll show you."

Christine turned and lay down on her stomach. Mayfridh searched the curve of her back with her hands.

"Tell me when I hit the spot," she said.

"Up a bit . . . there." Christine felt the warmth of Mayfridh's fingers through her shirt, and then a soft, lightly penetrating feeling like electricity. It spread the pain apart, making it lose its grip on her bones.

"Wow, that's amazing. How do you do it?" Christine asked.

"Magic often gets left over in my hands from using spells," she replied.

Christine closed her eyes and let Mayfridh's fingers work the area. The pain was still close by, threatening to swoop back into place the moment she took her hands away. It wasn't the same genuine freedom she felt in Ewigkreis, but it was a wonderful relief anyway. Much more effective than the drugs, which merely dulled the pain, dulling all her other senses with it.

"So, can I ask your advice about something?"

"Sure, go ahead."

"It's about my Real World parents. Do you think I should visit them?"

"Why do you want to visit them? I thought you'd forgotten about them."

"It's coming back to me, Christine, just as my memories and fondness for you came back. The longer I'm here, the more I think of them." In her distraction, Mayfridh had taken her hands from Christine's back. The pain returned.

Christine willed Mayfridh to continue the massage. "How would you explain what happened?"

"I'd just explain."

"They'd never believe you."

"You believe me . . . remember?"

"I don't know if it's a good idea to go around putting spells on people." Christine turned her head, saw that Mayfridh was sitting back, biting her lip, looking like she might cry. "Hey, don't listen to me, I'm just tired and snappish."

Mayfridh's fingers resumed their massage. "No, you're right. I can't go around putting spells on people. I didn't realize it before. Sorry."

Christine let her head hang forward again, taking comfort in the sweet soothing electricity. "Look, forget what I said. You probably really want to see your parents, and they'd be so happy to know that you're alive and well, whatever you've become. Maybe you should go. I can't see the harm in it."

"Eisengrimm sees much harm in it."

"Why?"

The magic was fading now as Mayfridh's last reserves were spent. "I'm sorry," she said, her fingers withdrawing. "I have no magic left."

"Don't be sorry. Thank you, it was great." Christine turned over and looked up at Mayfridh. "So what's Eisengrimm's problem with you seeing your parents?"

"Oh, he's just a grumpy thing."

"You once told me he was a wise counselor. He's got to have a reason for advising you against it."

Mayfridh hitched a sigh and sank down on her belly on the rumpled covers. Christine curled a finger into her hair and pulled it playfully. "Come on, tell me."

"It's not forever, Christine."

"What's not forever?"

"This favorable alignment. It's so rare."

"I don't follow you."

Mayfridh sat up. "You know I can't tell you where Ewigkreis is. Nor can I tell you where it will be next. It moves every season, to other places, other times. And wherever it arrives next, there's no way of contacting you even if

I remembered you. Any passage is binding—it restricts me in a fairly narrow circle."

"So you mean . . . that this passage between my world and your world . . ."

"Is temporary. Only until the last leaf falls on the birch outside the great hall."

"And you'll disappear."

"No, *you'll* disappear," Mayfridh said solemnly, "and I'll forget you."

"I'll forget you after a while too, I guess."

"No, no. You misunderstand. I'll forget you immediately. I'll wake up in the Winter Castle, and everything will be as it always has been in Ewigkreis, and my memory of you will be so far distant in the corridors of my thinking, that I will never trip over it and remember you. Unless, of course, our worlds align so closely again, which I very much doubt they will."

Christine started to realize what this meant: she had only limited time to escape from her pain in the autumn forest. "So we don't have long."

"No. Perhaps until early December. I'll be gone by Christmas."

"Eisengrimm—he doesn't want you to form a relationship with your parents that's doomed to end so soon, right?"

"That's right."

Such a longing filled Christine then, such a rolling, overwhelming desire to be thirteen years younger, to tell her parents not to take the shortcut, to keep her body whole and unbroken. Relief was slipping away from her, she was consigned back into her material limits. "He's wrong, Mayfridh," she managed to say. "He's wrong. Even the scantest moments of joy are worth the pain that follows."

"You really think so?"

"I know so. I know it with my whole heart. You should definitely try to find them."

Mayfridh beamed, threw herself on top of Christine and folded her in a hug. "Thank you, you're right."

"Just be cautious, okay?" Christine said through a mouthful of crimson hair. "They may have moved back to England. They may not be around anymore."

Mayfridh sat back. "I already looked in the phone book. There's a listing for Frith at my old address at Zehlendorf." Her face grew serious. "Though it only listed my mother's initials, and not my father's. Do you think that means he's dead?"

Christine thought that was exactly what it meant but didn't say so. "Just prepare yourself for any eventuality. That way, you won't get hurt."

Not that it really mattered if Mayfridh got hurt; she would soon forget it all when her miraculous, luscious faery world swung away forever. Christine struggled with this new despair; the journey had only just started and already it was coming to an end.

⌁

When Christine left for work, Mayfridh went looking for Gerda, but she was not in her apartment. She crept down the stairs and slunk through the gallery before Mandy, who was talking to a man in a suit, could see her. She knocked at Gerda's studio door but nobody answered. She knocked again, then pressed her ear to the door. Sometimes Gerda used electric tools and couldn't hear anything else. But all was quiet within.

"Gerda's not there."

Mayfridh looked up. It was Jude, leaning in the doorway of his studio, his head tilted to one side. Jude, impenetrable Jude. The spell Hexebart had given her had been utterly useless. There was no way into this secret of his, and she was unconvinced that Gerda was right about him, especially after what Christine had told her this morning.

He smiled. "Sorry, didn't mean to startle you."

"Where is she?"

"She went shopping, I think."

"Without me?"

Jude wiped a paintbrush on a cloth in his hand. "Maybe I'm wrong. Maybe she's somewhere else. Has Christine gone to work?"

"She left about five minutes ago." Half a second too much silence intervened between his sentences and her responses, too great a fraction of her mind was directed to admiring his dark, smiling eyes. "Sorry, I'm probably disturbing you while you're working. I'll go back upstairs."

"No, it's fine. I've finished."

"The painting?"

"Yeah, I finished it just now."

She felt her tongue hesitate, could imagine too clearly Eisengrimm's stern voice. Then said, "Can I see it?"

He seemed genuinely pleased. "Yeah, yeah. Of course. Come in." He held open the studio door and ushered her ahead of him.

She gasped. It was simply the most beautiful painting she had ever seen. Such an ache of clarity where dark swirling gray wheeled over bright white. Such somber, serious melancholy where brown and black collided. The colors so perfectly mixed that it looked as though a bright distant star pulsed weakly over the claustrophobic unions of gloomy shapes.

"You like it?" he said.

"Oh, it's the most beautiful . . . *beautiful* thing . . ."

He stood next to her, gazing at the painting. She felt the

warmth from his shoulder. "Thanks. I think it's the best I've ever done."

"You're a genius," she breathed.

Jude laughed. "I wouldn't go that far."

"No, no. Look at it, look at where this shape meets this patch of gray. It takes my breath away. It's so profoundly . . . so sad . . ."

He was gazing at her very seriously now. "You really mean it."

She met his eyes—such beautiful eyes—and had to swallow hard. "Of course I really mean it."

"You see it, don't you?" he said, filling up with tension. "You really see it."

Mayfridh nodded. "I really see it."

His mouth was open a fraction—surprise. She was overwhelmed with the desire to kiss him, but an instant later he was looking at his painting again. "What else? What else do you see?" He was agitated, alive with what appeared to be a desperate excitement.

She turned to the painting, feeling the pressure to say the right thing. "I see . . . this swirl of brown . . ." She touched the painting, felt immediately that the paint was still wet. "Oh, oh no!"

He was laughing, all the sudden intensity gone. "Hey, it's okay."

Her fingers were sticky and brown. "It's not okay. I've ruined it. I've ruined your painting!"

"No, really, it's okay." He was already picking up a brush, repairing the tiny blob of damage. "Look, it's fixed already."

"I'm so sorry, so very sorry." She could feel tears prick at her eyes. All she had wanted was for Jude to like her, and now she had smudged his favorite painting.

"Don't be sorry, it's all right. You weren't to know it was

still wet. Besides," he said, smiling at her with that wicked, knowing smile, "it's kind of nice that your fingerprints are under there now, seeing as how you love it so much."

She smiled back. "Thank you for being so sweet."

"All part of the service. Hey, you've got paint all over your hand."

In her distress she had balled her hand up into a fist and smeared the fingertip of paint everywhere. "Oh, dear," she said, moving to wipe the paint on Gerda's overalls.

He stilled her hand. "No, no, don't do that. You'll never get it out."

Before she could appreciate the touch of his hand on hers, it had been withdrawn. He went to the rickety table where his paints and brushes were kept, and returned with a dirty piece of cloth that smelled of chemicals. "Here," he said, "hold out your hand."

She did so, and he began to rub the paint off.

"You'll have to wash up afterwards. This stuff is toxic."

She couldn't answer, was struck dumb.

He finished wiping her palm and then turned her hand over, examining it for more paint. "Looks pretty clean."

"Thanks," she said, knowing it sounded forced.

His fingers lingered on her hand a moment longer, a slow brush of his index finger from the base of her palm, right up her middle finger, then, agonizingly, departing at the tip. A jolt of white heat. Had he done that purposely? So slowly, so sensually, the pad of his fingertip against hers, electricity. A big breath stopped in her lungs.

"There," he said softly. "There, that's better."

"Thanks," she said again.

"Anyway," he said brightly, "I might just . . . work a little longer on this." He wasn't looking at her now, he was folding the rag, organizing his brushes. "I want to make sure all the shapes are how I feel them."

"Certainly. I'm sorry to disturb you."

"I guess I'll see you at the party tonight," he said, over his shoulder, not meeting her eye.

"Yes. Yes, you will." And then when he said nothing further, "Good-bye, Jude."

He didn't reply. She backed out, closing the door behind her. The electricity was withdrawing now, and she felt mildly foolish. Confused. And besotted.

🦋

Mayfridh could hardly believe how many people had fitted into Mandy's gallery for the party. They jostled past each other to look at the art, glasses in hands, cigarettes on lips, a bubbling hubbub of conversation swelling the room.

"I'd bet everything I had on it," Gerda said, her words slightly slurred from an afternoon's preparatory drinking. "Mandy's got a crush on you."

Mayfridh turned to her and shook her head. "I'm sure that's not true."

"Every time I look at him, he's looking at you." Gerda glanced over her shoulder. "There! He's looking at you now."

Mayfridh cautiously lifted her eyes to find him. Gerda was right, but she denied it anyway. "No, he's not. He's talking with Jude and Christine."

"What do you think, Fabiyan?" Gerda asked.

"I think he looks at you, but it is maybe just an artist's interest."

Gerda rolled her eyes.

Pete slipped an arm around Gerda's waist. "I'm with you, Gerda. He's got the hots for Miranda." He made a growling-dog noise.

Gerda shrugged him off. "Get off me, you oaf."

Pete laughed and lit a cigarette. "She doesn't like me," he

said. "Gerda, look at the stats. There are too many gay men in Berlin for you to be so picky."

Gerda didn't laugh, pulling her cardigan tighter around her. "I wonder what Mandy's talking to them about."

Mayfridh found Jude and Christine again. Jude had his arm tightly around Christine's waist. She was leaning away from Mandy as he told them a detailed story. Jude swigged from a beer bottle and tried to look interested. Just seeing his fingers wrapped around the bottle brought back the memory of his touch from that afternoon. She shook her head to dispel the feeling. "It doesn't look like they're actually interested in whatever he's saying," she said.

"Nobody ever is," Gerda said with a wry smile. "He's universally despised."

"They're a good couple," Pete said, his cigarette dangling from his bottom lip.

"Who? Jude and Christine?" Gerda asked.

"Yeah, they're always together. They're really into each other."

Gerda offered Mayfridh a raise of her eyebrows. "I don't know that they're such a good couple. It seems unbalanced to me."

"What do you mean?" Fabiyan said.

"Jude's very good-looking and she's . . ." She trailed off meaningfully.

Pete sneered. "What are you talking about? Christine's all right. And Jude's not exactly a movie star."

"What do you think, Miranda?" Gerda said, turning on her suddenly. "Honestly, do you think they're well matched?"

Mayfridh was startled by this question. Gerda was becoming unpredictable. "I don't know what to say. Christine's a close friend whom I love very much, so—"

"Okay, forget I said anything."

Fabiyan said in a considered tone, "I think you are too hard on Christine. She is maybe not so glamorous, but she is very kind and very nice."

"Okay, okay!" Gerda said, thrusting exasperated hands upward. "I didn't mean she's ugly and I'm not denying she's a nice person. She just doesn't look like his type."

"He obviously loves her, so perhaps you just don't know what his 'type' really is," Pete said heatedly.

Gerda gave Mayfridh a tap on the shoulder. "Come on, Miranda, let's check out the eligible bachelors." Then she was dragging Mayfridh away from Pete and Fabiyan, farther into the warm crush of bodies. At every step she took, Mayfridh could feel Mandy Z's eyes on her.

❧

One moment, Christine was safely settled in the crook of Jude's arm enduring one of Mandy's interminable stories of gossip in the art world, the next Jude had been swept away by an American buyer who wanted a painting explained to him. Before she could move off with Jude, Mandy's hand closed around her wrist and pulled her nearer.

"I wanted to ask you something," he said, those small teeth bared in a smile.

"Um, sure, what is it?"

"Your friend Miranda . . . where is she from?"

Christine followed his eyes and realized that his distracted gaze hadn't been monitoring attendance, it was checking out Mayfridh. "England," Christine said warily. "Somewhere in Kent, I think."

"Have you known her long?"

"We were friends in childhood. She lived next door to me for a short time. Why? Is there a problem?"

Another smile. "No, no problem. You two are close?"

"We . . . I guess we're getting that way. But she won't be around for long."

His eyes grew anxious. "No?"

"No, she has to go home in a month or so. Mandy, is there some reason you're asking me all this?"

"I . . . well, yes there is." He swallowed, it was hard to say. "I wonder if she has a . . . you know . . ."

Christine felt her skin crawl. "A boyfriend?"

"Yes, a boyfriend." He laughed at himself. "Such an old-fashioned word."

Christine tried to process this information. Mandy had a crush on Mayfridh? Was that why he looked pale and slightly sick while talking about her? "There is someone," she said at last, thinking of Eisengrimm. "I would say she's definitely not available."

"I see," he said, not sounding particularly disappointed. Bravado, maybe. "And this boyfriend . . . is he here in Berlin with her?"

"No, he's back in her hometown."

"She's here alone?"

For indefinable reasons, this question unsettled her. Perhaps it was the almost imperceptible eagerness, the light shine of perspiration on his lip. "She's here with me," Christine said, "that's not alone."

"Indeed it isn't," Mandy said, nodding. "Indeed it is not."

"Look, if you want to talk to her, just go up and talk to her."

"No," he said quickly, "no, I won't. I'll leave it a while. She's very pretty, Christine."

Christine sought out her friend again, brightly colored and flawlessly beautiful. Just the kind of girl who would turn up in a painting. She smiled. "Yeah, she sure is. Makes me feel about as attractive as a stick insect."

Mandy laughed out loud now, and the tension between

them eased. "Beauty is more than surface effect, Christine. Every artist knows that. Jude knows that." He indicated across the room at Jude, who was being administered a cigar by the American buyer. "I'll let you join him. Thank you."

"You're welcome," she said, not sure what he was thanking her for, but glad to escape anyway.

She weaved through people, narrowly avoiding a collision with a drinks waiter. She tried to skirt around the edges of the crowd, only to trip over one of the iron poles that kept the viewers from getting too close to the paintings. She put her hands out, not believing for a second that she was actually going to fall, and next instant found herself crashing to the ground on her right hip. The streak of pain was instant and intense, setting her back throbbing.

"Christine, are you all right?" This was Fabiyan, helping her up.

"I . . . ouch, that really hurts." Her hands went to her back, and then Jude was there.

"Christine?"

"I fell over." She was as embarrassed as she was sore, seeing how many pairs of eyes were trained on her. "I tripped on the stupid . . ."

Jude's hands were on hers. "Are you badly hurt?"

"No, I've just set it off. It's not too bad."

Gerda, Pete, and Mayfridh were all there now, crowding around her solicitously. She waved them all away. "I'm okay, really. Don't make a fuss. It's embarrassing me."

"Don't be embarrassed," Gerda said.

"Yeah, easy for you to say," Christine snapped back, regretting it instantly. "Sorry, Gerda, I'm just—"

"It's all right," Gerda said.

"Do you want me to take you upstairs?" Mayfridh asked.

"I'll just see if I can . . ." She tried a few steps; pain jolted into her spine. "Um, yeah. I'm going to have to go lie down." She turned to Jude. "I'm so sorry, Jude. I've ruined your evening."

"Don't worry about it. I'll take you upstairs."

"No, Mayfridh can do it. You go back to your buyer. Make us lots of money." She smiled weakly and patted his arm.

He gave her a kiss on the forehead, and then Mayfridh was walking her out of the gallery and up the stairs—each step a jarring shudder of pain—and to her apartment. She fetched Christine's painkillers and put her to bed.

Once she had turned out the light Mayfridh sat on the bed and leaned over Christine. "Don't forget the twine," she said, her breath tickling Christine's cheek. "You still have it?"

"Yeah. I keep it in my purse. But I'd better lie still for a while."

"If you need somebody to help you out to the Tiergarten . . ."

"Sure, I'll come knocking."

Mayfridh gave her a kiss on the cheek. "I'll keep an eye on Jude for you."

"Thanks, good night."

"Good night."

A moment later she was gone. Christine closed her eyes and tried not to feel anything.

— from the Memoirs of Mandy Z.

My hands are shaking so much I can barely write.
There is one of the filthy things right here in my own building. No wonder I've had so many sleepless nights

of late. They have been hiding her from me, thinking I might prove to be too stern a landlord and charge her rent. I can't believe I didn't know before now.

So many problems, though. This is the first time I've met one who is a friend to others of my acquaintance. It is not like I can march down there to Gerda Ekman's apartment and drag her screaming into the hallway, cut her up, and dip her in the vat without expecting any consequences. It's so very tricky. I can't rightly discern either whether or not Christine Starlight knows her old childhood friend is from another world. She speaks of her returning home soon (not too soon, please), but without a flick of an eyelash that might give away a darker secret.

But then, Americans are such good liars.

Still, I know this much. She is here without other faeries, her friends don't expect her to stay for long, and there will be a moment, an unguarded moment, upon which I can prey. I need only be patient and clever. And I am nothing if not patient.

I am nothing if not clever.

CHAPTER ELEVEN

*C*hristine woke in the night, the pinching and pulling in her back flaring into life. She rolled over and tried to make herself comfortable, but the pain was insistent. In the dark, Jude was fast asleep, his relaxed, regular breathing a mocking reminder that deep, unfettered sleep was never to be hers.

For a few moments she lay on her side, gazing at the muted streetlight through the curtain. It would be cold out there; she could hear the wind gusting in the elms at the bottom of the street. But there was a place where this pain could no longer find her.

She checked on Jude again. He didn't stir, deep under the layers of sleep. In the three A.M. gloom, she slid out of bed and dressed, gathered the ball of twine from her purse, and slipped out into autumn streets. One block from home a blustering wind tore up the road and whipped her scarf from around her neck, sending it fluttering away behind her. She nearly turned back, but the pain was too stubborn and relief was more important than an errant scarf.

A half-emptied feeling inhabited the city at night. Rows of shop fronts, stoic and mute, were occasionally punctuated by the warm sounds and trickling crowds of nightclubs, or the yellow lights and greasy smells of fast-food restaurants. But as she drew closer to the Tiergarten, the blended scents of damp earth and rotting foliage completed the emptiness. She tramped through piles of fallen leaves to the dark, deserted corner where the passage lay. Leaves skittered around her like tiny insistent footsteps, and she felt very alone.

Christine spun the ball of twine out in front of her. It glowed faintly in the dark. She checked her watch, determined not to be gone more than an hour or two. Hand over hand, she began to follow the twine, and an eyeblink later, found herself in the dark twilight of afternoon in the autumn forest.

A few breaths, first, enjoying the freedom. Then she began to search for the golden twine among the drifts of fallen yellow leaves. She reeled it toward her, gave it a tug, and realized too late that the end was caught on a branch nearby. It sawed over the rough surface and nearly snapped. She gasped, gently released it from the snag, and inspected it. The twine was frayed almost all the way through. Did this mean she wouldn't be able to get home?

"Eisengrimm!" she called, carefully winding the twine around her wrist so she could find the fray easily again. She began walking toward the castle gate. "Eisengrimm!"

A flutter of wings. A crow perched before her on a tree. Christine fought down her first startled reaction and remembered her manners. "Eisengrimm? Is that you?"

"Of course it is."

She held out the twine. "I think I've broken it."

He hopped down a few branches and peered close. "I can fix it. Bring it inside." He fluttered to the ground and transformed to Wolf. "Follow me."

A gentle breeze moved the forest around her. More and more leaves descended from the branches above them, spinning and diving in random patterns toward the ground. Christine's eyes were constantly drawn upward to watch the branches shaking themselves bare in the long shadows. She thought about what Mayfridh had told her, about autumn ending and their worlds moving apart.

"Eisengrimm, what's the Winter Castle like?"

Eisengrimm did not look back, but his voice took on a warm fondness. "Ah, the Winter Castle is my favorite. It is gleaming white, and outside the branches are bare and glittering with frost and ice, and the world is buried in snow. We stay inside, and we have games and long dark nights of tale-telling and drinking by the fire and midwinter music."

"But I don't understand why you move from one castle to the other."

"Why does one season change to another anywhere? It just is as it is."

"So why do you have to forget everything?"

Eisengrimm stopped and turned to look at her. "We don't. We remember each other, we remember events that have taken place in Ewigkreis, and everything feels right and fresh and as though it has purpose. We simply don't remember the Real World and its people, if we have made contact in the season."

"Why not?"

"That I know not. But perhaps it is so that we do not grow too sad, knowing that many decades may pass before the worlds align again, knowing that our human friends will grow old and die while we stay young."

"I think it's sadder to forget them."

Eisengrimm turned and the castle gate swung open in front of them. "Come, I'll bring you to the spell chamber."

He led her inside the castle and along the main corridor, but when he started down a deep staircase she hesitated.

"Eisengrimm . . ."

He paused on the stairs and looked back. "What is the matter?"

"Are we going underground?"

"We are going to the spell chamber."

"I'm . . . I have a phobia." She wondered how that word would translate into their language.

Eisengrimm registered no confusion. "We're not going all the way to the dungeons."

"But still—"

"Christine, the spell chamber is below the ground, yes, but only barely. There is a window up near the ceiling, you can see the garden through it."

Christine swallowed hard, trying to fight the jitters. "Really?"

"You can see for yourself."

"Can we leave the door open?"

"Of course, if it makes you feel better."

Christine hesitantly moved down the stairs behind him.

"Could you bring in that lantern hanging on the wall?" Eisengrimm said with a nod of his head.

Christine unhooked the lantern. "I thought you said there was a window."

"It's only tiny. We'll need more light."

He nosed the door open and Christine followed him inside. There was indeed a window up high in the wall, and through it the long grass in the garden blotted out nearly all of the deep twilight. She dragged her eyes away from it a moment to examine the rest of the room. Dark, bare walls, a long table in the center of the room. Her breathing was shallow. She forced it to slow and deepen. Eisengrimm transformed back to Crow and hopped up on the table. He clicked his beak.

"Come, Christine, put the ball of twine here."

Christine carefully unwrapped it from her wrist and laid

it down, indicating the fray. "Here," she said. "Look, it's almost worn through."

"But it's not broken. I can fix it easily," Eisengrimm said. With one claw he held the twine, and with his beak he began to work the frayed threads.

Christine glanced up to the window again. "So, Eisengrimm, you said there are dungeons under here?"

"Yes. If you follow the stairs down further below the crypt, there's a deep, sloping corridor. The dungeons are very far beneath the castle."

Christine's skin crawled. "And are there people in them?"

"Rarely. We have little use for them. They're empty now." His beak kept working, pulling threads and winding them. "Why are you afraid of being beneath the ground?"

"My parents were both killed in a car accident. I was with them. It happened in a tunnel."

He cocked his head, his golden crow eyes round. "I find it very peaceful beneath the ground. The earth muffles out cares and concerns."

"It weighs on me, like being buried while you're still alive."

Eisengrimm went back to work. "Now I understand why you didn't want to see the dungeons on your last visit."

"Yeah, and why I won't use underpasses, tunnels, or subways. Sometimes it makes life complicated." She looked up at the window again. Even thinking about it had made her breath feel short and her fingers twitch.

"There," Eisengrimm said, "it's nearly finished. I just need to rebalance the spell."

He transformed to Wolf and as he did so, his front paw knocked the twine from the table so that it rolled away from him.

Christine bent to gather the thread. "Clumsy. I'll get it."

"Christine, don't—"

Christine was about to say, "Don't what?" wondering why Eisengrimm hadn't finished the sentence, but a sudden heavy blackness greeted her eyes, causing panic to flutter in her chest. Had the light gone out? Had the window been blacked by evening? She scooped up the thread and turned, but Eisengrimm was no longer there, and she realized with horror she was no longer in the spell chamber.

"Eisengrimm?" she called, her hand searching in front of her. Everything was blackness. She took a step, then another, her fingers found a wall, searched farther, found rough iron bars.

Christine screamed. She was in the dungeon.

"Eisengrimm!" She ran a few steps and came to another wall, her hands frantic upon it. "Eisengrimm! Help me!" *You're so far from the light, you're so far beneath the earth, your heart is thumping, your ears are filling up with the ache of your pulse, you don't know where you are, you're locked in, you'll never get out, your head is filling with white noise, your skin is buzzing, your pulse is throbbing in your eyeballs, you can't see a thing.* "Eisengrimm!" *You'll probably die, your head will burst open and madness will pour in, your body will fall apart, you can already feel it falling apart, that's what the pounding sound is, you can barely breathe anymore anyway, you should just sit down and wait to die.*

"Christine! Where are you?"

Oh God, oh God, oh God. "Eisengrimm, I don't know where I am," she sobbed.

"I can hear you, I'm coming."

"I can't see a thing."

"I'm nearly there. It sounds like you're in a cell. Is there a door?"

"I don't know."

A grinding, creaking noise and Eisengrimm's voice was in the room with her. Her eyes had started to adjust to the blackness, and she could faintly see his pale gray shape, but only if she looked just beside him. "Follow me, Christine."

"I . . ."

"Your breathing sounds strange. Try to breathe regularly."

She forced air into her chest. Eisengrimm was here, he was going to lead her out. Let go of the panic.

"Follow me, follow my voice if you can't see me. I'm sorry, but I haven't the ability to hold a torch. But I know my way around here." He was walking ahead of her now, his voice leading her in the dark. "We're lucky the dungeons are empty and unlocked. South gate." Iron creaked ahead of her, and they started to turn to the east. "There are four gates. If you follow the slope up and don't take one of the paths deeper into the dungeons, we'll find all four."

"How far are we from daylight?"

"Not far. Can you feel it? We're moving upwards now."

She could feel it, her legs growing tired. Another gate creaked ahead of them.

"I'm sorry we don't have lamps burning here all the time. You must have been very frightened. It was the twine, you see. I had been working it, but hadn't rebalanced the spell. It took you to the last place I had spoken of." Another gate. "I should have warned you, I'm sorry."

"Are we nearly there?"

"One more gate. You'll see the glow of lamplight from the stairs around the next bend. Ah, there it is."

She ran ahead of him, up the slope and up the stairs, and farther, into the main corridor of the castle and along it until she reached the garden. She threw herself down, gazing at the late afternoon sky, gratefully sucking in breaths of air. Eisengrimm appeared next to her a moment later.

"I am curious," he said.

"What about?"

"About how your body remembers the fear and reproduces it."

"Um, yeah. I guess you haven't had Freud here yet, huh?"

He curled up next to her, his face resting on her stomach. "Do you still think forgetfulness such a terrible thing?" he asked in his rich, mellow voice.

She stroked his ears, her breathing returning to normal. "Don't ask," she said. "I can't answer that."

Mayfridh woke in the dark, wondering what had roused her. She waited a few moments, began to drift off, then the knocking started again.

"Yes, yes, I'm coming." This was Gerda, her voice muffled through the bedroom door. Mayfridh slipped out of bed and pulled on the clothes she had been wearing that evening. She leaned her head out. Gerda was at the front door, fiddling with the lock. Another few sharp raps.

"Yes, okay, I'm here," Gerda said. She opened the door and Jude stood, dimly lit by the security light, on the other side. "Jude! It's four in the morning."

"Have you seen Christine?"

Gerda shook her head, confused. "What do you mean?"

Jude forced his way in, switched on the light. "I mean, have you seen Christine? I don't know where she is." His words were quick and breathless.

Mayfridh emerged from the hallway, shutting her bedroom door behind her, creeping closer.

"I don't understand, Jude," Gerda said. "Wasn't she with you?"

"Yeah, she was with me," Jude said, his voice growing

louder, "but I woke up five minutes ago and she wasn't there."

Mayfridh knew exactly where Christine was. She just wasn't allowed to tell. "Perhaps she went for a walk, Jude," she said, trying to imbue her voice with a reassuring tone.

Jude turned on her. "A walk? At four A.M. the same night she fell over and hurt her back and had to be helped to bed? A walk?"

"Just a suggestion," Mayfridh mumbled.

"So where else could she be?" Gerda asked.

"I don't know. I thought she might be here."

Gerda turned him around and faced him toward the door. "Go check with Fabiyan and Pete. I'll put a pot of coffee on."

Jude disappeared, and Mayfridh joined Gerda in the kitchen.

"He's worried," Mayfridh said.

"He's overreacting. I doubt she's been abducted by a psychopath."

"He's frantic."

Gerda spooned coffee into the filter and switched the machine on. "All the more reason for us to keep our cool."

Mayfridh pulled out a chair and sat down, dropped her head into her hands.

"Hey, I'm sorry," Gerda said, her hand on Mayfridh's neck. "I'm so sorry. That comment about abduction . . . I forgot about . . ."

Mayfridh looked up, took a moment to understand what Gerda was saying. "Oh. Oh, don't worry about me."

"No, it was insensitive. Christine told me that you were . . . you know . . . taken from your bedroom . . ."

"It's all right, Gerda. I'll tell you about it one day."

Jude burst back in, trailing Pete and Fabiyan. "She's nowhere in the hotel."

"Did you check with Mandy?"

"Yes," Pete said. "He said wait until daylight and call the police."

"I'll go crazy before daylight," Jude said, pacing now. "Where is she? What if she's wandered off somewhere and is hurt or—?"

"Calm down, Jude," Gerda said. "Do you want coffee? It'll be ready in a few minutes."

"No, I don't want coffee. I want to go out and look for her."

"Jude, you're panicking. Why would she be in any danger?"

"She was drinking tonight, and then she had painkillers. What if she woke up confused?"

Fabiyan put a hand on his shoulder. "Would you feel better if we went looking for her?"

Jude turned to him. "Yeah, yeah I would."

"Okay, you boys go off and take a walk round the block, but don't get too worried, Jude. I'm sure she's fine." Gerda bundled them out the door and closed it behind them, then turned to Mayfridh. "So, where do you think she is?"

Mayfridh shrugged. "Nowhere dangerous, I'm certain."

"It is kind of weird for her to wander off in the middle of the night." Gerda checked the coffeepot. "Want a coffee?"

"Yes, please."

Gerda placed a mug of coffee in front of her, and arranged four empty cups on the table. "I'm guessing they'll all want something hot to drink when they bring Christine home," she said.

"I suppose so."

Gerda sat across from her. "You could tell me now if you like."

Mayfridh was momentarily confused. "Tell you?"

"About when you were taken from your bedroom as a little girl."

Mayfridh smiled. "Gerda—"

"Go on. We've got some time to kill before they come back." She leaned in close. "I've always wanted to know."

"Christine said to beware of your questions."

"Christine is good at avoiding them too."

Mayfridh sipped her coffee. Gerda's eyes hadn't left hers. "It wasn't a big deal, Gerda."

"You were abducted and it wasn't a big deal?"

"I was abducted by people who thought they were my parents."

"Like relatives?"

"Not exactly . . . they were . . . it's hard to explain."

"Like one of those messy custody cases?"

"Yes, just like that. They loved me a lot."

"And they treated you well?"

Mayfridh laughed. "They treated me like a princess, actually."

"How long were you with them? Do you still see your real parents?"

"I—" Before she could answer, the door slammed open and Jude, Fabiyan, and Pete burst in. Jude was pale.

"What is it?" Gerda asked, and Mayfridh could tell that for the first time she actually thought Christine might be in danger.

Jude held out a pale brown scarf. "This is hers, isn't it?" The awful tremble in his voice touched Mayfridh's heart. He was suffering. She couldn't bear his suffering.

Gerda nodded. "It looks like the one she hangs by the door with her coat. Where did you find it?"

"About a block away."

"It might not mean anything—"

"I'm calling the police."

Pete interjected. "Maybe you should wait until daylight, like Mandy said. She could turn up."

"She could be dead!" Jude shouted. "She could have got up and gone somewhere and be dead, and it'll be my fault because I slept through it and didn't care enough to . . ." He trailed off, his shoulders slumping forward. "Guys, if anything has happened to her . . . I'd . . ."

Mayfridh knew she could fix it all. In an instant, in a sentence, she could end his pain.

"I'm sure nothing has happened to her," Gerda said.

"Are you really *sure*?" Jude asked. "Admit it, you're not sure. I'm calling the police. I'll go mad if I don't do something."

Mayfridh stood up, knocking the table and rattling the collection of empty coffee cups. They all turned to look at her.

"Jude," she said, "don't worry."

He stared at her as if he didn't even recognize her. It was so icily different from the warmth and excitement of the previous afternoon that a sob almost stopped up her throat. *He loves Christine, not me.*

"How can I not worry?" he shouted.

"Because . . ." she said, then licked her lips. Christine would be angry. But what could she do? It was within her power to make him feel better, and beyond her control to stop herself trying to please him. "Because I know where she is."

⌁

Christine checked her watch as she unlocked the front door of Hotel Mandy-Z. Five A.M. Good. She was getting the hang of it. Only two hours had passed and Jude would still be fast asleep. As she pushed the door gently with her shoulder, she assessed the twinge in her back. Could it be that it was actually easing? Or was it just that the few hours of relief had made it easier to bear? If that were the case, how was she to go back to living every minute in the Real World once Ewigkreis had moved on its way? She shook her head and refused to think about it, hung up her coat, and—

Noticed there was light spilling from Gerda's room onto the landing. And quiet voices, Jude's among them.

"Oh no, oh no," she said, hurrying up the stairs. What excuse was she going to make? An early morning walk to clear her head? A sudden craving for a foot-long at an all-night Imbiss? Moments later she stood at the threshold of Gerda's door. Fabiyan, Pete, Mayfridh, Gerda, and Jude were all there, drinking coffee and talking quietly. She knocked softly on the open door. Jude looked up, and a second later had his arms around her.

"You idiot," he said fondly, "I was so worried."

"I just went out for—"

"Christine, I told him." This was Mayfridh, standing next to her, touching her shoulder.

Christine shrugged herself out of Jude's embrace. "You told him what?"

"The truth. I told all of them."

Christine smiled, hoping that Mayfridh meant she had come up with a brilliant, plausible excuse for her absence. "Oh. The truth? And what . . . what is the truth?"

Mayfridh looked far too solemn, her hand a serious, cool pressure on Christine's arm. "The real truth, Christine. About who I am, and about where you've been."

Christine glanced around at the faces in the room.

Gerda scowled at her. "I should have thought you'd at least tell me I had faery royalty staying in my apartment."

Christine shook her head slowly. "Surely you didn't, Mayfridh?"

Jude had his arm around her again. "Come on, come to bed. This is too much excitement for me for one night."

"I'm sorry, Christine, but you would have done the same," Mayfridh said. "He was so worried, I couldn't stand . . . I wanted to let him know you were all right."

Once more Christine shrugged Jude off, tugging Mayfridh into the hallway with her. "Just give us a moment," she said to the others, closing the door behind them. She turned to Mayfridh, who gazed at her with guilty eyes. "*Believe* spells all round?"

"Yes. Though in the few minutes it took between when I told them and when I enchanted them . . ." Mayfridh trailed off and giggled in spite of herself. "Oh, you should have seen their faces."

"Mayfridh, you've made life so much more complicated for all of us."

Mayfridh snatched her hand away from Christine's. "That's not true. How can that be true? If anything, it makes things easier for you because you don't have to lie."

The door opened and Jude stood there, his eyes mistrustful. "Christine?"

Christine ran her hand through her hair. "I'll talk to you later, Mayfridh."

"Hey, Mayfridh." This was Pete, beckoning to her. "Come and tell us more stuff about faeries."

Mayfridh glanced from him to Christine and smiled sheepishly.

"Popular all of a sudden?" Christine said.

"The novelty's bound to wear off."

"Go on. I'm going to bed."

Mayfridh entered Gerda's apartment, leaving Jude and Christine on the landing together.

"Bed?" he said.

"Yes, please."

They lay for long silent moments awake, then finally Jude spoke. "I was still worried," he said, "even when I knew where you were."

"I was safe. I was with Eisengrimm." She frowned as she thought about the dungeons, but he couldn't see in the dark.

He hesitated before answering. "Christine . . . I want you to be happy, but I also want you to be safe. I also want you to be where I can look after you if you need me."

"I'm safe in Ewigkreis."

"You don't know that for sure. We don't even know if we can trust Mir . . . sorry, Mayfridh."

"She's really sweet, I've known her since I was a child." What would she do if he stopped her from going back? She had so little time.

"We know nothing about her, or her kind. Until two hours ago, Christine, I thought the only people who believed in faeries were children and madmen. There's a lot for me to digest here."

"But, Jude, it's so wonderful there. I feel no pain at all, I feel . . . like you feel every day."

He grew quiet, sighed deeply. "Christine, I can't stop you going, not if it brings you so much relief. But Mayfridh said that one day soon faeryland will move on. There's so much we don't understand about her and her world. It frightens me. What if you're stuck there? What if I lose you?"

She didn't answer, though she lay awake for a long time. Jude, she suspected, wasn't sleeping either. Was he right? The way that time moved there, out of sync and unexpected . . . could she guarantee she wouldn't be trapped in Ewigkreis, away from Jude forever? And was it hazardous to get used to the feeling of being pain-free, when it wasn't real? For thirteen years she had assiduously taken every precaution to avoid addiction to her painkillers, and here she was, after only three doses, addicted to Ewigkreis.

"I'll try," she said in the dark, not even sure if Jude could hear her, "I'll do my best to go without it."

☙

Mayfridh thought she was being so careful. That tiny gap between the bottom of the stairs and the foyer, the only place where Mandy could spy her, had been crossed with speed and success. But just as she was pulling open the door to the gray and yellow autumn day outside, he was standing there in front of her, key in hand.

"Good morning, Miranda," he said, baring a row of small round teeth. "I've been to fetch a paper. There is a review of our gallery party."

"I've got a train to catch," she mumbled, head down, trying to push past him.

"Would you like a lift somewhere? I can take you in my van." He didn't move so she had to brush against his belly.

"I'm going to Zehlendorf. It's a long way."

"It's not too far."

"I'd rather . . . I don't want to keep you from your work."

"Nonsense, the gallery doesn't open until one o'clock. Please, allow me to drive you to Zehlendorf."

A door opened above, and Pete called down. "Mandy, is that you? What does the paper say about my installation?"

Mayfridh slipped past Mandy and into the cool air outside. "Go on, Mandy, Pete needs you. I'm just as happy on the train."

"But . . ."

Pete was coming down the stairs, hands reaching for the paper. "Come on, Mandy, I'm dying here. Did they like it?"

Mayfridh hurried off, not looking back until she was at the end of the street. The door was closed, Mandy was gone. She realized she had been holding her breath, and let it go with a sigh. Alone with Mandy in a car? She'd sooner sit in the well with Hexebart.

Mayfridh tried not to look like a confused foreigner standing in front of the Berlin train map at Friedrichstrasse Station, but finally asked an English-speaking passerby to help her find Zehlendorf Station, and show her how to use the ticket machine. Within minutes, she was off, changed trains with confidence at Zoo, and settled down for the journey to her mother's house.

Strange how she had already accepted her father must be gone. Why else would her mother list only her own initials? D. K. Frith. Diana Kathryn. No "J. M." for James Matthew. Mayfridh realized she was jiggling her right leg so violently it was making the seat shake. She took deep breaths and told herself to be calm. Look how easy it had been to make all of Christine's friends believe.

Mayfridh watched as people got on and off the train, her mind so occupied with hopeful anxiety that she could barely distinguish between them—so distracted she nearly missed the stop. With apprehension, she stepped off the train.

She could still find her way from the station to her old home. Everything had changed, but she had walked this street so many times with her parents, down to the bakery and the markets, past the church, around this corner and . . .

There it was.

The house was shut up tight; not like she had remembered it, with windows open and curtains fluttering in the breeze. Except at night, of course, when her bedroom window had to be checked and checked and checked a third time before her mother went to bed. The garden had once been open and bursting with hedges and flowers. Now the hedges were overgrown, guarding the door, creating shadow where there once was sunshine, thorns wreathing the gate, and grass growing over the cobbles.

"Mother," she said quietly, feeling her heart beating in every nerve. A swell of sadness. She crossed the road, opened the gate, walked up the path, lifted her hand.

Knocked on the door.

Moments passed. She waited.

Finally, the door opened a crack. A thin, gray face peered out.

"Hello? Diana?" Mayfridh said warily. This was her mother? This pinch-lipped, sad-eyed creature?

The door swung inward. Diana Frith stepped back and stared at her.

Mayfridh held out her hand and tried a smile. "Hello, this is probably unexpected but—"

Suddenly, her mother's eyes rolled back in her head and she slid to the floor in a faint.

Mayfridh hastily made her way inside, knelt over the woman, and touched her face with frantic fingers. "What happened? Are you all right?"

Diana's eyes fluttered open. Her hand stole out to grasp Mayfridh's, her fingers cold in her daughter's warm palm. "Little May," she said, "I knew you'd come back."

CHAPTER TWELVE

Diana served tea in the lounge room. Mayfridh assessed the threadbare sofa she sat on, and the chairs and the dining table, and recognized them all, faded and worn though they were, from her childhood.

"Would you like sugar and milk?" Diana asked.

"I don't know. I've never drunk tea before."

Diana smiled and fiddled with the tea tray a moment longer, before handing her a cup. "Try this. It's how I have it. Perhaps you'll like it the same, as we're family."

Mayfridh sipped the tea. Too sweet. "It's perfect," she said, wary of her mother's fluttering anxiety. No need for a *believe* spell. Diana already believed it all.

Diana sat opposite her and pulled her teacup and saucer into her lap.

"Do you . . . live here alone?" Mayfridh asked.

Her mother frowned. "I expect you're wondering what's happened to your father."

"Yes."

"He's not dead. But he's not here."

"Where is he?"

Diana shook her head. "It's such a long time since you disappeared. How old are you now? Twenty-five?"

"Thirty-one. I've been gone nearly twenty-five years."

"Thirty-one. A grown woman!"

Where Mayfridh came from, she was considered barely out of adolescence. "I suppose I am."

"But now you're back. I knew you'd be back, just as soon as you could be." Diana smiled, revealing stained teeth. The years had been unkind to her. The skin on her face was as dull and lined as old paper, her eyes gray and hooded. Her smile disturbed Mayfridh. Eisengrimm's words were wiser by the moment. *Your mother and father have suffered enough. Do not make them lose you twice.*

"How did you know I'd be back?" Mayfridh asked gently.

"Because I prayed for it every day, and because God is kind to those who are patient."

"How did you know I'd been taken by faeries?"

"Because I knew the faery who took you. Queen Liesebet."

"You knew my mother?" As soon as the question was loose, Mayfridh wanted to recall it. Diana's face crumpled.

"Yes. I expect you think of her as your mother now."

"She's dead. Both my . . . faery parents are dead."

"Is that why you came to find me?"

"I came to find you because I missed you," Mayfridh replied, and it was the truth.

Diana's face glowed with pleasure. "As I missed you, dear child. As I missed you."

"Where is my father?"

"Back in England. Married to a vet named Ruth. They have two teenagers, boys."

"He left you here?"

"I chose to stay."

Mayfridh shook her head, setting her teacup on the table. "Mum, you'll have to explain it all."

"About your father leaving?" she asked, with a furrow of her weary brow.

"About me leaving. About Liesebet."

Diana dipped her head sadly. "Yes, yes, I should explain. I was careless, May. I didn't mean to lose you."

"Of course not." Then, when her mother remained silent, Mayfridh prompted her softly: "Go on."

Diana took a deep breath, leaned forward. "Do you know the reason your father and I brought you to Berlin?"

Mayfridh shook her head.

"Of course you don't. You were too little. James was very ill, May. He was being eaten alive by stomach cancer. The doctors back in Maidstone had given up on him, told him to expect six months at the most."

Mayfridh was aghast. "How could I not have known this?"

"We kept it from you. We protected you. We still hoped that he would live, and . . . we couldn't tell you. What words would I have used? How much of your beautiful spark would I have extinguished by telling you? May, we tried for years to have you. And we tried for years after to have a brother or sister for you. But we were only blessed once. You were so precious, your smile kept your father's spirits up. We couldn't have told you, it would have ruined you."

"So you came to Berlin for Dad's health?"

"Yes. A doctor here was famed for his experimental cancer treatments and his promising success rate. James left the army, and we sold everything to move. At first, it was worth every penny, every trouble. You settled in quickly and found a friend next door, and James responded well to the treatment. For nearly six months, my heart lifted every day. Soon after, it began to sink again.

"A routine test revealed the cancer had spread to his pancreas. The situation was dire." Diana shook her head. "I believed it might be all over. You may remember this, May. You walked into our bedroom one Saturday morning, early. Your father was in pain and slept poorly, so we were often awake before the sun had risen. We were lying in each other's arms, crying, and you came in and you took one look at us and started crying too."

Mayfridh nodded slowly. "Yes, I remember that."

"You were so distressed and you wouldn't stop asking us what was wrong and if everything was all right. So James took you for a drive to—"

"The pet shop! That was the day we bought Mabel."

"Yes, James bought you a puppy, hoping to take your mind off us. It appeared to work. You soon forgot seeing us crying, and your father was so cheered by your delight with Mabel that his pain eased for a week or so.

"But I had so little hope left in me by this time. I had prayed and prayed, and my prayers had been ignored and time was running out. I was desperate; I was clinging to a thread, trying to be a good mother to you, a good wife to James. I was drowning."

Diana fell silent, and Mayfridh watched her for long moments; her deeply lined face, her dull gray hair, her cheerless eyes. Mayfridh said nothing, waiting. A clock ticked in the kitchen, a flat thin pulse in the dusty room.

"One Wednesday afternoon," Diana said slowly, raising her head again, "you were next door at the Starlights' house, and I was vacuuming the carpet. I came downstairs to find your father motionless on the sofa. I thought the terrible moment was upon me, that he was dead. But no, there was the slow movement of his chest, and I found myself staring at him, imagining his breath stilled forever. The awful reality of his approaching mortality fell on me like a weight. The horror was so acute that I nearly screamed. I struggled to be free of it, but I was mercilessly trapped inside my mind and inside my body. James would die. Inescapable.

"I had to do something. I couldn't just stand there looking at him, losing my mind. I dropped the vacuum cleaner and I strode out of the room and to the door and out of the house and to the front gate where Mabel danced about my feet, thinking I was taking her to the park. I left her behind the gate, whimpering and yapping indignantly. I was a soul trapped in the electric moment of horror, and I walked away from the house and the street. A short time later, I found myself in the big park near your old kindergarten. I don't know if you remember it?"

"Yes, I do."

"It was empty. The sun was close to setting, and people were in their homes, cooking their meals, watching their favorite television programs. Not another soul in sight. I sat on the grass and then collapsed forward, and I sobbed and sobbed and sobbed.

"I truly believe I would have kept crying, perhaps until my lungs burst, if it hadn't been for the sound of a soft breath nearby. I gathered myself and looked up. Standing before me was a beautiful blond woman in a white sparkling robe, and her hair braided with white ribbon."

"Liesebet," Mayfridh said, fondly remembering her faery mother. "She'd come from the Winter Castle."

"She came from nowhere. I hadn't heard her approach. And the otherworldly smile on her face . . . May, I thought she was an angel. I thought God had sent me an angel."

"What did she say?"

"She said, in hesitant German, 'Tell me your woes, and it may be in my power to ease them.'" Diana smiled. "I'd hardly expected one of God's angels to speak German. I always assumed they were British."

Mayfridh laughed. Outside, the clouds had parted and a weak ray of sunshine probed the window, lighting on a stained-glass bird hanging from the sill.

Diana sighed and steepled her hands together. "I told her everything. While I spoke, she watched me with a very fixed and piercing gaze."

"I know that gaze," Mayfridh said. Liesebet had possessed a special talent for mind-reading. In the moment Diana was describing, the faery queen had been pulling thoughts from her mind.

"When I had finished, she said, 'I will grant you your husband's returned health, but in payment, you must promise to give me the first thing that greets you when you return home.' I considered this for a few moments. You were with the Starlights intending to stay the night, James was asleep on the sofa, and Mabel was waiting at the gate. Did I dare to promise her this payment?

"'I grow weary of waiting for your answer,' she said. 'Do you agree to the terms of payment?'

"I nodded. I said, 'Yes,' and she smiled and told me that my husband would be well very soon, but that I must return to her at the same time the next day to pay her. I agreed, and I ran home. I ran through the park and down the main road and up our street and . . . and I saw movement near the gate of the Starlights' house and began to panic. I knew I needed to get home while Mabel was still waiting, before I saw you or James or the Starlights' little girl, Christine, or anyone but the dog. Then I saw you . . . you were coming home to fetch your favorite teddy. I saw the back of your head. You hadn't seen me yet, and I began to sprint, to get to the gate and the puppy before you turned around.

"Just as I reached the edge of our garden, you turned. You saw me. You smiled and put your arms out and you ran toward me and grabbed me around the hips and said, 'Hello,

Mummy, where have you been?'" Diana's eyes had filled with tears. One of them spilled over and ran down her dry cheek, pausing on the tip of her chin. "Dear child, you weren't to know."

Mayfridh listened, entranced.

"I bundled you inside, and I promised myself that I wouldn't give you up, that I would find a way to keep you. I even started to think that perhaps the woman in the park was ordinary and mad and the agreement with her meant nothing. But before that evening was over, color returned to James's cheek and his appetite grew, and he declared he was feeling very well, and I knew that the angel was real and that James would recover.

"I didn't sleep that night, though James slept soundly next to me. I decided that I would take Mabel to the park the next afternoon. The puppy was all I intended to give away, and that would be the end of it. The woman in white hadn't seen me. She couldn't know that you were the first thing that greeted me." She paused, her lip caught between her teeth. "Foolish, I suppose."

"Liesebet knew," Mayfridh said softly.

"Oh yes, she knew. Yes, I understand that now. I returned to the park with the puppy, and sat in the same spot and waited for her. She arrived moments later, this time with a crow perched on her forearm as though it were a pet, a splash of black against her dazzling white dress. She wore such a look of triumph and disdain that I started to suspect she wasn't an angel at all, but something vastly different.

" 'Here, take the dog,' I said, not giving her a chance to speak.

" 'Is this the first thing that greeted you on your return home yesterday?'

" 'Yes,' I said, avoiding her gaze.

"Then the most incredible thing. The crow parted its beak

and spoke. 'She lies, Liesebet. The first thing that greeted her on her return was her daughter. I saw her.'

" 'Is this true?' Liesebet said, fixing me with her cold eyes.

" 'Take the puppy,' I said, holding out Mabel who wriggled and whimpered. 'I won't give you my daughter.'

" 'We made an agreement,' Liesebet said.

" 'I no longer wish to be part of the agreement.'

" 'I have cured your husband.'

"I took a deep breath. I had been afraid it would come to this. 'Then take back the cure. My daughter is more precious to me than my husband.'

"Liesebet pointed a finger at me and stood very still for several moments. I didn't breathe the whole time. Then she said, 'The cure will not be taken back. You will fulfill your part of the bargain.'

" 'I won't give up my daughter.' My heart raced and my hands shook, and Mabel wriggled her way free and dashed across the park.

" 'Why not?'

" 'Because she's my daughter.'

" 'No,' she said, very coolly. 'She is my daughter. Eisengrimm, do you agree?'

" 'The girl is clearly your daughter, Liesebet. Our kingdom is very blessed.'

" 'You hear that? *My* little girl, who will be heir to my throne. Bring her to me tomorrow, here at the same time. Good-bye.' She turned and strode off, the crow flapping behind her. I watched them go, and I vowed I would never give you up.' "

Here, Diana stopped speaking for long minutes. Outside, the sun disappeared behind a cloud. Mayfridh placed her empty teacup on the table and curled her legs underneath her. Her mother's face was a sad record of years spent alone, never expressing this story. Yet it was also the beloved face of her mother remembered from childhood, cherished unconditionally. She felt her heart swerve. To forget Diana again was to render this story once again unheard, to reiterate every line of sorrow that etched her mother's face. When time spun out and still Diana didn't speak, Mayfridh prompted her: "How did they get me?"

Diana shook her head, as if shaking herself out of a daze. She smiled, a sad eager smile. "You're back," she said. "That's all that matters."

"No, tell me."

Diana's thin, cotton-clad chest rose in a sigh. "I didn't go near that park again. For weeks, I heard nothing from Liesebet. James recovered. It all seemed like a bad dream, something my mind created at its lowest ebb. I became obsessive about you, of course. I wouldn't let you out of my sight; I locked your window every night. I even wanted to lock your bedroom door but James put a stop to it. If I tried to tell him about Liesebet, he would shake his head and say the shock of his illness had addled me, and that I would be feeling well enough soon. I urged him to return to England, but he insisted that it was the experimental treatment he was receiving—rather than magic—that was making him better. He wouldn't leave, he was too afraid of growing ill again.

"I tried to behave normally. I tried to believe James when he said I was suffering a nervous problem, that I was afraid of an hallucination. Until the morning I saw that . . . thing."

"The crow? Eisengrimm?" Mayfridh was tempted to defend Eisengrimm, to blurt out that he was her closest friend in Ewigkreis, but perhaps that could wait for later.

"Yes, the crow. I was in the front garden. You were with the Starlight girl next door. I could hear you laughing at the top of your lungs, and I was thinking about what a beautiful sound it was. I swept the previous night's light snowfall from the path, singing a song in my head. A shadow passed over me, and I looked up to see a crow sitting on a low branch. My heart jumped. I watched it for a few wary moments, hoping it was just an ordinary crow . . . but then he spoke.

"'Diana Frith, you owe Queen Liesebet something.'

"'I owe her nothing.'

"'If you pay her what you owe her, she will give you this pouch.' He reached his beak under his wing, and with a flash there appeared a red velvet pouch, strung on silver thread. He hung it from his claw in front of me.

"'I don't want anything from her.'

"'In this pouch is medicine. The smallest grain will cure any illness instantly. When you hand over your daughter to Queen Liesebet, this pouch will be yours.'

"'I don't want it,' I said. I blocked my ears with my hands and ran inside, locking the door behind me. When I peered out the window, he was no longer in the tree. I breathed a sigh of relief, but an instant later he was at the windowsill, and he called out, 'Be sure that I will come again.'

"I stopped going outside. I stopped letting you play at Christine's. Remember? I made her come here instead. Alfa Starlight began to think I didn't like her. I tried hard to keep myself together. I couldn't speak to James about it, I couldn't speak to you about it. I had to keep it all inside and protect you from the crow.

"Early one morning, while you were upstairs napping and James had left to go to the doctor, I was sweeping the front room when I heard a tapping at the door. I presumed it was Christine, she was always in and out of our house. I opened the door and a mad flapping of black wings sent me stumbling back into the room. The crow perched on the hanging light. Pale sunlight and a bitter winter breeze stole into the house, and the curtains swayed gently.

" 'Get out!' I hissed. I didn't want to attract your attention and have you run downstairs to see who I was talking to.

" 'Diana Frith, you owe Queen Liesebet something.'

" 'No, I don't. Leave me alone.'

" 'If you pay her what you owe her, she will give you this pouch.' Just like the last time, he reached his beak under his wing, and this time pulled out a blue velvet pouch. 'In this pouch is gold dust. The smallest grain will transform instantly into any amount of money you name. When you hand over your daughter to Queen Liesebet, this pouch will be yours.'

" 'I don't want it, I don't want it. Now get out. May's my daughter.' I brandished my broom and shooed him outside, but as he flew away he called, 'Be sure that I will come again.'

"Moment by moment, I felt a strange relief. He had come twice, enticing me with treasures, and he had been unsuccessful. Unsuccessful." Diana held her index finger up, a strange smile of wry cynicism on her lips. "I thought, May, that I had won. For certainly, if it were in her power to steal you from me, she would have done it by now. That's what I thought.

"Weeks passed. I grew more and more confident. Then, late one night, I was awoken by the sound of Mabel barking in the back garden. Yap, yap. Something had disturbed her. I knew instantly it was that crow. And I knew too that I wanted to go down there and tell him I wasn't afraid of him and his stupid queen. James was beginning to stir, so I said, 'I'll go down and quiet her.' I slipped out of bed, and into my dressing gown and slippers. I crept downstairs, and through the house, and out the back door. Mabel ran to me and cowered behind my legs. I scanned the cold garden in the dark, looking for the crow, but couldn't see him. Then his voice came from above me.

" 'Diana Frith, you owe Queen Liesebet something.'

"I looked up. He was perched on the gable, another pouch hanging from his claw, his eyes gleaming in the dark. 'I owe her nothing,' I said boldly, 'and you know that.'

" 'Queen Liesebet wants the child.'

"I scooped up Mabel. 'Let her have the dog. That's all I ever intended to give her anyway.'

" 'My queen has no shortage of dogs. It's a child she wants. She is barren.'

" 'No! I'm not giving you my daughter, and I don't care what you've got in your magic pouch this time. You can't take her, and you can't convince me to give her up. So just go.' I released Mabel and scooped up a handful of pebbles to throw at him.

"He flapped his wings and rose up, dropping the pouch, and took to the sky. I quickly seized the pouch and peered inside. It was full of nothing but crumbs. With a swoop and a flutter, he dived past me and snatched the pouch with his claws. 'Be sure,' he called as his shadow passed the moon, 'that I will come again.' "

Diana closed her eyes. The vertical furrows that surrounded her lips deepened. "And, oh," she said, "he came again. And he took you."

"How soon after?"

"Three weeks. Long enough for me to think I had won. Long enough for me to think that you would stay with me forever. But you didn't . . ." Her voice trailed off to a whisper.

Mayfridh leaned forward to take her mother's hand. "Mum. I'm here now."

"But for how long?" Diana's head snapped up, her gaze locked on Mayfridh's. "I've been watching you since you arrived. You're nervous, you're wary. You don't intend to stay, do you?"

"I . . . don't have long. I'll have to go back to my own world."

Diana shook her head and said softly, "*This* is your world."

"Not anymore. I've become . . . something different. Tell me about Dad."

Diana dropped her gaze to her hands in her lap, her fingers obsessively smoothing her faded skirt over her thighs. "He left me, May. After you had disappeared, when I kept insisting you had been taken by faeries, it all became too much for him. His illness was declared cured and he wanted to return to England. But I didn't want to go, because I thought you might still come back." She smiled a pained smile. "So he went without me, but I was right to wait, wasn't I? If you had come looking today and I hadn't been here . . ."

"I'm glad you were here."

"Was it awful, May? Was it awful for you being in another world, so far from me?"

Mayfridh chose her answer carefully. She and her mother had so little time together, there was no point in trying to explain to Diana how quickly she had been forgotten. "Liesebet and Jasper treated me very well. They loved me, and I grew to love them."

"How long have they been dead?"

"A very long time now. Many years," Mayfridh said solemnly.

"Then why didn't you come back earlier?"

"I didn't . . . it's not always possible to make a passage between your world and mine." Mayfridh didn't want to reveal that Diana had been forgotten.

"You're determined to go back, then?"

"I have no choice. I'm the queen."

Diana's expression was unreadable; somewhere between heart-wrenching disappointment and beaming motherly pride. "Of course," she said, "you're the queen."

"But I'll stay as long as I can," Mayfridh said quickly. "I'll stay until the last possible moment."

CHAPTER THIRTEEN

from the Memoirs of Mandy Z.

I have only once boiled a faery alive in my vat.

I had been living in Berlin for eight years, enjoying every moment that I drew breath. I set up the gallery and then the Zweigler Fellowship fund, and found that more and more of my sculptures were selling to galleries and private owners all over the world.

Beyond my wonderful public life, I had a delicious secret life that saw me drive off in my van two or three times a year to scour the forests of Germany and the newly opened countries of eastern Europe for faeries to kill. I often came back empty-handed, but I didn't mind so much. The disappointments served to intensify my enjoyment of those rare and special kills. I would kill them quickly, bundle them into the van, then bring their fresh bodies back here to my apartment, back to the vat for boning.

The vat is well hidden—upstairs through the sculpture room, beyond a small door and up another flight of dark narrow stairs—in a room I had purpose-built in the attic. The gabled windows are painted black, but two bright hospital-strength fluorescent lights are installed in the ceiling so I can always be certain of what I'm doing. The vat takes up half of the room. If I were to walk around it, I'd need eleven big paces to arrive back where I started. The vat itself is at hip height, constructed of thick black metal. The liquid inside— a cocktail of ghastly chemicals, which I've refined over the years to be perfectly suited to stripping faery bones—takes an hour to reach its optimum boiling temperature. When the motor that heats the elements starts up it can be frighteningly loud, so the room is soundproofed floor to ceiling.

Above it all, on the ceiling, there are two metal struts with aluminum cable running through them, attached to an iron cage. I took my time in designing the cage. It's large enough to fit a body bent or cut in two, and inside it is spiked with iron hooks to catch the smaller bones so they don't escape and fall through the holes. I load the body at the side of the vat. There are two large rubber buttons there. When I press the top button, the hydraulic mechanism pulls the cage into position above the vat; when I press the bottom one, the cage is dropped directly into the boiling acid. Because the room is soundproof, because it takes so long for the vat to reach boiling temperature, and because there is a danger of overboiling (if the vat overflowed into the shell and heating elements I could very well be electrocuted in my own home), I have two lights positioned above the door to the boning room. The top one flashes when the boiling temperature is reached, the bottom one if the temperature becomes critically high. (The fool who installed the lights and buttons for me made one of red and one of green so I could distinguish them. Me! I can't tell red from green any more than I can tell yellow from purple.) Four or five hours after immersion, I have a cage full of faery bones, stripped of their flesh and robbed of their scent. When they cool, they are ready to begin working on.

The faery who deserved boiling alive was a rare local

find. I was out at Kreuzburg, enjoying a meal in a tavern, when he walked in alone and bought a beer. I was sitting so far at the back of the tavern that at first I didn't know what he was. I noticed him only because he was very beautiful, even for a faery. I kept glancing at him, wondering if he were a movie star or a model. It was only as I paid for my meal and collected my coat that I smelled him—that horrible, wonderful smell. He noticed me staring at him, and gave me an inviting smile.

"Good evening," he said, his accent thick and French. "I'm Octave."

I was astonished that he was so forward. I know I do not possess a friendly countenance, and I was almost certain that my stare had not been amiable or pleasant. Then, a half-second later, I realized he had mistaken my gaze for sexual desire. And he was encouraging that desire.

How easy, then, it was to get him back to the hotel. He was a faery on an erotic mission, not afraid of breeding with humans (the results can be disastrous) because his sexual proclivities were toward the male of the species. Filthy, disgusting creature. When I brought him to my apartment, he fawned and preened like a teenage girl in love, and I endured his first caresses and his gooey-eyed gazes without shuddering, only by reminding myself in every moment that earning his trust would mean he would soon be material for my sculpture. Within minutes I had him blindfolded, with promises of erotic play, and I led him through the door and up the stairs to the vat, which I set to boiling with a clunk of the lever. I had a number of tools at my disposal to bludgeon him to death first, but I was so inflamed with rage by his sexual advances that I wanted to punish him.

I pushed him into the cage and now he started to panic and flail about, but the door on the cage was snapped shut, and then he began to scream. I wasn't afraid of his screams;

the room is perfectly soundproof. I left the cage suspended over the vat and went downstairs to bed to doze for a while until it reached boiling temperature. He was still screaming when I returned an hour later. I almost changed my mind and recalled the cage to silence him, but I was curious as to what it might feel like and sound like to boil a faery alive. Instead of hitting the top button, I hit the bottom one and the cage descended into the vat.

The screams intensified and were almost too much for me to bear, but then they stopped abruptly and I found myself strangely disappointed. My ears rang. The vat bubbled and boiled. I switched off the light and went to bed.

When I finally harvested the cool bones a day later, I was still plagued by the ringing in my ears. What I first assumed to be an effect of listening to Octave's deafening screams I now deduced must be an ear infection, and I phoned my doctor for an appointment the following day.

I cut and shaved and glued the bones into a block, which I then glued to the Bone Wife. This block was the original waist for my Wife, sculpted in a white heat while my ears rang and I congratulated myself on such an unexpected and successful kill.

It was only the next day when I returned home from the doctor—he gave me antibiotics at my insistence but was unconvinced there was anything wrong with my ears—that the trouble started. I was in my apartment, making phone calls and ordering supplies for the studios, when I heard the sound of someone crying far away. I barely registered the sound at first; I thought it was a child on the street, crying for something lost. The crying intensified into long gasps of anguish and finally shrieks. It jangled my nerves so I went to the window to look down on the street and call out to the child to stop.

There was no child on the street, but with my head out the

window, I could hear far more clearly where the shrieking was coming from. Directly above me, from the open window of my sculpture room.

I ran upstairs and pulled down both layers of glazing, looking around wildly for the cause of the shrieking. It was coming from Octave's bones, half-lumpen, half-sculpted, at the top of the sculpture.

I stood in front of the Bone Wife, my hands unable to find a solution. The screaming grew louder. It broke my heart, but I knew I couldn't keep these bones. A grand sculpture is not much use if it screams like a hurt child. I reached for the saw and began to saw away at the join, knocking off the portion of the sculpture made of Octave's bones and bagging it quickly to muffle the shrieking.

But worse was to come. Magic spreads between bones. I knew this and counted on it to enchant the whole sculpture. Almost as soon as I returned to the sculpture, other bones started ringing, gathering volume.

I took the saw and cut off another layer.

The screams collected themselves lower down.

I sawed again, despairing now. Was my whole sculpture infected? I sawed lower down, right through her thighs, hoping by this sacrifice of painful inches to save the whole sculpture.

And I did save her, but not before she had been reduced almost to her knees. I lost years of work. Damn Octave, damn him. I could weep just remembering it. My Wife is built to the waist once more now, but if it were not for Octave I may very well have been planning a graceful throat for her, and growing excited over what kind of face I might give her (it's my plan to give her my mother's face, but with the hard lines removed).

The bones kept screaming, and had to be driven miles away to a wood near the border of Poland for burial. For all

I know, they're still screaming in the rough sack two feet below the ground. Maybe someday someone will find them and be completely puzzled by it all. Or perhaps Octave has had his revenge and is now happy to rest in a peace he doesn't deserve.

I am very tired. Reminiscing isn't helping to take my mind off the problem at hand. It has been a very long two weeks. Miranda is still here and I cannot get my hands on her, and I cannot get her out of my mind, and it's torturing me. I see her darting past the gallery—like the others, she thinks I haven't noticed, that I haven't seen the flash of movement out of the corner of my eye—but I can't touch her because she's with Christine or with Gerda or with a gray-faced woman I don't recognize.

What a life she's leading! A faery, Germanic if the pronunciation of her (very weak) German is anything to go by, let loose on Berlin with some magically bottomless credit account to buy herself an endless procession of lace and brocade and velvet outfits, some in colors so bright I can almost see them. She sometimes takes plain little Christine Starlight with her, and brings the poor girl back dressed in a coat or a pair of boots that seem oversized and showy and make me feel embarrassed for her. Sometimes I hear her and Gerda giggling through the front door, returning from a beery lunch and no doubt making plans not to be heard or seen by horrible *me*. I even imagine sometimes that everyone else in Hotel Mandy-Z knows what she is, and that they believe it secret from me.

Most distressing of all, I think she may be a more important faery than I originally believed. Last Friday, when she and Gerda were out, I went into Gerda's apartment (I have keys to every apartment) and searched for some of her things to examine. The clothes were mostly new, but I found in the bottom of a drawer a dress woven through with fine bronze thread. Such craftsmanship speaks of faery nobility, maybe even royalty. She certainly isn't a common village faery. I pressed the dress to my face and sniffed it, drawing the faintest smell of her bones from between the threads. It was barely there. I bit a hole in the material in frustration, and almost decided to come back here at night while Gerda slept, and bludgeon Miranda and drag her up the stairs and cut her to pieces and pull out her bones and forget all consequences.

But I will not forget consequences. Miranda is known to too many people. I cannot spend my great fortune in prison. I cannot sculpt in prison.

Patience, now. I must have patience and wait for my chance. It will come. It *must* come.

❦

As the leaves fell down along Unter-den-Linden and Christmas decorations went up in stores, as the sky grew paler and the city grew grayer, Christine became increasingly fond of Mayfridh. It wasn't just her artless warmth, her childish affection, or her bottomless credit card that made her good company. It was also her rapidly returning memories of their shared childhood. Halfway through a sentence, Mayfridh would often interrupt herself and say, "Ooh, remember when Alfa cooked those scones with salt instead of sugar?" or "Didn't Finn have a coat exactly that color?" Christine hadn't realized how many memories of her parents she had buried with them; now Mayfridh was warming her cold afternoons with sunny recollections.

Christine still felt insecurities over Jude, but he gave her no reason for them to grow: if anything, he was offhand with Mayfridh, or ignored her. If Christine mentioned her, Jude would raise his hands defensively, claim he couldn't get his head around the fact that she was a faery; it was easier not to think of it. Christine reminded herself that he had painted Mayfridh out; been attracted to her colors, then obliterated them for the monochrome he was more comfortable with. No couple went through life together, she supposed, without jealousies. Christine refused to let hers interfere with the sweet moments she and Mayfridh shared.

"What now?" Mayfridh said as they stepped out of the heated department store on Kurfürstendamm and into the autumn chill. "Do you want more clothes?"

"Um . . . no. I'm fine for clothes." Christine had already accepted too many presents from Mayfridh that she knew she would never wear. "Sorry, I know I'm not as much fun to shop with as Gerda."

"That's not true. Gerda gets bossy," Mayfridh said. "As for my mum . . . you've never seen someone take so long to make up her mind about a pair of shoes."

"Let's get coffee. I know a good cafe near where I work. I can stop in and check my roster."

They walked through the bustling crowds, past shiny shop fronts and shedding trees, down side streets to an Italian cafe. Its outdoor tables drowned in yellow and red maple leaves. Christine ordered while Mayfridh considered her from across the table.

"What?" Christine asked as the waiter returned inside. "Too cold for you out here?"

"No, I like the fresh air."

"Why the frown?"

"I saw you wince as we sat down. Your back's hurting."

"It's always hurting."

"It's hurting more than usual today. I'm tiring you out."

Christine smiled. "It's not you. It's just a bad-back day. I get them from time to time."

"So why don't you go to Ewigkreis?"

Christine hung her head, watching her hair trail over her shoulders. "I don't know . . ."

"You haven't been for ages. Not since the night I told Jude and the others. Is something wrong? Did Eisengrimm offend you in some way?"

"No, no. I like Eisengrimm, he makes me feel . . . safe."

Mayfridh pushed a crimson curl behind her ear. "Then what is it?"

Christine bit her lip. "I kind of got afraid."

"Afraid?"

"You say that when the last leaf falls the worlds change."

"Yes."

"What if I'm stuck there?"

Mayfridh reached across the table for her hand. "Christine, the last leaf won't fall until December . . . almost Christmas."

"But you know time in your world and mine is different. What if I misjudge?" Christine pointed at Mayfridh. "What if *you* misjudge? Will you be stuck here?"

"No, I'll be pulled back through the passage."

"But if I was in Ewigkreis and the worlds changed?"

"You'd be stuck, yes. The passage only anchors and retrieves faeries."

Their coffees arrived and both fell silent until the waiter left.

"See? I'd be stuck."

"But that's not going to happen for ages. It's barely November."

Christine stirred sugar into her coffee. "I don't know . . ."

"Is there something else?"

"Jude doesn't want me to go."

Mayfridh lifted her eyebrows. "Jude? But surely he wants what's best for you?"

"He's worried I'll never come back. He doesn't know what it's like and . . . hey, can I take him with me?"

Mayfridh was shaking her head before the question was out of Christine's mouth. "Eisengrimm would have a fit if I brought another human through."

"But you're the queen."

"I'm a queen who takes good counsel. Having more than one human at a time in Ewigkreis starts to upset the rhythms of our world, the balance of the seasons." Mayfridh smiled brightly. "He could come through alone. Eisengrimm could show him around. Or I could go back for a day or two." The smile turned to a frown. "Lord knows, Eisengrimm's probably wondering where I am."

"Jude would say no," Christine said. "I think the whole concept frightens him."

A chill breeze swept down the street, driving a flurry of spinning leaves in front of it. Christine pulled her scarf tighter.

"Christine," Mayfridh said, "how well do you know Jude?"

"I've known him for four years. We've lived together for three. Why?" What a weird question, and something about the guarded way Mayfridh asked it unsettled her.

"I'm not implying anything," Mayfridh said, blue eyes wide-open innocent. "You don't have to snap."

"Did I snap?"

"You did."

"Sorry. It's just a strange thing to ask me."

"Anyway, after four years I suppose you would know everything about someone, wouldn't you?" Mayfridh finished.

"Maybe, maybe not." Christine drained the last of her coffee. "Do you think you know everything about Eisengrimm?"

"Yes, of course. He's my closest friend in Ewigkreis."

Christine felt a strange shift in her stomach. Mayfridh didn't know Eisengrimm's secret; Christine could be equally oblivious to some mystery of Jude's heart. Was that why she always felt he didn't really love her? Or were those feelings just the clumsy imaginings of a girl who knew her lover was far more beautiful than she?

❧

"Christine!"

Jude's voice reverberated around the apartment, the door slammed behind him. Christine emerged from the bedroom, sheets in hand ready to take to the laundry.

"What's up?" she asked.

He brandished a sheaf of papers in front of her. His cheeks were flushed. "How would you like to go to Australia?"

"Um . . ."

"Come here, look." He laid the papers on the table and beckoned her over.

She rolled the sheets into a ball under her arm and approached warily.

"Pete gave it to me. It's a fellowship with the National Gallery in Melbourne. They want an overseas artist to come spend a year there, from June next year. I'm perfect for this one, I know it. And it starts right after this fellowship finishes. I tell you, it's meant to be."

"Australia?"

"Yeah, Melbourne. It's where Pete lives. Better than Berlin. We'll know the language and have someone to show us round."

"At least Berlin's in the same hemisphere as home. Don't you want to go home?"

"We've got plenty of time to go home when we're old

and gray. Come on, Christine, what do you say? Can I apply?"

Christine stared at the application form as though it could provide her answer. Jude was a painter, he had a gift. It wasn't her place to hold him back, even if it did mean following him to the other end of the planet. "I suppose you should."

Jude grabbed her in a quick hug. "Yes! I knew you'd say yes." He turned his attention back to the forms. "This closing date is very soon. Christine, can you ring the post office and see how long their express air to Australia takes? My German's not good enough."

Christine dumped the sheets on the sofa and did as he asked. The answer wasn't encouraging.

"Basically," she said, returning to the table where Jude was already filling in blanks, "if you want it there by the due date we'll have to post it today. This afternoon."

"Today!"

"Can you fax it?"

"No, look . . ." He pointed to a bold-type line on top of the form. "Faxed applications not accepted."

"Maybe you can call them and—"

"No, I'll just get it done today." He was out of his chair now, rummaging in the drawer under the bookcase. "I think I've got photos somewhere."

"Photos?"

"My paintings. They have to see my paintings." Old letters, travel documents, and bank statements were dumped on the floor. "Damn! I can't find them. Only these." He flung out a handful of photos that looked perfectly fine to Christine.

"What's wrong with these?"

"The light's bad, the color's all wrong."

"Do you want me to—"

"Mandy," he said, suddenly whirling around. "Mandy will have my best photos from my application for this fellowship."

"You sent Mandy your best photos? He's color-blind."

"I didn't know that at the time." His eyes darted from the photos on the floor, to the application form at the table, and then to Christine. "Christine, would you mind going up and asking him for them? I've got to write this entire application in, like, two hours."

Christine cringed. She still hadn't forgotten Gerda's description of Mandy's unexpectedly naked body: *molded by preschoolers out of old dough and copper wire.* But Jude was looking at her with pleading eyes. "Yeah, okay," she said.

"Thanks. Thanks so much." He returned to the table, his head bent over the forms, his brow furrowed with concentration. Christine left the apartment and headed up the stairs. The lamp in the stairwell was out, and Mandy's door waited in dim gray light. She raised her fist and knocked sharply. *Please let him have clothes on.* She had never been to Mandy's apartment before. He had a monthly meeting for his artists—where they drank champagne and ate expensive hors d'oeuvres—to which she had never been invited. Artists Only. Very Important Artists' Business.

Mandy didn't answer the door. She knew his apartment was large, extending up into the attic. She rapped harder, thought about going back to Jude empty-handed, and decided she couldn't. She tried the door; it opened inward. She stepped inside and called out, "Hello? Mandy? Are you here?"

Mandy's apartment was lavishly furnished in such an array of mismatching colors that Christine almost laughed. He had no idea that he'd thrown an orange rug over a blue sofa on a green carpet. She imagined for a moment what this room must look like to him: black and white. How sad that somebody who loved art so much couldn't appreciate color. The heavy scent of sandalwood hung in the air. A set of stairs led up to the next floor. Perhaps that was where he was, so involved in sculpting something that he couldn't hear her.

"Mandy?" She took the stairs slowly, feeling guilty and apprehensive and strangely curious. But he must be home, or at least not far away, because he'd left the door open. "Mandy, are you around?" She found herself standing in his working studio. Half-finished sculptures leaned unevenly on each other around the walls. A large mahogany desk sat under the window. In the center of the room, one particular sculpture caught her eye. She approached, forgetting momentarily about Jude's photos as she admired the work.

It was the bottom half of a woman, so exquisitely carved Christine felt certain that if she touched it, it would feel like warm flesh. But, no, it was cool and smooth. What was it carved from? It was neither stone nor plaster. The substance gleamed like nothing she had ever seen before. For an instant, all her aversion toward Mandy disappeared. It was unbelievable that he could carve something so beautiful and delicate from a hard substance. Christine knew nothing about art, especially not Jude's abstracts, or Gerda's bewildering "installations," or Pete's videos, or even Fabiyan's distorted clay nudes. Mandy's work was different: sheer beauty, pure perfected craft. Christine found herself tracing the contours of the woman's knee with her fingers, before realizing that Mandy wasn't here.

"Mandy?" she called again. She looked around her. A narrow door faced her, painted with black glossy enamel. Two lights—one red, one green—hung above it. Three deadlocks lined its edge. She tried it anyway. Of course it was locked. Where did it go? To the attic? If so, why did it have three deadlocks on it? Was he keeping his billions in barrels up there? She ran her fingers over the edge of the door.

A creak from downstairs startled her. Mandy. And here she was snooping around his apartment. She dashed to the stairs and started down, only to find Jude standing in the doorway.

"I wondered where you'd got to," Jude said, holding up a handful of photos. "I found them."

"Mandy's not here."

"Then what are you doing up there?" Jude smiled his wicked smile.

"Poking around. Come on, we should get out of here."

They were halfway down the stairs to their own apartment when they ran into Mandy heading in the other direction.

"Hello, Jude, Christine. Were you looking for me?"

"We were, but we're okay now," Jude said.

Christine couldn't meet his eye. What had come over her, snooping like an eight-year-old? His eccentricity didn't preclude his right to privacy.

"I'm sorry that I wasn't home for you," Mandy replied with a nod of his head. "I was downstairs in the laundry." Then he continued up the stairs.

"See, you should have just let me wash the sheets. I would have found him anyway," Christine said as they let themselves into the apartment.

"Then you wouldn't have got a chance to see inside his place," Jude said, flinging the photos on the table. "I've never been up to his studio, what's it like?"

"Like a big room full of sculpture. He does nice work, doesn't he?"

"Not particularly adventurous," Jude said dismissively. "He's not an explorer, he follows well-worn paths."

"Oh . . . well, I like his stuff. Maybe I'm not an explorer either." Jude wasn't listening; he was arranging his photos and Christine found herself wondering again where that narrow black door in Mandy's apartment led.

≈

Mayfridh woke to an empty apartment. Gerda had left a note saying she had been struck by early morning inspiration and was going to exorcise it in the studio. This, despite her having promised to go shopping for new boots today. How unfair! Still, Mayfridh wasn't queen in this world and had to get used to people occasionally letting her down. Even though Christine wasn't as much fun to shop with, at least she was good to talk to on the bus. Maybe they could go out to Zehlendorf together and visit Diana. She dressed in her favorite blue lace blouse and black velvet skirt, put on her makeup—she was an expert at applying it now, and had determined to take a lifetime's supply of liquid eyeliner back to Ewigkreis—and headed upstairs to Christine's apartment.

She knocked. Waited. Knocked again. Heard footsteps inside. Then the door opened, and a sleepy-eyed Jude stood there.

"Sorry, did I wake you?" she said, taking an embarrassed step backward.

"Um . . . yeah. But it's pretty late. I should get to work." He was wearing loose-fitting gray track pants and a pale blue shirt, unbuttoned. His feet were bare.

"Is Christine here?"

"She's at the bookshop."

"Oh. I must have my days mixed up. I thought she was off today."

"She was supposed to be. Somebody's sick." He ran a

hand through his blond hair. "Do you want to come in? I can make coffee."

Mayfridh knew she should say no, but found herself nodding anyway. No Gerda, no Christine. What else was she to do with her morning? "Yes, thank you."

He closed the door behind her, then scuffed into the kitchen, buttoning his shirt and yawning. She moved to the table where a handful of photos was strewn. Jude's paintings. She picked one up and studied it, astonished by its dark beauty.

"They're the bad photos."

Mayfridh turned around. Jude was very close, his dark eyes flicking from her face to the photo. "Sorry?" she said.

"I sent the good ones away with a fellowship application. The colors didn't come out in these."

She leafed through them. "I think they're beautiful."

"We've only got instant. You have milk and sugar?" He shook a half-full coffee jar in front of her.

"No, black, thank you."

"Sit down," he said, returning to the kitchen bench. "I've got an old Danish in here, if you want to share. I know it's not much to offer a royal faery but . . ." He laughed to himself, uncomfortable.

Mayfridh barely noticed. "Hmm? No, I'll have breakfast later. I'm never hungry in the mornings."

"Me neither. But if I don't eat I can't seem to paint."

One by one she studied the photographs. Every single painting was a masterpiece, a shadowy enchantment. How she longed to see them for real.

Jude set down a cup of coffee in front of her, then sat beside her. "You like them?"

"I love them. Where are they all?" she asked, placing the photos carefully on the table.

"Mostly in New York. In galleries. A couple are in

Washington. I've got one in London but it's not hanging. Two downstairs, and . . . I've forgotten where the others are. Oh, yeah. One in a university in Barcelona, and four in some merchant bank office in Texas. They put them in glass frames. I hate that. It changes the texture."

She raised her eyes to steal a glance at him, but he wasn't looking at her. He was concentrating instead on his Danish. His hair was messy and his hands looked warm.

"Could I . . . buy one of your paintings?" she asked. To take with her; to hang in the great hall so she would have some small piece of Jude forever, even though winter would obliterate any memory of his face and voice and personality.

"Really? You want to buy one? They're expensive."

"I have a lot of . . ." She was bragging and she knew it, but couldn't stop herself. "Money isn't a problem."

"Real money? Not magic faery money that will disappear when you do." He was smiling, teasing her.

"Yes, real money," she said. "I'd pay any price to own one of your paintings."

"Well, sure. But I've already sold the two I've done here. You might have to wait for the next one."

"I can wait." She felt embarrassed now, as though she had said too much. She bent her head to the photographs once more, spreading them out on the table in front of her.

A few moments passed, then Jude said to her softly, "Which one do you like best?"

Mayfridh caught her lip between her teeth. This was like a test she had to pass to make Jude like her. From the corner of her eye, she could see him finish the Danish and dust his fingers off. His hand stole out and he plucked one of the photos from the spread.

"This one?" he asked. "This is Christine's favorite."

Mayfridh shook her head. *Christine's favorite. He belongs to Christine.* "I think I prefer this one." She reached for the picture that had touched her heart, a scratchy white line not perfectly centered on a canvas of dark swirling colors.

"Really," Jude said, his voice gentle. "This one?"

"Why? Don't you like it?" Her gaze met his. His eyes were dark and deep.

"The opposite. It's my favorite too."

Encouraged, she continued: "Can I tell you what I see in it?"

"Of course. I'd love to know."

"It reminds me . . . it reminds me of how I feel back home at an official banquet, when I'm surrounded by people and they're all telling me how much they love and admire me, but I feel completely and utterly alone." She pointed to the white line. "This is me. I hear them saying my name, but I don't even know who I am and why that name should fit me. I'm as lonely as a distant star." She indicated the swirling gray and brown patterns around it. "This is them, and they're all pushing at me and wanting something from me, stripping me bare, and never knowing the delicate core of who I am. Never caring that they're obliterating it in every second."

She ventured a glance at him. His expression was unreadable. At first she thought he was in pain, but perhaps it was confusion. "Jude?"

"Mayfridh, that's *exactly* it."

Mayfridh repressed a self-satisfied smile. "Really?"

His hand reached toward hers on the table, then drew back. She glanced from his fingers to his eyes.

"Mayfridh, can you promise me something? If I ask you what I'm going to ask you next, will you promise that you'll tell me absolutely the truth?"

The weight of his words sobered her. "Yes. Of course."

"Do you *really* see that, or have you used some kind of faery magic to read my mind?"

Her heart fell. He thought she was trying to manipulate him. "It's not possible for me to read minds," she said, knowing she sounded irritated. If only he knew how often she had tried to get inside his head without success.

"I didn't mean to offend you, but it's important," he said. "You see, I spend my whole life trying to put a feeling into an image. Most of the time, nobody can see what that feeling is. But you see it, you *know* it. It's like, my work has finally reached its audience."

"It has. It really has." Electricity was growing in the two-inch space between her hand and his on the table. "Jude, I'm not lying. I'm not tricking you."

"I feel like that," he said, nodding toward the photograph she still held. "That's how I feel."

"Lonely? You're lonely?"

"I am," he breathed, barely audible, "sometimes."

"And sad?"

He nodded once, his eyes fixed on the table.

A tide of half-confused feelings and half-formed questions washed through her. Danger had twined with the blood in her veins. She felt his fingers move, glanced down. The back of his hand, his knuckles, brushed the side of her index finger. Deliberately, slowly. Her whole body was a held breath.

He belongs to Christine.

Mayfridh snatched her hand away and shot out of her chair, dropping the photo on the table. The bewildered guilt on Jude's face stopped her from running out as she'd intended. She stood tensed in front of him. He looked up at her, that same expression of pain and confusion on his face. The longer she stood there, the harder it was to pull herself away.

"Jude . . ." His name came out strangled and breathless.

Jude reached for her hands and pulled her one step toward him. He closed his eyes, his thumbs stroking her fingers. Then he leaned forward and—slowly, so slowly—pressed his face into her belly, kissed her through the blue lace and black velvet. The heat of his lips expanded through her, singing in her stomach and her lungs and her heart, gliding like electricity up her throat and into her brain. She gently shook off his hands and touched his hair, an awful pain of desire coiling between her ribs. His own hands curled around her hips. It was all she could do to keep breathing. Bliss, utter bliss.

Then his shoulders hitched, and she realized he was crying.

"Jude, what's wrong?"

Suddenly, he tore himself away, turning from her, leaping from his chair and hurrying from the room. She stood in empty space, her body and heart bereft.

He belongs to Christine.

She had to go. She had to get out of here, go home where she couldn't hurt people, couldn't hurt herself. In her hurry to leave, she tipped over a chair, left it lying on its side in Christine's kitchen.

This wouldn't happen. She wouldn't let it happen. Her heart ached, but all would be forgotten soon if she could just get home and wait quietly.

Winter was coming.

PART TWO

Oh lift me as a wave, a leaf, a cloud!
I fall upon the thorns of life! I bleed!
"Ode to the West Wind," *Percy Bysshe Shelley*

"Aye, granny, what are you doing there?"
"I'm scraping intestines, my child. Tomorrow I'll
scrape yours as well!"
"The Castle of Murder," *Jacob and Wilhelm Grimm*

CHAPTER FOURTEEN

Heedless of the cold air outside, Mayfridh threw open her bedroom window and let the fresh wind bite her cheeks and nose. A gust moved the gauzy canopy and curtains, which fluttered white like desperate flags around her face. Four deep breaths later she was buried in the white layers of her bed, sobbing and sobbing. Leaves torn from the trees outside skidded into the bedroom.

She cried for Christine, who loved Jude and whom she had betrayed. She cried for Jude, who was lonely and sad and whom she had led to disloyalty. But mostly—as the red and brown and yellow leaves pattered onto the floor like rain and settled on the white blankets and pillows and caught in her crimson hair—she cried for herself. And no matter how many times Eisengrimm bumped on the door to her room and pleaded with her to let him in, she called out "No" and continued to cry until the room wore a carpet of dead leaves and her face was flushed and hot despite the autumn chill.

"Mayfridh."

His voice was close this time. She sat up and looked toward the window, where Eisengrimm perched as Crow.

"Leave me alone," she said, her voice hoarse and her own language heavy on her tongue. She palmed tears from her cheeks.

He hopped to the floor and transformed to Wolf, placed his paws on the sill, and pushed the windows closed with his nose. "You'll catch a bite in your lungs by letting all this cold air in."

"I don't care!"

He jumped up onto the bed next to her. "Mayfridh, what has happened? Why are you so distressed?"

Even though she knew he wouldn't approve, her heart ached to tell somebody her sad story. She threw her arms around his neck and confessed the whole tale, even found some more tears inside her. When she had finished, she sat back and waited for his stern lecture.

Instead, he gazed at her with soft silent eyes.

"Well," she said, "say something."

"I'm sorry, Mayfridh. It hurts me to see you so unhappy." His deep, honeyed voice was tender.

"You're not angry at me?"

"I think you behaved unwisely, but love makes people unwise."

"I do love him, Eisengrimm," she said, choking on the words. She took a deep shuddering breath to try to regain her composure. "And he loves me, there can be no doubt."

"He hasn't said he loves you."

"Eisengrimm, *I felt it*. He loves me, and he can't bear to love me."

"Does he not love Christine?"

"Yes, I think he does love Christine. But not as he loves me. Perhaps he once loved her as much, but now he loves her as a brother might love a sister. She doesn't understand him or his wonderful paintings. They aren't a good match for each other, and now that he has fallen in love with me—"

"Wait, wait. Do you know all this for a fact?"

"Yes."

"But he said nothing to you about Christine."

"Words aren't everything," she snapped. "I'm right, Eisengrimm. He does love me."

Eisengrimm paused and seemed to be choosing his response carefully. "Mayfridh," he said at last, "humans are . . . humans can be driven by feelings other than love."

"What do you mean?"

"Do you understand what sexual desire is?"

Mayfridh grew annoyed. Now he was treating her like a little girl. Of course she understood sexual desire; she felt it herself. "Do you think that because I am a virgin I am a complete fool?"

"Be not angry, Mayfridh. I only suggest that perhaps Jude's feelings are not love, but desire. A man can love one woman and desire another. Desire quickly turns to distaste once an attempt to fulfill it is made. Love remains. Love endures."

Mayfridh closed her eyes and slumped back on her bed. Leaves crackled and turned to dust beneath her. She should never have expected Eisengrimm to understand. She knew that Jude loved her, as certainly as she knew that the sun lived in the sky. Eisengrimm curled up next to her, and she put her arms around him, suddenly bone-weary.

"I feel I haven't slept for days," she murmured.

"Then sleep now, and I shall keep you warm."

"My heart hurts, Eisengrimm."

"In just a few weeks we'll move to the Winter Castle. You will forget."

"But it's so sad to forget things that matter." She thought now not just of Jude and Christine, but of her mother, Diana.

"Imagine how much worse it could be, Mayfridh. Imagine if you loved somebody in this world and couldn't have that person. No change of seasons could ever make you forget."

"Hush, Eisengrimm, don't make me even sadder. What a terrible thought." She curled on her side against his warm back, her fingers spread in the fur over his ribs, and fell into a deep slumber.

Eisengrimm was waiting when she emerged the following morning, the golden chain and medallion of his office as counselor fastened around his neck. Mayfridh took a step back.

"No, not official business. Not today."

"My Queen, you have been absent for a number of weeks. There are angry questions in the village, and Hilda says the domestic staff have started to doubt your fitness to rule us. You must make an appearance this morning, you must show that you are still the queen."

"Of course I am still the queen!" she snapped. "How dare they question my activities?"

"Because you have not been here, Mayfridh," he replied forcefully. "The seasons must turn soon; the citizens of this world require your magic and your blessings. They grow worried that you aren't preparing them sufficiently for winter." He dropped his voice, gentle now. "Little May, to be queen involves responsibilities."

Damn Eisengrimm and damn the rest of the world! The change of seasons never faltered. Plenty of time still remained for her to distribute the magic and make the blessings. Were they all nervous old ladies? How could she even think about official duties while nursing a broken heart?

"My Queen?"

"Yes, yes, I'm coming."

"Official robes, Mayfridh. I doubt the others will deem your current attire . . . appropriate."

Now she wanted to cry. The Real World was slipping farther and farther away from her every moment. "But Eisengrimm . . ."

"Please, Little May. It will make matters easier."

She retreated to her bedroom and slammed the door, pulled off her tartan pinafore, replaced it with her yellow gown and bronze robe, hung her keys about her waist, and scraped her hair beneath a scarf. With as much dignity as she could assemble, she descended the stairs to the great hall and took her place on the throne. This was where she had sat that first day, when Christine had unwittingly wandered into her world. What a twisted and miserable path life had taken since then.

"Majesty," Hilda said with a curtsy.

One by one the others in the gloomy hall acknowledged her: Thorsten the village mayor, the three village aldermen (she never remembered their names), Brathr the hatchet-faced reeve, and Eisengrimm.

"Well then," Mayfridh said, "why the sudden meeting?"

"Majesty," Thorsten began, "we are only weeks away from the turn of season, and haven't received our winter magic yet."

"We still have time," she said, irritated.

"The villagers grow restless," one of the aldermen said.

"You may feel there is plenty of time, Queen Mayfridh," Hilda said, "but the opinion of your subjects and your staff is not to be ignored."

How petty this was. She fantasized about enchanting them all into silence, then remembered she hadn't a single spell left. Damn Hexebart.

"Eisengrimm," Mayfridh said, turning her attention to him, "do you not think we have plenty of time still?"

"Your Majesty, I agree that the opinion of your subjects is a pressing issue."

"But we have many weeks, do we not? And the magic and the blessings can be administered in a day."

"That is true," Eisengrimm conceded.

Thorsten turned hostile eyes on the wolf. "Perhaps another issue we might discuss is the issue of counsel."

"Counsel?" Mayfridh asked, watching Thorsten carefully. "What do you mean?"

"The issue, my Queen, of an adviser who sees no harm in your being from your home and duties for weeks at a time."

Mayfridh quickly examined the faces assembled around her. Each had turned suspicious gazes on Eisengrimm, and she was gripped by guilt. Had Eisengrimm been fending off their questions and accusations all this time, while she enjoyed herself in the Real World? "Eisengrimm's counsel is not in question," she said firmly. "It was my own decision to spend time in the Real World. In fact, Eisengrimm discouraged me from being away for so long. But now I am returned."

"For good?" Brathr asked.

"I . . . I believe so."

"Majesty," Thorsten said, taking a penitent step forward, "be not angry with us. We have all been bearing the weight of the many questions asked of your behavior. Your subjects are not happy, but they remain loyal. Some gesture must be made to reward their continued loyalty."

Mayfridh nodded. Outside, a fresh wind from the west rattled branches in the dawn half-light.

"What do you have in mind?"

"A royal autumn parade, Queen Mayfridh," Hilda said. "You can distribute the winter magic and the blessings, but more importantly, you can be seen by your people. They will be reassured by your presence."

"We all recommend this plan, your Majesty," Thorsten said firmly.

The thought made her weary. Dressed in royal garb, waving and smiling and meeting the villagers, when all she wanted to do was curl up in a dusty corner with her fervent imaginings of Jude until the winter erased him from her mind. She turned to Eisengrimm, knew her voice sounded plaintive. "Eisengrimm? Do you also recommend this?"

He took a few paces forward, transforming to Fox and jumping into her lap. "Yes, Little May. It will be for the best." Then, secretly, in her ear, he added, "And it will take your mind off other matters."

"Very well," she sighed. "Make the necessary arrangements."

The gathered assembly exchanged relaxed smiles.

"I will go to Hexebart for spells. Eisengrimm, will you come with me?"

"We will need Eisengrimm for the parade committee, Majesty," Hilda said.

Mayfridh groaned. She hated dealing with Hexebart alone.

"Just be firm and don't lose your temper," Eisengrimm said to her softly.

Mayfridh placed Eisengrimm on the floor and stood, smoothing her skirt. Today was already growing more complicated than she could endure.

🦊

The temporary twilight of evening and morning twined about the garden with the thorns. Mayfridh lingered a moment to watch a spider spin a web amongst the branches of an elder bush, its silvery thread glistening in the dim light. The air was chilled, and deep in her bones she could feel winter nearby. Soon.

Hexebart's well cast a long shadow across the grass. Mayfridh approached and called down to her.

"Witch, come up here. I need blessing spells."

Mayfridh was expecting the usual stubborn refusals and abuse but, to her surprise, the cage hoisted itself up immediately. Hexebart sat among the iron bars, smiling a crooked smile.

"Why are you smiling?" Mayfridh asked, her eyes narrowing instinctively.

"Perhaps I'm happy to see my queen."

"Is this some trickery?"

"I have a few spells for you. Hold out your bag."

Mayfridh paused. Hexebart had never been this compliant.

"Go on, Queen." She spat the word like an insult. "Hold out your bag."

Suspicious, Mayfridh held out the woven bag. Hexebart gathered up a handful of spells and tipped them in.

"It's not enough for all the winter blessings, but I'll make more soon," the witch said, all sweet-voiced again.

"Thank you," Mayfridh said, grudgingly, moving to tie off the top of the bag. As she did, Hexebart's bony hand slipped out and clamped around Mayfridh's wrist. Mayfridh gasped and tried to pull away.

"What are you doing?"

"Shh, fool, I shan't hurt you," Hexebart said. "Where's dog-chops?"

"Eisengrimm is back at the castle. Let me go, what is the meaning of—"

"I know his secret."

Mayfridh was shocked into silence. Surely she couldn't mean Jude.

"Well," Hexebart said, "what do you say about that, little sow?"

Maybe she'd misunderstood. Maybe Hexebart was talking about a secret Eisengrimm was keeping from her. "What are you talking about? Whose secret?"

"The boy you love in the Real World."

"But you gave me a mind-reading spell. It didn't work."

"You asked for the wrong spell. I made the right spell. And I know his secret."

"Then tell me."

Hexebart bared her crooked teeth and replied in a sing-song voice, "No-oh, I don't believe I sha-all."

Mayfridh's stomach clutched tight with anger and frustration. "Tell me, you hideous creature."

"And why should I? Why should I do you a single favor? You are nothing but a cuckoo in the nest, a dirty little changeling, a pile of perfumed puke. Why, I should be delighted to see you suffer for the rest of your days for what you have done to me, and what you did to the real queen."

"I am the real queen. Liesebet disappeared."

"Conveniently for you."

"Tell me, witch. It is not for you to keep secrets from the queen. You are my servant. You are at my command."

"Even the thoughts of slaves are free," Hexebart spat. Then she leaned back in her cage and closed her eyes. "Hmm, I'm thinking about his secret this very second. Hmm, hmm. What a terrible thing he's done."

Mayfridh could feel her blood growing hot. "Tell me!" she shrieked. "Tell me immediately."

Hexebart opened her eyes. "We could, of course, strike some kind of a deal." Her voice was cool and measured in contrast to Mayfridh's.

"How dare you be so—" Mayfridh stopped abruptly. Shouting never got her anywhere with Hexebart. Although it undermined her role and her dignity, she clenched her teeth and said, "What do you want in exchange for Jude's secret?"

"I am sick of living in this well."

Mayfridh almost laughed. "Witch, I am not setting you free. You have the royal magic. You are doomed to be imprisoned until you return it."

"I will return it when Queen Liesebet asks for it."

"Then you will be in the well until you die."

"Perhaps I don't mind being imprisoned so much as I mind being in the well," Hexebart said slyly.

"What do you mean?"

"Perhaps the dungeons would be more comfortable. Fewer frogs."

Mayfridh considered. Hexebart had been confined to the well as a cruel punishment for her recalcitrance. She could do her spell weaving and be safely incarcerated just as easily in the dungeon, though she hardly deserved the space and shelter. And yet, granting the witch some comfort was a small price to pay if it meant Mayfridh would finally learn Jude's secret.

"There would be conditions," Mayfridh said slowly.

"Like what?"

"You would be forbidden to tell Eisengrimm why we have struck this agreement."

"I wouldn't tell him a thing, the pompous dog's breath."

"And I'd need some guarantee that you'd keep your side of the bargain. A magical oath that you would tell me the secret."

Hexebart's hands emerged between the bars once more. Her fingers danced against each other as she spun a spell. When it was complete, she closed her fingers over it and said, "I swear that as soon as the dungeon door is locked behind me, I will tell you the secret." When she opened her hand, the spell had disappeared. Hexebart was now magically bound.

Mayfridh couldn't help smiling. "We shall organize the

transfer immediately." She turned to leave, but Hexebart's croaking voice called her back.

"One other thing," the witch said.

"What?" Mayfridh said, turning back with a frown.

"I should like to see the whole dungeon."

"What do you mean?"

"You swear that you don't have the real king and queen imprisoned. I should like to prove that for myself."

Mayfridh shook her head. "No. The agreement is I transfer you from the well to the dungeon and that's that."

"Perhaps if you can prove they aren't there, you might not need to imprison me at all. Perhaps when I see with my own eyes, I might be prepared to give the royal magic back."

Mayfridh peered at Hexebart closely in the morning gloom. "Are you serious?"

"Of course. Why would I waste my breath otherwise?"

"We might arrange it after you've been moved to the dungeon. I will consider it."

"I won't tell you the secret."

"You're sworn to tell me the secret."

"Only after you've locked me in the dungeon. I can refuse to go. I can tell dog-chops what's really going on and he'll let me stay here in the well."

Mayfridh wanted to grab the cage and shake it until Hexebart bounced around inside. "You can't add a condition after you've sworn to something."

"I can. What difference does it make to you? I expect I'll be bound and you'll have guards all around me."

Mayfridh pressed a hand to her brow. Hexebart was right. She would be bound, there would be no chance of escape, and for years the witch had accused her of imprisoning her parents. Jude's secret was so large and pressing in her mind, it hardly mattered to Mayfridh whether Hexebart peered into the empty cells or not.

"Very well, then," Mayfridh said, "but you will be bound."

"I want you to swear on it, as I swore on my end of the bargain."

Mayfridh reached into the bag for a spell, held it gently in one hand while considering.

"Go on," Hexebart said. "I swore. You'll get your precious secret."

"I swear, then," Mayfridh said, quickly in case she changed her mind. "I swear that you will be allowed to view all the dungeons before we lock you in one." She opened her hand to show that the spell was gone.

"Good," Hexebart said. "I look forward to you returning soon." The cage began to lower itself into the well. In the first glimmer of sunrise, Mayfridh thought she saw Hexebart smile, and wondered if she had done the right thing.

❦

Eisengrimm's face never gave much away, but Mayfridh could have sworn he looked completely bewildered.

"But why?" he said, for the fifth time.

Mayfridh watched him pace in a circle around the bedroom. "Because she's been living in the well so long it's making her difficult and bitter," she said. "Because if we take her to the dungeons we can show her once and for all that my parents are not there."

He stopped and turned to face her. "She will simply say that we have them imprisoned elsewhere."

"She said she might consider returning the royal magic to me."

"Hexebart is dangerous and hostile. I don't trust her."

"It's too late. I swore to it."

Eisengrimm's ears pricked up in alarm. "You *swore*?"

"I didn't want her to change her mind. She seemed very

serious. I thought it would be a chance to regain the magic that's rightfully mine."

"If you have sworn, we have very little choice in the matter," he said gruffly. "I should never have let you go to Hexebart alone."

"What do you mean by that? Do you not think I can manage her alone?"

"You have done a very foolish thing. I would have counseled you against it."

"I am not bound by your counsel, Eisengrimm. I am the queen and may do as I please."

Eisengrimm fell silent and bowed his head. "That is true, your Majesty. Meet me in the garden in ten minutes. I will assemble some guards to accompany Hexebart to her new home."

He slunk out, leaving Mayfridh sitting on the edge of her bed, fiddling with the keys on her belt. Her heart was hammering and she felt unsafe and unsatisfied. Why did Eisengrimm have to put so many doubts in her mind? She moved to the window and peered down through branches to the leafy slope behind the castle. The well sat silent and remote like a painting. Hexebart was in there, no doubt singing to herself and preparing for the move to her new space. Mayfridh went over the details in her head. Hexebart would be bound so that her hands couldn't perform magic; Eisengrimm would organize at least four guards; the dungeons were as inescapable as the well. Nothing could go wrong.

She pulled herself away from the window and headed down the stairs to the garden. At the end of all this, in that moment when she locked Hexebart's dungeon with her own fingers around the key, she would know Jude's secret. She was both thrilled and terrified. Hexebart had said Jude had done something terrible. What if she couldn't bear it? What if he *had* slept with Gerda, or with a million other women? What if that intense passion she had sensed he felt for her was nothing more than lust, as Eisengrimm suggested? Perhaps Hexebart was lying, and his secret was of some pure and noble nature. Mayfridh would only remember it for little more than a month, but at least she would know it. She would tuck it away with the dark sweet ache of her love for him; the love that could not be realized.

Eisengrimm was waiting for her with four royal guards. They greeted her dourly and she led them out the gate and down the slope to the well. Hexebart must have heard them coming, for the cage was already above ground when they arrived.

"Hexebart," Eisengrimm said in a stern voice, "you must cooperate with us at all times."

She nodded solemnly.

Eisengrimm turned to the chief guard, a burly fellow with a bright yellow beard. "When the queen unlocks the cage, pull the witch out carefully. Never let the fingertips on one hand touch the fingertips on the other. That's how she works her magic." Eisengrimm nodded at Mayfridh. "Go on, Little May. Open the cage."

Mayfridh unhooked her belt of keys. Unlike ordinary keys, they did not correspond to particular locks and doors. Each key was enchanted, just as each lock in the castle and dungeons was enchanted. No ordinary lock could hold Hexebart. Ironically, it was the witch's own spell that held her captive; she had built all the enchanted keys and locks while still in Liesebet's service many years before. Mayfridh stilled her hands as she approached. The cage hadn't been opened in decades and the lock was flaked with rust.

"Hexebart, spread your arms apart," Eisengrimm said. The witch complied.

The door to the cage sprang open, and two of the guards roughly bundled Hexebart out, keeping her arms spread wide apart. Eisengrimm instructed them as they twisted her arms behind her back, turned her hands knuckle to knuckle inward, then tied a block of wood between them. Then her hands were bound tightly from her fingers to her wrists. Mayfridh watched anxiously. The knots were secure. Hexebart endured it all in angry silence.

The burly guard gave Hexebart a shove. "Come on, witch," he said, "time to inspect your new home."

With Eisengrimm in front, two guards on either side of Hexebart, and Mayfridh following them and never taking her eyes off Hexebart's bound hands, they made their way back through the trees and the garden and down the stairs toward the dungeons. The first gate swung open. Hexebart's feet shuffled and scuffed obediently, a counter-rhythm to the marching guards. Mayfridh's skin itched with tension; the danger, the secret. The party continued through the other three gates, and finally arrived at the cells.

"Walk her past them all, one by one," Eisengrimm instructed. He let the guards go ahead of him with Hexebart, hanging back with Mayfridh.

"You see," she said, "it's all working out."

Eisengrimm's eyes were following the progress of the witch up the corridor as the guards lit each cell for her to peer inside. He returned his attention to Mayfridh. "She is suspiciously silent."

"Perhaps she really is considering giving my magic back. Perhaps it's the penitence we've dreamed of for so long." Mayfridh was still hopeful that this would prove true; then Eisengrimm couldn't look at her sternly and think her foolish.

"Perhaps," Eisengrimm said, sounding not in the least convinced.

"We've looked in all the cells, your Majesty," the burly guard called from the other end of the corridor.

"Very well, bring her back and we'll lock her up." She took a key between her trembling fingers. As soon as the others were gone, she would know. *She would know.*

Guards flanking her tightly, arms bound behind her, the hag shuffled down the corridor with her head hanging down.

"So, witch," Eisengrimm said. "You have seen all the cells and they are empty. What do you say now?"

Hexebart lifted her head and parted her lips. Mayfridh saw the glimmer of light on her tongue too late. There was a horrid spitting noise and a flash of blinding light, and then she was on the floor, confusion and darkness and shouting all around her.

"Where is she?"

"What happened?"

"Run after her!"

"It's too late. We've all been sleeping for an hour." This was Eisengrimm's voice.

Mayfridh opened her eyes and rolled over. Eisengrimm stood above her.

"Are you hurt?" he asked.

"I . . . feel a little bruised."

"She had a spell in her mouth."

"I saw it. At the last moment."

"She's gone, Mayfridh."

Mayfridh sank back on the cold floor and groaned. No secret of Jude's; no magic for the winter blessings; Hexebart on the loose. She didn't want to be queen anymore. It was all too hard. She wanted to go shopping with Gerda and drink coffee in Christine's kitchen.

"My Queen?" Eisengrimm said.

"Send out a search party," she replied. "We have to find her quickly."

*   *   *

Hee hee hee, Hexebart is free! Silly little queen. Did she really think Hexebart would be well behaved? Did she not remember how despised she is? Hexebart laughs and laughs, nearly doubles over. Into the Eternal Woods she plunges. They could search for weeks and never find her in here. Hexebart checks all around. There! A hollow in a tree. Hexebart squeezes herself in, leaving her bound hands dangling out behind her. Damn them for the block they tied between her fingers. Just the lightest touch of fingertip to fingertip and Hexebart could work her magic. But the bossy wolf is too smart, too smart.

And yet not smart enough. Just a stupid dog in the end. Hexebart is free.

It won't take long to fix. Hexebart is clever and Hexebart is patient. See? If she rubs the ropes on the rough edge of this hollow, they will eventually wear right through and drop off. Then Hexebart will clap her hands with glee and make magic with her fingers, and who can stop Hexebart then? Nobody. Certainly not a smelly little changeling princess and her dog.

Ha, ha, la, la, la,
Hexebart is going far.

My, that's a cold wind. Brr! Hexebart tries to wriggle her fingers. They are icy on the tips, poor things. But never mind, because Hexebart won't be here for long, no. Hexebart is going somewhere where the houses are warm and the windows don't let in drafts and people don't have to live in cages. Hexebart is going to the Real World.

Over There, Over There,
Who but Hexebart would dare?

Hexebart isn't afraid. Hexebart knows people there and will be sure to visit them. Especially that girl with the long brown hair . . . her name is . . . Christine, that's right.

Hexebart has a little story to tell Christine.

CHAPTER FIFTEEN

"*Where's Miranda?*"

Christine took a wary step back from Mandy, who stood outside her door, wild-eyed and with his shirt only half-buttoned. His pale, hairy belly was exposed. "I don't know," Christine said, "I haven't seen her for nearly a week."

"Gerda told me she left. Did she say she was leaving? Is she coming back?"

A thread of unease curled in her stomach. Mandy sounded desperate. Christine had no idea he had fallen so hard for Mayfridh. She also had no idea why Mayfridh had gone. She hadn't left a note and the suddenness of her departure made Christine wonder whether the seasons had changed early back on Ewigkreis, and whether her friend had disappeared forever with them. Already she had fielded three frantic calls from Diana Frith, who also suspected the worst.

"Mandy, she could be gone forever," Christine said, hoping this would end the conversation definitively. "It was always a possibility."

"Forever?" His voice was forlorn, a child who'd seen his favorite teddy washed out to sea.

"I'm sorry, I didn't know you'd grown so fond of her."

He turned away without answering and started up the stairs. Christine gratefully closed the door, leaning back on it with a sigh. Mandy was becoming weirder and weirder. It made her wonder if there was more to him than simply a few disgusting habits and a lot of money.

And if so, what more was there? She shuddered. What an unnerving thought.

Gerda was relating the name and physical dimensions of every man she had ever slept with—an astonishingly full and thorough list—when Christine realized she had lost Jude.

She stopped Gerda mid-sentence and turned to check the dark, slick street behind her. "Where are the boys?"

Gerda turned with her, keeping the umbrella steady over-head. "They must have stopped to buy cigars. Remember we were all talking about it at dinner? Come on, let's keep going. I don't want to stand out here in the rain."

They set course for home, and Christine said, "Go on, Gerda, you were saying?"

"I've forgotten where I was up to."

"Lars, seven-and-a-half inches," Christine reminded her.

"I'm tired of it now."

"I wish they'd told us they were stopping somewhere. The rain's getting heavier."

"We wouldn't have all fitted under one umbrella," Gerda said, giving the umbrella a twirl. "This is pretty, Miss Starlight. Where did you buy it?"

"Can't remember. I've had it for years." Christine glanced over her shoulder again.

Gerda punched her arm lightly. "Don't worry about Jude, he'll be fine. Pete will look after him."

Christine raised an eyebrow. "Pete? Look after anybody?"

Gerda giggled. "I see your point. Hey, have you heard from Mayfridh?"

"Not a word."

"I miss her," Gerda said, "she was a lot of fun."

"You miss her because you're not getting free clothes anymore."

"That too. But I do miss her."

"So do I." More than she could put into words.

"It was weird, wasn't it, how she just disappeared?"

Christine sidestepped a puddle. The rain was heavy now, infringing on the dry space under the umbrella. "I expect she had to go back. You know, with winter coming."

"She told me she'd be here for weeks yet. At least a month."

"Perhaps something happened back in Ewigkreis."

"You'd think she'd leave a note."

"It's strange."

"You could go and see her."

"Jude's worried that winter has already started there. That I'd get stuck."

Gerda frowned. "Not yet. Hey, give me the twine. I'm not afraid to go."

Christine couldn't bear the thought of Gerda being able to share in her precious journeys to Ewigkreis. She'd convince Eisengrimm to smoke cigars and the locals to build a jazz club before a week was out. "Sorry. Mayfridh made me promise not to give it to anyone else," she lied.

Gerda showed no signs of disappointment. "Mandy's taken her disappearance badly."

Christine shivered, but it may have been from the sudden

cold wind that roared down the street, chilling the rain on her sleeve to ice. "What has he said to you?"

"He just asks about her a lot. Where did she go? Is she coming back? Did she say anything before she left?" Gerda fished a cigarette out of her pocket and jammed it in her mouth. "What do you think it's all about? Was he in love with her?"

"I guess so. He's been freaky since she left. On edge. Watching me closely." Christine laughed. "I thought he was creepy before, but it was only the tip of the iceberg."

"Oh yeah, he has unknown depths of creepiness," Gerda said. Her lighter flashed in the dark, then sputtered out. "Damn rain," she said.

"Here, let me help."

Christine stopped and cupped her hand around Gerda's while she lit her cigarette. She took the opportunity to check behind her again. Where was Jude? Normally she wouldn't worry, but he'd been so vague and withdrawn lately. She could easily imagine him stepping out in front of a car without seeing it.

"Still," Gerda said as they turned into Friedrichstrasse, "you must be a little relieved that she's gone."

"Relieved?"

"She had her eye on Jude. Didn't you notice?"

"Many women before her have had their eyes on Jude," Christine said. "Nothing ever comes of it."

"Any as beautiful as Mayfridh?" Gerda smiled and poked her elbow in Christine's ribs. "Apart from me, of course?"

Christine took the poke with good humor. "I don't know if beauty comes into it, Gerda. You've seen what he paints."

"Ouch, Miss Art Critic," Gerda said, pulling the umbrella away. "You can walk in the rain for that remark. You're talking about Jude the genius."

"Don't, Gerda, I hate getting wet."

"Sorry." The umbrella was restored. "Has Jude said anything about Mayfridh going?"

"No. I told him she'd disappeared and he just went back to his painting."

"So you really think he doesn't notice other women?"

Christine thought about that splash of red, so hastily painted out. "Sometimes he doesn't even notice me, Gerda."

"Maybe he just pretends not to notice them. Maybe he has a secret other life where he indulges all his sexual fantasies."

Christine gave Gerda a cautionary frown. "Don't put ideas like that in my head." For an instant she imagined finding out that Jude had slept with Gerda. It would kill her.

"Sorry, didn't mean to be nasty."

"You never do." She checked over her shoulder once more before they turned into Vogelwald-Allee. "Look, there they are."

Gerda turned and waved madly at Jude and Pete, who were huddling together in the rain about two hundred yards behind them. "Christine," she said, "wait here under this awning. I'll take them the umbrella."

"But—"

A second later, Gerda was tearing off down the street and Christine had to slip under the awning of a music shop to protect herself from the downpour. The movement pulled a muscle in her back, and she pressed her hand against it. From here, she could see diagonally across the road to Hotel Mandy-Z. She supposed she could dash the distance in the rain; it was only about fifty yards. As she looked at the front of the building, her eye was drawn upward to the gabled window at the top of the building. The attic. Mandy's attic. She remembered the door with the three deadlocks. That was where it led.

The streetlight over the storm drain, obscured by the

swinging branches of the big elms, reflected in the window but illuminated nothing within. Everything was black behind it. What was in there?

The gurgling of the storm drain and the thundering of the rain on the awning meant she didn't hear the others approach. When Jude grabbed her in a wet embrace she nearly shrieked.

"Sorry, babe. Didn't mean to scare you."

"It's okay. I was thinking about something unpleasant." She touched his wet curls. "You're soaked."

"Let's go inside and dry off," Pete said.

"Good idea."

The four of them squashed together under the umbrella and made it across the street to Hotel Mandy-Z, then inside where it was warm and dry.

Early the next morning, before Jude was awake, Christine dressed and let herself out of the building. She stood under the elms in the drenched dawn and looked up at the gabled window again. No wonder it had been black the night before. The window was painted over. She returned to her apartment and lay down on the bed next to Jude, wondering why someone would need to lock an attic up with three deadlocks, and paint the window black.

from the Memoirs of Mandy Z.

I am so filled with frustration and anger. Where is Miranda? Why can't anyone give me an answer? I go to sleep thinking about her, I dream about her, I wake up with her name on my lips like the bad aftertaste of an ill-digested meal the evening before.

So much of this frustration and anger is misdirected too. I also feel enraged with myself, because I know that whatever is in Miranda, whatever it is that makes her a creature apart from the human race, it is in me in small measure. I am, remember, the product of a union between human and faery. Thirteen generations ago, yes, but not necessarily thirteen generations diluted. Have you never seen a painting of a distant ancestor, and marveled at how his teeth are prominent like your teeth, or how her eyes are heavy-lidded like your eyes? Each of my twelve male ancestors in a direct line from the faery has been blind or color-blind as I am. I know, whether I'm comfortable with it or not, that it is in me.

Now humans don't normally breed with faeries. The story of my family's original union with them goes like this. In the far north on the borders with Denmark, there lived a wealthy man with two sons named Oswald and Diebolt. The man thought it would be good for his sons to go out into the wide world and try their fortune. He gave them each a knapsack with food and gold coins in it, and waved them off on their adventure.

The younger son, Diebolt, walked for a day through forest and found a little cottage in bad repair. The dense shade allowed only a few stains of sunlight to shine on the rotted panels and abandoned birds' nests. Beyond, in the distance, he could see the turrets of a castle. The sun was low in the sky and he wondered if he should stop for the night at the cottage, or make for the castle even if it meant spending a night in the forest. The choice was taken from his hands when a strange-looking little man—a dwarfish fellow with thin wrinkled arms and a tuft of white hair—popped out of the cottage doorway and said, "I am old and poor, but you may stay here the night as long as you give me half of what's in your knapsack."

Diebolt looked at the dwarf, who was indeed very old, and at his rundown cottage, and thought, "Why should I have so much more than this little man? Half the gold and food in my knapsack is a high price for a night's rest, but he needs it more than I do. I'm young and strong."

So Diebolt agreed. He came inside and laid out all the food and coins from his knapsack on the table, divided them carefully in half, and gave the dwarf his share. Then he set about helping the dwarf prepare a meal, swept the hearth, and fixed a leak in the roof. He became exhausted soon after and the dwarf led him to a warm, soft bed, where he slept soundly.

The next morning, as he bade the dwarf farewell, the dwarf pulled a shining object out of his pocket and handed it to Diebolt.

"What's this?" Diebolt said, examining the object. It was a gleaming red jewel strung on a silver chain.

"It's a token of my gratitude. Wear it always and it will bring you good fortune."

Diebolt thanked the dwarf warmly and hung the jewel about his neck. Then he hoisted his knapsack on his back and went on his way.

Now Diebolt's brother Oswald had been lazy and slow in leaving his father's home, and was many hours behind him. As Diebolt was leaving the dwarf's house, Oswald arrived. He saw the jewel about Diebolt's neck and said, "Where did you get that beautiful jewel?"

Diebolt explained how he had spent the night with the dwarf (Oswald had spent it at an expensive inn not far from his father's house) and how the dwarf had rewarded him with the jewel.

"Now, if you'll come with me," Diebolt said, "we can

share in my good fortune and take on the wide world together."

"No, thank you," Oswald said, for he had another plan, "I'd prefer to travel at my own pace." Then they waved each other good-bye and went their separate ways.

Oswald eyed the dwarf's house. How could someone in such a tumbledown house have such a fine jewel, and if he had one, might he have another? Oswald knocked on the door and the dwarf appeared.

"I would like a jewel like the one you gave my brother," Oswald said.

"I am old and poor, but you may stay here the night as long as you give me half of what's in your knapsack," the dwarf said.

Oswald could barely contain his laughter. Half of what was in his knapsack for a bed in this hovel! Then he thought of a way to trick the dwarf so he agreed.

They went inside and Oswald took from his knapsack one loaf of bread. "This is all I have," he said, "but you may take half of it."

The dwarf took the bread gratefully and asked Oswald to sweep the hearth. Oswald thought that sweeping the hearth was beneath him, so he did it halfheartedly and accidentally spread ashes onto the floorboards. Then the dwarf asked him to fix a loose window, but he was growing tired from all the work, so he pretended to fix it by stuffing the gap with a rag. Then, although it was only midday, Oswald said he was tired and where was the bed he had been promised? The dwarf led him to a soft, warm bed and he spent all day in it, dreaming about the jewel that the dwarf would give him and feeling very pleased with himself.

The next morning, Oswald awoke early and was so impatient for his jewel that he rose and made a lot of noise to wake the dwarf up.

"I'm going now, little man," Oswald said. "I know you paid my brother handsomely, and expect the same courtesy."

"Ah, I see," said the dwarf. "Very well, hold out your hand." And the dwarf handed Oswald a shining jewel strung on a silver chain. "There you are, it's what you deserve."

Oswald hung it about his neck and set off in the early morning light.

About a mile from the cottage, he noticed a strange buzzing noise. He looked around but couldn't see where it came from. He took a few steps farther, but the buzzing was growing louder. In fact, it seemed to be coming from under his shirt. He pulled open the front of his shirt and the jewel on the silver chain was gone. In its place was a piece of string with a fly tied to it.

"Argh!" he cried, tearing the string from around his neck and flinging it to the ground.

The fly slipped the knot and took flight, but not before it darted toward Oswald's face and, in the very voice of the dwarf, said, "You lied and were lazy and greedy. You have received precisely what you deserved."

Oswald was so angry that he stomped through the forest, cursing and breaking branches with rage. He walked so fast that he managed to catch up with Diebolt, who had spent the night in the forest, and was incensed to see that Diebolt's jewel still hung around his neck

"How is it possible that your jewel hasn't turned into a fly?" Oswald demanded.

"What do you mean?"

"The dwarf gave me a jewel too, but because I only shared a loaf of bread with him, and spread the ashes rather than sweeping them, and fixed the window with an old rag, it turned into a fly and flew away."

"If you lied and were lazy, why would you deserve a jewel?" Diebolt said. "Come, brother, don't be sad. I'll share my jewel with you. You see, it's magic. Last night when I realized I'd have to spend the night here in the forest, I just held the jewel and wished for a warm bed, and one appeared in front of me. In the morning, when I woke, the bed disappeared again."

Now Oswald was even more angry. A magic jewel! He didn't want to share it, he wanted it all to himself. So he raised his staff and hit Diebolt over the head. When Diebolt fell to the ground, he stole the jewel and hung it about his own neck, then proceeded on his way to the castle.

When Oswald arrived at the castle, he was greeted by a beautiful young woman whom he took to be the king's daughter.

"Good day, my lady," he said, bowing deeply, "I wish to see the king to show him something wondrous." He thought the magic jewel was his opportunity to impress the king and win some favor.

The king's daughter, whose name was Konstanz, wrung her hands together and said, "Alas, the king is terribly ill and cannot leave his chamber."

"Then take me to his chamber and I will demonstrate there."

Princess Konstanz agreed, and led him to the king's chamber. The king was indeed very ill and pale, propped up in his bed with many servants around him attending to his every need.

"Father," Princess Konstanz said, "this young man says he has something wondrous to show you."

"What is it?" said the king irritably.

"A magic jewel, sire. Watch." He held out the jewel and said, "I wish for a table of food." A moment later, a table appeared in front of him, laid out with hot bread and jam and pickled fish.

The king sat up with a start. "Then you have finally

come! It is said that when a young man with a wishing jewel arrives at the castle, he is to marry my daughter and conceive this very night a son and heir, who shall be born before I die."

Oswald thought himself very lucky to have won the hand of the princess and to have been proclaimed father to the throne's heir. He imagined he would have a very nice life indeed under these circumstances and agreed immediately to a hasty wedding, very eager to partake of the wedding night pleasures. He didn't think of his brother Diebolt once.

In the meantime, the dwarf, walking through the forest to find firewood, stumbled across Diebolt lying unconscious on the ground. He helped him to his feet and asked, "What happened to you?"

"My brother hit me and stole the jewel you gave me, and I believe he has gone to the castle."

The dwarf twisted his little face into a grimace and said, "Then I know what has happened, because of the ancient prophecy associated with the wishing jewel. He must be punished." Because, of course, the dwarf was of the faery race, and they are unforgiving and irrational people, among their many other faults. He didn't suggest that Diebolt go to the castle and explain the situation, but plotted instead his own revenge.

Knowing that Oswald would, that very night, lie with the king's daughter and produce an heir, the dwarf summoned up a friend of his, a faery hag, to help him. As evening approached, the faery hag bound and hid the princess and then took her place in the bed.

When Oswald neared the bedroom with a lit taper in his hands, the faery hag called out, "No, my husband, put out the light. Let us share our pleasures in the dark."

Oswald did what he was told and climbed into bed next to the hag. He touched her bosom and belly, and thought that her skin was very saggy and thin for a beautiful young princess.

"Princess Konstanz," he said, "your skin is not as silky and plump as I imagined it."

"That is because I waste away with desire in every second you do not kiss me," she said.

He was surprised by her being so forward, but complied and kissed her. Her lips felt very hard and whiskery for a beautiful young princess.

"Princess Konstanz," he said, "your lips are not as smooth and full as I imagined them."

"That is because I waste away with desire in every second you do not poke me."

Again he was surprised by her forwardness, but complied and eased himself on top of her and slid inside her. She felt very dry and loose for a beautiful young princess.

"Princess Konstanz," he said, not quite sure how to phrase his next statement, and trailed off into an awkward silence.

"What's the matter, my lord? Is my hole not as wet and tight as you'd imagined it?"

He instantly realized this was not his sweet young princess and he tried to pull away, but the hag locked her bony legs and arms around him, and using some disgusting magic she milked him of his seed over and over again, for many, many hours, until he finally had none left in him. She cast him aside, and then jumped out of bed and ran to the king's chamber. By this time, her stomach was already swelling with the child of her union with Oswald.

"My King, my King," she said, "see the offspring that young Oswald has brought into the royal line."

With no further warning, she lay upon the ground naked and spread her legs and pushed and pushed until a hideously mutated child emerged and lay shrieking upon the floor.

And that, my friends, was my long-ago tenth great-grandfather.

I expect you're wondering what happened to them all. The mutant son was large of head and shriveled of feet and completely blind. The faery hag disappeared as soon as she had birthed him, and the king called for his retainers to collect the mutant son and abandon him in the woods. He demanded that Oswald explain what the faery hag had meant, but Oswald denied any knowledge of the faery hag and had, indeed, found the bound princess by this time and threatened her with violence unless she denied it too. So the king believed that it was nothing but a mischievous faery tale, and allowed Oswald to stay in the castle.

Within a few months, it became clear that the prophecy had not come true, and that Konstanz was not pregnant with a son and heir. The king cursed and swore, demanding to know if the young people had lain together on their wedding night. They had, they said, and every night since, but still no child was forthcoming. The king, who was very sick and in pain and just wanted to die, knew he would have no relief until an heir was born.

Meanwhile, in the forest, the mutant son lay puking and mewling for a day before Diebolt found him and took pity on him, and decided to raise him as his own dear son. He carried the child back to the dwarf's cottage, but the dwarf was nowhere to be found. Presuming the dwarf wouldn't mind, he set up a little bed for the child and called him Rudolf.

The dwarf never returned, and Diebolt wondered if perhaps he had died. It seemed very sad to him, as the dwarf had treated him more kindly than his brother had. Rudolf grew very fast and was remarkably developed, and although he could not see, he could speak before he was a week old, and walk within a month, and was the size of a full-grown child within a year.

On his first birthday, Rudolf asked Diebolt if he could have a special present.

"What is it, my child?" Diebolt replied.

"I would like to visit the castle and meet the king."

And because it was the only thing Rudolf had ever asked for, Diebolt agreed that he would take him to the castle and ask to meet the king.

They walked all day to the castle and when they finally arrived a guard at the gate stopped them and tried to turn them back.

"No, you can't come in and see the king," he said. "Nobody sees the king except his daughter."

"Then let his daughter come down and we shall ask her," Diebolt said, determined to grant Rudolf's wish.

Princess Konstanz came down to greet them. Diebolt had never seen anyone so beautiful, but he didn't know that her beauty had been marred by the previous terrible twelve months, stuck in a marriage with a man who was cruel and whom she didn't love, worried about the awful pain her father was in, and trying over and over to conceive a child who would not come. But when she saw Diebolt's face, she felt kindly toward him.

"My lady," he said, "my son's dearest wish on his birthday is to meet the king."

Princess Konstanz took one look at the poor blind, deformed creature and agreed. "Of course. Come in, I will take you to his chamber myself."

"I have a story to tell the king," Rudolf said, excitedly dancing about next to Diebolt as Konstanz led the way to the king's chamber.

"I'm sure he will delight to hear it," Konstanz replied. A

few minutes later, they were standing within the king's chamber.

"Father, a blind boy wants to meet you."

The king sat up. He was very weak and gray, and in great pain. He didn't recognize the child, of course, as it had been a newborn babe just a year ago when he last saw it.

"What is your name, child?" the king asked.

"Rudolf," the child answered, "and I have a story to tell you."

"Go ahead, Rudolf," the king said.

Rudolf opened his mouth and told him the whole story about Oswald and Diebolt and the ugly little dwarf. The king listened in stunned silence, but Konstanz sobbed all the way through. Then the king turned to Diebolt and said, "Is this true?"

Diebolt replied, "Yes, it is, but you must believe me when I tell you that I did not put the child up to this. I have been happy with my lot in life."

The king ordered that Oswald be brought in for questioning, and he denied everything.

"Show me the wishing jewel," the king demanded.

Oswald handed it over, giving Diebolt a black look. The king examined the jewel closely. "How am I to tell," he asked, "who is your rightful owner?"

At that instant, the dwarf appeared out of nowhere. "I am the rightful owner of the jewel, your Majesty," he said, "but as to the story you have heard here today, every word of what the blind child said is true."

So the king immediately ordered Oswald's marriage to Konstanz invalid and offered her instead to Diebolt. They conceived that night an heir to the throne and the king now knew he could die a happy man. The king ordered that Rudolf be made a knight of the realm, and he was also given a huge area of land on which was bestowed many gifts from the faeries who pitied his deformities: diamond mines and hot springs and magnificent manors, all of which were the basis of my family fortune. Rudolf then lived happily to an old age and had a son with his beautiful wife. We are an unbroken line of only sons.

As for Oswald, well, the king was angry and vengeful over his deception and planned a fine punishment for him. An iron mask in the shape of a donkey's head was cast and bolted over his head. Then his head was forced inside the royal oven that was used to roast pigs and sheep. The oven was lit, and his head was cooked while he was still alive. Only, I assure you, he did not remain alive for long.

And so ends the tale. Not a particularly happy ending, for despite the great fortune that I still enjoy, it seems to me that I have been deprived of something the value of which I can only imagine. Color. I admire form and shape so much, color would have been among my favorite things in the world. Instead, I have only shades of gray.

It is surely not too much to ask for a little pleasure in its place, even if that pleasure might seem cruel.

❧

Somehow, they'd all ended up in a punk club in Prenzlauer Berg, very, very drunk for this early in the evening. It hadn't looked like a punk club when they'd followed the HALF-PRICE SPIRITS sign that afternoon, but now a very loud band was playing songs to a crowd of mohawks, chains, and dirty tartan.

"Look at these kids," Gerda shouted over the music. "I feel old."

"I feel older," Fabiyan replied.

"Pete seems to be enjoying himself," Christine said, indicating in front of the stage where Pete jiggled furiously to the music.

"Is someone keeping an eye on the time?" Gerda asked.

Christine checked her watch. "We've got an hour." They had organized to meet Mandy for a late dinner nearby. Christine was apprehensive. Every time she had seen Mandy lately he seemed jangled and desperate, and always wanted to bring the conversation back to Mayfridh.

Jude returned from the bar and distributed drinks. "Apparently there's going to be twelve bands on tonight," he said. "I don't like our chances of getting Pete out of here."

"He'll wear himself out shortly," Gerda said. She turned to Fabiyan and asked for a cigarette, and for a few moments the two of them were lost in a conversation that Christine couldn't hear.

Christine leaned her head on Jude's shoulder and sipped her drink. It was vodka number six and, as always with spirits, the drunkenness was creeping up on her slowly but comprehensively.

Jude touched her hair. "You okay, babe?" he said, close to her ear.

"I'm drunk."

"Me too."

"It's weird without Mayfridh here. I miss her."

Jude didn't answer. She sat up straight and looked at him. He was lighting a cigarette. "Do you miss her?"

He shrugged. "Not really."

"Did you like her?"

He shrugged again. "Why do you ask?"

"Sometimes I'm worried about her. You know, she disappeared so suddenly."

"She probably had her reasons."

"But what if something bad has happened to her?"

"She strikes me as the sort of woman who can look after herself. It's not as though she was the smartest or most rational person we ever met, Christine. She probably broke a fingernail and was so distraught that she had to go home to that wolf guy."

"Eisengrimm. He's not a guy, he's just a wolf."

"Whatever," he said, dragging deeply on his cigarette.

"You make it sound like he's a werewolf or something."

"Again, Christine, whatever," he said, his voice rising almost imperceptibly, his hands moving emphatically. "None of it matters anymore because she's gone and it's all over."

But it wasn't all over, because Christine still had the ball of twine and winter wasn't here yet.

As though reading her mind, Jude held up a cautionary finger. "I really don't want you going there."

"I know, I know." Maybe if she just disappeared to Ewigkreis for an hour or so, just to check if Mayfridh was there and well and happy. Otherwise, how would Christine ever know if her friend had got back safely, and hadn't just fallen prey to some accident here in the Real World?

"I mean it, Christine. I don't want to lose you."

"I heard you the first time," she mumbled, turning her shoulder to him.

His arms enclosed her waist. "Don't be angry with me," he said softly in her ear.

"Jude . . ."

He turned her to face him and kissed her deeply. His mouth tasted of rum and warm tobacco. God, she loved him so much.

"Come on," he said, "cheer up. We've got to put on our happy faces for dinner with Mandy."

She drained her drink. "I'll need more vodka before then."

❦

Christine ended up so drunk that she became paranoid about crossing the road. She checked and checked and checked that there were no cars coming, afraid to trust her eyes, while the others gestured and ridiculed her from the other side of the street.

"Come on!" Gerda called. "We'll be waiting all night."

This was the fourth intersection she had held them up on. Jude dashed back across the road, put his hands over her eyes, and walked her across briskly.

"Don't, Jude," she said, trying to struggle free. "You're drunk."

"I'm drunk. You're drunk. We're all drunk."

"But what if you misjudge the distance?"

"We're here now."

He uncovered her eyes and they were safely on the pavement. Spirits-drunk. It messed with her head every time. The world seemed to tilt beneath her. "How far?" she asked.

"Just there," Gerda replied, pointing out a bustling Indian restaurant ahead of them. Some diners were braving the autumn chill at the outside tables. The inside was cavernous and smelled of rich spices. In the very farthest back corner, Mandy sat at a table set for six, alone, checking his watch.

"Are we late?" Jude whispered guiltily.

"Twenty minutes," Gerda replied.

In those few moments before Mandy spotted them, Christine felt a stab of pity for him. Sitting lonely in the restaurant, waiting, watching the time, while they were all getting drunk and laughing at him. But then he saw them and stood, and smiled with his tiny teeth, and that ineffable loathsomeness of his pushed pity out of the way.

"Good evening, all," he said.

"Sorry we're late," Gerda replied, taking the seat at the farthest end of the table.

Christine didn't get to a seat fast enough, and found herself sitting next to Mandy. In her drunken state, the ginger hair sprouting from his pallid knuckles became nightmarish. She couldn't stop staring at it.

"Are you well, Christine?" he asked, leaning close.

She jerked her head up. His eyebrows were the same color as the hair on his hands, a terrible mismatch with his dyed and greasy black hair. "I, ah . . . yeah. Yeah, thanks, I'm well."

"Heard anything from Miranda yet?"

"No." She shook her head, then wished she hadn't because the room kept moving after she stopped.

"If you do hear anything let me know," he said, averting his eyes. Was he embarrassed? "I'd like to know how she is."

"Yeah, sure," Christine muttered. "Who do you have to bribe to get a beer around here?"

Mandy kept her close at the crook of his elbow all night, leaning toward her, including her in his asides from the main conversation. Jude sat diagonally opposite, conversing inaudibly with Gerda and Fabiyan, leaving Pete—drunken and full of useless statistics—to assist her with Mandy. A combination of inebriation and eating too much of the most astonishing butter chicken she had ever tasted had left Christine heavy-stomached and queasy, and the beer she was throwing on top of it wasn't helping.

"So you see," Pete was saying as the plates were cleared, "Berlin is one of the safest cities in the world. You want murder, you go to New Orleans."

"Fascinating, Peter," Mandy said, leaning back to let the waiter clear his plate. "How do you remember all these things?"

"There's nothing else in his head to get in the way!" Gerda shouted from the other end of the table. Everyone laughed.

Pete smiled, proud of himself. "I have a photographic memory for numbers. If I see it once, I remember it forever."

"Are you good at math?" Jude asked.

"Yes, I was declared a mathematical genius at age nine," Pete said. "My mum still has the photo of me from the newspaper. She keeps a scrapbook."

For some reason, Christine felt stupidly defensive of Jude, who hadn't finished high school. "But genius is about more than remembering facts and figures and regurgitating them later, right?" she said.

It seemed everybody turned to look at her, and all those eyeballs focused on her face made her feel vulnerable and giddy.

"Of course," Pete conceded quickly.

"So, you can tell us how many murders have been committed in any city in the world," Gerda said, "but you can't tell us why they were committed."

"Not at all. I have no ability to understand something that far out of my personal experience." Pete shook his head. "Just before I left Australia, a guy I went to primary school with was charged with murdering his girlfriend. I couldn't believe it. Nothing about him as a child indicated that that's where he would end up."

"So," Gerda said, "how does a person get to that point, where suddenly taking another life becomes a reasonable option?"

Mandy sputtered to life beside Christine. "Perhaps you don't understand because you have never hated somebody deeply enough to want them dead."

Attention turned to Mandy.

"I mean . . ." he said, his voice taking a smoother tone, "that murderers may not see murder as a reasonable option so much as the *only* option."

"Well, I still don't get it," Pete said, and then promptly changed the topic. "Hey, are any of you guys interested in going back to that punk bar?"

They teased him and argued over the rest of the evening's entertainment, but Christine's eyes were drawn back to Mandy's pale, small hands, grasping the water glass in front of him. No mistaking it, his fingers were shaking. Talking about murder had agitated him for some reason and, drunk and paranoid as she was, that agitation unsettled her profoundly.

CHAPTER SIXTEEN

*M*orning had nearly broken on the third day of the search for Hexebart. Mayfridh knew that they wouldn't find her in time for the parade. Only a few hours remained until she had to descend the slope; the horses and open carriage were being dressed. Hexebart was nowhere to be found.

Mayfridh sank to the ground beneath a tree. In the distance Eisengrimm and three of the royal guards combed the Eternal Woods, though their stealth meant she couldn't hear them. She looked up through the half-bare branches. The sky was pale yellow, the shadows deep around her as dawn gathered itself out of the ashes of sunset. She missed night, its long soft darkness and secrets, but at the Winter Castle she would soon grow sick of it and start longing for the fresh sunshine of spring.

The future, stretching out empty before her. What would Jude be doing while she was at the Winter Castle? At the Spring and Summer Palaces? She would have no concept of their parallel lives, he would be entirely forgotten. Perhaps, one morning when she painted on her Real World eyeliner, she might feel a twinge of memory: *Why is there a trace of excitement attached to this object?* But soon after it would be gone, and the things she'd brought back with her would feel as though they had always been with her; eternal, natural, ordinary.

Surely it was impossible that her soul could really forget his. Surely they were connected always, far beneath the swirl and tide of memory and forgetfulness. Would she continue to ache, deep and low under her ribs, without even knowing what she was aching for? A gust of wind rushed overhead, sending a shower of leaves rattling down on her. A dry leaf tip grazed her cheek and she closed her eyes and thought of Jude, of the feel of his hot breath through her clothes and the unutterable melancholy of his admission that he was lonely, that he was sad. And she believed she would understand it all if she captured Hexebart and pried Jude's secret from her.

A rustle nearby made her sit up and open her eyes. Too large to be a squirrel, too nimble to be a man. "Eisengrimm?"

"There you are," he said, emerging from the bushes and approaching her.

"Have you found her?" she asked glumly.

"Three men are still looking for her, but you and I must return to the castle to prepare for the parade."

She covered her eyes with her hands. "Oh no, the parade. I won't have enough blessing spells. Everybody will hate me."

"Nobody will hate you."

She dropped her hands and met his gaze. "Eisengrimm, some days I don't want to be queen. Some days I can't stand the official duties, and the clothes, and the blessings. I just want to be a Real World woman with a job in a department store and friends over on the weekend and a man to love."

Eisengrimm settled on his back legs next to her. "Jude?"

"Yes," she sighed, "Jude. For my entire life, Eisengrimm, I've been able to get whatever I want. But now, the thing I want most in the world I can't have."

"That's because he's not a thing, he's a person. You can't make somebody love you."

"He does love me."

Eisengrimm remained diplomatically silent. The first rays of sunshine broke over the tops of the trees, tracing the leaves with glittering gold.

"The sun," she said.

"The parade," he replied.

Her hands were cold. "I'd like to stay here. Just here."

"Come, Little May. Time to be a queen."

❧

Halfway down the slope on her decorated carriage, Eisengrimm as Crow perched on her shoulder, Mayfridh could hear the noise of the crowd in the village below. The autumn festival had begun at dawn. The town well had been decorated with vines, and music and noisy drinking took place in the street. Now the royal procession descended from the hill. Mayfridh wore her finest bronze and gold gown, her crimson hair pinned under a golden scarf. Before her, five black horses trod proudly; behind her, the royal guard marched. The sight of hundreds of villagers mingling in the street made her catch her breath with fear.

"Eisengrimm, they are so many. I haven't enough blessings." She patted her woven bag, woefully thin under her fingers.

"It matters not if we run out of blessings," he said close to her ear. "It only matters if they know that Hexebart has escaped. Just tell them you will return to see them individually with blessings in the next few days."

Mayfridh recoiled. "Visit the villagers individually? In their homes?"

"Little May, you are not in a position to be intolerant. Once we find Hexebart, we will get more spells and we will deliver them as we must."

Mayfridh fell silent. The crowd below roared with laughter and shouts of joy. Music floated up on the breeze. A group of villagers had seen her and started to chant her name.

"Mayfridh! Mayfridh!"

Eisengrimm took to his wings and sailed down amongst them, urging them left and right and left, clearing a path for the royal carriage. The music grew louder and some folk had started singing. Most of them were already drunk. The Queen began to wave, mustering her most dazzling smile. The crowd cheered. Moments later, she was among them.

"Your Majesty! Your Majesty!" they called, individually trying to catch her attention.

"A blessing for my home, Queen Mayfridh!" Crowding in on the left.

"A blessing for the harvest, Queen Mayfridh!" Pushing on the right.

"A blessing for my sick mother, Queen Mayfridh!" All around her, pressing in on the carriage, supplicating faces and hands outstretched. Isolating anxiety and dread loneliness: they all wanted something from her, and cared nothing for her own wants. She reached into the bag and produced a spell.

"A blessing for you!" she called, blowing on the golden ball and watching it float and disappear like a bubble over a farmer's head.

"Thank you, my Queen, thank you!"

Young girls were showering her with colored leaves, collected at the turn of the season, red and gold and russet brown.

"Queen Mayfridh," one of them called, "the leaves!"

Mayfridh gritted her teeth. It would waste a spell, but the young ones expected it. She threw a spell in the air, it exploded overhead, and suddenly the leaves cast above her turned to glittering foil, dazzling down on her in the slanted sun. A cheer arose from the crowd. They pressed in on her, demanding their blessings, as Eisengrimm ducked and glided overhead. A tall, lean man thrust his pregnant wife in front of him. "A blessing for our unborn child!" he called. She obliged. Others joined the chorus. She reached into the bag over and over, fingers finally closing on the last spell.

"Here!" she cried, flinging it into the crowd. A well-being spell, to relax everyone there. She ordered the carriage to stop, and stood, shaking the colored foil leaves from her clothes.

"I shall return and call upon you individually within a week," she announced, "to hear your cases and give out the blessings you need."

The villagers applauded, a small child called out, "All love to you, Queen Mayfridh." For a moment, smiling in the sunshine, Mayfridh believed all would be well. Then an unshaven, crook-eyed man stepped in front of the carriage, his arm tight around a white-haired, gray-faced woman.

"A blessing for my mother, Queen Mayfridh," he said, a cruel smirk on his face. "She is very ill."

Mayfridh's smile froze on her face. "I have said I will return to you personally, perhaps even tomorrow."

"She may not live until tomorrow," he said.

Mayfridh glanced at the old woman. She looked ill, but not near death. In fact, she shared the gleam in her son's eye. What was this about?

"I'm sorry," Mayfridh said. Eisengrimm came to rest on her shoulder. "I have no more blessings today, but tomorrow—"

"Then go to Hexebart tonight. Go to her now. We shall wait for you."

The crowd had grown silent around him. One person murmured, "Leave her be. She'll do as she pleases."

"I do not wish to return to Hexebart today," she said, gathering her queenly demeanor, "and I am not in the habit of taking orders from villagers. Your mother will be well until tomorrow. Now step aside so my carriage may pass."

"Is it true, my Queen," the crook-eyed man said, not yielding his position, "that Hexebart has been accidentally set free?"

A collective gasp moved through the crowd. Mayfridh felt Eisengrimm's claws tighten on her shoulder. One of the royal guards moved forward and accosted the man, forcing him off the path. But it was too late, the question had been asked.

"Is it true?" another man called, anxiety keen in his voice. "Is the royal magic no longer under your control?"

"Tell them," Eisengrimm whispered in her ear, "only make it sound as though you are not concerned."

"There is some truth in that rumor," Mayfridh said, hoping her voice wasn't shaking as much as her knees were. "Hexebart has escaped, but we expect to find her before the end of the day and then the royal magic will—"

"The magic is gone?" a panicked voice cried.

"We won't have blessings for the season!"

"Will we be safe to move to the Winter Castle?"

"How can this have happened?"

Such a hubbub of angry and anxious voices ensued that Mayfridh had to press her hands over her ears. Eisengrimm hopped from her shoulder, transforming to Wolf and coming to land near her feet.

"Hear me!" he cried. Then when the noise continued, "Hear me! Hear me, all of you!"

The crowd quietened.

"Hexebart is not lost," he said, his rich voice ringing clearly on the crisp air. "We know where she is and we are simply waiting for the right moment to apprehend her. She will be back safely in our custody before the sun rises again. I promise you."

Disapproving murmurs circulated.

"Now we return to the castle. You will hear from us, within days, with your blessings. Do not concern yourselves. Your queen is good and your queen is wise. She will not disappoint you." With that, Eisengrimm gave the order for the carriage to turn, and moments later it was rattling back up the slope to the castle. The crowd dispersed with angry whispers and pale faces.

"What shall we do?" Mayfridh sobbed. "You have made them a promise we may not be able to keep."

"We shall keep it," Eisengrimm said through gritted teeth. "I shall make sure of it."

"How? We've already searched for her for days."

"I do not trust the royal guard to find her. They are not keen enough hunters. They make too much noise and they cannot follow a scent. I can be a fox, the stealthiest of hunters. I will go out there by myself."

"But how will you capture her? She's strong and unpredictable. You need their help."

"I need not remain a fox, Mayfridh." Eisengrimm glanced away, his yellow eyes narrowing against the light. "I've not yet met a witch who is any match for a bear."

Hexebart is snakes-in-the-blood angry. These hands are still twisted and tied and ouch! she saws and saws at the edge of the broken tree, and the ropes hold fast. Nasty little dog! He knew how clever Hexebart was, and he had them tied and tied and tied again.

One part of the rope breaks, another knot holds it firm. Hexebart is hungry—she eats leaves and drinks dewdrops, but Hexebart wants to taste that Real World food that is hot and saucy and salty and goes on a plate. Her guts squeeze tight just thinking of it. She saws her ropes on the tree trunk again.

> *Back and forth, back and forth,*
> *To the south and to the north,*
> *Forth and back, forth and back,*
> *Drown old dog's breath in a sack.*

Hexebart won't give up. They'll never find her. She can hear them stomping past like elephants, thinking that they're quiet. Thud, thud, stomp, stomp, shhhh. It will take a wilier hunter than that to catch Hexebart. She's had enough of Ewigkreis.

It was once so different and Hexebart sighs. Once, she loved Queen Liesebet who was soft and pale and pretty, and how she misses Queen Liesebet! Hexebart begged Queen Liesebet not to take the little changeling redhead. Hexebart even offered Queen Liesebet her own daughter. But Queen Liesebet wanted a pretty child; that was all she cared about. How Hexebart wishes Queen Liesebet was still here. Then Hexebart would be living in a warm chamber and eating red soup and bread with butter, and not freezing outside in a tree trunk with her hands twisty-tied. How Hexebart hates the little princess for disposing of her parents and taking over. And how Hexebart hates hates hates that nobody else suspects Mayfridh of anything wicked.

It's not fair. Hexebart saws at the ropes again. Something gives, but another knot holds her. Not fair, not fair, not fair. Hexebart despairs, Hexebart is very, very hungry.

Mayfridh and Eisengrimm waited until the afternoon drew long and shadowy before approaching the Eternal Woods alone.

"You should return to the castle," Eisengrimm said as Mayfridh sat herself against a tree.

"I want to be here for you. You'll be in pain." When Eisengrimm changed to Bear the pressure on his joints and organs would bruise him for weeks. "Besides, I want to see Hexebart dragged out of the wood by a bear, with my own eyes."

"You must be silent."

"I won't move a hair. I'll breathe like a mouse."

"She'll hear a mouse. Breathe quieter than a mouse."

"I have magic left in my hands. I'll work a silent glamour."

"Good. Good." His wolf eyes flicked right and left. He was nervous. "Now, I haven't changed to Bear for many years. I'll take a moment here, where I'm safe, to practice."

"Go on." Mayfridh smoothed her blue skirt—one of her Real World favorites—over her knees and tucked her feet beneath her.

Eisengrimm took a breath, then pushed up on to his hind legs. With an awful creaking noise, like the sound of joints under strain, his gray fur shimmered brown and his body began to grow. In an eye blink, a large bear stood before her. Eisengrimm let out a sigh of pain.

"Dear friend," Mayfridh said, climbing to her feet, "does it hurt terribly?"

He came down on all fours and grunted. "Yes, but I can endure it for long enough to catch the witch."

"Stand again, Eisengrimm," she said, gazing with wonder at his new shape.

He reared on his back legs again, balanced steadily.

She spread her arms. "In this shape I can hold you, almost as if you were a man," she said, moving to embrace him.

"Don't, Mayfridh," he said.

"Surely it won't hurt to hug you," she insisted, sliding her arms around his middle. "Go on, you can hold me too."

A reluctant pair of Bear arms encircled her waist. She snuggled against his warm, large chest. Twilight shadows moved over them in the breeze and a dim ray of sunshine glinted on his fur. She breathed in deep and sighed. For the first time in years, she felt she had found safe haven.

"It's wonderful to hold you," she breathed.

He did not reply. The rhythm of the wood around her pulsed in her veins: the creaking of tree branches, the flutter of leaves, the lift and stir of the debris beneath them. His heart beat a steady cadence. She remembered a song from her childhood and hummed a few bars, fitting it to the pulse around her. Eisengrimm's arms tightened, one of his paws pressed into her back. She sang a few lines out loud, then laughed.

"Come, Eisengrimm," she said, stepping back and taking his Bear paws in her hands. "Let us dance."

He tore his paws away and returned to the ground, shaking off Bear and shrinking down to Fox. "I haven't time, Mayfridh," he said gruffly.

Mayfridh pouted, but didn't protest. Perhaps the pain had made him irritable. "Very well," she said, resuming her position under the tree. "I shall wait here for you, as silent as magic can make me, and relish seeing you drag the hag screaming from the wood."

"I won't fail you," he said. Was that a catch in his voice? Eisengrimm was very moody this afternoon.

"I don't doubt you, old friend," she said.

He slunk off into the woods and disappeared from sight.

She listened hard, but he was perfectly silent. With the magic left in her hands, she worked a silent glamour, so that none of her movements would cause the tiniest noise for Hexebart to hear. She leaned her head against the tree and waited.

Mayfridh wondered what Jude was doing at this moment. And Christine too. And Diana. The Real World continued without her. Did they think about her at all?

She sighed, but the silent glamour ensured that no sound emerged. Of course they thought about her. Jude was in love with her, she knew that. Diana would be grieving, having lost her again. Christine would be worried. . . . But then, if she was worried, why not come through to Ewigkreis to check on her? Mayfridh suspected that Christine was frightened to do so.

Perhaps it was better if Mayfridh didn't see Christine again. She felt tears prick at her eyes. To lose such a dear friend twice was careless. But how could Mayfridh look at Christine knowing that Jude's heart was errant? Mayfridh closed her eyes. *Come, winter. Come, forgetfulness.* Life would be bearable and sane again, soon. All of these people would slip from her mind, and things would be as they always had been, and Mayfridh would be oblivious to the emptiness that created inside her.

A shriek, deep in the woods. Mayfridh sat up with a start, her eyes flying open. Was it Hexebart? Had he found her already?

Far away, coming back to her on the breeze, she heard a stream of broken abuse. "Dog-chops . . . boil you alive . . . Princess Putrid . . ." Oh yes, he had caught Hexebart.

Mayfridh stood, heart thumping. Not simply because Hexebart had been caught and the royal magic was safe, but because once that dungeon door shut behind her, Hexebart had to tell.

Thumping and crashing through the woods they came, closer and closer, until Eisengrimm emerged, his Bear arms clamped around Hexebart, who hung upside down and wriggled and squirmed and shrieked.

"Let me go, pig's breath," she screamed, her white hair flying as she struggled against him. Then when she saw Mayfridh waiting, she began to spit and curse all the more, her face turning deep red. "Changeling! Cuckoo! Nothing but a turd with a crown."

"Well done, Eisengrimm," Mayfridh said.

"Let us get her to the dungeon quickly," Eisengrimm replied. His voice was strained, betraying the effort of maintaining Bear so long.

"Gladly." Mayfridh hurried along behind him as he loped unevenly through trees, skirting the village. He leaned left, then right, clutching Hexebart soundly around the thighs. Hexebart screamed and cried the whole way, but ran out of steam as they approached the slope to the castle. Mayfridh knew Eisengrimm must be growing tired and sore, but he kept his steps quick, bringing Hexebart to the dungeon only ten minutes after dragging her out of the forest.

"There," he cried, throwing Hexebart to the floor and slamming the door behind her. Mayfridh pressed in with the key, only breathing freely when she heard the lock clunk into place. When she turned around, Eisengrimm huddled, a fox, against the wall behind her.

"Eisengrimm?"

"I'm so very sore, Mayfridh." He hunched his shoulders up and shivered.

Mayfridh's heart clutched. "Come, you poor fellow. I'll take you to my bedroom and feed you treats until you feel better." She glanced over her shoulder at Hexebart, whose dark eyes gleamed deep in the dungeon. The witch was under oath; Mayfridh could ask her right this instant for

Jude's secret and she had to give it. Yet how could she when Eisengrimm was so ill and needed her attention?

And how could she when Eisengrimm was well again? After this last disaster, he would never leave her alone with Hexebart again.

Something soft brushed against her ankle. She looked down. Eisengrimm sat on the edge of her foot.

"I've got you," she said, scooping him up in her arms.

He winced. "Mayfridh, be—"

"I'll be gentle."

She cradled him carefully against her chest and left Hexebart behind.

"Will you be back?" Hexebart called. "I have something to tell you."

Mayfridh steeled herself and didn't answer. In a few days, Eisengrimm would be feeling better. He would be well enough to make a trip to the Real World for her, long enough to check on those she had left behind.

Long enough to leave her a few hours alone with Hexebart.

⌁

Work had been hellishly busy, the train hellishly crowded, and Christine ached all over by the time she turned into Vogelwald-Allee. She hoped that Jude hadn't drunk all the beer in the house already. He was struggling with some immense creative issue that she knew she couldn't hope to understand. He spent hours in his studio painting savage slashes of dark color as though he hoped to damage the canvas with them, as though art were physical instead of mental. Four afternoons in a row he had been back upstairs by four, drinking and chain-smoking and clicking his tongue and tapping his fingers. She hadn't probed him. He went through this periodically, and preferred it if she let him sink into it for a few weeks. He always resurfaced eventually.

Christine had her keys in her hand, ready to try the lock, when a flash of red caught the corner of her eye. She glanced to her right. Something moved among the long grass growing around the storm drain. A dog or a cat or . . .

A small fox-shaped head peered out.

"Eisengrimm?"

He ducked into cover again. She hurried over. It must be Eisengrimm; surely foxes weren't running loose in the city. She crouched next to the gutter inlet and looked inside.

"Eisengrimm, is that you? Come out."

He slunk forward. "Hello, Christine."

"You didn't come all the way down from the Tiergarten like that?"

"I flew down as Crow. But I'm a bit sore for such a small shape so—"

"Sore? Here, follow me into the trees." She indicated the overgrown parkland that tangled around the end of the street.

"Can you carry me?"

Christine was surprised, but picked Eisengrimm up without questioning him. She carried him several yards into the trees and placed him carefully in the grass, sitting cross-legged next to him. He winced as he sat.

"You're in pain."

"I became a bear not two days past. It bruises every inch of me."

"Then why are you here?"

"Mayfridh sent me."

"Even though you're in pain?"

"She insisted. She's worried about you."

"More than she's worried about you?"

Eisengrimm sighed and leaned his snout on his paws. "I don't mind. She was very agitated."

"Is there anything I can do for you?"

"No. Only time can help. I'll be fine in a week or so."

She stroked his nose gently. "I'm glad Mayfridh's been worried about me. I've been worried about her."

"She wanted me to let you know she's well. She wanted to know if you were also well."

"I'm fine. Why did she go so suddenly?"

"Urgent matters at home."

"Really? None of us said or did anything to offend her or upset her? Or frighten her?" She was thinking about Mandy now; Mandy with his strange habits and locked attic.

"No, no. She is the queen, and she has duties."

"I get it. I'm glad she's okay."

"She wanted me to ask, too, about her other friends."

"They're all fine."

"And Jude?"

"He's okay, but he's having some artistic dilemma. Keeps muttering about how nobody understands him." She laughed. "He's like a teenager sometimes."

"And her mother?"

"Diana's frantic, but I can phone her and tell her that Mayfridh's okay. Is she coming back?"

"I don't know," he said. "She hasn't decided. Are you coming back to Ewigkreis?"

Christine glanced into the trees. She could hear a train speed past in the distance. "I don't know either."

"She would love to see you again. Before . . ."

"Before winter? Before she forgets about me forever?"

"Yes."

"I'd like to see her too." She met Eisengrimm's eyes again. "Will you forget me too?"

"Yes, I'm afraid so."

Christine shrugged. "I won't disappear, you know. Just because you don't remember me doesn't mean I won't be here living my life." She knew that Eisengrimm already understood that, but some nameless fear made her say it anyway, as though saying it made her more concrete, less likely to disappear into a crack.

Eisengrimm didn't answer. He stood and gingerly shook himself. "I must return. I've grown very tired."

"Tell her I miss her."

"I will."

"And I miss you too," she said, rubbing his ears. She uncrossed her legs and stood.

Eisengrimm transformed to Crow, and fluttered up to perch on her shoulder. She made her way out of the park and back onto the street.

"I hope you're feeling better quickly," she said, gently touching his feathered chest.

"Come and see us again, soon," he said. "Mayfridh would love you to visit."

"It's safe?"

"Perfectly. For at least a few more weeks."

"I'll think about it, then."

He spread his wings and took to the sky. She watched him wheel above her, then disappear from sight. When she turned her attention back to the hotel, she saw Mandy standing on the front step staring at her.

"Hi, Mandy," she said, trying to sound casual. Had he seen her talking to the crow?

"Good afternoon, Christine." He hurried inside without another word, and Christine felt her ribs contract. He seemed agitated, but then, he was often agitated. Usually more talkative, always wanting to chat with her about her day, about whether or not "Miranda" was coming back.

She glanced up at the sky again, but Eisengrimm was

long gone. Hopefully he was nearly back at the Tiergarten, nearly home where he could rest his aching body. She locked the front door of the building behind her.

Upstairs, she heard Mandy's hasty footsteps and the squeak-thump of his apartment door. Almost as though he were running away.

Hexebart will kill someone. Hexebart will kill them all.

At least her hands are free now. At least she's warm again.

But, oh! the Real World still beckons Hexebart. She smooths the blue fabric between her fingers. A tiny, tiny scrap of Real World from the bottom of Princess Putrid's skirt. Hexebart found it hanging in the doorframe. Hexebart has sharp eyes and never misses a clue.

Hexebart is supposed to be weaving the winter blessings, but takes a moment to enjoy the blue scrap. Pulls a thread, weaves a spell. The ugly changeling bought this in a shop. Bright lights and warm air. Hexebart screws her eyes tight and thinks tight. Hmm. The ugly changeling didn't buy this at all, someone bought it for her. Somebody she loves in the Real World. Think tighter, think tighter.

Her mother!

Hexebart is confused a moment, and tears prick her eyes. Hope swells and falls. But no, not Liesebet. Liesebet is gone. This mother isn't a faery mother, this is a stupid skinny sad human mother. Hexebart flings the spell into a corner of the dungeon. Stupid skinny sad human mother. Liesebet is gone.

If Hexebart ever makes it to the Real World, Hexebart will find this human mother and feed her burning coals. Hexebart will find every one of Mayfridh's human friends and hurt them all.

Hexebart's heart is clutched by sadness. The dungeon is locked up tight; she knows she will never leave.

She weaves more spells, her fingers splitting and bleeding. The changeling princess will come soon to hear the awful secret. Hexebart knows this because she can smell that dog-chops is not at the Autumn Castle. Mayfridh is afraid of the dog's opinion. Ha! Some queen! Hexebart can't understand why the ugly queen cares so much about those Real World people, but Hexebart shines with warm happiness inside that the secret will hurt her. Even if she weren't under magical oath, Hexebart would tell. Hexebart relishes hurting her.

What's that? What's that?

Footsteps, footsteps. Here she comes.

— from the Memoirs of Mandy Z.

My hands are almost shaking too much to write.

Did I really see what I think I saw? Hear what I think I heard?

Imagine if you will, dear reader, the pale sky of twilight, streaked with gray clouds. The outlines of the trees, their few last sad sick leaves clinging in a November breeze. A pale, thin woman of indeterminate attractiveness in a coat and scarf, with a black crow perched on her shoulder.

Then imagine that, made curious by this sight, you shuffle a few paces past your front door to ensure you're really seeing it. A crow? I'd seen Christine Starlight concerning herself with a crow once before, only that time she had been unnerved, complaining of it following her home. Nothing had excited me on that occasion. She had seemed just a girl with a silly neurosis about birds.

But today, as I shuffled a few paces past my front door to ensure I was really seeing it, voices came softly to me on the breeze. One, Christine Starlight. Asking after his health. I had nearly laughed. Christine talking to a crow.

But *then*. Another voice. The crow's voice. "Come and see us again . . . Mayfridh would love you to visit." The rest of the conversation was, for me, inaudible for the rushing of excited blood in my head.

First, crows don't speak. Unless they're animated by some magic. And the only magic I know truly exists is faery magic.

Second, his invitation to visit means one searing, indisputable truth. Christine has a passage. "Come and see us again." Come to faeryland again as you have in the past. It explains the odd faery smell that I thought I had mistakenly detected on her. It also means that she knows precisely where Miranda—or Mayfridh as is her real name—has gone, and that's why she hasn't displayed the slightest furrow of concern in all the long exchanges where I've questioned her.

A passage. I apologize for all the emphasis, but I don't believe I have ever been more excited in my life. Let me spell it out. Faeries in unlimited supply. Faery *bones* in unlimited supply. All waiting for me, unsuspecting, on the other side of the passage.

And then, my heart trembles like the heart of a man who has seen there is only one place in the lifeboat and the rest of the crowds on the *Titanic* block his way. *It might slip beyond my reach.* I need to find Christine's method of passage, and if I can't, then this brilliant imagining will remain forever an imagining. There is no point in searching her apartment. She could be conjuring the passage with a button or a pin, or any number of ordinary-looking objects. Instead, I will follow and watch her closely. Her exchange with the crow leads me to believe she may attempt a passage soon.

Please let it be soon. This ship is sinking.

❧

Mayfridh made her way down the dimly lit corridors of the dungeon. Only two or three lanterns burned between each gate, the flames' reflections sucked up by the black walls. Her heart was a frightened bird. Or an excited bird. Or both. She would soon be alone with Hexebart, and the magical oath would be collected.

She fumbled with the gate; it squeaked open. In the distance, she could hear Hexebart laughing.

"What are you laughing about, hag?" Mayfridh called.

"I know something you don't know," Hexebart replied, her voice faint and far away.

Yes, but not for long. Not for long.

She advanced up through the other gates, watching her step on the sloping, uneven ground. She didn't have much time. Eisengrimm would return soon. He had been in so much pain when she sent him through that she'd almost cried with guilt; but his errand was quick and simple, and when he returned she would be upstairs waiting with soothing balms to rub into his joints and magic spells to ease his pain.

Mayfridh rounded the last bend and stood in front of Hexebart's cell.

"Well, witch," she said, "you are under an oath to tell me Jude's secret."

Hexebart moved close to the bars in the window of the door. "I'll gladly tell," she said, her eyes gleaming dimly in the dark. "Gladly."

Mayfridh's pulse thudded in her ears. She steeled herself in case it was bad news. "Go on then."

"Put your ear close to the bars, my Queen," Hexebart whispered. "Such a secret should only be told in a hush."

Mayfridh warily moved close to the door and leaned her ear against the window. She could feel Hexebart's breath close to her hair. The witch inhaled, and then shrieked loudly, directly into Mayfridh's ear.

Mayfridh jumped back, clapping her hand to the side of her head. Hexebart was cackling and her ear was ringing, and she burned with anger. Before she could protest or lash out, Hexebart said something utterly shocking and Mayfridh was stunned into silence. The words were so astonishing that, for a moment, Mayfridh could barely make sense of them.

"What?" she gasped. "What did you say?"

Hexebart smiled her crooked smile. "You heard me," she said. "Jude killed Christine's parents."

CHAPTER SEVENTEEN

*T*here's someone out front to see you."

Christine looked up. Natalie, the afternoon casual, stood in the door to the storeroom, indicating over her shoulder to the front counter.

"It's not that South African guy again, is it?" Christine asked, placing aside the pile of books on her lap. The one who had first come in back in September and probed her about the car accident. He'd returned today to pick up a book, asking after her. She'd avoided him so far, and now, ten minutes before knock-off time, she had no intention of answering to his ghoulish curiosity. Not today; two bad nights of sleep in a row, a dull throbbing growing sharper by the hour, the growing cold easing wicked fingers into her back. She predicted the blue tablets by the end of the week. Just getting through the day was an ordeal. And the aching had no knock-off time; it would come home with her.

"No, it's a girl. A woman. Really amazing hair."

Christine rose gingerly and a second later spotted her friend browsing between two bookshelves. "Mayfridh!"

Mayfridh turned. Her smile didn't make it all the way to

her eyes. Still, she advanced and held out her arms, enclosed Christine in a hug.

"I was worried about you," Christine said against her hair.

"Me too. About you." Mayfridh stood back.

"What's wrong?"

"Nothing's wrong," Mayfridh said, and this time her smile worked.

"You can't fool me," Christine said. "You look tense." She tilted her head to the side, examining Mayfridh's face. "And kind of pale. Are you sick?"

Mayfridh shook her head and sighed. "A few problems back home with Hexebart, with the villagers. It was hard to get away at all."

"I'm glad you came. Are you staying long?"

"I don't . . . look, I came to speak to you about something. Can we go somewhere?"

Christine glanced around the shop: Tuesday-afternoon quiet. "I'm sure nobody will mind if I leave a little early. Wait here." She went back to the storeroom to explain her early departure to Natalie and to collect her purse and coat. A few moments later, she and Mayfridh were heading up to Zoo Station.

"A bit slower," Christine said, unable to match Mayfridh's agitated pace.

"You're in pain."

Christine waved a dismissive hand. "So what do you need to talk to me about?"

"Eisengrimm said you were concerned about traveling back to our world."

"Well, Jude is concerned more than me. But, yes, when you disappeared so suddenly I thought that winter had already come."

Mayfridh plunged her hands into the pockets of her long

blue coat. "No. In fact, it's still at least a month away. It's been warm; the trees are shedding quite slowly."

"Still, Jude said that—"

"Jude doesn't have to experience your pain," Mayfridh said firmly.

Christine was puzzled. Mayfridh had never said a bad word about Jude before. "No, that's right."

"I didn't mean to be rude," Mayfridh continued. "You have a month left. In that time, you can be without suffering. Then you have the rest of your life to spend with it. Go. Go to Ewigkreis. Enjoy it. Eisengrimm will look after you."

"Eisengrimm? Not you?" They stopped to wait for traffic lights.

Mayfridh smiled, turned her palms up. "I need to see my mother."

"Your mother's been frantic. She'll be glad you're back."

The lights changed and they crossed the road, fought their way through swelling Christmas crowds on Kurfürstendamm.

"So will you go?" Mayfridh asked.

"I'll talk to Jude and—"

Mayfridh was already shaking her head. "No, no, no. He'll talk you out of it again. Trust me on this. Trust me." Mayfridh took her hand. "Go. You must have missed it."

"I—"

"Go now. Look at you . . . you're hobbling like a cripple. You're in terrible pain."

Christine bit her lip. Instant relief; no blue tablets.

"I'll explain to Jude. I'll reassure him." Mayfridh was intense. It was suspicious, but also persuasive.

"Why are you so concerned that I go?" Christine asked.

"Because I care," Mayfridh said simply. "I care a great deal, and genuinely. You still carry the twine around with you?"

Christine patted her purse. "Yeah, it's right here."

"Then what's stopping you?"

Christine took a deep breath. Eisengrimm and the beautiful woods, and that gorgeous, free, floating feeling of being *normal* and *whole*. Oh, she'd missed it, all right. She'd missed it for thirteen years. She shrugged, offered Mayfridh a smile. "Nothing's stopping me, I guess."

❧

Sometimes, since Hexebart had spoken that horrible sentence, Mayfridh had felt like her body might be shaking to pieces. Starting slowly, deep inside, with a shuddering ache of disbelief, then disappointment, then disavowal.

It simply could not be true.

Yet, Hexebart had sworn it under magical oath. Again and again, she had repeated the same sentence. *Jude killed Christine's parents.* How could it be true? How could such a fact exist in the world without angels weeping? If it were true—

It can't be true.

—then why was he with her? How could he pretend in every moment that he had nothing to do with the accident?

Mayfridh still had the key to Gerda's apartment, the key to the front door of the hotel. She let herself in, checked nobody had heard or seen her. No Mandy in the gallery. She crept up the stairs. Only one way existed to know if the awful thing were true: to ask Jude. To hear it directly from his traitorous lips.

She knocked on the door to the apartment. This was the real reason she had urged Christine so strongly to leave for Ewigkreis. The winter blessings had been distributed and a celebration would take place that evening in the village. She had asked Eisengrimm to take Christine down the slope, to fill her full of wine and firelight and dancing, to keep her there as long as he could; long enough to dig for the truth behind those horrible words.

Jude killed Christine's parents.

She raised her hand, ready to knock again. Footsteps inside. Then the door swung inward.

He looked at her, speechless.

"Hello, Jude," she said. "Can I come in?"

"I . . ." He had a towel wrapped around his waist. His hair was damp. "I was in the shower."

"I'll wait for you to finish. I need to speak to you."

His eyes darted about nervously, but he let her in. "Christine will be home any minute," he said.

"No, she's gone to Ewigkreis, she's . . . look, just go and get dressed. It's important that I speak to you."

He narrowed his eyes. "What's this about? Did you tell her to go?"

"Please. Get dressed. I don't want to have this conversation with you in a towel."

He still looked dubious, but backed away toward the bathroom. Mayfridh sat down heavily at the kitchen table, closed her eyes, and saw his torso again. Damp, warm, smooth. Desire lurched through her. He was back a moment later, dressed in jeans and a black T-shirt.

"Okay," Jude said, standing in front of her, arms folded. He looked defiant; like a young boy. "What's all this about?"

Mayfridh swallowed, her mouth dry. There was no other way to ask. "Did you kill Christine's parents?" she managed, her voice squeezed tight and flat.

She saw the blood drain from his face. He was ashen in an instant. His hand reached for the back of a chair, then he fell into it. Thud.

Mayfridh felt a violent trembling in her legs. "Jude?" she

asked. To hear it from Hexebart was one thing; to see him like this was terrifying her.

"Please," he said, his voice little more than a hoarse gasp, "please, don't tell Christine."

❧

Christine had to wait a few minutes for a group of rowdy school children to go by. When their cries died off in the distance, she sank into the shadows of the elm, the ball of twine clutched in her right hand. A shiver. Yes, she was nervous. Understandable, really. For weeks she had stopped herself from performing this act, convinced she would become lost somewhere in the swirl of faerylands forever.

She checked around her once more. She thought she saw a dark shape dive off the path, but when she peered among the trees she could see no other movement. A bird? Or the shadow cast by a shower of leaves, shivering off branches under the persuasion of a cold draft? Thirty seconds, forty . . . no further movement. She was safe.

Christine opened her fingers and released the twine.

❧

The horror subsided, leaving only disbelief. Mayfridh noticed that somehow he was managing to make coffee for them both. How could he make coffee as though today were an ordinary day? But then, she realized, he'd been pretending things were ordinary for a long time now. He had been making coffee for Christine for four years, all the time knowing. All the time remembering.

He came to the sofa and placed the coffee in front of her, sitting opposite. His hand shook. The coffee splashed, made a puddle on the table.

"I'll clean that later," he said, thinking aloud.

She took up her cup to give herself something to do with her hands. "You have to tell me everything," she said.

"I know." He closed his eyes a second. When he opened them, he wouldn't meet her gaze. "You must be thinking . . . I mean, I know what you're thinking, but whatever your opinion of me is right now, it can never be as low as my opinion of myself. Never."

"Just explain it to me from the beginning," Mayfridh said, growing impatient.

He sighed. "So simple and yet so complicated," he said. "It started when I was born, I guess. I was christened Julian Brown. My father left, my mother died, I was raised by an uncle who drank and didn't care about me. I was always in trouble. I stole things, I wrecked things, I got into fights, I flunked every year of school. I ran away from him at twelve, lived in eight different foster homes, squatted in old warehouses, spent four months living in a sleeping bag under a bridge in California. . . . This isn't to make you feel sorry for me."

"Go on." She did feel sorry for him.

"Okay, fast-forward to November 1989. I'm fifteen. I steal a car. I drive it all the way across country to New York. I'm planning to sell it, right? To get some money to set me up in a new city. I'm driving it through a tunnel when I lose concentration for a second and—BANG! I hit someone. I stop. I look in the rearview mirror. The car behind me is a total mess, mashed against the wall. I freak out. I drive away." He dropped his head. His fingers were spread out over his knees. "I drove away."

"That was the accident that . . . ?"

He nodded. "If it had been anyone else in that car, maybe they wouldn't have found me. But it was Alfa and Finn Starlight. Everyone wanted blood. They traced the wreck of the car that I'd sold for parts, hunted me down. Found a scared kid, someone they couldn't even name in the press. I went to juvenile detention, was released two years later."

Mayfridh didn't know what to say, so said nothing. She placed her coffee cup on the table, waited for him to continue.

Jude lifted his head and met her gaze with an attempt at a smile. "I knew by this time what a bad person I was. So I changed everything. I changed my name, I changed my focus, I started to paint. Life improved, gradually."

"And you met Christine."

"Yes, I met Christine."

"It's incredible. A coincidence that you should meet."

He pressed his lips together a moment, thinking. Then said, "It wasn't a coincidence."

"What do you mean?"

"One of the gossip columns did an article on her. You know, 'Reclusive daughter of seventies pop stars lives tragic, empty life' . . . something like that. I became obsessed with it; so guilty. I knew she was lonely, I knew she was in pain, and I knew it was my fault."

Mayfridh realized she was holding her breath. The first horrible truth had at least been an accident, a careless moment in a wild youth. But what was Jude confessing to now? "You mean, you found her on purpose?"

"Yes."

"Why?"

"So she wouldn't be lonely anymore."

"And then you fell in love with her? Right?"

Silence.

"Jude?"

"No," he said.

"You don't love Christine?"

He squeezed his eyes shut, as though trying to block out a harsh light. "It's hard to explain," he said.

"You've started now. You have to finish."

He opened his eyes again. "Yes, I feel love for Christine. She's great: kind, generous, unassuming. No, I never fell in love with her. I'm responsible for her; I care very much what happens to her; I don't want her to suffer another instant in her life. I want her happiness above all things."

"But it's all because . . . ?"

"Of my guilt," he confirmed. "I've never been in love with her."

Mayfridh sank back on the sofa, bewildering emotions tumbling inside her. The deception was immense, even cruel, but she sensed no cruel intent behind it. Looking at him now, she still saw only beautiful Jude, perhaps even more beautiful now he had revealed how troubled and conflicted he was.

"I've tried," he said quietly. "I've tried to be in love with her."

"Four years."

"I haven't been counting. I'm determined to do this for the rest of my life. To atone. I've done it for reasons that are pure and true. I never want to hurt her again. I've been faithful. I haven't even looked at another woman." His eyes dropped, embarrassed. "Well, until . . ."

Mayfridh suddenly saw her own role in this drama clearly, and recoiled from herself, despised her attempts to make Jude fall in love with her. The flirtation, the dropping-in when Christine wasn't around, the subtle faery glamour she turned on whenever he was near. But no, that wasn't fair either. She and Jude had connected; beneath all the silly games she had played to be near him, they had connected.

"I'll marry her when I can afford it. I'll raise a family with her," he continued. "I'll go to my grave loving her the way I always have. It just won't be the way love is usually meant to be."

"And if you fell in love with someone else?" Mayfridh asked, challenging him with her gaze. "For real?"

His eyes met hers and didn't waver. Desire rushed upon her and she cursed herself for thinking about her own happiness when his and Christine's were so distant.

"I never thought that could happen," he said. "I could never imagine that there existed a woman in the world who could sway me from my purpose. I thought I was making the sacrifice for life." He paused. "I still believe in that sacrifice, Mayfridh."

These last words stung her. Whatever he felt for her— and he'd all but admitted that he felt the connection as much as she did—he was determined to deny it. He was determined to continue in his deception, and how could she persuade him otherwise? The alternative was to tell Christine the truth.

"Mayfridh," he said, leaning forward, his voice dark and serious, "Christine can never know."

"Of course."

"Only you and I know this story. I will never tell her."

"Nor will I. She's . . . I don't want to see her hurt."

"Yes. Yes, exactly. And she's got enough pain in her life. You'll go. You'll be back in faeryland and you'll forget all this, and I'll be left here with this life that I've created for myself, and I'll get through it and it won't be so bad. But she can't know, not ever."

"Our little secret," she said, humorlessly.

"Until winter. Then just *my* secret again."

A sudden knock on the door startled them both. Jude jerked to his feet, smoothing his hair back, muttering, "I wonder who that is?" Mayfridh felt guilty and flushed, hoping it wasn't Christine, then realized Christine wouldn't have knocked.

Jude opened the door. It was Gerda.

"Hi, Jude," she said. "I wondered if—oh, hi, Mayfridh." She peered into the room curiously. It had begun to grow dark but Jude had switched no lights on. Mayfridh realized she looked anxious and guilty. Gerda, with her keen eye, hadn't missed it. "What are you two up to?" she asked, only the thinnest veneer of humor over her words.

"Nothing," Jude said, his casualness returning. "We just got talking while waiting for Christine to come home."

"Where have you been, Mayfridh?" Gerda asked. "We've all missed you."

Mayfridh rose from the sofa and joined them at the door. "I had some problems back home," she said. "I won't be staying long." She shot a glance at Jude, who ignored it.

"But you're staying tonight, right?" Gerda asked. "Come on, Garth sent me a bottle of Swedish vodka—trying to make up with me—and you're just the girl to help me drink it."

Mayfridh tried to smile, realized it wasn't so hard to do. "Yes, I'd love it."

Gerda switched her attention back to Jude. "I wanted to borrow some laundry powder. I'm all out."

"Um, sure. Wait here." Jude disappeared into the bathroom.

Gerda fixed Mayfridh with her eye. "You look guilty."

"Do I?"

"You did when Jude opened the door."

"You're imagining it."

Jude returned with a box of laundry powder and handed it to Gerda. "Here."

"Thanks." She hooked her elbow through Mayfridh's and dragged her into the hallway. "Come on," she said, "you can help me with my laundry."

"Good-bye, Mayfridh," Jude said.

Mayfridh glanced over her shoulder. Jude at the door,

like the first time she had seen him. Perfect, dark-eyed, tangle-haired Jude.

Before she could say good-bye, he had closed the door.

☙

Three A.M. came and still Mayfridh was no closer to sleep. The vodka had been the only way to distract Gerda from asking insistently what she and Jude had been "up to." Now, lying in bed with a narrow band of streetlight that fell through the crack in the curtain, Mayfridh's mouth tasted sour and her head throbbed lightly. Her body, so saturated with uncomfortable thoughts and feelings, could not find a smooth or restful position in the bed. She tried her right side, her left, her back. It was like trying to sleep on a handful of pebbles. She sat up.

What was she even doing here? So close to Jude. Just one floor below him. Was he sleeping?

Three A.M. seemed the perfect time to contemplate secrets and deceit and betrayal. The gray darkness and the shadows. Mayfridh dropped her head into her hands. Hexebart had really only told her half the secret: Jude had killed Christine's parents. The most awful half of the secret was that he had spent four years pretending to love her, and intended to spend the rest of his life living the same deception. She knew she should be angry with him; he lied to Christine with every beat of his heart. Yet Mayfridh felt nothing but sadness and pity and worry and *love* for him.

In the distance, a police siren wailed and ebbed. She shouldn't be here. She should be far away from Jude. Every second they were together they were coconspirators, sharing too much unspoken intent, but she couldn't go back to Ewigkreis yet. As soon as she returned Eisengrimm would persuade her to unburden her miserable heart, and he would have only scorn for Jude. And so he would mutter and mumble and sermonize until winter came, and every precious sensation she felt for Jude would be spoiled.

Her mother's house, then. With a guilty twinge, she realized she hadn't even contacted Diana since her return. Mayfridh swung her legs over the side of the bed and stood up. This early hour of the morning wasn't the most polite time to show up at Diana's door, but she had to get away from Hotel Mandy-Z and from Jude and from Gerda with her endless questions.

In the bathroom, she rinsed out her mouth and splashed her face with cold water. The clothes she had worn the previous day were hanging on the towel rack and she pulled them on. The light from the bathroom reflected past Gerda's open door. Mayfridh paused in the doorway, considering whether or not to wake Gerda and tell her she was leaving. Gerda was fast asleep, sheets and bedspread askew, wearing a white singlet, her arm thrown up over her pillow, revealing a hairy armpit. Snoring, ever so gently. Mayfridh smiled and backed away, closing Gerda's bedroom door behind her. She picked up her shoes and let herself out of the apartment and down the stairs.

In the foyer she paused. A faint glow from the gallery. She glanced around the corner. Light, coming from under Jude's studio door.

The next few moments stretched out like elastic, and it seemed she had stood there forever, knowing that Jude was awake in his studio, knowing that she should just leave as she had intended, but being pulled toward his door. Hanging on to the threshold of the gallery as if it could hold her back.

Her feet decided for her, and she was moving barefoot, her shoes still in her hands, toward the light. The dark gallery was cluttered with paintings and sculptures, and yet it seemed so empty as she crossed through it, the abandoned emptiness of a room where someone has died and left his possessions, meaningless, behind. Her hand was on the doorknob; she turned and pushed.

Jude looked up. The first thing she noticed was his legs, long and pale and bare. He wore only a white shirt, unbuttoned, and a pair of boxer shorts with cartoon characters on them. Then she noticed his eyes. Dark smudges under them. He hadn't slept either.

He said nothing. The room was in chaos: the easel on its side, a canvas thrown down, paint tubes spread about. He had a large paintbrush in his hand, dripping brown paint. Behind him, the wall was a mess of monochrome shapes, still wet.

"You've painted the wall," she said, knowing it was an empty nothing to say, but needing to say something. She closed the door behind her.

"Yes," he replied. "The canvas wasn't big enough for . . ." He didn't finish his sentence, but she knew what he meant.

"I'm sorry," she said.

He dropped the brush and moved toward her, reaching for her. She took a step back but he caught her and pressed her against him so hard it pushed her breath from her lungs. "Hold me," he said.

Was there anything else she could do? Her arms went around him. His lips were on her throat and something long trapped inside her rose up with her breath and gasped out of her. "I love you," she said.

His lips moved to her cheek, her nose, and finally her mouth. He pressed his lips against hers fiercely, and she let him crush her in his arms. His tongue tasted of tobacco and whiskey. She tried to say "I love you" again, but the sweet violent kiss barricaded the words inside her. She twined her fingers in his hair. His own fingers were descending down her blouse, popping the buttons free one by one. He stood back, slipped the shirt from her shoulders to reveal her bare breasts. Then his lips were on her nipples, kissing, biting, sucking.

She shuddered with an acute sense of vulnerability. No man had ever seen her breasts before; no man had ever kissed her before. Jude raised his head and pressed her to him again, and this time she could feel the hard warmth of his erection through the silk of his shorts.

"Jude," she said, her voice unsteady. "I've never . . ."

He stood back a pace, his eyes curious. "What?"

"I've never done this before."

"Never?"

She shook her head. A silent moment passed between them; his fingers were drawing away from her body.

"But I want to," she said hurriedly. "I want to do everything. I want to do whatever you want me to do. You just have to show me."

Jude's gaze dropped to her breasts. He moved closer again, his hands at the zipper on her skirt. It slipped over her hips and fell to the floor. He lifted her against him and carried her to the wall of the room, pressed her bare back into the still-wet paint. His hands pinned her shoulders as he kissed her throat, her breasts, her belly. The paint felt sticky and soft and slimy all at once. She tried to keep her head bent forward, to keep her hair from trailing in the paint, but he stood and crushed his mouth against hers again, forcing her head back, pushing her whole body into the wall.

"Will you forget this?" he murmured against her lips, her chin. "Will none of this have ever happened?"

"I'll forget everything," she said, the sadness a cold barb. "I'll forget you."

He kissed her and kissed her until her breath was short and her head dizzy. Then he grabbed her hand and pulled her to the sofa, tipped off the rags and the empty paint tubes, and laid her down. The paint on her back stuck and pulled on the rough material of the sofa. Still he kissed her, as if he never wanted her to breathe again. She almost wanted to suffocate, surrender all under the weight of passion. His hands were all over her body, smudging her with paint. His lips left her face and descended between her breasts. He removed her knickers and wiped his painty hands clean on them, casting them aside into the chaos on the floor of the studio. The swelling feeling of vulnerability returned. The most private parts of her body, areas she had never even explored, and he was down there with his eyes and his fingers and his tongue and, oh, what a velvet searing pleasure rocked her body then, and somehow the vulnerable feeling became part of the pleasure, a strange liberation. He lifted her ankle and rested it on the back of the sofa, and she lay there with the paint gluing her to the sofa and her hair tangling into sticky clumps and closed her eyes and Jude was doing the most *incredible things* to her body and every hot nerve was shuddering and trembling and tensing tighter and tighter and—

Mayfridh covered her face with her hands so she wouldn't shriek and wake up everyone in the building. The pleasure was almost unbearable. And then, strangely, thankfully, it released in warm rhythmic waves. Her heart pounded in her ears, her toes trembled.

Jude covered her body with his. "I'll be gentle," he said. "Do whatever you like," she gasped.

He fumbled himself out of his shorts and moved into her slowly. She let her body relax and mold to his. A different pleasure this time, a feeling of wholeness and rightness and emptiness leaving, like the most perfect embrace it was possible to know. She wrapped her legs around his back and his breath was very hot on her neck.

"Don't forget me," he said.

"I won't," she said, even though it was a lie.

"I love you," he said.

"I know." She clung to him, feeling his hot skin through his shirt, allowed herself to be loved, to be embraced, as she knew she may never be loved or embraced again.

They lay there for long minutes afterward. She thought about the paint drying in her hair but didn't worry. She thought about the door to the studio being unlocked but didn't worry. There was nothing after this moment. This was the only moment, and nothing before or after could ever count.

Then he pulled himself away from her and readjusted his clothes and sat slumping forward with his hands crossed between his knees.

She sat up, looking for her clothes. They were strewn about the room. She left them there for the time being. "Jude? Are you okay?"

He raised his head. She noticed for the first time that he had paint smudged all over his face. She touched her own face, presuming it would be the same.

"I'm not okay," he said.

"What's wrong?"

"Everything."

She reached for his hand, but he pulled it away gently and stood up.

"Where were you going?" he asked.

"Pardon?"

"When you came down here, you were dressed. You were going somewhere." He picked up her clothes as he said this, and handed them to her.

"I was going to stay with my mother." She dressed herself quickly, awkwardly, while he watched her.

"Good," he said. "We can't . . ."

She took a deep breath. "I know we can't. But we did. And you told me you loved me."

"I have to be with Christine." Her name came out very softly, as though he almost couldn't bear to say it.

"Don't be guilty."

"Aren't you?"

She nodded.

"It will mean nothing," he said. "You'll forget."

"You'll remember."

"I already have lots of guilty secrets to remember," he replied, "but you have to go now, and we should never see each other again."

Reality swerved in on her, and the last shred of that beautiful moment in his arms was snatched away. He was right. This was ending, this was already over. The pain in her heart paralyzed her.

"Go, Mayfridh, please," he said, and he blinked as though tears might be approaching. "Please go, it's hurting me."

She picked up her shoes. Her body felt stiff and awkward. "I'll go," she said.

"Please."

She took a step toward him, stole one last kiss from his lips. "Good-bye," she said

"Forget me," he said.

And then she was moving back through the empty gallery, out the front door with her coat, and into the cold, dark street.

CHAPTER EIGHTEEN

*C*hristine lay down among the fallen leaves in the autumn forest and breathed, deep and full. The relief. *The relief.* She almost regretted coming; coping day to day with the reality of the pain had driven this feeling toward forgetfulness, so she hadn't missed it as keenly. Now, knowing she would soon have to bid good-bye to the freedom for always, a niggle of anxiety—maybe desperation—worked its way into her stomach.

She opened her eyes and she was startled by how different the forest looked. The trees were almost bare, and the rich colors had faded. Now everything appeared to be gray and sickly yellow. She sat up and peered into the layered mist. Some of the trees were completely naked. Winter was drawing very close.

"Eisengrimm!" she called. She wanted to see the birch outside the great hall. If it was as stripped of its leaves as some of these trees were, she feared that the last leaf was only hours away.

The gate opened, and Eisengrimm appeared, his gait still stiff.

"You're not recovered yet?" she asked, standing to follow him inside.

"Nearly. Just a few bruises left. I feel fine unless I have to change, so I just stay Wolf and hope that Mayfridh doesn't need me to fly off somewhere."

"The giant birch," Christine said. "I need to see it."

"You can see it from the chamber window. Winter is still weeks away. You're not to worry."

Christine stretched her arms over her head. "It's divine to be here again."

"I've missed you," he said. "Tonight the village is celebrating the winter blessings. Will you accompany me?"

"I don't know. I probably shouldn't stay long."

"There will be dancing and singing and plenty of hot mead. Have you danced since your accident?"

They were entering the castle now. Eisengrimm led her up the corridor to the winding stairs.

"No," she said, "but that's okay because I was never a good dancer. Two left feet."

The last phrase troubled Eisengrimm, even though it had translated into his own language. "Two of the same?"

"It's just an expression," she said, giggling. "Sorry."

"Oh, I see. Here." He indicated Mayfridh's white bedchamber. "This is your chamber for as long as you choose to stay. Mayfridh insisted."

Christine flopped down on the bed. "This bed is so comfortable."

"The chest under the window is full of Mayfridh's old dresses, from when she was in her teens. She thought they might fit you. Choose one you like for the party. I'll come for you in an hour or so. That's if you've decided to attend?"

Christine bit her lip. It sounded like fun, and both Eisengrimm and Mayfridh had reassured her she still had plenty of time to get home. "Okay. Okay, I will."

"I'm glad. Make yourself comfortable. I'll be back soon."

Christine rose from the bed—so much easier without the ache in her back—and flipped open the chest. The dresses were mostly in shades of gold and russet. She wriggled out of her work clothes and pulled out a dress of tawny red. The weave was rough against her skin but a quick search of the rest of the chest revealed they all had the same texture. Right down at the bottom of the chest she found a gold circlet for her hair. She went to the window in her new clothes and gazed out. Sunset was deep gold; the birch had lost only half its leaves. She let herself relax. From far away the scent of wood smoke drifted. The quiet was all around her; no traffic, no voices, no hum of electricity. Just leaves in the wind, faint birdcalls, the steady rhythm of her own heart. Peace eased into her bones, made her spirit warm. Only now, in such a moment of tranquillity, could she appreciate how jangled—physically and emotionally—she usually felt.

And this moment was temporary. And there was a Real World full of people and commitments to remember.

She sighed and turned her back to the window. Another trunk near the bed caught her eye. Eisengrimm wouldn't return for an hour. Surely it would be all right to explore a little.

In the trunk she found books, all written in English. So this was how Mayfridh had kept her native language. The collection was strangely anachronistic in this medieval setting; mostly eighteenth- and nineteenth-century volumes, but some more recent editions of children's books by Enid Blyton and C. S. Lewis. Christine wondered how she had acquired these, or maybe Liesebet had acquired them for her. They were dusty and looked like they hadn't been touched for years.

She lay on the bed with a Famous Five book and waited

for Eisengrimm to return. By the time he opened the door, she was nearly dropping off to sleep.

"Christine?" he said gently.

She sat up and yawned. "Sorry. I was just so comfortable."

"I'm glad you were comfortable."

"I've never slept without pain. Not in thirteen years."

"Do you still want to come to the party?"

"Absolutely."

"Come on, then. I have a carriage waiting."

"A carriage?"

"It's the appropriate way for a special guest of the queen to travel."

Christine smiled. "Oh yeah? The first time I came you had me brought to the castle in a pig sack on the back of a cart."

Impossible to tell if Eisengrimm was smiling as well.

The carriage stopped at the bottom of the slope where the cobbled village road started. Eisengrimm leapt off and urged the driver to help Christine down. At first she opened her mouth to insist she needed no help, but then she told herself to enjoy it. Let them treat her like someone special. She'd spent a long time being someone very ordinary.

Half-timbered cottages with thatched roofs lined the street. Deep shadows advanced along the road in front of them. People bustled in and out of their homes, taking firewood down to an enormous bonfire near the town well. Christine and Eisengrimm arrived at a low-roofed tavern, overflowing with noisy drinkers.

"Come, Christine," Eisengrimm said, leading her toward the door, "I shall introduce you to some of the villagers."

Christine thought they would have to push through the crowd, but everyone stood aside to let Eisengrimm pass. Merry and happy, they bent to stroke his tail or touch his back, saying, "The best of the winter to you," and "Many blessings." At the bar, Eisengrimm stretched his paws up and ordered Christine a drink. When he returned to all fours, he called out, "Good afternoon, everyone."

Every pair of eyes in the room was suddenly turned toward him and a hurried hush fell.

"I'd like to introduce Christine Starlight," he said, "a visitor from the Real World and a special guest of the queen."

The crowd broke into cheers and applause and began to huddle and gossip again. Christine took a sip of her drink— warm, spiced wine, rich with the scent of cloves—and was glad to be in a bar not choked with cigarette smoke. Apart from the woody aroma of a few pipes, the air was clean. There was something organic about the tastes and the smells, and she relished it.

The door to the tavern opened, and two musicians with pipes pushed through the crowd to a square of empty floor under the mullioned window. More cheers. They cramped themselves into a corner and started to play merry music. Within seconds dancers were crowding into the space.

"Is everybody drunk?" Christine asked.

"Yes, except you and me."

"I'll do my best," she said, lifting her glass and draining it. "How about you?"

"No, I'll stay sober and look after you," he replied with a twinkle in his eye.

A tall man with a gingery beard approached them. He was dressed in a plain brown tunic and pants. "Did I hear your name was Starlight?" he asked.

"Yes," she replied warily.

"It's a beautiful name. Care to dance?"

Christine shrank back from him. "I don't know . . . I can't dance and—"

"Can't dance? Have you never learned?"

She glanced at the dancers, who were whirling and stomping around each other to the music. "I don't know the steps," she said.

"We've all had our winter blessings," the man replied. "I can enchant your feet."

"Enchant my . . . ?" Christine turned to Eisengrimm. "Is that safe?"

"Perfectly," he said. "Go on, Christine. Dance. It's not difficult."

The man was holding out his hand for her to take. She drew a deep breath and grabbed his fingers, and he pulled her onto the crowded dance floor.

"I'm having the first dance with Starlight," he announced, though his voice was nearly drowned out by the music.

"I want to dance with Starlight too," somebody else called.

"Me too!"

"Well, I'm first!" The man bent to the ground and touched Christine's feet. "These are strange shoes," he said.

Christine looked down at her shiny patent leather Mary-Janes. "Um, they're Real World shoes."

"Real World shoes," he repeated, awestruck.

Then a warm tingle suffused her feet and they started moving without her. She almost shrieked, the feeling was so strange and frightening. She was no longer in control of her own feet, and resisting the movements put her off balance.

Her dance partner stood and steadied her. "You must surrender to your feet," he said. "Otherwise you'll fall over."

Christine tried to do as he said, and found it wasn't so hard. It reminded her of when she was a little girl and her father had danced with her toes balanced on his. The memory was achingly sweet and she tried to enjoy it in the split second before the other, less pleasant memories of her father came. But then her feet started moving, and there was nothing to think about except the dance.

Soon she was whirling and stomping and kicking up her toes with the rest of them. The first time her feet took her spinning expertly to the edge of the dance floor and back she nearly doubled over laughing. Her dance partner was laughing too, and some of the others around her. The music changed to a more stately tune, and another man was bending to touch her feet, and she was performing a slow, measured dance with him. On and on the music went, now slow, now fast, now soft, now loud, and everybody wanted "to dance with Starlight": old men, tall boys, fat women, toothless twins in hats made of thatch. Her feet were enchanted over and over again, and she laughed and surrendered to the dance, grabbing frantic sips of mead whenever someone handed her a cup. The experience was marvelously physical. She couldn't have put her body through this for even five minutes in the Real World without her back moaning. Her very blood seemed hot and merry, and she suffered a moment's guilt thinking of Jude back home waiting and worrying about her. She pushed the feeling aside and danced, and danced, and danced as the last of the amber sunset faded through the little diamond panes and lamps and lanterns were lit all around. Finally, though, she was exhausted. She saw Eisengrimm waiting at the edge of the dance floor and approached him.

"Could you unenchant my feet?" she asked, as they were already tapping to the music.

"Your feet haven't been enchanted since the third dance," he said. "They're all having a joke on you."

Christine realized she could stop her feet tapping if she willed it. "Oh," she said, laughing. "You mean I've been dancing for real?"

"I told you it wasn't difficult."

Her first dance partner approached to thank her, and handed her a cup of wine before disappearing back into the crowd. The wine . . . that was why her head was starting to spin. A warm, cheerful feeling. The door to the tavern burst open and a little girl called out, "The bonfire is lit! The bonfire is lit!"

With these words, the crowd began to surge toward the door.

"What's happening?" she asked Eisengrimm.

"The winter bonfire. It's a custom. They all sing thanks for the harvest and ask for grace in the winter. Come, bring your wine. We'll find a good place to sit."

Eisengrimm led her through the crowd to the road outside. The huge bonfire had roared into life, at least six feet high with the flames peaking above it. The evening had descended, that brief window of almost darkness before the pale sun rose once again. At a safe distance around the bonfire, rugs and mats had been laid. A shiny-faced woman, whom Christine thought she might have danced with, beckoned her over.

"Here," she said, "you and the counselor may share my mat."

"Thank you," Eisengrimm said, sitting down and resting his head on his paws.

Christine joined him. The dancing light of the fire, the noisy crowd, the taste of the warm alcohol; she closed her eyes for a moment and that sense of peace she had felt standing at the chamber window returned.

A hush fell over the crowd. Christine looked around. A beautiful pale-haired young woman in a white dress had taken up a position in front of the fire.

Eisengrimm leaned close. "That's Klarlied, Hexebart's daughter."

"Hexebart's daughter?" Christine whispered.

"When her mother dies, she'll be our new witch."

"She's so beautiful."

Then Klarlied opened her mouth and began to sing. Her voice was pure and bell-like, and she sang of winter and snow and ice. When she had finished, everyone applauded and she commenced another song, but this time, after the first line, people all around began to join in.

"This is the biggest campfire sing-along I've ever been to," Christine laughed.

"Faery folk love music," Eisengrimm said. "You can join in if you like."

"I don't know the words," she replied. "Besides, I sing worse than I dance." She lay back on the mat and gazed at the sky. Scattered across the dark velvety blue were a few pale stars. The fire crackled and popped, ashes and sparks rising up into the twilight air.

Eisengrimm turned and lay down next to her, his nose close to her ear.

"Eisengrimm, can you see many more stars here when it's night?"

"Of course. On a clear night in winter you can see millions."

"Are they the same stars I see back in the Real World?"

"I don't know," Eisengrimm said. "Do you recognize any?"

"It's hard to tell. They're so pale."

"They have been washed out by the proximity of the sun; dawn is about to break. When the sun is far away, starlight has its own brilliance."

She turned on her side to face him. "Tell me about winter," she said. "Is it dark the whole time?"

"Most of the time. The nights are very long and the days gray and hazy."

"Does everyone get depressed?"

"No, people stay inside and tell stories and make music and warm themselves next to fires." He paused a moment before saying, "Though Mayfridh sometimes becomes melancholy."

"Really?"

"When the snow comes, she can't go wandering in the forest." Flickering shadows from the firelight moved over him. "But spring is never far away. Winter isn't long or brutal."

A new song had started, sweet and sad. "Eisengrimm," she said, "what does it feel like to lose your memory?"

"We don't lose all our memories. Only memories gathered in the Real World."

"I know, but what does it feel like to lose them? And what does it feel like to move to the Winter Castle?"

Eisengrimm pondered for a minute, then said, "It isn't a perfectly pleasant feeling, and most people suffer at least a little anxiety in the days leading up to the move. We usually know when it's going to happen because we have someone watching the birch, but we don't make it happen. We have to surrender ourselves to the season."

"And when the leaf falls?"

He closed his eyes, trying to articulate the details. "It's like being pulled downwards, somewhere dark, a loose spiral. The sensation of having nothing beneath your feet. Your thoughts seem like sounds . . . I can't explain it better than that. It's as though the words in your head echo around you, and some thoughts—memories of the Real World—echo off into the distance and disappear. You have a sense of losing something, but not being able to comprehend what it is you've lost. That feeling can make people anxious, but it lasts only a few moments. Then, an eye blink of complete darkness—no light, no sound, no thoughts—followed by a shock of arrival. The new season rushes upon you, all bright and noisy. It takes a moment to readjust, and you realize it's not bright or noisy, just a normal winter's day and you're in the Winter Castle."

"I still can't comprehend it."

"You'd have to experience it to comprehend it."

"What happens to those memories, though? Will Mayfridh know she's forgotten something?"

Eisengrimm opened his eyes. They glowed yellow in the firelight. "Oh, she'll have a faint sense of it. It will not be pressing, and within a week or so it will be gone."

"And if she finds an object she's brought back with her from the Real World?"

"It will seem as though she's always owned it."

"What if I left her a letter, reminding her of things?"

"She would not have any sense of recognition. She may read it and wonder how long she had owned it, perhaps amuse herself imagining what she might have done. But you, the deep essence of you, will be gone from her memory. There's a small chance she'd remember you if our world aligned with where you are again."

"Is there any chance of that?"

"There's no predicting it, Christine. It could happen in five years or fifty years or not at all."

Christine settled into silence. Sadness threaded through her sense of peace. She would miss Mayfridh; Mayfridh wouldn't miss her.

"Don't be sad," Eisengrimm said. "One mustn't be sad when the world is what it is."

"I'll miss her. I'll miss you. I'll miss Ewigkreis and the magic and the adventure."

"But you have so much else to look forward to. Life with Jude, children, friends."

"Yeah," she said. Her eyes were growing sore from the fire. "Yeah, I suppose you're right."

"You look tired. Would you like to return to the castle?"

"I should go home."

"No, stay here with us tonight. You said you had never really slept without pain. Sleep here, sleep long and deeply."

Christine considered: this might be her last chance to enjoy Ewigkreis. "All right," she said, "I will."

They left the bonfire—at least a dozen people called out, "Good night, Starlight"—and made their way back to the carriage. The sky was lit with pale dawn light, the sun poised behind the horizon, as the carriage rattled back up the slope. Christine felt herself lulled by its movement, dozing in short fits. Back at the castle, Eisengrimm led her to the white chamber, where she sank among the covers.

"Good night, Christine," Eisengrimm said, settling on the bed next to her.

"Do you sleep here too?" she asked, opening her eyes.

"I always sleep next to the queen. But if you would prefer I didn't . . ."

"No, no, I love it that you're here." She put her arm around Eisengrimm's ribs. He was very warm. "Though I don't know what Jude would think of me sleeping with another man," she joked.

"I am a wolf," Eisengrimm said, "with no man's desires. You are safe."

"I know," she replied, too tired to worry if she had hurt his feelings. "I know."

She felt herself drifting off. What bliss to sleep without pain.

"Close your eyes, Christine," he said, drawing a deep breath and settling on his paws. "Sleep peacefully."

And she did.

━ *from the Memoirs of Mandy Z.*

This could be my last entry for some time. I have quite an adventure to set out upon.

My Bone Wife, ever unfinished, can dance. It's true, although there's only half of her. I was experimenting with her—lift, step, lift, step, fall—when I became so frustrated with her that I went up and put my hands on her hips and tried to guide her forward. As I stepped back, she stepped forward, matching the distance exactly. Intrigued, I took a step forward, and she stepped back. I stepped to the side, she likewise, and so on, until I had her waltzing unevenly for nearly two minutes. Then she clattered to the floor as she always does, and I had to repair her knee which had become chipped. I have never laughed so much in my life, but then I'm in a fine, merry mood today.

When I've finished her—and I know it won't be long now—I have a new fantasy to fulfill. I always imagined that I would top the Bone Wife off with a face sculpted to look like my mother's. But now, I'm imagining her quite differently.

Now I know I want Mayfridh's head.

I will use her gleaming skull, and fill it with plaster and smooth over its surface and repaint her features lovingly. I will use her hair, her real hair. How it drives me mad, that hair, because its color is so bright I can almost see it. I shall dance with her every day.

For now, the Bone Wife has been moved upstairs to the boning room, under lock and key. I will be away for an uncertain amount of time, and I want her to be safe until I return.

You see, I saw Christine Starlight in the Tiergarten. I followed her there. I have been following her for days. I saw

Mayfridh turn up at the store where she works, I saw Christine bid her friend farewell on Friedrichstrasse, and I saw her find a dark hollow where she thought she wasn't seen. I saw her pull out a ball of golden twine and unravel it in front of her, and then I saw her disappear.

The twine is the passage.

I came back here to work and to write. I had thought I would simply go into Jude and Christine's flat one evening when they are both out and steal the twine, but I'm too impatient. She hasn't returned. I visited Jude Honeychurch— dazed and seedy—in his apartment this morning and he said Christine had gone away for a short while, but he expected her back very soon. I'm going to the Tiergarten to wait. I don't care if I have to wait for hours. I don't care if it rains on me (today is very overcast and cold). I'm going to faeryland. Who knows how long I'll be there, with so many raw materials to gather?

Farewell. (I'm laughing as I write this.) *I go to a better place.*

***

Christine found she was clamping her jaw against the expected rush of embodiedness as she left Eisengrimm behind and wound out the twine in front of her.

"Good-bye, Christine," he said, "I hope to see you again before winter."

"I hope so too," she said, picking up the thread.

She stepped into the pressure on her back, and traffic sounds and the smell of the city enveloped her. She gathered the twine, stood up straight and—

"Mandy?" Where had he appeared from? He stood in front of her, grinning. Her skin prickled.

"Christine," he replied, as though there were nothing at

all unusual about him standing in the Tiergarten two feet from a woman who had just appeared out of nowhere.

She moved to tuck the twine away in her coat, but he stopped her hand and forced it toward him. Her blood sizzled with fear. Was he going to rape her? Kill her? She fought to regain control of her arm.

"What are you doing?"

He turned his head away from her forearm as though disgusted. "Ugh, you smell just like one of them."

"One of what? What are you doing?" She struggled with him but he overpowered her, wrenched the twine from her fingers and rolled it in front of him.

"No! No, Mandy, don't," she cried, frantic now. "You don't know what you're—"

One moment he was there. The next, he was gone.

CHAPTER NINETEEN

*C*hristine slammed into the apartment and dropped her keys with a clunk on the table. "Where's Mayfridh?" she asked Jude.

"What? Why?" He rose from his seat with a nervous jerk of his shoulders.

"I need to find her. Is she with Gerda?" Christine was halfway back to the door.

"I think she's at her mother's. Why? What's wrong?"

Christine ignored him, picked up the phone, and started scrabbling through the mess of papers in the bookcase drawer. Diana's number was in there somewhere.

"What's wrong, Christine?" Jude asked again, his hand on the small of her back. "Did something happen in faeryland? Are you okay?"

"I'm fine," she said, her fingers closing over the phone number, "but Mandy's not."

"Mandy?"

"As I came back through the passage, he was there waiting for me. He stole the twine and now he's gone through."

"To faeryland?"

"Yes, to faeryland." She dialed the number. "I have no

idea what he intends, or if he knows what he's doing. But I have to tell Mayfridh." At the other end the phone rang once, twice.

"What the hell was he thinking?" Jude asked. "He didn't know about Mayfridh, did he?"

"No, last time we spoke he still called her Miranda. Hang on."

Diana picked up the phone. "Hello?"

"Hi, Diana. It's Christine Starlight. I need to speak to May urgently."

"Of course. May!"

Christine waited, tapping her foot. By now Mandy would have found the autumn forest. Would Eisengrimm still be there? What would Mandy do? She wished she could trust him, but he had always seemed so very sinister to her.

"Hello?" Mayfridh's voice.

"Mayfridh, something terrible has happened. Mandy stole my magic twine and he's gone to Ewigkreis."

"What?" It was almost a shriek.

"I don't know what he intends, I don't know if he knew about the passage—"

"He couldn't have, could he? None of us told him."

"But it was an open secret among us. Maybe he overheard something. Maybe Gerda said something, I don't know. She can be such a gossip. I'm worried, Mayfridh. He's had that weird crush on you—"

"And he doesn't know I'm here. He's gone looking for me."

"Eisengrimm will find him," Christine said. "Will he send him back?"

"I don't . . . I'm not sure. He won't do any harm, will he? I mean, perhaps he's just curious," Mayfridh said.

"Probably. I'm nervous about it, though. He practically

wrestled me for the twine." At this Jude's face darkened with concern. "Will you go back straightaway?"

"Yes. I mean, not immediately. I can't. It's . . ." Mayfridh's voice dropped to a whisper. "It's my mother's birthday. We're in the middle of dinner."

"You can't just let Mandy invite himself to Ewigkreis without going after him."

"Eisengrimm can handle him in the short term. I'll get away in about an hour. Mum's not going to like it, though."

"Well, let me know as soon as you're back in the Real World. And let me know if there's anything Jude or I can do, okay?"

"Yes, sure. It will be fine, Christine, don't worry. He's eccentric and he's nosy, but I don't think he's a monster. Eisengrimm will keep him safe somewhere until I can get there, and then I'll send him back."

Christine replaced the phone and turned to Jude.

"Did he hurt you?" Jude asked.

"No, but he frightened me. I don't like him, Jude, and I don't know if it's worth being at Hotel Mandy-Z with such an unpredictable person. He's probably got keys to this apartment. I think we should consider leaving."

"But the fellowship?"

"You don't need the fellowship. You're got an international reputation. You don't need this gallery."

"We can't live off your salary alone."

"We can go back home. We can leave Berlin."

"But . . ." Jude trailed off, nodded. "Let me think about it."

"I'm telling you, Jude, Mandy is more than just eccentric."

"I believe you. You're right; we can't stay." He didn't sound convinced.

Christine sat heavily on the sofa. Her back was throbbing, her head was aching, her heart was sick with worry. So different from the uncomplicated peace she had felt sitting by the bonfire with Eisengrimm. What did Mandy have in mind? She knew she wouldn't relax until Mayfridh returned.

❧

Mandy had expected the passage to make a far greater impact on his body and mind. Instead, he took two steps and simply arrived somewhere else. A rural quiet descended and he looked up to see he was no longer in the Tiergarten. He laughed. "I am in faeryland," he said.

He turned in a slow circle, his eyes taking everything in: trees, leaves, grass, sunset. A crow sitting on a bough, eyeing him impassively. Pretending to be an ordinary crow, and perhaps it was, but Mandy had seen Christine Starlight speaking with a crow at the end of Vogelwald-Allee and was immediately suspicious. He looked away from the bird, feigning a lack of interest. Tucked into the back of his pants he had a canvas sack, expressly bought for the purpose of collecting faery bones. He eased it out and shook it. Glanced at the crow. It had hopped closer. Mandy lifted his left foot, as though to take a step away, then turned at the last instant and, with lightning speed, reached out to seize the bird. It flapped madly, but Mandy had it by the leg. He yanked it toward him and straight into the sack.

"Good birdie," he said, tying off the sack. It flapped about as he slung it over his shoulder and headed in the direction where the trees began to thin. What a beautiful day it was. The weather clear and cool, the breeze fresh but not gusty, and oh, the clean air. Mandy took a deep lungful. Fine weather indeed.

In a matter of minutes he spied the castle. Its narrow, crooked turrets rose above him. All that stood in his way was the rusty gate and . . . yes, with the application of a sharp stone and his considerable weight behind it, the lock gave and he had entry to the castle grounds. Faeries, clearly, were not fussy about security. Why would they need to be? They probably reveled in each other's foulness and saw no reason to hurt one another, not even the queen. No faeryland could possibly be prepared for the arrival of Immanuel Zweigler. He strode with his chest puffed out. He was the hero of a faery tale, come from another world to exterminate a terrible evil by turning it into art. Bones, so many bones, must be clicking and clacking around in this castle, separated from his hands only by a few inches of soft flesh.

The garden was untended and overgrown. He stepped into the shadowy depths of the castle; a dark place with a smell like lime or damp or yeast. The ceilings were high above him, dotted with tiny windows that barely admitted enough light to break the gloom. He stuck close to the wall, wary of attracting attention, but the castle appeared to be empty. He stopped and listened; no sound. Ahead was a long corridor. He slunk along it carefully, peering into rooms on the left and right. The sound of footsteps sent him for cover in a room that was empty except for a faded rug and dust. He eased the door almost closed behind him, waited until the footsteps passed, then cautiously reemerged in the corridor. Alone again. The smell of food floated up from downstairs. Kitchens. His stomach rumbled. He hadn't eaten for hours, sitting in the park waiting for Christine. It would be his next stop, as soon as he found Mayfridh.

Mayfridh's bedroom was likely to be upstairs. He peered up the dark narrow turret, listened for any signs of life. The bird in the sack had become very still. Either it was in shock or it was trying to be clever. Not clever enough, however. Mandy pondered: would a crow's bones be useful to him at all? Probably too light and bendable. Perhaps for some fine detail work, to make eyebrows or lashes. His feet scuffed lightly on the stone steps as he wound up and up, finally discovering a chamber decorated in white. He slung the sack on the floor and flopped onto the bed.

Ah, yes. He could smell her. The profane scent of her bones had permeated the linen. It was a scent both repulsive and impossibly attractive. It turned his stomach but invited his nostrils to breathe deeper. Mandy had recognized on-lookers at car accidents succumbing just as shamefully to the magnetic pull of the awful sight. He rubbed his face in the sheets, his lips, his tongue. Felt himself grow flushed and sat up, guilty and angry all at once.

Beside the bed, flung carelessly on a low table, a belt of keys. He snatched them up.

Keys to the castle! It truly was his lucky day.

❧

Christine didn't sleep well her first night back in the Real World. Where falling asleep in Mayfridh's chamber had been pure careless bliss, here in Hotel Mandy-Z the ever-present niggling pulls and stiffness plagued her. She woke again and again during the night. Was the discomfort worse now than it had ever been? Or was her imagination magnifying the difference between the freedom of Ewigkreis and the reality of the bed she shared with Jude?

She slept fitfully until dawn, then a cold emptiness in the bed brought her all the way to wakefulness. She rolled over. Jude wasn't there. At first she thought he might be downstairs in the studio, but then she could hear his footsteps, hear him running water in the kitchen. Yawning loudly, she eased over onto her back and considered the day. Hopefully Mayfridh would call soon. Christine would never relax in Mandy's company again. His behavior yesterday was confirmation of all her worst fears about him; he was eccentric enough to be dangerous.

The door cracked open and Jude peeked in. "You're awake."

"Only just." She gingerly stretched her arms over her head. "How long have you been up?"

"Couple of hours," he said, pushing the door open all the way.

"Couldn't you sleep?"

He shook his head. "Do you want a cup of coffee? Some breakfast?"

"A bit early to eat, isn't it?"

"Coffee coming right up."

She wriggled into a half-sitting position and propped herself up with pillows. Coffee in bed with Jude. It made the return to the Real World worth it. A few minutes later, he brought in a steaming mug.

"Here," he said, handing it to her.

"Thanks, Jude." She took a moment to inhale the deep aroma, then sipped it gratefully.

Jude lowered himself onto the bed and lay on his side. "Christine," he said, "there's something really important I need to say to you."

"Wow, that sounds serious," she said, putting her cup down.

"It is. It is serious."

Christine frowned, her heart held its breath. "Okay. You'd better say it then."

"Christine . . ." He sat up, took her hand in his. "Christine Starlight, will you marry me?"

All of a sudden, her face didn't seem big enough for her smile. "Really? You're for real?"

"I wouldn't kid about something like this." Jude still looked very serious; his eyes were dark and he wore no trace of a smile.

"Jude, is this what you really want?"

"Yes."

"Then how come you're . . . how come you don't seem very happy?"

"Because you haven't said yes."

She ruffled his hair. "Dummy. Of course I'll marry you. I'd love to marry you. I'd marry you every day until I'm seventy if you kept asking me."

Now he smiled, a relieved smile. "So that's a yes."

"That's a yes."

He leaned forward to embrace her, hard, like he was afraid she might slip out of his arms. She felt such a swell of warmth and contentment then, like she used to feel back home, before Berlin, before Mayfridh, when the pain was still bad but she'd accepted it and grown used to it. It had been so long since she felt that way, she'd forgotten it was even possible.

"So when?" she said, sitting back and picking up her coffee again. "And where?"

"Whenever you want, wherever you want."

"Back home. Soon."

He sighed. "I suppose we'll have to leave Berlin. You were right about that."

Christine felt a twinge of suspicion, only momentary, but enough to take the edge off her happiness. Yesterday she'd urged him to leave Berlin and abandon his fellowship. Without it, he'd have to go to work teaching art classes or worse. But now they were getting married, he knew she'd access the trust fund. Convenient timing. That's what Gerda would say.

"What's wrong?" he asked.

"Nothing."

"You went all quiet."

"Just thinking about organizing a wedding. We don't have to do a big performance, do we?" She was being paranoid. Jude wasn't after her money, and besides, she didn't mind sharing it with him.

"No, I'd prefer not to, actually."

"Jude," she said, trying not to sound suspicious, "why are you asking me to marry you?"

His eyebrows shot up in puzzlement. "Why? Because I love you."

"Yes, but why *now*? Why this morning?"

"I missed you while you were away. I worried about you. I didn't have a good time without you here. It's something I've wanted to ask you for a long time, but I've always put it off, not sure if it's the right time. But I love you and I know I want to be with you and take care of you. So now; now is the right time."

"Yeah. Sure is."

He sank onto the bed next to her, wrapped his arms around her. "We make a great couple, Christine. We'll be happy."

"I'm already happy," she said, snuggling into him.

He kissed her cheek. His breath was warm. "Wife."

"Husband. To be."

"I'm all yours."

Mandy found an iron cage the perfect size to contain the crow. At first he thought the creature was dead, it had been still for so long in the sack. But when he'd reached in to grab it, it wriggled and pecked him, though not in the brainless, instinctive way that an ordinary bird would. Its movements were too precise and calculated. Mandy knew that this was the enchanted crow and he intended to keep it safely in his possession. Now, peering between the sturdy black bars, he tried to coax the bird to talk.

"Come on then, Mr. Crow, say something."

Silence.

"Mr. Crow, you're being very naughty. I know you can talk, I heard you speaking with Christine Starlight."

Still, the bird did not answer. Mandy smiled at it. "Very well, have it your way. I'm hungry now, and I'm going to the kitchen to have something to eat. And you, my new pet, will come with me." He picked up the cage and headed down the stairs, patting the key belt under his shirt. A wild bravado had gripped him. He knew he should be careful: these faeries outnumbered him vastly, wherever they were. But the castle was deserted and he felt strong and sure of himself with the keys, the enchanted crow in the cage, and his empty sack waiting to be filled. He stepped into the kitchen. It smelled cold and sour like old potatoes. A woman, hard-faced and fair-haired, stared up at him.

"Who are you?" she asked, in a guttural version of Middle High German he recognized from his university days.

"A special guest of Mayfridh," he replied, mixing some new German with the old and hoping that the message would come across clear enough.

"The queen hasn't told me of any guest."

Mandy sat the crow on the large wooden table in the center of the room. "She told me that if I wanted something to eat I just had to come to the kitchen and ask."

The woman leaned over the table and peered into the cage. "Is that Counselor Eisengrimm?"

"No," Mandy said, happy to know the crow's name, "it's a crow I found in the woods. It doesn't speak."

"I shouldn't have thought the counselor would be happy to be kept in a cage," she said with an ironic smile. "A bit too fancy for that."

Mandy was growing exhausted from trying to keep up with the language. "Just make me food, woman," he said in German. Whether it was his words or his manner that startled her into action, he didn't know, but at least she had gone to a cupboard and pulled out a loaf of bread. With a large carving knife, she began to hack off a piece.

The knife blade was dark and stained, not the shining steel he was used to in his own world. Something about its rudimentariness appealed to him. He listened carefully near the door. There was nobody else around. He smiled at the crow again, and approached the woman.

"Here, let me help with that," he said, reaching for the knife.

As he struck the first blow, a voice cried out "No!" behind him. He turned. The crow.

"So you have revealed yourself, bird," Mandy said, letting the woman's body fall to the floor.

The crow began to shout. "Help! Help!"

Mandy picked up the woman's body and folded it into the sack. A lot of blood; it was a messy job. He hated messiness usually, but in this raw and uncivilized place it had a pleasing coherence. He stored the sack behind the door to pick up later, and seized the cage.

"Come along, Counselor Eisengrimm. I'm going to find a place where I can keep you quiet."

"Help! Somebody!" the crow called, but Mandy had already found another set of stairs, leading underground. The bird's voice was swallowed up by the stone.

"Where are we going, then?" Mandy said. "Perhaps there's a dungeon under here."

He came to a gate. It was unlocked. Another gate. The bird was quiet. Mandy made his way along the dimly lit passage. "How far to the cells, bird? What, not so talkative now?"

"What do you intend?" said the crow, in English.

"I intend to kill everybody I can kill and clean off their bones to use in a sculpture," Mandy said, opening another gate. "And I intend to capture Mayfridh and cut off her head. I don't know what I'll do with you, but if you're a counselor of some sort, perhaps you can advise the queen not to leave balls of magic twine lying around for anyone to find."

He had found the cells, eight of them, lined up four and four in the dark. He kicked a door open and deposited the cage on the floor.

"Now," Mandy said, "tell me where I'll find Mayfridh."

"Hexebart!" Eisengrimm cried. "Hexebart, you must help!"

Mandy looked behind him. "Is there someone else down here?" he asked. He hurried out of the cell and slammed the door behind him. He peered into other cells, finding in one of them a hunched hag with dirty hair.

"Hello," he said, "are you Hexebart?"

The hag twitched. A ball of pale light shone in her hands. She licked it and smoothed it over her ears. Then said in his own language, "What is your name, traveler?"

"Immanuel," Mandy said.

"Immanuel," she repeated, savoring the word. "What have you done to upset Birdbrain?"

Mandy chuckled. "I've put him in an iron cage and threatened to kill his queen."

"She is not the queen," Hexebart spat. "She is a nasty little impostor. One day I'll pull out her teeth and make a necklace of them."

Mandy was curious. He hadn't expected to find an ally. "Why do you hate her so much?" he asked.

"Because she had the real queen killed so she could get her hands on the royal magic."

"Is that so?" Mandy had counted on Mayfridh having royal magic. It would make the Bone Wife much better able to perform all her duties around the apartment. "I don't know if you could tell me where I'd find Mayfridh? I'd like to kill her."

"Certainly. If you let me out I'll show you where she is." She smiled. "I know all the secret passages of the castle."

Mandy considered. The hag's bones would be far too old and brittle to use in the sculpture, and her hatred for Mayfridh might make her a decent assistant. He tried a key and popped the lock, held the door open for her.

Hexebart shuffled to her feet and moved to stand near him. She peered up at him in the gloom, one eye twitching closed. "Immanuel, you have very beautiful hair," she said.

"Thank you," he replied.

She reached up and plucked a hair from his head and tucked it away in the bodice of her ragged dress.

Mandy laughed, heard his own nervous note. She was obviously crazy. "Which way?" he said.

"To where?" she asked.

"To Mayfridh," he replied, impatience touching his voice.

She clapped her hands together in front of her face. A strange pale light shone between them.

Mandy frowned, suspicious now. "What are you doing?" he asked.

She opened her hands. He saw her twisted smile through a delicate ball of light suspended between her fingers.

"Passage," she said. And disappeared.

🐀

Mayfridh shifted from foot to foot on the train platform, rubbing her hands together against the morning cold. Early light streaked the sky through the clouds. Diana stood next to her, sucking her bottom lip nervously.

"Really, Mum, I'll be back before you know it."

"You've said that before and then disappeared for weeks. How do I know this isn't the last time I'll see you?"

"Because I promise." Mayfridh buttoned her coat and tucked her scarf down inside it. Every breath of wind was laced with ice. "It's getting so cold."

"Winter's nearly here."

Mayfridh looked at her mother and tried to smile. What a powerful coercion guilt was. She should have returned to Ewigkreis last night, directly after Christine's phone call. But Diana and her trembling jaw kept her here in Zehlendorf, producing soothing reassurances. Layered on top of that was guilt about leaving Eisengrimm to deal with Mandy. And, of course, the guilt over her betrayal of Christine.

The train slid into the station.

"Bye, Mum," she said, enclosing Diana in a brief hug.

"Will I see you again?"

"I promise you will. I've just got a little problem to take care of back home."

"Don't be gone too long."

Mayfridh stepped with relief into the heated carriage. Diana waved good-bye from the platform, then disappeared from view. Mayfridh put her head between her hands to think. When did life become so complicated? Soon she would have to say good-bye to Diana forever. She would forget; her mother would remember forever. Twenty-five years hadn't healed the first loss. Mayfridh recalled Eisengrimm's original warning against seeking out Diana. Damn him for always being right.

And what of Eisengrimm? She had left him in charge, a de facto wolf king to defend her land against Immanuel Zweigler. Not that she thought Mandy was anything but harmless. Despite Christine's anxieties, it was clear to Mayfridh that he'd developed an infatuation and gone to find her. She felt such a raw pity for him; she knew love without any hope of a union. She trusted Eisengrimm to be kind to him, but Mandy would have to be told firmly to leave. An uninvited intruder might upset the balance of the seasons, precipitating an early winter. She shuddered. The last thing she wanted was to have him stuck in her world forever.

Mayfridh raised her head and watched suburbs speeding past in the gray light. Forever unraveled before her in her imagination. She had such a long time left to live. Four hundred years now seemed like a torture. Humans had the perfect life span: long enough to grow old with someone, yet short enough to inspire them to find meaning. She thought about Jude—the warmth of his skin, the weight of his gaze—and the space under her ribs felt bruised by the longing. He had made it clear: this love was impossible.

Now she had to convince Mandy his love was impossible too. Hopefully he wouldn't cause a scene. She wasn't in the mood for dealing with that.

CHAPTER TWENTY

*E*isengrimm?" *Mayfridh warily ascended the circular* staircase to her rooms. Eisengrimm hadn't been in the forest to greet her, so perhaps he was busy with Mandy. Maybe he had taken him to the village.

Mayfridh went to her bedchamber window. Through the branches of the giant birch, she could see the village in the slanting sun. Smoke rose from chimneys, children played in the streets. No sign of Eisengrimm and Mandy. Perhaps they had stopped at the tavern for a drink. What kind of adventure was Mandy on? Had he anticipated any of this? She wondered what he had expected when he stole the twine from Christine. Did he know, for instance, that Mayfridh was the queen of a race of faeries? She allowed herself a smug moment; how impressed he must have been when Eisengrimm told him. Surely he would realize she could never love him in return.

A sound near the door caught her attention. She turned around.

"Mandy?"

"Hello. Surprise." Mandy tried a smile. He wore a brown tunic—far too tight for him—leg wrappings like the villagers wore and a rough cap on his head. His hair was damp and he carried a muddy, stained sack. When he saw her looking at it, he dropped it on the floor and something inside rattled and clattered. "I went for a swim in the stream," he said. "I got my own clothes wet. I stole these. They were hanging on a tree branch."

She allowed a little smile. "Oh. Well, you'll have to make sure you return them before you go. Where's Eisengrimm?"

"He had something to take care of."

Mayfridh was surprised. It was unlike Eisengrimm to leave a stranger unattended wandering around the castle, but perhaps he had decided Mandy was little threat. She took a deep breath. "Mandy, we need to sort a few things out."

"Yes. Yes we do."

"I think I've guessed how you feel about me."

"You have?"

"Yes."

"That's good. Now I don't have to tell you." His eyes gleamed, and Mayfridh felt a twinge of unease.

"Nothing can come of it, though," she said quickly.

"No? You're sure?"

"I'm sure. Faeries and humans can't form relationships." She thought this simple truth the easiest way to let him down, but even as the words left her lips she realized that her encounter with Jude had been twice as foolish as she had believed. *Faeries and humans can't breed.* Now what? How could she make sure that no monstrous child had been conceived? Damn. She would have to tell Eisengrimm; he would know what to do.

Mandy was saying something, but she had missed it in her moment of preoccupation.

"Pardon?" she asked.

"I said that I thought that might be the case."

"So why did you come here?" she said. "How did you find out? Did you hear all of us talking about it?"

"All of you?" he said, and she saw his fingers tighten by his sides. "You mean *everybody knew*?"

"Um . . . yes. At first only Christine knew, but then I told the others." Why did she feel so guilty? Poor Mandy: everybody avoided him, nobody told him anything, and yet he was generous and patient with them all. "I'm sorry. The opportunity never came up to tell you, and I knew that I wouldn't be around for long."

He fell silent, gazing at her across the room. Outside, the shift and scuttle of leaves.

"Mandy," she said gently. "You have to go. You can't be here."

"I'd like to stay a little while."

"I know you're fond of me. Perhaps you've even fallen in love with me—"

"You have no idea how I feel," Mandy said, smiling ruefully.

"But it's never going to be possible for us to be together," Mayfridh continued. "It would be best for everyone if you went home and tried to forget about me."

He dropped his head. Released a quiet breath. "Yes. Perhaps it would be best."

She waited a few moments. She was anxious for him to leave, but she felt a great pity for him too, and pity was such a tyrant.

Mandy met her gaze again. "Mayfridh, could I have just one tiny favor?"

"Certainly. What is it?"

"Could I embrace you? Just once. I'd like to know what it feels like to hold you in my arms."

Her skin crawled, but she forced a smile. "I . . . well . . ."

"Please. And then I'll go, I promise. I'll go home, I'll leave you alone, and I'll deal with my feelings."

"Very well, then," she said, opening her arms halfheartedly.

He came to her, big and rough and hairy, and she closed her eyes as his arms circled around her and he pressed her to him. He sniffed her hair, a long, passionate inhalation. Then she moved back to break the embrace.

He didn't let go.

"Mandy, let me go now."

"I don't think I will." His arms tightened on her, and he began to propel her backward. She shrieked. Was he intending to rape her?

"Eisengrimm!" she called, struggling frantically against him.

"He can't hear you, he's in the dungeon," Mandy said.

"Let me go!" Her arms were pinned by her sides, her heart thundering. She should never have trusted him, never let pity cloud her judgment. "There are guards and . . ."

She twisted her neck to see where they were going. Surely he wasn't going to throw her out the window? Then he picked up the heavy brass bear on the chest.

With a sickening pain to her head, blackness descended.

❧

Christine mused that there must be a better venue for an engagement party than Super Jazz. The loud music was making it hard to talk and the thick smoke was making it hard to breathe.

"Okay, okay," Pete said, shooting out of his seat and raising his beer bottle. "We should have a toast."

"Yes, a toast," Gerda replied, clapping her hands together. "Everyone stand up."

She and Fabiyan stood, beer bottles at the ready, while Christine and Jude exchanged smiles over the tabletop.

"These guys are just perfect for each other," Pete said, "and I wish them many happy years together. To Jude and Christine."

"Jude and Christine," the others chorused, and clinked their bottles together.

Jude bumped his bottle against Christine's. "To us, Christine."

She took a swig of beer, relaxing into the evening. She still hadn't heard from Mayfridh, but the worry seemed farther away right now. It was easy enough to convince herself that Mayfridh was showing her castle to Mandy and that they would return together soon.

"And another announcement," Jude said as the others sat down. "I heard back from Australia. I made the short list for the fellowship."

Pete whooped and leaned over the table to hug Jude, knocking over Gerda's beer.

"Hey, watch it," she shouted, jumping out of her seat. A large beery stain was spreading over her shirt.

"Sorry," Pete said distractedly, before sliding back into his seat. "Jude, it would be so cool if you came back to Melbourne with me. You could stay with me and my mum. And Christine too, of course."

"I'm not in yet," Jude said, hands in the air. "Just on the short list."

Gerda was inching her way out from behind the table. "Don't worry about me. I'll just go and wash the beer out of my two-hundred-euro dress."

Pete waved a dismissive hand. "Big deal. Mayfridh bought it for you with faery money, anyway."

Christine rose and joined Gerda. "Come on, I'll help

you." She accompanied Gerda to the toilets. In here, the music was at a reasonable level for conversation.

"Pete really pisses me off," Gerda said as the door slammed behind them.

"He's just a kid."

"He's a *spoilt* kid." Gerda turned a tap on and splashed water over the stain. "The worst kind."

Christine caught sight of herself under the bright lights over the mirror and turned her back on her reflection. "Why does it have to be so bright in here?"

"They've had all the lights fixed," Gerda said. "Scary, huh?"

"Sure is."

"Anyway, what have you got to worry about? You've scored the most beautiful man in the world until death-do-you-part." Gerda wrung the moisture out of her skirt.

Christine couldn't help herself smiling again. Since this morning, it was all she could do. "Yeah, I know." She braved the mirror once again and fixed a smudge of mascara.

Gerda punched the button on the hand dryer. It didn't turn on. "Typical," she muttered, pulling a handful of paper towels from the dispenser. As she blotted her dress she caught Christine's eye in the mirror. "So why do you think he proposed?"

"Because he wants to marry me." Christine fought the irritation in her voice. Gerda had a habit of touching the most exposed nerve. "I guess."

"Sorry, Miss Starlight, I didn't mean to be rude. I meant, why *now*? We all knew you'd get married someday, but why now? Is it that Australian fellowship?"

"No, he only got the call this afternoon. And it's not for certain." *And I don't want to go to Australia.* Christine rested her back against the bench. "He said it just felt like the right time for us to get married."

Gerda inspected her skirt, bent over, and pulled it up to her face to sniff it, revealing her ample thighs in cherry-red tights. "Still smells like beer." She went back to the basin and rinsed the stain again. "I'm going to make Pete pay to have it dry-cleaned."

"He's never got any money. He owes Jude a fortune."

"So," Gerda said, toweling her skirt, "I take it you haven't heard from Mayfridh?"

"Not yet."

"Do you think she's okay?"

"Probably." Christine shrugged. "I mean, she's the queen. I guess there are people there to look after her, and Mandy—"

"Mandy's probably harmless," Gerda said. "I agree."

Christine thought about how he had wrestled the twine from her hands. "I don't know about harmless. But I don't think he intended any harm, if you see the difference. I think he's just in love with her and he's acted rashly."

"Easy to fall in love with, right? She's very beautiful."

"Yes, she is."

Gerda paused with a thoughtful twist on her lips.

"What is it?" Christine asked.

"Well . . ."

"Go on, tell me."

"I'm sure it's nothing," Gerda said, "but I'll tell you anyway."

Christine felt her stomach sink. What gossip did Gerda have up her sleeve this time?

"The other night I dropped in at your place to borrow some laundry powder," Gerda said, "and when Jude opened the door, your apartment was all dark and Mayfridh was just sitting there on the sofa."

"In the dark?"

"Yes. Maybe not completely dark; around twilight. But

no lights on in the house. And I swear she looked really guilty."

"How does someone look guilty?" Christine thought about how forcefully Mayfridh had convinced her to go to Ewigkreis that day.

"You know, kind of twitchy. Nervous, glancing around." Gerda demonstrated; Christine had to agree she looked guilty.

"I'm sure it was nothing," Gerda continued.

"Did Jude look guilty too?"

"No."

Christine tipped her head to the side and considered Gerda. "Okay, so what do you think it all means?"

"I don't know. I just thought I should tell you."

"Do you think I shouldn't marry Jude? Is that why you're telling me this?" Her annoyance with Gerda couldn't be contained beneath the usual excuses she made for her.

"No! God, no. I think Jude is great. I just think Mayfridh is after him."

Christine tried to get her smile back, tried to dilute the imagined scenario: the two of them alone in the dark. "It's probably nothing," Christine said. *I'm not giving him up.*

"Exactly."

"Come on, let's go back. My beer will be going flat."

"At least you have a beer to go back to. Mine's all over the floor."

The others had moved to a different table—Pete citing the reason as spilt beer—and Jude had bought Gerda a fresh drink.

Jude curled his arm around Christine's waist and pulled her into the seat next to him. "Now, seriously, guys. I need to talk to you about Mandy."

"Mysterious Mandy," Pete said.

"We're thinking of leaving the hotel," Jude said.

Fabiyan clattered his beer bottle to the table in shock. "No, don't go!"

"I don't know if it's safe to stay," Christine said. "The way he wrestled that twine out of my hands . . ."

"It's understandable you feel a bit shaken," Gerda said, "but that wouldn't frighten me enough to leave."

Christine curled her fists in her lap. Gerda had a talent for the casual put-down.

"Where would you go?" Pete asked.

"Back home," Jude replied. "We want to get married in New York anyway."

The taped music stopped and the live band cranked up. It became difficult to hear. They huddled closer around the table. The smoke from Gerda's cigarette made Christine's eyes sting.

"It is not as good here without you," Fabiyan said, "but I see that Christine is uncomfortable with Mandy."

"But do you think Mandy's dangerous?" Gerda asked him.

"How can anybody see? We do not know him so good."

How can anybody see? Christine turned Fabiyan's words over in her mind. That was the problem with Mandy, wasn't it? He was so unlikable that nobody had bothered to get to know him better, nobody had bothered to peel back the surface and take a look inside. Perhaps when Mandy had fought her for the magic twine she had really seen him for the first time. And now the black windows, and the locked door, and the faintly malicious smile took on new significance. She wondered if Mayfridh was all right.

"Look," Gerda was saying, "nobody would blame you if you left. But I'm staying. A fellowship like this only comes along once in a lifetime. Unless I thought he was going to murder me in my sleep I'd stay."

"I would too," Jude said. "But . . ." He glanced at Christine and she felt her veins zing with angry warmth. Surely he wasn't going to make her feel guilty about their decision to leave Berlin.

"But what?" she said, a challenge in her voice. "But my crazy girlfriend won't let me?"

"No, Christine." A soothing hand on her shoulder. "That's not what I meant. I have a responsibility to protect you—"

"A *responsibility*? You make it sound like I'm a baby. Or a mental patient in your care."

"Wedding's off," Pete declared cheerily, slurping at his beer.

Jude turned to the others. "We are leaving," he said firmly. "We are."

"When?" Gerda asked.

Jude turned to Christine, eyebrows raised expectantly.

"Soon," she said.

"You don't want to wait until Mandy gets back and give him a chance to apologize?" Pete asked.

"We'll wait until Mandy gets back, but only to see if Mayfridh's okay," Christine said.

"Can we have a big send-off party?" Pete asked.

"Of course we will," Gerda said. "And we all respect your decision to go. But Mandy's not a psycho. I'd bet all the money I had on it."

"I'm with Gerda," Pete said.

"You don't have any money," Jude replied, laughing.

Pete smiled. "Then it's a safe bet."

Hexebart likes the Real World.

Oh, what smells! Oh, what sounds! Oh, what shapes and colors! Hexebart is swamped by them.

Oops! Hexebart avoids a shiny metal speeding object

("car" *is the word . . . it was all in the potion made with Immanuel's pretty hair) and sees, for the first time, Hotel Mandy-Z. This is Immanuel's house. He shares it with others, but he has a room at the top of the stairs. Hexebart hopes it's a big room. Hexebart hopes it's warm.*

Big and warm, warm and big,
Room enough to dance a jig;
So much for the preening pig!

Hexebart could laugh until she cries thinking about the changeling princess and her featherbrained friend left behind in Immanuel's clutches. A fitting end for them both. Perhaps now they'll understand how Liesebet and Jasper felt. Mind, that Immanuel fellow is not to be trusted. Oh, no. Hexebart is not a fool.

She approaches the front door. No key. Never mind. Hexebart has magic fingers from years of weaving spells. See, she can make them long and narrow and her pointiest finger fits right in the lock and—snap!—it pops open.

Shhh, now. Hexebart steps inside and listens the house. Nobody home, not even a mouse. Hee hee! It's warm in here. Much cozier than dungeons and wells and other places Hexebart has lived lately. She creeps up the stairs, one foot in front of the other. The stairs creak once. She runs her hand along the banister; so smooth. Real World smooth. She lowers her nose and sniffs the wood. Pretty smells. Everything so pretty. Hexebart could grow intoxicated with Immanuel's house.

Here, a door. Hexebart can see many more stairs in front of her. This door isn't Immanuel's. She touches it and tries to imagine inside it. A boy lives here. Another door. A girl lives in this one. Hexebart will learn all their names. She will listen the house carefully until all the secrets come thrumming up the beams and shivering into her ears. More stairs. Another door. A man lives here. And across the hall . . .

Ah, Christine lives here. Jude lives here. Hexebart feels she already knows them from the time their secrets were in the pea shell, all the way in the bottom of the well. Their essence is so familiar. She breathes it in and her eyelids flutter. Oh, it will be so much fun to meet them. Won't they be surprised when they find out she knows their secrets! Hexebart can taste the fun upon her tongue.

Top of the stairs. Immanuel's door. The lock pops open around her elongated finger, and then she is inside a room so warm and big and sweet-smelling that she almost cries for joy. The door closes behind her. A large, colorful, soft thing makes her eyes grow round with wonder. A "sofa." Oh, the joy of a sofa! Hexebart sits on it, reclines on it, lies down on it, hugs it. So soft. So warm. Hexebart closes her eyes. She hasn't slept in more than twenty years. Weariness paralyzes her bones. Hexebart sighs.

Come, sleep. Come, sleep.

Christine woke from dark dreams that fled from consciousness as soon as she tried to catch them. What had disturbed her so much? The sticky web of disquiet clung to her. The bedroom was still dark, but morning was not far away. The streetlight outside flickered off. The curtain let in a soft gray light. Streetcars and buses and trains moved in the distance. Christine closed her eyes, trying to recapture the last shreds of her dreams.

Something about Mandy. Something about the door with the three deadlocks and the room with the black windows. Not surprising that she should weave them into a nightmare. He had become so sinister and dangerous in her imagination. Why hadn't Mayfridh returned? Sleep backed away.

Christine opened her eyes and watched the curtains grow paler as dawn seeped into the room. Her head ached faintly, a low coarse hum of insufficient sleep and excess beer. She listened to the city waking up around her.

Jude stirred. She cuddled up against his smooth warm back and dropped a soft kiss on his shoulder.

"Christine?" he said groggily.

"Don't wake up," she replied.

He turned onto his back and his eyes opened, two bleary cracks. "God, we drank too much."

"We always drink too much. It'll have to stop when we go home."

"What time is it?"

"Too early to be awake. Go back to sleep."

"Why are you awake? Is your back hurting?"

She snuggled under his arm. "No. Just a bad dream."

He stroked her hair and silence settled in the room again. Then he said, "What did you dream about?"

"Mandy, I think. I can't quite remember."

"He's really got to you, hasn't he?"

"Yes. You could say that."

Jude kissed the top of her head. "Don't worry. I'm here to protect you."

"Who's going to protect Mayfridh?"

"You're worried about Mayfridh?"

"Desperately. It's been two days. I haven't heard a thing."

Jude wriggled into a sitting position and rubbed his eyes. "Didn't you say time passes differently over there?"

"Yes."

"Well . . . perhaps it hasn't been two days over there. Perhaps it's only been a few hours."

"I suppose."

"She can look after herself. And she has Eisengrimm."

"Yes," she said, wondering if the unsettling dreams had

made the situation seem worse than it was, "but I wish that I knew if—"

"Shh!" Jude said sharply, his head cocked to the side. "Did you hear that?"

Christine shook her head and listened.

He pointed up toward the ceiling. "Upstairs. Listen."

Unmistakably, faint footsteps on the floorboards, from Mandy's apartment. He was pacing.

"He's back," Christine said, at once relieved and troubled. "When did he get back?"

"He's probably been there all night and we just didn't know," Jude said, then yawned broadly. "You want some coffee?"

"Mmm, yes, please."

He rose, found a shirt on the ground next to the bed, and pulled it on.

"Can I have toast and peanut butter too? I didn't eat last night."

He leaned over and kissed her cheek. "Sure."

Christine lay still, listening for the light footsteps above. Pacing and pacing. If Mandy was back, why hadn't Mayfridh called? Christine buried icy fingers under the bedclothes. The nights were growing colder. Winter was a few bare weeks away.

Jude returned shortly with a tray and climbed back into bed with her.

"Breakfast in bed. My hero," she said, reaching for the coffee. She warmed her hands on the side of the cup. "Is it going to be like this every morning when we're married?"

"Better," he replied, sipping his coffee.

"Why do you think Mayfridh hasn't called me to say everything's okay?" she asked. "She must know I'm worried."

"Since when has she been the queen of good manners?" he snapped.

Christine looked at him sharply. "I'm just wondering aloud. No need to get snippy with me."

"I'm not snippy."

"You sounded snippy."

Jude opened his mouth to say something, then laughed instead. "You're right. I did sound snippy." He brushed his fingers gently over her forehead. "I'm sorry. Of course you're concerned about her. Look, she's probably at Diana's."

"Why wouldn't she come back here? Why wouldn't she call?"

Jude shook his head. "That's probably my fault."

"Your fault?" Christine grabbed a piece of toast and took a bite.

"Yeah. The last time I saw Mayfridh, we didn't part on good terms."

"I don't understand."

"We argued. Gerda walked in on us in the middle of it. I'm surprised she didn't tell you. She's such a gossip."

So that was what Gerda had seen. Mayfridh had looked guilty because she had fought with Jude. "What did you argue about?"

"About you." Jude brushed crumbs from his fingers and sat back. "I was angry with her for convincing you to go to faeryland. She took offense. She thought I was casting doubt on her judgment, and on the wolf's ability to take care of you." He looked sheepish. "I was pretty hard on her."

"You scared her off?"

"I think so. I know I should have held my tongue, but you know how worried I get about you, and you know what she's like. She never really stops being a queen."

"What do you mean?"

"Okay, so she might not have a throne and a crown here in our world, but one way or another she likes throwing her weight around. She's manipulative. She uses people."

Christine was surprised at this judgment. "I can't say I'd noticed."

"Because you always see the best in everybody." He dropped a kiss on her shoulder. "That's why I love you."

Christine leaned back into her pillow and yawned. Sleepiness was catching up with her. "Well, I'll wait until a decent hour and then I'll call Diana's. But if Mayfridh's not there, one of us has to go up and ask Mandy about her." She smiled at Jude. "Mandy's someone I've never been able to 'see the best' in."

"I'd noticed."

"Last night I got the feeling that you don't agree with me about Mandy. Or about leaving."

"I was drunk last night."

"Are you sure that's all? I mean, I'd want you to tell me if you'd prefer to stay. I don't want you to be resentful."

Jude sighed and turned over on his side to face her. "Christine, I'm happy to take you home because I care about your feelings and I know you're not comfortable here anymore. But, yes, there is part of me that would like to stay."

"Why?"

"It's not about Mandy. It's about independence. You know that when we go home I'm going to have to live off you for a while if I want to keep painting. If I get this Australian fellowship, it doesn't start until July next year. I don't like being a leech."

"Oh, Jude, you're not a leech. I've always said that when I get married I'll access the money. We have so much."

"No, *you* have so much."

"But it's enough that you won't be depriving me of anything."

He nodded, resigned. "I know, I know. And, as I said, I'm happy to take you home. But if you sense any reluctance, that's why."

She reached out and tangled her fingers in his hair. "You'll earn your keep," she said playfully. "In housework and sexual favors."

He closed his eyes, a soft smile on his lips.

She wriggled closer and pressed her body against him. "You can start practicing now if you like," she whispered.

"Sorry, not in the mood," he mumbled.

Never in the mood anymore. She returned to her side of the bed. Her eyes felt heavy and raw from lack of sleep. She let them close. As she drifted off, she could hear footsteps again from above. They seemed far too close; she almost couldn't bear to hear them.

CHAPTER TWENTY-ONE

*M*andy was surprised by how peaceful this faery world was. He had imagined a land of chaos, of noisy preening faeries, of endless chatter and tantrums. Instead, the rural quiet pervaded his senses, filling him with a dreamy warmth and contentment. In many ways, it was so much better this way. It meant his hunting and killing and boning could take place in serenity.

He had watched the village from high on the slope above, studying its layout carefully. All the houses on the main street were too close together; hunting in one of them would alert the whole street. A low profile was imperative; he still wasn't sure where the hag from the dungeons had gone, and eventually somebody would notice the queen and her counselor missing and raise the alarm. The wheel of roads leading away from the main street were marginally more promising for hunting, with trees and spacious gardens between them. But there were cottages farther out on dusty roads, leading into the forest and farmland, which caught his eye. The faeries living inside would be easy prey. So he pulled his hat firmly upon his head, hoisted his hunting bag over his shoulder—the kitchen maid's bones were stored in Mayfridh's bedroom—and headed down through the forest.

It was cold today, but rural cold was somehow different from the urban cold back in Berlin. No tall, cool buildings to block the sunlight, and the peaty smell of smoke seemed to warm the air. Or perhaps his blood was just a few degrees warmer here, full of satisfaction and anticipation. Dried leaves crunched under his feet. He was most pleased with himself and felt compelled to whistle a little tune. Normally he was too embarrassed to whistle or sing, even when he was alone. An ear for music was not one of his gifts, and he could hear that there was something wrong with the melody, though he didn't know what.

A few hundred feet ahead the trees parted onto the back of a little garden and he paused a moment to survey it. Overgrown with thornbushes, with a sagging wooden gate. Sitting in a sunbeam on her back step was an old woman, her white hair untidily escaping a loose bun. She threw bread crumbs out in front of her and watched, smiling, as gray birds gathered to eat them.

Mandy considered. She was old; old bones were porous and snapped too easily. He slid down to the forest floor among the leaves and sat, his back against a tree, to think. In his own world, he wouldn't hesitate to catch her and kill her, but in a place like this, where he had such a wide selection to draw from, he should conserve his energy for only the best kills. Mayfridh he was saving until the very last, but not because of some misguided infatuation that allowed him unconsciously to want her to escape (oh, no, she and the crow were far too securely guaranteed against that). The decision was purely practical. He couldn't carry corpses back and forth to Berlin from here, so he had to bone in the river. Boning by hand was an inexact science, especially the volume he intended to do. He knew he could easily chip or scrape or splinter a bone. Mayfridh's bones, imbued with royal magic, were too precious to damage. She had to be scalped and dunked in the vat, simple as that. He plucked a long blade of grass absently and chewed on it. The sun was mild, but far away, and a breeze high up carried its warmth into the distance. He shivered and pulled his hat down harder.

Voices drew his attention and he glanced back toward the old woman's garden. A young, dark-haired man leaned in the doorway, talking to the woman and helping her up. Mandy smiled, pulled himself to his feet, and headed toward the cottage. By the time he had made his way through the sagging gate, they were inside.

"Good morning!" he called as he approached the door. He peered into the dark room. The two of them sat at a rough wooden table.

"Good morning," the old woman called sweetly.

The young man was more cautious. "Good morning," he said. "Can we help you?"

Mandy knew his uneven grasp of their language might draw suspicion. "I am a stranger in this land," he said, "a special guest of Counselor Eisengrimm."

The old woman beckoned him inside. "Are you lost?" she said, smiling a toothless smile at him. "I often get lost."

"Yes, I am lost," he said, moving inside the door and waiting politely near the end of the table. "The counselor sent me out for a morning walk and I've strayed too far from the town. Could you show me how to get back?"

"A friend of Counselor Eisengrimm," the old woman said, staring at him with shining eyes. "Sit down and join us and tell us of life at the castle. Have you met the queen?"

"Yes, I have," he said, concentrating hard to keep up with the conversation. Next time, he was going to have to murder someone in their sleep; this was too difficult. He avoided the seat offered—their smell was too strong—and leaned on a cutting board under a mullioned window, planning in his head. The woman would scream if he attacked the young man, but perhaps didn't have it in her to run for help. She was very frail.

"I've met the queen four times," she boasted. "Haven't I, Sig?"

Sig smiled fondly at her. "If you say so, Oma."

"Is Liesebet not beautiful?" the old woman said to Mandy. "So much more beautiful than her mother."

Sig patted Oma's hand and winked at Mandy. "My great-grandmother gets confused. She forgets that Liesebet is gone and Mayfridh is now our queen."

"Is that so?" Mandy smiled to himself. Liesebet was Mayfridh's mother. How clever he had been to kill her, and how much prouder he would be when Mayfridh was dead at his hand too. Immanuel Zweigler: slayer of royal dynasties.

"The queen is very beautiful," Mandy said, "and so was her mother."

Oma popped out of her seat and came to the sideboard. She was more agile than Mandy had given her credit for. Would he have to kill her too? Her smell was strong now, almost acrid.

"Here," she said, "have some cake before you head on your way." With a rusted cake knife she hacked some uneven chunks of food onto a plate and offered it to him.

"No, thank you." The thought of eating here repelled him.

"Ah, well. I shall give it to the birds, then." She shuffled out of the room and through the back door into the garden. Birds sat on the gate waiting for her.

Sig smiled at him. "She's a dear old lady. Three hundred and thirty next week."

"Good lord," Mandy said, suddenly slipping into modern German. He had had no idea that faeries lived that long.

Sig joined him at the window and together they watched Oma through the tiny, thick panes. Her body was distorted by them, oddly dislocated and misshapen. Mandy felt at his belt for the kitchen implements he had stolen from the castle. Cleaver, knife, mallet. He slipped one into his hand and while Sig was still gazing lovingly at his great-grandmother, pulled it out and raised it.

Sig saw him, his face registering horror. He reached for the cake knife; there was a struggle, a cry, and a great deal of blood. Oma saw none of it. Suffocating her with the sack directly after was very humane, Mandy thought, as he hurried down to the river with his sack full of warm faery. It would save her the shock of coming inside and finding her great-grandson's hand left neatly on the cutting board.

Twenty years of nightmares all in one night. Oh! Oh! Hexebart didn't sleep well at all!

Now the morning is here and Hexebart feels a little better. Hexebart can't quite get used to being inside and warm and comfortable. Every surface is soft and she could sleep and sleep. She won't, because of the nightmares. She tastes Immanuel's food and likes it, then sits down on the hard floor and listens to the house some more. Hexebart can hear Jude and Christine talking, has to make a quick spell to understand the language. Then Hexebart can hear a woman in another apartment, talking to nobody. No, she's talking on a telephone. But Hexebart can't hear anything else and the warm is making her sleepy again. Hexebart suddenly longs for the outside, for the cool air and the fresh ground.

Careful now, quiet now. Don't let anyone know who's here. In the Real World it's not allowed for old ladies to go into people's houses and eat their food and sleep on their soft things. One step, two. Creeping past all the doors and out into the street. Hexebart spies trees and grass and birds, and heads in that direction. Here's a place to sit and take big breaths of morning. In . . . out . . . in . . . out . . . But the Real World smell is on everything and suddenly Hexebart feels homesick.

Silly old woman. Hexebart bites her own fingers to scold herself. The Real World is full of fun and promise, and Hexebart won't be put off by a little homesickness. She watches people walking up and down the street. Some of them look at Hexebart and smile, but Hexebart darts her eyes away and hums an absent tune. Then the door to Immanuel's house opens and a boy steps out, and Hexebart knows immediately that this is the boy Jude.

"Hoy!" she calls. He doesn't turn around so she stands up and calls, "Hoy, hoy!"

The boy Jude turns and cocks his head like a bird.

"Hoy!" she calls again, beckoning him.

And he comes, just like that. Hexebart follows him closely with her eyes; Hexebart is clever enough sometimes to read people, but this boy is unreadable. This boy has many layers covering his secret self. Hexebart is glad she had the magic stuffs in the pea shell, or else she would never have found out his secret.

"Come here, boy," she says, in his language.

"What's the matter? Can I help you?" he says, and he is wary and he should be wary because Hexebart doesn't like such pretty boys who hide secrets.

"I'm lost," Hexebart lies, making her bottom lip tremble. "And I have no money and I am all alone in this place."

Jude won't stand too close and Hexebart can see he is holding his breath away. Ha! So he thinks Hexebart smells bad, does he! Well, Hexebart thinks that his whole world smells bad. Perhaps she should tell him that!

"Could you help me?" she asks.

He reaches into his pocket and fetches money. Hexebart grasps at it and tries to touch his hand but he pulls away quickly. "Here," he says, "it's all I have."

Hexebart wishes she could tell if he's lying. She suspects he is; she knows he's a liar. Hexebart doesn't like liars. Hexebart doesn't like Jude.

He turns to go.

"Wait!" she says.

"What is it?" he says. He's trying to be patient with Hexebart. He's trying to be patient with the crazy hag.

"I am alone," Hexebart tells him. "Are you alone?"

He pauses, and shakes his head. "No," he says, "I'm not alone."

She touches the very edge of his sleeve and he flinches but doesn't pull away. "Do you love someone? Do you have a beloved?"

Now Jude smiles, he's decided that the crazy hag is harmless, perhaps even amusing. "Yes, I do."

"And what is your beloved's name?"

"Christine."

"And does Christine know?"

"Know what?"

Hexebart's fingers move to his warm wrist. "You know what I mean," she says.

"Yes, Christine knows I love her," Jude says. Hexebart is so amused by his stupidity that she laughs loudly and suddenly Jude is not so sure and is trying to pull away.

"I meant," Hexebart hisses, "does Christine know you killed her mother and father?"

Jude twists and wrenches and jumps back and he is simply horrified. Hexebart doubles over with mirth. "Hee, hee," she says, "I've got your secret."

"Who are you?" he cries.

But she turns and scurries away from him, into the trees. He tries to follow her, but she uses a little glamour to make herself blend among the trees and he searches for her in vain before heading back to the street. Hexebart climbs onto a branch and sits there a while, thinking about Jude. Ha ha, that was fun. How many more friends does Mayfridh have here in the Real World that Hexebart can play tricks on?

Hexebart isn't homesick now; not even a little bit.

The blackness gave way to a paler wash of gray, and consciousness rushed on Mayfridh with a gasp. She opened her eyes. More blackness. No—a little light seeped from somewhere. Firelight? Was she in her room? But the air felt dank and stagnant and her whole body ached and shuddered. She certainly wasn't in her bed. Why did she feel so dazed and—

Mandy!

Mayfridh sat up, regretting it instantly. She put her hand to her throbbing head. She tried to focus; where was she? The darkness, the smell, the hard floor.

Of course. The dungeon.

She scrambled to her feet and grasped the door, shook it soundly and called out, "Help!"

"No, Mayfridh!" It was Eisengrimm's voice, from nearby. "Don't touch the door."

She jumped back as though scalded. "Where are you? What's happening?"

"Look through the bars. You'll see."

Mayfridh peered through the bars of the door and into the darkness. Opposite, she could see an amber glow like firelight.

"He's run a rope from your door. Can you see?"

Mayfridh spotted it. A rope had been attached to the bottom of the door. It ran up to the ceiling where it slid over a rudimentary pulley made of an old cart wheel and some kitchen hooks, then back down through the window of the dungeon opposite. "Yes, I see it."

"It's rigged up to an iron cage and I'm inside. If you open your door, it will drop the cage. He has a drum of burning coals beneath me. I'd be roasted alive."

Now she could make out the shape of Eisengrimm, as Crow, behind rows of bars. Behind him, his shadow moved eerily in the firelight. An overwhelming tide of dread and helplessness surged through her. "Oh, no," she managed to gasp in the dark.

"So don't shake the door. I don't know how secure these knots are, and I don't think Mandy much cares whether or not I die."

"Eisengrimm, I'm so sorry. This is all my fault. I don't know what's wrong with him. I don't know what he wants."

"I do," Eisengrimm said, and his voice sounded so serious that Mayfridh's stomach flipped over. The horrible reality of the situation rushed upon her, and she slid to the floor, trying to catch her breath.

"Mayfridh? Are you all right?"

"I . . . my head hurts. He hit me."

"I thought you were dead when he brought you in. When he spent all that time rigging up the cage I was almost glad. He wouldn't bother securing your imprisonment so carefully if you were dead. I knew you'd wake eventually."

"What does he want, Eisengrimm? What has he told you?"

Eisengrimm fought hard to keep impatience out of his voice. "Did you never suspect, Mayfridh? Did you overlook all clues to his true nature?"

"Eisengrimm, you're frightening me. I thought the worst

Mandy was capable of was embarrassing me with a declaration of love."

"Love, Mayfridh, is the last thing on his mind. He is full of hatred."

"For me? What did I do?"

"Not just for you, for all of us. For faeries as a race. He's a hunter of faeries, Mayfridh, and he collects their bones in the name of art."

Her disbelief was electric. "What?"

"He's a killer. I saw him murder Kat in the kitchen without even blinking."

Kat. Which one was Kat? Her head was spinning and it was hard to focus on Eisengrimm's words.

"For bones?" she said. "He murders faeries for their bones?"

"He murders faeries because he hates them. He bones them for his sculptures. He explained it all as he hung me above this fire."

"Then why hasn't he murdered me?"

"I don't know," Eisengrimm said quietly.

"Perhaps he won't," she said, fear boiling icy in her stomach. "Perhaps he is in love with me and—"

"It won't be long before someone notices we're missing and comes for us," Eisengrimm said quickly. "You must be brave and you must be cool."

Cool! Mayfridh would have laughed, only her throat was too constricted with terror. Her ears rang and her head throbbed, and a wall of gray descended on her.

"Mayfridh!"

Eisengrimm was calling. What was happening? She shook her head clear, realized she had lapsed into unconsciousness. "Yes, yes, I can hear you," she said. "The blow to my head is still affecting me."

"Are you bleeding?"

She touched the wound. Her hair was matted with dried blood. "No. I'm fine. Are you injured?"

"No, though this fire is very warm."

"How did he capture you?"

"Mayfridh, he has the speed and reflexes of a beast. It's uncanny and horrible to watch. He caught me in his bare hands in the forest and stuffed me in a sack. I didn't know what he intended, and assumed he didn't know who I was, so I lay very still to wait for a chance to fly away. If I'd had any idea what kind of man he was, I'd have transformed to Wolf and torn him to pieces immediately."

"And now? You can't change?"

"The cage is iron. It may crush me."

Mayfridh felt keenly her body's own vulnerability; so easily ruined, the life within so easily extinguished. Eisengrimm, her protector, couldn't help her. Who else could help her? She had royal guards somewhere in this village, for all they were untrained and chosen for their good looks. Where were they? Or had Mandy killed them already? She remembered the filthy clattering sack he'd had with him in the bedroom. Kat's bones?

"Don't despair, Mayfridh," Eisengrimm said, reading her silence perfectly. "He's spared you so far, he may yet. Someone may notice us missing and come searching for us."

"Or Christine," Mayfridh said, cheering suddenly. "Christine will worry when I'm not back and—"

"No, Mayfridh. Christine has no way of getting to us now. Mandy took her twine."

Her heart sagged again. She leaned her head against the door and forced herself to breathe naturally. Why was this happening? A primitive suspicion that her infidelity with Jude was being punished by a vengeful god overpowered her. She groaned.

"Mayfridh?"

She couldn't bear the terror in his voice. "I'm fine," she snapped.

"I can't see you," Eisengrimm said. "I've been waiting here for hours for you to return to consciousness. You must forgive me for my concern."

Her guilt intensified a thousandfold. "Of course, Eisengrimm. I'm sorry. I'm well, I'm whole, I'm conscious." A sob threatened to erupt through her sentence, and she hitched her shoulders to hold it in. "But I've done an awful, awful thing, Eisengrimm. You will hate me for it."

His voice became tender. "How could I hate you? You're my Little May."

"I did something hateful. In the Real World."

There was a long silence in the dark and Mayfridh felt the tears dry in salty tracks on her face. She palmed them, sniffed loudly. "Do you not want to know what it is I did?" she asked him.

"I think I can guess."

"Can you? Do you think so little of me that it's the first conclusion you draw?"

"Your voice and your words give away much, and you've been in love with Jude for a long time." His voice was resigned, sad.

"Are you very disappointed in me?"

"It's not for me to show disappointment or approval to my queen."

His words, his detached tone, froze her. "No, no. I'm not your queen. I'm your friend. Your very dearest friend. Please, speak to me freely."

"Mayfridh," he said softly, "I can never approve of what you have done. And yet, I can understand that love is a mighty engine that drives men and women to foolishness and ruin."

"Are you glad, then, that you are a wolf and not a man?"

"I am glad to be what I am," Eisengrimm replied quietly, "as anyone should be, no matter what their form or circumstance."

Mayfridh buried her head in her hands, her curls tumbling forward. "How can you still be so wise and composed, even at a time like this? I feel I shall go mad."

"You must take heart, Little May. At any moment, someone may come to find us."

"I can't stand not knowing. What do you think he's doing out there? Is he killing everybody?"

"I don't know, I don't understand him or his intentions," Eisengrimm said, "but I expect we will find out soon enough."

Christine's work send-off was ruined by Mayfridh's continued silence. While her boss toasted her with cheap sparkling wine and she munched her way through a German pastry, her mind kept reaching for explanations as to why her friend hadn't been in touch. Diana hadn't seen her (it was a mistake to call her, because she had grown extremely anxious and upset); Gerda hadn't seen her; she hadn't sent Eisengrimm to say she was fine. Christine knew that she would have to ask Mandy what had happened. Loathsome Mandy. Maybe she could convince Jude to go.

She arrived home to an apartment in chaos.

"What's going on?" she asked, stepping over a bag of rubbish tied up near the door. Jude was in a cleaning frenzy.

"Can you believe we've only been here five months and already we've collected so much junk?" Jude said. He crouched in front of the bookcase, pulling out papers and sorting them into piles.

"Are you cleaning?"

"I'm packing."

"Packing?"

"We're leaving, remember? We're leaving as soon as we can."

Christine slung her purse on the sofa and joined Jude at the bookcase. From here she could see into the spare room. The suitcases were open, starting to fill up with clothes and books. "Wow, you're seriously packing."

He looked up. A lock of hair fell over his eyes. "Is there a problem with that?"

"No, no. I just assumed we'd pack together. In a week or so when we've organized the flight home."

"I've organized it," he said. He rose to his feet and dusted his hands on his jeans. "Kind of."

"Kind of?"

"We can fly out on Sunday but—"

"Sunday? Today's Friday. That's very close."

"I thought you wanted to leave soon."

"I do, but . . . Why the sudden urgency?"

"I booked the tickets."

Christine ran a hand through her hair. If she asked Mandy about Mayfridh tonight, if they had a send-off tomorrow night, yes, they could make a flight home on Sunday. "Okay, we'll go Sunday."

"I haven't paid for them," he said.

"Sorry?"

"They cost a lot because they're such short notice. The airline wouldn't refund our original tickets. We bought them on a special cheap fare." He handed her an old pizza menu with his handwriting in the corner.

She blanched when she saw the figure. "That much?"

"Our other option is to wait a week, and I know you don't want to wait. I would have put them on my credit card, only it's maxed out. I hoped you could pay for them. I mean, seeing as how we're going to access your parents' money when we get home anyway."

Christine looked closely at Jude. For the first time she suspected that he was nervous. His eyes darted here and there, his words were quick and rambling. "Jude? Is there something you're not telling me?"

"No. What? What do you mean?"

She pulled him gently to the sofa and sat him down, sitting on the coffee table in front of him. "This morning you were still reluctant to leave at all. This afternoon, you want to spend thousands of dollars rushing home before we've had a chance to say good-bye to our friends. Before we've seen if Mayfridh is all right."

"I thought you wanted to go."

"I do," she said. The profound and undeniable truth. The idea of going home on Sunday, though only new to her, was dazzlingly appealing. Her own home, her own city, her own life; leaving all this confusion and wondering behind. "I want to know why you do. Tonight. When you didn't this morning."

His gaze fixed on hers a few moments, and she couldn't read his expression. Then, to her surprise, he began to cry. She had never seen him cry before.

"Jude?"

He buried his head in her lap and sobbed. She reached for him, smoothed his hair with her hands, both bewildered and afraid.

"Jude, for God's sake, you're frightening me. What's wrong?"

"I want to go home," he said, his voice rumbling against her stomach. "I've had enough of this. I just want to go home."

"I don't understand. You've had enough of what?"

"Of faeries and other worlds and magic. I'm overwhelmed

by it. I can't stand to think of it. It feels like I'm going crazy."

He sobbed harder and she soothed him with her hands, staring straight in front of her. Could it be that Mayfridh's *believe* spell had a use-by date? Was it wearing off, leaving only confusion and disbelief? Her own sense of belief was still strong, but she had experienced Ewigkreis firsthand.

"It's all right, Jude," she said, "we'll go. I'm happy to go on Sunday, I'm happy to pay for the tickets. It's all right."

He took a deep shuddering breath and sat up, wiping his face with his hands. "I'm sorry," he said.

"Don't be sorry. It's fine. I'm the one who wanted to leave, anyway." She patted his thigh. "But I'm not leaving before I ask Mandy what's happened to Mayfridh. He's probably got a message from her that he hasn't passed on yet."

"He's not there," Jude said, shaking his head. "I went up this morning after you left for work, and phoned again this afternoon. He's not around."

Christine frowned. "Where is he?"

Jude shrugged. "Maybe he had something else important to do. We'll try again tomorrow. He's always around on Saturdays."

Christine felt suspicion rise, but pushed it back down. Jude was out of his seat and handing her the pizza brochure with the airline's phone number in the corner. "They'll only hold our tickets until seven o'clock. You'll have to ring them right away."

"Sure, of course," she said, reaching for her purse to find her credit card. "Jude, what if Mandy's not back at all? What if he never came back from Ewigkreis?"

"We heard him upstairs," Jude said. "He's back. He's around somewhere, don't worry."

Don't worry. "Yeah, right."

CHAPTER TWENTY-TWO

Those nasty human people have been knocking on Hexebart's door and ringing on Hexebart's telephone all day. Can't they tell she doesn't want to speak with them? Can't they guess that Immanuel isn't home? They must surely be the stupidest of all races.

Hexebart is bothered by them. She is trying to listen the house.

Oh! Of course! They must be hearing Hexebart's feet, up and down on the wooden floor. Hexebart curses her own silliness and enchants the floor to make it very very silent. Then she presses her ear to the boards and listens.

At first, the house is quiet. Hexebart can hear her own heart, beating a dance in her ears. Then a voice, here, there. Sounds of water running. She centers in on Christine's voice. Christine doesn't know what to wear tonight. Jude is telling her she looks nice in blue.

> *Blue, blue, Christine trusts you,*
> *Does she know you killed her parents too?*

Hexebart cackles at her own song. Delightful, delightful! In another apartment she hears a man whistling, the sound of him shaving. He is saying nothing so Hexebart centers in on another voice, the other woman, Gerda. Hexebart likes to listen to Gerda talking on the phone to someone named Garth.

"Of course it's suspicious," Gerda is saying. "He proposed so suddenly and now they're rushing back to New York. I just know that something is going on. . . . Christine doesn't know, though . . . Well, I think Jude has run into some financial crisis . . . Yes, I've always said that he only wants her for her money. She's such a mousy little thing . . ."

Hexebart laughs. Gerda is saying spiteful things about Christine, but Hexebart has heard Gerda talking to Christine in a different voice altogether. Gerda pretends to be Christine's friend. How deliciously wicked!

But, oh! Hexebart has an idea. Hexebart knows just the punishment for a spiteful gossip. She smiles just thinking about it. Gerda the gossip, gossiping Gerda, Gerda groaning and griping to Garth. But Gerda will have a nasty shock very soon.

Hexebart listens. Voices die off, doors open and close. They've all gone out. Hexebart has the whole house to herself.

She sits back and holds her finger up in front of her. It grows long and thin, just right for picking a lock. She creeps down the stairs and finds Gerda's apartment door, and lets herself in.

This room is full of warm soft things, but not as many as Immanuel's. Hexebart sings a tune to herself as she looks around. In one of the rooms a sense of familiarity grips her, and she pauses, listening, smelling, looking.

Aha! The nasty little princess has been here. Hexebart can feel it in her bones. She approaches the bed. Yes! The preening pig has slept right here, in this warm bed. Hexebart crawls into the bed and imagines Mayfridh sleeping here, while Hexebart was back in the well with the frogs and lizards. Oh, oh, she hates that changeling so much it burns! Hexebart clicks her tongue on her teeth and can't even think of words for a song to sing about how angry she is. She hopes that Immanuel is torturing her slowly and pulling all her fingers and prickling all her toes. Hexebart only wishes she could do the same—what satisfaction!

Hexebart turns over and thrusts her hands under the pillow, burying her face in it. She bites it, angry, angry. And her hand comes to rest on something smooth and cool. What's this, what's this?

Hexebart draws out a picture. No, a photograph. In it, Mayfridh wears Real World clothes, and a thin gray woman next to her smiles a pained smile. Then Hexebart remembers: Mayfridh has a Real World mother. This is her.

Hee, hee. Hexebart pops the photograph in her pocket. Later, she'll make a spell to find out where this Real World mother is, and perhaps she'll pay a visit, yes, perhaps she will. Hexebart has many people to call on here in the Real World, many new friends to fit into her busy schedule. She pops off the bed and returns to the warm sofa, curls up on it and amuses herself with thoughts of how surprised Gerda will be to see Hexebart when she gets home.

❧

You see, Sig," Mandy said to the dead faery as he pulled out his bones, "if one is going to invade a country and take control of it, it should always be a peaceful country. They are far less prepared for such an eventuality." His hands remembered the task and the blood flowed away into the river.

Mandy waded farther out. The next part was messy, and he preferred to do it with the body deep underwater. He was up to his thighs now and, despite the cold, he enjoyed the labor, feeling both masculine and refined, both powerful and finely adept. Back to nature, that was the feeling. People went camping for the same reason: to feel they had returned to the basics, to touch once again that source of fundamental human practicality that urban living, with its shrink-wraps and its delivery services, removed them from. "Your own country, Sig, is woefully under-defended. I note that you, as a race, have become very peaceful. You all like each other. Nobody threatens the status quo. The royal guards are little more than dress-up dolls with swords and axes. I've easily avoided the one that rattles around the castle, and nobody has even noticed that the queen and her counselor have been missing for a day."

He pulled a gleaming bone free and threw it onto the riverbank. It landed with a whump. Sig wasn't listening to him anyway. Mandy was growing weary. He couldn't risk sleeping in the castle, so he had slept curled up at the base of a tall beech tree with stolen blankets and pillows. Not comfortable.

Mandy sighed as his hands worked under the water. He wasn't a young man anymore, and his original fantasies of killing at least a dozen faeries now seemed vastly ambitious. Perhaps he would only kill another three or four, and then take their bones back to Berlin, along with Mayfridh. She waited for him in the dungeon. What a clever idea of his to make escape mean certain death for Eisengrimm. Mandy wasn't sure of the extent of her magic powers, and she certainly hadn't used them to fight him off in the bedroom; even if she could open locks without keys, she wouldn't dunk her companion in a barrel of burning embers. Mandy had been in to stoke them up an hour or so ago, and had enjoyed not answering a single one of her desperate questions. His silence had unraveled her, and she had still been screaming when he left.

One thing she had said, though, was troubling. "Winter

will come, the worlds will slide apart, you'll be stuck here. Go home now, while you still can." This was something he didn't understand. He realized he had little comprehension of many aspects of faery worlds. Could it be that Mayfridh's warning was true? Or was it simply a ploy to scare him out of her kingdom?

This job was taking too long. He'd come to rely too heavily on his boning vat. The back-to-nature satisfaction was growing dull as the muscles in his arms and hands began to tire. Just a few more faeries, then. That would be enough, including Mayfridh, to finish the Bone Wife. No point in being greedy.

I'm afraid to die, Eisengrimm."

"Everyone is afraid to die, Little May."

Mayfridh leaned on the door, her face pressed against the barred opening. From here, she could see Eisengrimm's crow shadow, obscured by bars and shifting in the firelight. It gave her some comfort. Otherwise his voice, disembodied in the dark, started to feel imagined, as though she were completely alone. "I'm glad you're there, Eisengrimm. He's going to kill us, isn't he?"

"He might not. He might give us a chance to escape. If he lets me out of this cage for even a moment I'll tear him to pieces."

"Is the fire too hot? Does it cause you pain?"

"No, no. I'm at a sufficient distance from it." He sighed. "Mayfridh, you are the queen. You must be saved. I matter far less."

"Nonsense. I'm nothing without you at my side."

"I think you should try to open the door."

"I am locked in."

"We don't know that for certain. I didn't see if he had the enchanted keys. Indeed, how would he find them?"

Mayfridh winced, knowing she had left the keys carelessly beside her bed.

Eisengrimm continued: "Perhaps he set up this contraption precisely because he couldn't lock you in."

"But if I open the door, I'll plunge you into the fire."

"Yes. I know. But you would be free. You could save yourself."

Mayfridh's fingers clutched the rusty bars. "Eisengrimm, how can you suggest such a thing?"

"Because you're the queen."

"I'm sick of being the queen."

"Then, because of the great love I bear you."

"And I should repay that love by being the very person to burn you alive to secure my own survival? I would never even consider it."

"He knows that," Eisengrimm said, his voice so quiet she almost didn't hear. "He is counting on that."

"I know we are locked in. I left the keys where they could easily be found. I also know that somebody will save us," Mayfridh said. "Somebody will catch him, or notice we're missing." She knew, as Eisengrimm did, that this was not necessarily true. The entire village was in the process of gathering and storing the last harvest, preparing for winter. At this time of year, even her royal guards were sent down to the fields and the mill and the granary to help and only one maid was kept in the castle: poor Kat who was now dead. "We must have courage, Eisengrimm."

"I feel I have failed. Failed measurelessly."

She tried to focus on his shadow: his beak, the hunch of his wings. "It isn't your fault."

"I could have done more. I was too trusting."

"You only had my description of his character to base your assumptions on."

"You left me in charge, and I let something evil go free in our world."

"I gave Christine the magic twine. I made it possible for him to gain passage."

Eisengrimm fell silent and Mayfridh closed her eyes. They had gone over this ground a hundred times already: the self-recriminations of the condemned. For a long time the only sounds were her breathing, her heart, the occasional pop of a burning coal.

Then Eisengrimm said, "I wonder if I could break out of this cage."

She opened her eyes and located his shadow again in the dark. "How? It's made of iron."

"But surely a large powerful creature could break it open. If I changed to Bear—"

"You could be crushed to death."

"Or I could escape."

"You'd fall into the fire."

"Bear's too big to fit in the barrel. I'd just knock it over. Perhaps I'd burn my paws, but I wouldn't burn to death. And without the cage to constrain me, I could flee from the coals as soon as they spilled. I could break down this door, and yours too."

Mayfridh was tempted. In just a few minutes they could both be free. Her desire to survive overrode her reason. "Do you think the cage would break?"

"I think there's a good chance. Bear is large, the cage is small."

"But if the cage doesn't give . . ."

Eisengrimm pecked at the bars. Mayfridh could hear how sturdy they were. She had once kept a canary in it, until the contrast of its soft pale feathers against the black wrought-iron twists had distressed her so much that she had set it free. She thought of those sharp angles, biting into Eisengrimm's flesh. "I think it's too dangerous," she said.

"I could try it, and if I meet too much resistance I'll shrink back."

"Can you do that?" She knew that Bear was a hard form for him to control.

"I can. Mayfridh, I have to try something."

"We could wait. He might let us out to take us somewhere and then—"

"Mayfridh, I am in a cage," Eisengrimm cried out. "I cannot help you from this cage. He could kill you before my eyes and I would be helpless."

Mayfridh bit her lip, a sob rising in her throat. "But we can—"

"We can do nothing as we are."

"I don't want you to die."

"He could come back in ten minutes and plunge me directly into the barrel. I may die anyway. Let me try this."

For a few moments, Mayfridh felt as though her mind and her heart couldn't stand the situation any longer. Surely she would start screaming, and scream until her heart burst and she died. She tried to force air into her lungs. "You'll promise to shrink back the moment you're injured?"

"I'll have to press against the cage with my body. I may be a little injured."

"Before you go too far, then. Don't be foolish. You are more use to me alive than dead."

"I promise, Mayfridh. This isn't an attempt to extinguish my own life. It's an attempt to set us both free."

Mayfridh's voice trembled. "Very well, then. Good luck, old friend."

Clutching the bars, Mayfridh focused on his shadow. It trembled and the crow features suddenly expanded, forming a black blob against the firelight. With an excruciating sound of bones and ligaments creaking, the black shape swelled, shuddered against the bars of the cage. Mayfridh heard a loud snap.

"No, Eisengrimm! Stop."

Another snap, a horrible groan—half a bear's roar, half a crow's hack—and the shape shrank again, all the way down to a crow, which fell with a soft thud to the bottom of the cage.

"Eisengrimm?" Mayfridh cried. "Eisengrimm, are you hurt?"

"I think I . . ." He wheezed. The sound chilled her.

"Eisengrimm, what's wrong?"

"I think I have broken . . ." His voice trailed off to a gasp and then he was silent.

"Eisengrimm? Eisengrimm? What have you broken?" He didn't answer. Sobs pulled out of her chest. "Eisengrimm, answer me." She tried to focus in the dark. Was that movement shallow breathing, or just an illusion of the shadowy firelight? "Eisengrimm? Speak to me!"

The cage was silent.

❧

Christine had never seen Jude so drunk and it alarmed her.

"Come on, honey, one foot in front of the other." He leaned on her heavily, her back twinged, but she had to get him up the stairs to the apartment somehow.

"Can't," he said, grabbing for the banister, missing it and dropping.

Christine released him immediately. Holding on to him would cause too much pain. He landed on his backside on a stair, and rested there. His skin was flushed and his eyes were glazed and he stank of cigarettes and whiskey. They had been the first to leave Super Jazz—after Jude had thrown up on Sparky in repayment for the free drinks. Gerda, Pete, and Fabiyan were still at the club, no doubt speculating on why Jude got himself so wasted.

"Jude, honey. Come on. Not far to go. Then you'll have a nice warm bed to pass out in."

"Can't," he said again, leaning his head against the stair railings. "I'll just sleep here."

"No, you won't." She grasped his hand and pulled, causing her back to shriek at her. She dropped him quickly, her fingers going to her spine.

"Christine?" His drunken hands were fluttering up now, his voice all panicked and guilty. "Christine? Did I hurt you?"

"Please, Jude, just get up and come to bed."

"I didn't want to hurt you."

"Come on. We're nearly there, just a little further."

"I'm tired." He sighed and put his head on his knees. "I'm . . . so . . . tired."

She pulled his arm. "Come on, Jude, please. I'm not going to leave you here on the stairs and I can't carry you."

He straightened up, stood unsteadily. "No, of course. You can't carry me. We'll be home soon. It'll be nice to be home, won't it, Christine?"

"Do you mean home here in Berlin, or back home in New York?" she said, her hand under his elbow to steady him as they took the remaining stairs.

"Home where nothing ever happened to us," he slurred. "Home where it was easy."

"Okay, whatever." She had the key in the door. "Come on. Inside."

He shuffled in and she guided him to the bedroom where he sprawled on the bed, eyes closed. With a sigh, she unlaced his shoes and eased them off, unbuckled his belt, and took his wallet and keys out of his pocket. Then she turned him on his side and pulled the covers up. By now he was fast asleep; the absolute-and-entire sleep that only babies and drunkards know. Christine sat on the edge of the bed and watched him: his tangled hair, his pale fingers clutching the pillow. She was tired too, weary to the bone, but she couldn't sleep without knowing if Mayfridh were safe.

Mandy was nowhere to be found. He hadn't opened the gallery, answered his door, or picked up his telephone all day. Either he was hiding, or he hadn't returned from Ewigkreis and the footsteps upstairs had been boards settling, or rats, or something. Christine was worried sick. Mayfridh hadn't contacted her and Christine didn't trust Mandy.

She left Jude sleeping, switched off the light, and closed the bedroom door. Checked the answering machine; nothing from Mayfridh. She sat on the sofa and looked up at the ceiling. Mandy's floor. No footsteps tonight. In fact, she hadn't heard them at all today. So far, only Jude had tried Mandy's door. She checked her watch. It was one in the morning.

Before she could think better of it, she was on her feet and heading up the stairs to Mandy's apartment. She knocked. No answer. She knocked again. Remembered that the other time she had been here, his door had been unlocked. She tried it.

It opened.

Either he was too rich to care about burglars, or he was doing laundry at one A.M. She nervously backed down a few steps, leaned her head over the railing, and listened. Not a sound: no whir of a washing machine, no footsteps nearby.

Taking a deep breath, she went inside and switched the light on. One glance told her why the door was open, and what the footsteps had been: Mandy's apartment had been broken into. It was a mess. Blankets were draped over the sofa and floor, books had been pulled out and left haphazardly over the tables and chairs, food scraps lay on dirty plates everywhere she looked, and the smell of stale rubbish and old sweat hung in the air. Someone had been camping here. A quick check of the television and stereo told her it hadn't been thieves, but the state of the room told her it hadn't been Mandy.

He wasn't back. He was still in Ewigkreis with Mayfridh. What the hell were they doing there? Christine glanced at the mess around her and balled her fists in frustration. How could she go home to New York without knowing what had happened to Mayfridh?

She shouldn't be up here, especially if someone had recently broken in. Whoever had made this mess might still be here or intending to return soon and, besides, she should call the police.

"Anyone here?" she called, advancing into the kitchen and turning on the light. More food scraps. The intruder had eaten a lot for someone who had only stayed one night. Bugs buzzed around the sink. She checked the bedrooms and the bathroom. The apartment appeared to be empty.

She hesitated on the stairs up to the second floor. What precisely was she looking for? But she knew: she wanted to see if that narrow door was still locked. She wanted to know what Mandy was up to.

"Hello?" she called, taking the steps slowly, peering around the doorway to see if anyone waited for her up there. "Hello?" Nobody. In fact, the room seemed much emptier than last time she was here. She gazed around. Of course, the beautiful statue of the woman's body was gone. Mandy must have sold it, even though it was unfinished. Or perhaps it was finished. Perhaps Mandy thought half a woman's body made a good sculpture. This thought made her shudder, and she became aware of how vulnerable she was up here alone, with an unconscious Jude the only other person in the building. Christine grabbed a sculptor's mallet from the shelf and held it firmly in her right hand. She went back to the stairs, leaned over the railing, and listened. Silence. The locked door awaited.

Perhaps because the front door of the apartment had been unlocked she presumed the mysterious door would be too. It wasn't. Every deadlock was in place. No access

Christine ran her fingers over the door, frustrated. The enamel paint was very thick and had dried in a pattern of dribbles. The door itself was narrow and short; Mandy, surely, would need to duck his head and take a deep breath to get through it. A little door, leading to . . . where? A little staircase to a little room where the windows were painted black.

She turned to survey the room. Perhaps a set of keys hid in the mahogany desk. Hefting the sculptor's mallet in one hand against imagined enemies, she sat at the desk and began to search it. Pens, pencils, papers, but no keys. She slammed the last drawer closed in frustration.

"What the hell am I doing here?" she muttered. Mandy wasn't here; Mayfridh certainly wasn't. In less than forty-eight hours she had to catch a plane to New York and she couldn't see how that was possible if she hadn't heard from either of them. But coming into Mandy's apartment and searching his desk was not going to help her.

She halfheartedly checked the drawers again. One of them had carefully stacked notebooks in it, and she pulled them out to leaf through the pages. Perhaps Mandy had stashed the keys between the covers. Most of the books were art journals, full of sketches. One was a ledger of accounts for the hotel. The book at the very bottom, a scrappy spiral-bound notepad, was filled with Mandy's handwriting. She glanced at the front: *from the Memoirs of Mandy Z.*

Christine almost laughed. Trust Mandy to embark on

something so narcissistic as an autobiography. He considered himself something of a celebrity. Curious, she opened to the first page and began to read.

Within moments, her blood had chilled. She turned the page: *I have a measureless loathing for faeries. And I am the Faery Hunter.*

"Oh, my God," she gasped, flipping forward, scanning the pages. Mayfridh was in terrible danger. Did she know it yet? Or was she still assuming Mandy had an innocent crush on her? She read a little farther, sickened by the details. A surreal panic lurched through her. It was one thing to believe in faeries—Mayfridh's spell had helped to cope with that—but it was beyond imagining that the wealthy billionaire had devoted his life to hunting and killing them. Her head spun, and she had to grab the edge of the desk to reassure herself that what she was experiencing was real. Somewhere downstairs, she heard people arrive home. Gerda and the others. It barely registered as she flicked quickly through the notebook reading snatches here and there. Her stomach clutched against the awful helpless fear. There was absolutely no way for her to get to Ewigkreis to warn or help Mayfridh.

A scream broke into her train of thought. At first she believed she had imagined it; that it was the scream inside her head that she hadn't let escape. But then it came again. A woman's scream from somewhere in the hotel.

Clutching Mandy's book under one arm and the sculptor's mallet in the other, she hurried downstairs and out of the apartment.

The scream came again, this time followed by a frantic voice. "What have you done? What have you done?" Gerda. Commotion on the landing as Fabiyan opened his door and leaned out, as Pete raced across the landing to Gerda. She stood there, crying, "Where did she go? Did you see her? She's disappeared!"

But something was very wrong, because every time Gerda spoke, she spat something from her lips. Christine peered down the semi-lit stairwell as she came down. For a moment, she was reminded of a rabid dog she had seen once, spitting foam left and right, distressed.

"Gerda?"

"What the fuck?" This was Pete, taking two steps back from Gerda in horror.

Gerda turned to him, her eyes wild with terror. "What has she done to me?" And as she spoke, two tiny frogs jumped from her lips and pattered to the ground. Christine looked around her feet: frogs, lizards, locusts, all scurrying away from the loud voices and the panic.

"Who did this?" Christine gasped. "Who did this to you?"

"Oh, God! You have to help me," Gerda shrieked, and a shower of locusts sprayed from her mouth. "She said her name was Hexebart."

CHAPTER TWENTY-THREE

W here's Jude?" Pete asked, as Christine searched for a bucket under the sink.

"In bed. Unconscious." She approached Gerda, who sat at the kitchen table in Christine's apartment, her face flushed and her eyes teary. Christine put a bucket in front of her. "Here."

Fabiyan, who sat across from Gerda, watched her in awe. "Where do they come from?" he asked.

Gerda shook her head, tight-lipped.

"Okay, Gerda," Christine said, pulling up a chair, "so Hexebart did this to you?"

Gerda nodded.

"Where? Outside? In your apartment?"

A nod.

"She followed you home?"

No.

"She was waiting for you?"

Yes.

"And she said her name was Hexebart?"

"Who is she?" Gerda said, and a lizard plopped into the bucket.

"That is so amazing," Pete said, leaning over the bucket. "Can I get my video camera and film this?"

Christine pushed Pete away in irritation. "Hexebart is a witch from Mayfridh's world. She's supposed to be imprisoned. I have no idea how she got here, but it must have something to do with Mandy." She slapped the notebook on the table. "The guy is a homicidal freak. He's been hunting faeries for decades. None of us had any idea, least of all Mayfridh."

"What are you talking about?" Pete asked.

"I'll explain in a minute. Gerda, did you see where Hexebart went?"

Gerda shook her head.

"Did she leave by the door, or did she just disappear?"

"Door." A tiny frog jumped from her lips. Pete caught it and put it in the bucket.

Christine ran a hand through her hair. "I have to find her. She's my only hope of getting back to Ewigkreis. I have to warn Mayfridh. Or save her, if it's too late to warn her."

Pete held his hands up, a "slow down" gesture. "Wait, Christine. You're seriously going to try to find this witch? Look what she's done to Gerda."

"Gerda's still alive, at least. Mandy wants to kill Mayfridh and use her bones for a sculpture. I bet Hexebart was squatting at Mandy's. Maybe she'll go back there."

"Will she take the spell off?" Gerda said, spitting locusts and frogs.

"I don't know. But if I find Mayfridh, she can take the spell off."

Fabiyan was flicking through Mandy's memoir. "Where did you find this?"

"In his desk."

Pete leaned over his shoulder, reading a line Fabiyan

pointed out for him. "Oh, my God. Is this for real? This guy is a psycho."

Christine's eyes ached and her heart sped. "I feel so helpless."

"We will help if we can," Fabiyan said. "Anything you say."

"Okay. Right, Fabiyan, can you go up to Mandy's and keep an eye out for Hexebart? If you see her, don't approach her. Just call me. Trap her up there if you can, lock her in. Pete, can you take Gerda back to your place? Don't make her say anything and don't film her." She handed him the bucket. "Gerda, hang in there. It may only be a temporary spell. If not, I'm sure Mayfridh or Eisengrimm will be able to fix it." She glanced back toward the bedroom. "I'd better wake Jude and tell him what's going on."

Pete led Gerda out and Fabiyan warily took the stairs up to Mandy's apartment. Christine closed the door behind them. Her knees shook and for a moment she had to steady herself against the doorway. Was Mayfridh already dead? The thought was unbearable; Mandy preying on her like a cat preys on a butterfly. But then, if Mayfridh were dead, surely Mandy would have returned by now. She clung to that thought. Until he came back, she could convince herself that Mayfridh was still alive.

Christine entered the bedroom and sat on the edge of the bed. Jude, in exactly the same position she had left him, was fast asleep.

"Jude," she said, shaking his shoulder lightly. "Jude, wake up. It's urgent."

"Mmm?"

"Wake up," she said, her voice cracking over a sob. "It's life or death."

He reached out a hand for hers. "Christine? Are you okay? Are you hurt?"

"No, I'm fine," she said, sinking down next to him and letting the tears come, "but Mayfridh's in terrible danger."

"What? What are you talking about?"

She explained as fully as she could through her helpless tears. As her eyes adjusted to the dark, she could see Jude's face take on a bewildered desperation as sobriety crashed in on him.

"Oh, Jesus," he said when she had finished, pressing his fingers to his forehead. "Oh, God."

"I have to find Hexebart, I have to—"

"No!" he cried. "No, I don't want you anywhere near her. Stay away, stay far away."

"But she might help."

"From what you've told me, it's more likely she'll turn you into a frog."

"I have to get to Ewigkreis."

"I know, I know."

"Mayfridh's in terrible danger."

He raised his voice. "I know!"

She drew back, startled. "Jude?"

"I can't take this anymore. I don't want you to go to Ewigkreis. What if Mandy kills you too?"

"He hunts faeries, not people."

"You just told me he boils faeries alive. I can't predict where he'll draw the line."

"You can come with me, then. If we can find a way to get across, you can come and we'll find Mayfridh together."

"Yes, but how? How does Mayfridh get back and forth?"

"The passage." Christine snapped her fingers. "Yes! It will stay there until the winter comes. Mayfridh doesn't need twine; perhaps we can try it."

He sprang out of bed. "Okay, I can't just lie here and talk about it. I have to do something. Let's go down to the

Tiergarten; let's try the passage. I'll go crazy if I have to sit here useless another moment."

"Agreed." She watched him lace his shoes. "Jude, I can't bear to think of what Mandy's doing to her. What if he's torturing her, or killing her slowly, or—?"

He reached out and pressed his fingers to her lips. "Don't paint pictures in my head," he said gently. "Please, Christine, don't make it worse than it already is."

Hexebart is cold, but she doesn't mind so much. She's having trouble getting used to all the soft things and warm spaces, and out here in the branches of this tree, with the stars and the wind above her, Hexebart feels a little more like her old self.

Besides, there's a special kind of thrill in being outside looking in. Oh, yes.

> *Through your window, through your curtain*
> *Hexebart can see you certain,*
> *Sees you sleeping in your bed,*
> *Not a worry in your head.*

Ha! This is fun. This woman's name is Diana, and she is the nasty pig princess's mother. She is old and ugly and sleeps in a yellow dress with bare elbows. Nothing special at all about her. But Hexebart can make her more special.

Hmmm, let's see. She'd be more special if she only had seven fingers, or eight toes. She'd be more special with no nose and only one ear. She'd be very very special with a head like a donkey. . . . Where should Hexebart begin?

Yes, yes, Hexebart knows she's taking out her hatred of the little princess on this sour old woman. But Hexebart has been down a well for years and years, and she misses Liesebet so sorely, sorely so. Diana isn't Liesebet. Diana is just a stupid human with ten fingers and ten toes, and Hexebart

will fix that soon, you'll see. Everyone will see. Such fun,
oh, such fun, rum-a-dum-dum.

❧

Dark and windy, and faraway sounds of trains and streetcars, and leaves falling and skittering, and moonlight shifting and flickering in the blustery shadows. Even though
Christine was certain she stood precisely where the passage
lay, nothing happened when she took a step forward. She
readjusted her starting position and tried again. Nothing.
Without the twine, it was useless. Jude sat a hundred feet
away, reading Mandy's diary by the light of a torch. He
glanced up.

"Christine, you've been trying for half an hour," he
called. "It isn't going to work."

Christine sighed. "I know. But I can't go home. I can't
just leave her."

Jude closed the diary. He raised it with his right hand.
"How could we not have known?"

"Until Mayfridh came along nobody believed in faeries."
She joined Jude on the bench. "If we'd found it we would
have called it imaginative fiction. Grisly, in keeping with his
horrid personality. But fiction."

"When Mayfridh gets back, we won't show it to her. I
mean, that stuff about her parents . . ."

"It's horrific. She doesn't need to know."

Jude slid his arm around her waist. "It's cold. We should
go home. Think of another way."

"Yes. Yes, I know." Still they didn't move. The silence
between them drew out, filled with the sounds of the trees
moving and shivering. "Jude, Hexebart may be able to
help."

"I don't see how."

"She's got all the magic. She could send us across to Ewigkreis."

"Yes, but she wouldn't help us, Christine. You've told me: she's bitter and full of hatred and she despises Mayfridh. Why would she do anything to help?"

"Because Mayfridh's the queen. She's under some kind of magical oath, but I'm not sure how far it extends. We know Hexebart is around here somewhere. If we can find her we could ask. The worst she could do is say no."

"The worst she could do is turn us all into frogs."

Christine put her head in her hands. "I'm so tired I can't think," she said. "What time is it?"

"Four o'clock."

"I'm afraid to go to sleep. I'm afraid to stop searching for an answer even for an instant, in case that's the instant he chooses to kill her."

"We'll think better after a few hours' sleep. Come on." He rose and held out his hand to her. She took it reluctantly and they walked to the edge of the park.

"Promise me we'll only sleep a few hours," she said. "And promise me that we'll look for Hexebart tomorrow."

"I'll look for her. We'll leave Fabiyan up at Mandy's, and I'll search for her. You can finish reading Mandy's notebook in detail, in case he's left any clue."

"How will you search for Hexebart? She could be any-where."

"I'll start in the park at the end of the street," Jude said. "I don't think she's 'anywhere.' I think she came to play with Mayfridh's friends. Why pick on Gerda otherwise? I think she's nearby."

That thought was both comforting and frightening. "I should be with you. If you find her, I should be there to talk to her."

"No. No point in both of us being put under some horrible spell." He squeezed her against him as they approached the road. "Promise that if a lonely little frog comes knocking at the door, you'll take him in and treat him well? Just in case it's me?"

Christine managed to smile. "Don't joke, Jude."

"I'll be careful. Let's catch a taxi home."

Sitting in the back of the warm, quiet taxi, Christine's mind still raced and her pulse still hammered. She didn't see how she could ever sleep. But a short time later, lying in bed next to Jude, the weariness began to override the worry. She dozed and woke, dozed and woke until dawn's gray light began to seep into the room. It was only then that she noticed Jude wide awake next to her, staring at the ceiling. She considered him through half-closed lids, then turned over to let sleep come again. But not before she had seen such a look of horror on his face that it made her heart chill. He was worried about Mayfridh; desperately worried. All that talk in the past of Mayfridh being able to look after herself, his descriptions of her as irrational and spoiled, clearly had been a feigned nonchalance. Jude was worried like a man in love.

Christine thought she knew, now, why Jude had wanted to leave Berlin in such a hurry. Perhaps even why he had proposed to her so hastily. Those red and fuchsia brushstrokes may have been dutifully painted out, but they were still under there somewhere. Strong and bright as ever.

Mandy took the long walk down to the dungeon with a spring in his step. In his stained sack he had the bones of three faeries. He had stacked them under a tree near the lake, but this morning had found them disturbed and a number of them stolen. Wolves, probably. What dog could resist a bone? So he'd thought long and hard about where to put them, and come up with a solution that was both safe and entertaining. If he piled them outside Mayfridh's cell door, she'd have to look at them every time she wanted to talk to her crow! What a lovely reminder for her of what she'd be reduced to soon enough. But carefully, with her; in the vat, not this business of hacking flesh from bone. His fingers, usually so careful with his sculptures, were growing careless in his excitement. He had cracked and splintered two bones already. He couldn't risk that happening with Mayfridh's, not with all the magic infused into them.

"Good morning, Queen and Counselor!" he called cheerily as he advanced down the final hallway. No answer. He hadn't expected one.

He dropped the sack with a clatter, then began to pile the bones halfway between Mayfridh's door and Eisengrimm's. "Are you well, Mayfridh?" he asked.

Again, no answer. A moment's panic. Was she still there? One glance into her cell reassured him. She sat against a back corner, disheveled and broken.

"What's the matter, Mayfridh? You look terrible."

"Leave me be," she spat in her own guttural language.

"Is there something wrong?"

"Let Eisengrimm go."

"Why?"

"He's injured. He's no use to you, his bones are too small."

"Injured?"

She choked back a sob. "He might be dead."

Fear seized Mandy. If the crow were dead, she'd try to escape. He glanced over his shoulder into the other room. "I'll check for you," he said, releasing the rope from the ceiling and pulling it toward him. The cage swung up to the barred window of the cell. Eisengrimm was indeed lying motionless on the bottom of the cage. Mandy slid a finger between the bars and poked the bird. No response. "Well, now, it's hard to tell. Was that a twitching foot?"

Mayfridh was at the window to her cell. "Leave him be. Let him go."

He was fairly certain Eisengrimm was dead, but didn't want to let her know that. "I won't let him go, Mayfridh. He's my insurance policy." He peered close. The crow was breathing, shallow and slow, but breathing. "He could very well be alive, you know. It's difficult to say for sure." He let the cage swing back into place and replaced the rope on the hook. "You'd better be careful you don't roast him. Don't open the door, will you? I'll stoke this fire up nicely to keep him warm while he recovers."

"Is he really alive? Are you lying to me?"

"I don't think I'll tell you."

She shook the cell door in frustration. The rope jiggled and the cage swayed.

He held up a cautionary finger. "Be careful now, Mayfridh. I'm not much of a handyman. That cage could drop at any second if you're too rough with the door."

But now she had caught sight of the bones, piled artistically with the three skulls sitting on top. Her face grew pale.

"Oh, no . . . who . . . ?"

"Ah, this is the start of my collection. I hope to add to it before I leave. I can't tell them apart now, of course. All faeries look the same once you pull their skin off. But one of them is a woman from your kitchen, one a young man named Sig from the outskirts of the village, and the last was a farmer I caught wandering the edges of his field alone, looking for his dog." He glanced up, a smile on his lips, to see if she was listening. Her knuckles were white around the iron bars, her eyes glassy and frantic.

"Mandy," she said, her voice little more than a choked whisper. "Has it grown very much colder outside?"

Mandy frowned, a finger of fear touching his heart. "Yes, it has. Why?"

"Has the west wind grown stronger? Are the last leaves being torn down?"

"Yes, why?"

"What you're doing is upsetting the balance of the seasons. Winter is coming early."

"Why should I care?"

"Because when winter comes our world will move; you'll be trapped here forever. And if you stay, you'll eventually become one of us. One of the very creatures you loathe so much."

"You'd say anything to make me go."

"I'm telling the truth."

He watched her for a moment, transfixed. Then shook his head and pointed to the pile of bones. "There's your view. I'll add to it later today. Enjoy it in the meantime, and careful you don't cook the bird." He turned and stalked back up the corridor, angry with her for making him fearful. Carefully, carefully, he checked the long hallway before emerging aboveground, then darted out into the wild garden.

Mandy turned an eye to the sky. The clouds were slate gray, making the late afternoon prematurely dark. A frosty bite hung on the air. And, in the almost-bare branches, a cruel wintry wind began to play.

~~

Christine put down Mandy's notebook memoir on the coffee table and rubbed her eyes. She had read every ghastly word now, and was more frightened for Mayfridh's safety than before.

The door to the apartment opened and Jude walked in.

"Any news?" she asked hopefully. He had been checking

with Fabiyan, who still kept a vigil at Mandy's, hoping for Hexebart's return.

Jude shook his head. "She hasn't been back. No footsteps on the stairs, nothing. Gerda's nearly out of her mind, convinced she's going to be spitting worms for the rest of her life."

Christine tapped the notebook. "This makes for interesting reading."

"I know. I glanced through it."

"But you didn't read it in detail." She picked up the notebook and flipped it to the last page. "He's absolutely ghastly."

"I believe you, Christine. I don't want to hear it."

"Listen," she said. " 'Now I know I want Mayfridh's head. I will use her gleaming skull, and fill it with plaster and—'"

In three quick steps he was across the room, tearing the notebook from Christine's hands and slamming it shut. "I said I don't want to hear it."

She'd done it on purpose; she knew she had. She wanted to see how he would react. "Sorry," she said.

He handed back the notebook and grabbed his coat off the back of a chair.

"Where are you going?"

"Back to the park at the bottom of the street."

"You've already checked there twice."

"I've just got a feeling Hexebart might show up there."

Christine shrugged. "It can't hurt."

He pulled his coat on. "Be careful. If Fabiyan calls, if Hexebart turns up at Mandy's again, I don't want you to go anywhere near her. Let Fabiyan deal with it until I get back."

"But Jude—"

"Christine, you've suffered enough. I won't have you suffer more. She could put some awful spell on you."

"Or you."

"But it's my job to protect you. Just let me do that, okay?"

Christine gazed at the cover of the notebook, feeling like a useless, pitiable creature. *His job to protect me.* As though he were a kindhearted social worker. "Okay, I'll stay away," she said.

He closed the door quietly behind him. She dropped the notebook on the floor next to the sofa and stretched out, closing her eyes. She had slept only a few fitful hours, her mind turning over the problem again and again. They had pinned too many hopes on finding Hexebart. First, Hexebart might not even help. The witch hated her queen: why should she do a single thing to benefit Mayfridh or her friends? Second, and most pressingly, Hexebart had disappeared. She hadn't returned, there was no trace of her anywhere. So if Hexebart didn't make another appearance . . .

Christine sat up, the agitation sparking to life once more in her stomach. She needed to get to Ewigkreis. Even if she had no idea what she'd do when she got there, she needed to go. And if Hexebart wouldn't help her, and if Mandy had taken her ball of twine, and if only faeries could use the passage that Mayfridh had drawn between their two worlds, what could she do?

She took a deep, shuddering breath. There was one other method of getting there. She knew this, because it was the method she had used the very first time.

Pain, extreme pain.

Her back twinged just thinking about it, and all the nerves in her body resisted the idea. She eyed the edge of the table. It could all go wrong: she wouldn't hit herself hard enough; she'd flinch at the last moment and cause horrific pain with no passage across to Ewigkreis to relieve it; or she'd misjudge and hit herself at the wrong angle, in the wrong place, causing more damage. Her eyes were drawn to Mandy's sculptor's mallet, still resting on the table. Jude could do it. He knew the spot exactly from years of finding it to massage the pain away, and he'd be able to judge the force and distance better than she could. If he'd do it. If she'd let him do it.

Hexebart was still their best option. Mayfridh had told her about an oath the witch was under. Perhaps that was a bargaining point. Christine pulled herself up off the sofa. She wondered if Fabiyan had had any luck getting past the locked door to the attic. Presumably, if Hexebart could open Mandy's apartment door, she could open that one too. She might even be up there right now, listening to their conversations and laughing at their distress. Despite Jude's warnings about approaching Hexebart, Christine knew she was the only person who could deal with the witch.

Fabiyan looked up as she opened the door to Mandy's apartment, alarm quickly replaced by relief. "Oh, it's you," he said.

Poor Fabiyan, on witch-duty by himself.

"Hi. Do you want me to get Pete up here to relieve you for a while?"

"He takes care of Gerda. It's better if Jude come and stay with me."

"Jude's gone down to the park to look for her." She sat down on the sofa, next to him.

"Again?"

"Yeah, for some reason he's convinced that's where he'll find her."

"I hope he is right. I have never like witches."

Christine smiled at him. "You speak as though you've always believed in them."

"The village where I grew up, many miles outside of Svislach, tells stories about a witch named Chyornaslova."

"A local legend?"

Fabiyan nodded. "She comes to children in the night and leans over them, and if they smell her breath they must pretend to sleep and not open their eyes. If they open their eyes, she says a word to them, and that word make them go mad and kill their sisters and brothers and parents."

"And do you think she's real?"

Fabiyan's eyes dropped to his lap. "Perhaps," he said. "When I was ten, I wake up one night because I hear breathing nearby. I keep my eyes closed very tight, afraid of Chyornaslova. I still hope this is only my mother or father. But the person sit very close and still next to bed. She smells different from anyone. She smells stale and old and like onions. Then, I feel her lean on bed, her weight pressing against my chest and her breath hot in my face. I want to scream, or push her away, but I remember the stories and so I pretend I sleep. Not for me is going mad and kill my family. Already, I can see very clearly how I do it. I can take knife from kitchen and I can cut them up and there would be very much blood and screaming. The imagining won't go away and my heart almost burst of fear." He shook his head. "After two hours, she finally leave. By the morning, I say myself it is only nightmare.

"Years later, when I took my own little boy to visit at the village, my mother told him about Chyornaslova and I wished she hadn't, because he was only five and very fearful. He slept in our bed that night, buried under the covers like frightened little animal. I told him again and again, 'Evgeny, there's no such thing like witches.'" Fabiyan paused with a sigh. "I lie to my son. What will I tell him when I go home?"

Christine touched his shoulder. "You're very brave and kind to wait up here when you're afraid."

"What else can I do? Mayfridh, she may die."

"That's right."

"She is beautiful person."

"Easy to fall in love with," Christine sighed.

"You are beautiful person too, Christine. I would wait here the same for you."

"Thanks, Fabiyan. But right now, I need your help trying to get into that doorway to the attic. I suspect Hexebart might be up there."

"I have looked everywhere for key." He swept his arms around him. "It is nowhere here."

"Let's check the desk upstairs again. We'll pull out the drawers. Maybe he's stuck the key to the bottom of one."

They ascended to the next floor and emptied Mandy's desk. Christine shook every book; Fabiyan crawled around on the floor checking underneath drawers and in crevices and crannies. Still no key.

"Such an important key, maybe he keeps close to his heart. He wants nobody to go up there." Fabiyan hitched his thumb toward the door. "Christine," he added quietly, "what is up there?"

"A vat for boiling flesh off bones. I'll loan you the notebook to read."

"It is in English, I read it only slowly," he said with a self-conscious laugh.

She went to the door and peered down the crack between door and jamb, touched the locks as if they could give her any clues. "What a pity we can't just call the police. We have evidence of multiple murders by Mandy, of a break-in and assault by Hexebart . . ."

"Faeries and witches. Not so much police business, you would say?"

Christine laughed. "No, not so much. I'd better get back home. Jude will kill me if he knows I'm up here. I'll send him up as soon as he gets in, so you don't have to wait alone."

She ran into Jude on the landing. He lowered his brows. "Where have you been?"

"I dropped in on Fabiyan for a moment."

"I thought I told you not to go up there."

"Sorry. Any luck in the park?"

He opened the door to the apartment and shrugged off his coat. "No, nothing. I'll go back later."

"You need to go upstairs and wait with Fabiyan. He's frightened to death alone up there."

"Okay, okay, I will." He ran his hands through his hair, making it stick up at odd angles. "Christine, please stay away from the witch if you see her."

"Jude, I don't think we're going to see the witch. I think she's avoiding us, or she's into some other mischief elsewhere. I hate to think what."

"But we have to find her. How else can we get to Mayfridh?"

"I've thought of a way."

His eyes grew puzzled. "What way?"

She quickly explained; his expression grew increasingly horrified. "No way, Christine. Not a chance."

"But Jude—"

"I've spent the last four years trying to help you with your pain. I'm not going to risk injuring you worse than you are already."

"It's our only hope."

"Look, Hexebart was in this building just last night. She'll be back."

"Jude, I really think—"

"No!" he shouted, and she almost jumped backward from shock. "No, I won't hurt you." He turned quickly, embarrassed. "I'm going upstairs. Call me if you need me."

She waited in silence while he left, then sank into the sofa. *No, I won't hurt you.* Too late for that.

Knock, knock, there's someone at the door.

Hexebart waits for Diana to turn off the vacuum cleaner. It's a cool, clear morning and Hexebart likes the sun on her back. Footsteps. Then, the door opens.

"Can I help you?" Diana asks.

Hexebart smiles. Diana is all unsuspecting and smiles back.

"Can I help you?" she says again.

Hexebart thinks for a while, her bony finger poised on her lip. What could she say now that would be the very funniest thing? The very shockingest thing? The very nastiest thing?

Diana's smile is beginning to fade and Hexebart must think quickly. "Who are you, and what do you want?" Diana says.

"I'm Hexebart, and I'd like to eat your toes," Hexebart says.

Diana's face goes pale, her lips pull down, her eyebrows shoot up. Hexebart laughs and pops a spell from between her fingers and Mayfridh's mother falls to the ground with a thump.

"I'll teach you a lesson," Hexebart says, dragging Diana toward the kitchen. "I'll teach you for giving your daughter to Liesebet."

Diana moans. How funny. How excruciatingly funny.

CHAPTER TWENTY-FOUR

*M*andy couldn't get the smell off the bones.

Normally, one good scrub was enough to remove the scent almost completely. But he'd been scrubbing his two new sets for two hours, and still he could smell it, faint but permanent. He even sneaked into the castle kitchen and stole a lemon, cut it in two, and squeezed the juice onto a cloth to rub the bones with. He sat, waist-deep and shivering in the river, scrubbing and scrubbing. The smell lingered everywhere. He sniffed the sack. Was that where it was coming from? Dunked the sack, rubbed it vigorously under the water.

The damned smell was everywhere, he couldn't escape it.

"What did you expect, Immanuel?" he muttered bitterly. "You are in faeryland." The sickening smell was wearing him down, making him nauseous, irritated. It was the kind of detail that might eventually send a man crazy, like a ringing in the ears or an itch under the skin.

"Damn it!" he cried, flinging a collarbone away from him in despair. It bounced on the muddy bank and came to rest under a tree. He forced a big, shuddering breath into his lungs. It would not do to lose his wits. Quite clearly, it was time to return to Berlin. He had five sets of bones, and he had Mayfridh. It was enough. He rose from the river and walked to the bank, wringing water out of his pants. For a few excited seconds, as a cold wind tore past, he thought the smell was gone. But no, as the air stilled, there it was. Not fainter. Growing stronger.

This was like a nightmare.

He was freezing. He had to get back to the dungeon and warm himself on Eisengrimm's fire. Slinging the bone sack over his shoulder, he began to contemplate how he could get Mayfridh out safely. Perhaps two trips to Berlin? One with the sack, and one with the queen. He pulled the ball of twine out of his top pocket; it glinted in the sun. What a clever little device. As long as he kept it, he could return anytime he wanted to this place and hunt more bones. Fantastic!

Unless Mayfridh's threats of the worlds moving apart were true. He looked to the sky. It had become wintry since he had been here. That first day, the sky had been sunset colors. Now it was dark gray and leaden. The air had a bite to it, but perhaps he was just feeling that because he was wet. How he longed to be back in his warm apartment, on his soft sofa, with his new treasures spread around him.

Voices in the distance. Mandy frowned. All the time he had been in faeryland, he hadn't heard another soul here near the river. He shrank into the shadows of a tree, pushing the twine back into his pocket, and listened as hard as he could.

". . . go towards the river, the others can go . . ."

Someone was coming. Mandy glanced around frantically. Where could he hide himself and his treasures? A rock jutting over the water caught his eye. He dashed toward it and stuffed the sack of bones beneath it, then he looked about for a place for himself.

About five steps away, beyond the mud of the bank, he

spotted a deadfall all overgrown with moss and weeds, part of a large tree trunk on its side, and an arc of thorny bushes. He dived toward it. Scrambling on his belly, he tried to hide himself under the curve of the log. Thorns caught and scraped at him and he had to stifle a cry of pain. When he thought he was sufficiently hidden, he lay very still on his front, cold and sore. A drop of blood fell onto his hand from his forehead with a splat. For a few moments all he could hear was the sound of his own breathing.

Footsteps approaching. Men's voices. Mandy tried to count them. Three, no four. Four men, heading purposefully this way.

"Now, you search the riverbank," one said. "I'll search for him among these trees."

Mandy struggled to keep up with the language. They were looking for someone. With an awful lurch of fear, he wondered if they were looking for him. He tried to shrink back farther but found an unbroken section of log. Too tight a squeeze.

He listened, trying to catch their conversations, as they began to search nearby. Running footsteps came pounding down to the bank. They stopped near enough for Mandy to hear the exchange that followed.

"Einar? What's the matter?"

"I've been following you for twenty minutes. Didn't you hear me call?"

"No."

"We checked Oma's house. I found Sig's hand."

A shocked silence. "His hand?"

"On the cutting board. Sig didn't murder Oma, somebody else did."

Oh, this was a bad sign. They hadn't been looking for Mandy at all. For some reason they had deduced that Oma was murdered (though why the death of a woman already three hundred and thirty years old should be a matter for investigation was beyond him) and that the murderer was Sig, because he had disappeared. Damn. Mandy should never have left the hand there on the cutting board. He'd allowed his sense of drama to override his reason. Now, the hunt would be pursued even more vigorously, and Mandy was the prey.

The other voices drew near. They crowded around Einar, and spoke rapidly. Mandy couldn't keep up except for a few key phrases.

"Who would do this?"

"Is it an outsider?"

"This explains the weather."

Again, the weather. Mayfridh was telling the truth; winter was coming early. Let it come. This afternoon he would be gone, with his stash of bones and his faery queen.

"Resume the search!" a man cried.

Once more, the footsteps began to circle near his hiding place. He dreaded to think what they would do if they found him. Kill him? Drag him down to the dungeons? He couldn't finish his sculpture in a filthy prison in faeryland, and he'd never escape the horrible smell. Mandy was overwhelmed with such a tide of self-pity that he almost began to cry. He inched backward, managed to get his legs into the log.

"Here! Here!" One of the men was shouting frantically. The footsteps pounded past, and Mandy allowed himself a breath of relief. They were heading in the other direction.

A commotion ensued, and Mandy couldn't make out much of what they were saying. They were speaking too fast, and their voices were being carried away on the wind. He strained his ears.

Then he caught a single word, "bone," and realized what had happened. The collarbone he had thrown aside in his earlier tantrum; he had forgotten to pick it up and now they had found it. The footsteps grew closer again; and a rhythmic, heavy beating sound.

"He must be nearby," somebody said. *Thump, thump . . . thump.* They were beating at the hedges and undergrowth with a heavy object, hoping to find him, hoping to drive him out.

Mandy cowered under his crumbling log and deadfall. The bark above him was thin and he didn't trust it to save him from a blow. He inched farther inside the log. His legs were compressed horribly; the crude pants he wore ripped and he could feel his flesh torn. But still he wriggled in all the way to his waist, and then his belly wouldn't allow him any further access, no matter how hard he tried. He went limp, tucked his head under, and hoped the roof of bark above him would hold.

Thump, thump, thump.

Closer and closer they drew. Mandy clutched at the dirty bark beneath him. Termites and tiny brown beetles crawled over his fingers. He set his teeth. He didn't like bugs.

Thump, thump, thump. They were standing not more than a few feet away, hacking at the deadfall, cutting through the thorns.

Thump, thump, thump. This from the other end of his log, sending shuddering pulses along it, dislodging flakes of bark which bounced into his eyes.

Thump, thump, thump. Now they moved on. He was too well hidden, they hadn't found him. Ha! Why did he suspect for a moment that faeries could outsmart him?

He lay very still now, and listened for a half-hour as they beat and searched the bushes and moved away into the forest. When he was very sure that they were all gone, he closed his eyes and rested his forehead on his hands. A close call. But when he thought of his stash of bones in the river and in the dungeon, perhaps such danger was worth it. He was a hero, a braver of peril in the name of art.

As he began to relax and become more aware of the sound of his own breathing, he noticed the smell. The horrible, horrible smell.

His eyes flew open, he pressed his nose to his hands and sniffed. The smell of faery bones. On his skin.

No. No, no. Not on his skin. It hadn't the power to cling so tightly to his skin, not after all the scrubbing and the soaking and the rinsing. And besides, he could tell the smell was coming from beneath his flesh and his veins.

The smell was coming from his own bones.

He cried out. His first instinct was to flee, but he was still too firmly tucked inside the log to move very far. *And if you stay, you'll eventually become one of us.* He sniffed as far along his arms as he could. Without any doubt, his bones smelled distinctly like faery bones. His breath became panicky and shallow in his lungs, and a shot of bile rose in his throat. He remembered now the evening that Christine Starlight had sat next to him, and he'd thought he could smell the faintest scent of faery. She had been here. Mayfridh was telling the truth. Humans who came to faeryland became faeries. No! No! He had to get home. Immediately.

Mandy heaved himself forward. He moved a half-inch, maybe even less, then stuck.

"What the—?"

Heave. This time, he didn't move at all. Frantically, he jerked his body forward. But he was stuck fast inside the log.

Mandy fell forward on his hands and let out a sob. Tried to wriggle his legs, tried to contract his buttock muscles, cursed his hips. At their broadest measure, they had become lodged behind a dip in the bark. No matter how hard he pulled against it, it wouldn't give.

"No!" he cried. His field of vision spangled with gold and black spots, and he realized he was breathing too shallowly. He forced deep breaths into his body, was horrified all over again by the smell of himself. Despair washed over him. He collapsed forward, tasted the ground beneath him as he sobbed and drooled. He could barely control the impulse to chew his own skin and liberate the bones within. *I will change back, I will change back,* he said over and over in his head, hoping it were true, needing to be home.

When he had sobbed a while and calmed himself, he remembered the ball of magic twine in his pocket. Perhaps he could use it, right now, to get home. He could come back for the bones another time. The thought made him glad, relieved, and with a shift and a wriggle he managed to free it from his pocket and hold it before him.

The damage was apparent immediately. His pocket must have been shredded by thorns and bark, and the twine had been frayed. He attempted to roll it out in front of him. Loose threads spun off it, and the twine itself separated into three strands, then broke completely. Desperate, still hoping for escape, he pulled on the twine and attempted to heave himself forward.

Nothing moved, not him, not the space around him. He was not back in the Tiergarten; he was still trapped inside a dead log with the bugs and the ghastly, ghastly smell of his bones.

See how very clever Hexebart is? Oh, yes, there are surely not many who could adapt so well to the Real World and all its shrewd devices. Of course the spell helped, but Hexebart is very bold and sharp, and look what she has mastered: electric frying pan, refrigerator, television, CD player . . .

well, that's all for now. Diana has many other things that Hexebart would love to learn about, but that will do for now.

"Once the mince has browned nicely, add the crushed tomatoes and half a cup of water."

Hexebart thinks that the meal the television man is cooking looks very tasty, and her own rather lackluster in comparison. She glances at the frying pan. Yes, she has chopped onion and garlic and fried them in butter. But she has no mince to brown and no crushed tomatoes to add. Oh, oh! Only four poor toes. She supposes she could have cut off all the fingers and toes that Diana has, but she may be here for a few days and wants to ration herself on fun.

"Stir and allow to simmer uncovered for about ten minutes."

Hexebart keeps a close eye on the television on the bench and hums along with the tune playing on the CD player. The cooking-show music doesn't go with the CD music, but it drowns out those annoying little mews that Diana is making.

"Mew, mew!"

Hexebart marches to the cupboard, flings open the door, and glares at Diana. "You be quiet!" she shouts.

Diana, her feet all bleeding and bandaged with tea towels, looks up with haunted gray eyes and a tear-streaked face. She has been screaming and screaming, but Hexebart has used a silence spell. The only sounds that Diana can make now are kitten noises.

"Mew, mew!"

"I'll drown you in a sack!"

"Mew, mew!"

Hexebart slams the cupboard door shut and returns to the frying pan. She samples a toe. It's very tasty, despite the fact that it isn't a real "spaghetti bolognese." A new man is on the television now. There is a breeze on Hexebart's back *from the refrigerator so she closes the door and warms her hands over the frying pan, picking at the food inside.*

Oh, what a merry adventure! This is so much more fun than Ewigkreis, and Hexebart never never never wants to go back. She's glad that Mayfridh is in a dungeon, far away. Because if Mayfridh catches Hexebart and locks her up again, all the fun will stop. Liesebet's rules. Ah, how Hexebart misses Liesebet.

Diana thumps from inside the cupboard. She's kicking the door again, despite her bandaged feet.

"I said be quiet!" Hexebart shrieks. The music on the CD reaches a crescendo and dies off. The pan sizzles and a woman on the television reads the news. Diana is quiet at last. Hexebart turns to the book of pictures she has found. Here, Mayfridh as a tiny little girl, like she was when she first arrived in Ewigkreis. Why on earth had Liesebet chosen such an ugly little child? Why hadn't Liesebet chosen Hexebart's daughter? Klarlied is much more beautiful, of that Hexebart is certain, even though she hasn't seen her in many long years.

Hexebart's eyes fill with tears as she remembers the day, many many years past, when she offered Klarlied to Liesebet to adopt and keep forever as her very own child.

"No, no," Liesebet said. "She's a witch. A witch can't be queen!"

But a human could? Just because she has pretty red ringlets and eyes like sapphires?

Hexebart reaches for the carving knife. Suddenly she is hungry again.

Jude held Mayfridh while she sobbed.

"I'm so tired and thirsty," she said.

His hands were warm in her hair and she tried to sink into him, to disappear into him, but something black and iron and cold was in the way. . . .

Mayfridh woke, her neck uncomfortably crooked, her arm pinned under her on the filthy bed of straw. The sick disappointment of being brought back to her reality, of warm Jude disappearing from her arms, stole her breath from her lungs.

Still in the dungeon.

"Eisengrimm?"

He didn't answer, and she began to accept that he might be dead. She pulled herself up into a sitting position, her knees under her chin, and let her tears fall. When long minutes had passed with only the sound of her own crying, she rose and went to the door. If Eisengrimm were already dead, she would be foolish to stay locked in here. She pushed the door hard. No, it was as she thought. Mandy had locked her in. That meant he had the enchanted keys and was the only person who could set her free.

She stood at the barred window for a few minutes, watching the still figure of the crow in the cage, silhouetted in the firelight. She felt her face contort into a sob, but no sound emerged and no tears moistened her eyes. A huge guttural scream was trapped between her throat and her face.

"Good-bye, friend," she managed to whisper, and returned to the pile of straw.

She closed her eyes and thought about Eisengrimm. Liesebet and Jasper had brought her to Ewigkreis just before the change of season. Those first bewildering days of deep winter, when the sun never shone and Mayfridh was confused and screaming for her parents all the time, soon passed into the warm colors of the Spring Palace. There, the sense of always-belonging had first embraced her, and Liesebet had begun to introduce her as Princess Mayfridh, heir to the throne.

It was at the Spring Palace that she had first met Eisen-grimm. He had seemed very forbidding and serious, with his yellow wolf eyes and solemn demeanor. Truth be told, she was afraid of him for a long time. But then Queen Liesebet's favorite bracelet had gone missing, and Eisengrimm had transformed to Fox to search all the nooks and crannies of the palace. Mayfridh had been enchanted with him in this form; small enough to pick up and cuddle, like a pet who could teach her and converse with her. By the time summer came, she wanted him with her all the time. The friendship had been good for both of them. While he had helped her prepare for the duties that would all too soon be thrust upon her, she had helped him become more light of heart, not so serious and somber.

And now he had gone beyond death's incomprehensible barrier, and become as deaf and unknowing as a stone. Mayfridh opened her eyes and sat up, clutching the straw in her hands and knowing it could not save her from falling into death. Mandy would return, he would kill her, and the moment of horrified realization was so hot and bright upon her that she yelped. But it was only a moment, and then death became ordinary again, something that happened to everyone. Yes, she was afraid of dying, wondered if it would be painful or filled with frightful noises and sensations, but death, once it came, was resolution. Acceptance. She slumped back into her bed of straw and closed her eyes again. If only she had died in that moment with Jude, lying in his arms after making love, feeling whole and warm and embodied, feeling as though she had found the one place where care and woe were not permitted to enter. With a sigh she re-created the scene in her mind, replacing the cold darkness with a pair of warm arms; the still body of her dear friend with the live presence of her one love, her only lover. If Fate intervened and she saw Jude again, she would not let him go. Friendship, royal duty, his history of lies—nothing could persuade her to give him up again.

❧

She would still marry Jude. Once Christine had decided that, she felt an enormous sense of relief. Yes, he had fallen in love with someone else, but Mayfridh belonged to another world, another race of beings. Despite the anxiety Christine felt for her now, Mayfridh would soon disappear, never to think of Jude again. Christine should concern herself about Jude having feelings for Mayfridh no more than she should about him developing a crush on a movie star. Mayfridh was unattainable and forever distant.

Perhaps, from time to time in their lives, Christine would catch him with a faraway look in his eye and know he was thinking of Mayfridh. But she was used to him seeming far away, and once they had settled into comfortable affluence and had children, he would stay and he would be happy with her. Of course he would. If eighty percent of his heart was all he could give, she would take it. She loved him too deeply, too desperately and too wholly, to demand more or to choose nothing.

But for now, whatever feelings he had for Mayfridh were exploitable. Christine had to convince him to hit her by pushing every guilt and fear button she could find.

She descended to Gerda's flat. Inside, Gerda sat tight-lipped on the sofa while Pete sketched furiously in his notepad.

"Hi," Christine said, brushing hair from Gerda's eyes. "How are you?"

She shrugged. A bump and a croak came from the bucket

on her lap. Christine peered in to see a frog, two lizards, a locust, and a handful of worms. "It's still happening then?"

Gerda nodded. Pete looked up from his notebook. "That's my fault. She was determined not to say anything, but then I started drawing her." He turned the sketch around. Gerda's face in thick pencil lines, perfect bewilderment on her brow, a locust leaping from her lips.

"Pete, will you go up to Mandy's and relieve Jude? Tell him I need to speak to him."

Pete put the sketchbook aside and rose. "Sure, but if I see that witch, I'm going to run screaming. I have a hard enough time socially without spitting reptiles when I speak."

He closed the door behind him. Christine sat on the sofa next to Gerda and slid an arm around her. "I'm so sorry, Gerda."

Gerda nodded, her lips pressed together hard, tears welling in her eyes.

"I will do my best to fix it. I'm going after Mayfridh."

Gerda turned questioning eyes on her.

"The first time I went across was when I knocked myself out. I've got to convince Jude to hit me in the back."

Gerda reached for Christine's hand and squeezed it softly. "You'll be hurt," she whispered, and a lizard pattered into the bucket.

"She may be killed. You may be stuck like this for life. It's the only way." Christine took the bucket to the window and emptied its contents down into the street. "Gerda," she said, "if Jude won't do it, will you?"

Gerda nodded.

"I'd rather Jude did it, because he knows the exact spot. But if I tell him you're willing it might convince him."

She nodded again, reaching for the bucket and cradling it against her.

Christine sank onto the sofa. "I think he's in love with her, Gerda."

Gerda didn't answer; her expression was unreadable.

"Now you shut up?" Christine said good-naturedly. "Just when I need you to talk?"

Gerda smiled.

"Okay, let's get Fabiyan out of Mandy's apartment and lock it up. The poor guy is scared to death anyway. I'll go to Ewigkreis without Hexebart's help."

The door opened and Jude entered. "Christine? Is everything okay?"

Christine rose from the sofa. "Come on, Jude. We need to talk." She led him upstairs to their apartment, Jude with a puzzled look on his face.

When the door was closed behind them, she handed him the sculptor's mallet.

"Oh, no way, Christine," he said, "not this idea again."

"It's the only hope we have."

"Christine, I'm not going to hurt you."

"Gerda said she'd do it."

"No, I won't let that happen either."

"Every moment you do nothing, he could be killing her." Silence.

"He could be killing her right now," she said.

"He could kill you too."

"I'll be careful. He doesn't know I'm coming. I'll take a knife, that big one from the kitchen."

Jude's face was flushed with anger. "I can't believe you're even asking me this."

"You're the only person who can do it. You know exactly the spot to hit. I won't feel a thing once I get to Ewigkreis, and when I come back . . . so, I'm laid up on painkillers for a couple of weeks."

"I could cause permanent damage. More pain, for the rest of your life."

"But she may die. Dead is forever."

"Okay, I'll hit myself. I'll knock myself out and go."

"It's got nothing to do with you. I ended up over there because Mayfridh and I made that stupid blood-sisters pact when we were kids. You'd just end up unconscious."

Again he fell silent.

"Jude," she said softly, "only you can save her."

Jude scowled. "Don't say that."

"You are the only person who can save her. Every moment you hesitate is a moment he can kill her. It only takes a moment to die."

"I—"

"Now, Jude. I'll get the knife." She went to the kitchen, opened the cutlery drawer with shaking hands. Tried to force down some air. All her nerves were screaming. He was going to do it, he was really going to do it. She tucked the knife into her waistband and returned to Jude. "Are you ready?"

"I can't do this, Christine," he said, and his bottom lip was trembling.

"You can, you will." She turned her back to him. "Go on, you know the spot."

"Christine . . ."

"I'm waiting."

A long silence drew out behind her. She heard him hitch his breath on a repressed sob.

"Okay," he said on a long shaky breath.

Christine closed her eyes and forced her body to go limp. "Don't tell me when, don't count down, don't—"

The blow was sharp and swift and excruciatingly precise. In an instant, she was falling between worlds.

PART THREE

So pure and cold the wind breathes.
It pares the flesh from the bones of the land—
finds at last the essential shape.
                    "Autumn," *Kate Humphrey*

"Hee, hee, hee! Circle of fire, circle of fire!
Spin, spin, circle of fire! Merrily, merrily!
Puppet, ha, pretty puppet, spin, spin!"
            "The Sandman," *E. T. A. Hoffmann*

CHAPTER TWENTY-FIVE

I'm too late, winter's here.

*C*hristine *sat up slowly, dread clutching at her heart.* The sky was leaden, the branches all but bare, the light dim and low on the horizon. The air was very still, and gravity, rather than movement, sent leaves plummeting to the ground. Winter seemed poised to rush upon her in any instant.

And yet, she hadn't forgotten anything about the Real World—not Jude, not Mandy's diary, not the awesome promise of pain that waited for her to return—which meant the worlds hadn't moved yet. She needed to see the giant birch. Instinct told her it was unwise to call for Eisengrimm—Mandy didn't know she was here. She checked that the knife was still tucked into her waistband, and almost laughed at herself; she was no action hero.

Up through the forest and past Hexebart's empty well she found the garden wall. The lock on the gate had been smashed to pieces. A shiver of trepidation. The gate was never locked; in Ewigkreis there was no need to bolt intruders out of the castle. The only person who didn't know that was Mandy, and he'd struck this lock with a violence that betrayed the brutality in his heart.

Prepare yourself for the worst, Christine. Mayfridh might be dead, Eisengrimm might be dead—hell, *everybody* might be dead. She steeled herself as she passed through the garden and into the long shadowy corridor of the Autumn Castle.

On tiptoe, careful not to make a sound, she checked the rooms off the corridor and the great hall. The birch outside appeared sad and bare, but leaves still grasped its branches in many places. Soon, very soon, winter would be here. But not today.

Christine moved toward the staircase. The strange emptiness of the castle was magnified by her fear. Dark, silent shadows gathered in corners, a hollow cold rose from the kitchen, and her footsteps echoed around the narrow turret as she made her way up to Mayfridh's chambers. No sign of anyone. From Mayfridh's bedroom window she gazed down on Ewigkreis. Out in the fields, people were scything and gathering and tying bundles onto carts. Even though it seemed very distant, the bustle of activity heartened her. Mandy hadn't killed everyone. Mayfridh and Eisengrimm might still be alive.

She turned, and noticed the brass bear lying on the floor. She crouched to pick it up. There was blood on it. A veil of frost stole over her heart. "Mayfridh," she whispered, pulling herself to her feet. But where was she, what had Mandy done with her? A burst of frantic energy seized her. She raced down the stairs and across to the other turret. Nothing. Through the kitchen. Nothing. The spell chamber. Nothing, nothing, nothing. And then she paused at the stairs.

Christine knew where she had to go. Christine knew where Mandy had stashed her friend. Yet, here she stood just above the dungeon, and she couldn't make her feet move, not even an inch.

Underground. A bad place. Bad things happened there.

She took a deep breath.

Couldn't move.

This was ridiculous. She'd had Jude hit her with a mallet to get here, and now she was balking at a short walk in the dark.

Not just the dark. The weight. The silence. The dread finality.

Christine pressed her palms into her eyes in frustration. Her fingers were trembling. Why was she even here? Why suffer so much pain and trauma to rescue a woman whom Jude had fallen in love with? Perhaps Christine had fallen a little in love with Mayfridh too, with her warm breath and her soft fingers and her childlike eyes.

One foot, then, onto the stairs. And another. Descending slowly. Into the dark tunnel.

Can't breathe can't breathe can't breathe.

Christine stopped. Turned. Saw the faint light spreading from above the stairs. Breathed. See, not far from the air, not far at all. She clung to the wall and began to back up the tunnel, keeping her eyes focused on the light above her. The wall was cold and rough beneath her fingers. Gradually, the floor sloped away, and the square of gray light narrowed to nothing. Slowly, so slowly, she turned her back on the exit and faced the path to the dungeons. The light of a burning torch illuminated the bars of the first gate. No going back. Her trembling hands reached for the gate. She was awash in memories.

They had been coming home from a party. Christine had won a stupid bet with Finn, and so she sat in the front passenger seat beside her mother. Finn sat in the back, singing a silly song. Alfa was laughing. Christine was pretending to be embarrassed.

She pushed her legs forward, one then the other. Her breath was short and she could feel her shoulders hitched up so hard that the bones in her chest compressed.

It was very late, or very early. The black night and the lights of the city and the abandoned streets. Alfa and Finn bantered about the route to take home. Finn changed the words of the song to be about Alfa's shortcut; how it was really a circuit to another dimension where men were always right.

Next gate. The dim tunnel seemed to constrict in front of her. Her windpipe felt as if it were closing at the same rate.

And then the bang and the jolt and the bewildering dislocated suddenness of pain and horror, as though a switch had been thrown: in one second the world had integrity and in the next it was broken to pieces. The car had been clipped, had hit the wall; her father was crushed, her mother had been thrown through the windshield and had returned in ghastly fragments. Christine, the only one wearing a seatbelt, could feel something hard and sharp bent into her back. Her head was swimming and life had taken on a surreal, dimly colored cast.

Deeper and deeper in she moved. A third gate. The squeak of its opening was wrapped in cotton wool, coming from a long way away. Sweat on her top lip, hands clammy, nerves shrieking.

The sounds were awful. Wheezing and groans and metal fatigue and the engine screaming in horror. The headlights caught his taillights. He had stopped. The letters and numbers of his license plate burned themselves into her brain. (She still remembered them today. She had not really needed to write them down.)

One more gate. Christine's lungs shook with the effort of breathing.

And as he sped away, the weight of the tunnel and the dark crashed down on top of her, pushing her deep inside herself, certain she would suffocate in death's black tunnel. And the light receded from her forever. There was only heavy, grinding pressure, endlessly descending on her brain and her lungs and ears and . . .

She hit the ground before she'd realized the dizziness had stolen over her. She cried out, a girlish shriek that sounded both desperate and distant.

Then, not far off, she heard Mayfridh's voice.

"Who's there? Is someone there?"

"Mayfridh?" she managed.

"Christine? Is that you, Christine? Come quickly. I don't know when Mandy will be back."

Christine stumbled and stood. Only a few more minutes and she could be out of here. She forced herself forward.

Mandy hadn't breathed properly in hours. His weight pressed on his lungs, and his legs were growing numb. One small triumph: he had managed to work free his cleaver, which had been pressing against his belly uncomfortably. Now he hefted it in his left hand and wondered if it could be of any use to him in gaining freedom.

In this uncomfortable, twisted position it was difficult to find any leverage, but he tried to chip away the log from around his legs with the blade. A few splinters of bark flew away, and he wriggled forward a half-inch. He tried to twist more onto his left side, to take the pressure off his stomach, but a sharp pain in his right thigh told him that he had become stuck again, even less comfortably. His legs were squashed against each other and his hip pressed into something hard and sharp.

He slumped forward, closing his eyes and groaning with frustration. How long was he destined to be stuck here? Would he die before anyone found him? Mandy was perfectly certain that he didn't want to die, especially not smelling like a faery. Then that thought shocked the breath from his body, because if he became a faery and faeries lived a long, long time . . . Could he be stuck here in this log, under this deadfall, for hundreds of years? Could faeries starve to death?

Mandy opened his eyes and every morbid imagining fled because he saw something so amazing, so incredible, so wonderful that there wasn't room for anything else.

Green.

He had heard that grass was green, so that must be the strange sensation in his eyeballs that wasn't what he normally saw. Color. The grass was colored. It was colored green.

And then his astonishment and delight were ruined by the repulsive, sick knowing that this too was a product of his becoming the very thing he despised. His bones were transforming into faery bones, his eyes into faery eyes.

He gazed around him. Spots of warmth were growing among the gray and black and white. Colors forming. He couldn't bear to close his eyes. He watched the green as though it might escape from him, crying and crying in happiness and in horror.

🐟

Mayfridh was roused from numbness by footsteps. Mandy returning? She scrambled to her feet and leaned against the door, ears straining. No rattle and clank of bones in the sack.

Was he coming back to kill her? Her heart raced and she felt dizzy with fear.

But then there was a loud gasp and the sound of someone falling. A woman's voice, not a man's. She called out and Christine replied.

"Christine? Is that you, Christine? Come quickly. I don't know when Mandy will be back." The footsteps came closer, and in a moment Christine was leaning on the cell door, panting and pale in the dim light.

"I'm so glad to see you," Mayfridh said. "How did you get here? Have you seen Mandy?"

No answer, just the panting.

"Christine? What's wrong?"

"I . . . I . . ." Her top lip was sweating and her eyes were glazed.

"What's wrong? Are you sick?" Then Mayfridh remembered Christine's phobia of tunnels. She reached her fingers through the bars and stroked Christine's hair. "Shh, shh, be calm."

"I can't . . . I need to get out . . ."

"I'm locked in here. I don't know when Mandy is returning." Then a thought struck her. "Christine, Hexebart was in the neighboring cell. She may have left spells. If you fetch me one, I'll try to calm you down with it."

Christine swallowed hard and nodded.

"That one," Mayfridh said, indicating the next cell.

Christine nodded again, pulled herself up straight and disappeared from sight.

"Can you see any?"

"No."

"Look behind the door. She hides them."

"Okay. Yes, there are eleven."

"Grab them all. Stuff them in your pockets."

A moment later, Christine was back. She passed a spell through the bars to Mayfridh.

Mayfridh rolled it between her fingers. "Lean your head against the bars. Take a deep breath. It might not completely dissolve your fear, but it will help."

Christine leaned her head against the bars. Mayfridh reached out gently with her fingers and stroked Christine's forehead. "Be *calm*," she said. "Be *calm*."

Christine expelled a long breath and her shoulders fell.

"Better?" Mayfridh asked, touching Christine's hair.

"A little, yes. But I need to get out of here, really quick."

"So do I. Christine, I think Eisengrimm is dead."

"What?"

Mayfridh indicated the cage, hanging still in the sputtering firelight. A sob stopped up her speech. "He's . . ."

Christine went to the cell, eyed the rope above her and pulled it to bring the birdcage close to the bars. She tied a knot to hold it there. "Mayfridh, he's breathing."

Relief leapt into her heart. "Breathing?"

"I can feel his heart. He's alive."

"Eisengrimm? Can you hear me?"

"He's not conscious. Is there someone in the village who can tend to him?"

"Klarlied. If you get us out of here . . ."

Christine was trying the door.

"But . . . Mandy has the keys."

Christine turned on her heel and gazed across at Mayfridh. "Mandy has the keys."

"That's right."

"You can't use a magic spell to get out?"

"The locks are all enchanted. Only the keys will open them."

"Where is he?"

"I don't know. I dread to think what he's doing. He hasn't been back for a long time."

"It might take forever to find him. What if he's hiding in the Eternal Woods?"

"You have to find him. I can't do anything in here."

"What if I miss him and he comes back here to kill you?" Christine approached the cell door and pulled a spell out of her pocket. "Can you find him with one of these?"

"I don't . . . well, yes. Yes, I could. I can locate a foreign presence, and that's exactly what he is. Here. Hand it to me."

Mayfridh's fingers closed over the spell. Her brain was racing—Christine here, Eisengrimm alive, spells to use— but she concentrated as hard as she could and let her eyes roll back, seeking out the foreign presence in Ewigkreis. In her mind's eye she scanned the land, like a bird might see it, rolling off east and west and into the shadows. A dim splash under the castle: that was Christine, such a veteran of her visits to Ewigkreis that she barely made an impression. Mayfridh took a moment to examine the shadow. Christine was changing rapidly. If she stayed as little as a month she'd be all faery.

Scanning again across the land. A dark cancerous speck caught her attention down near the river. She homed in on it, down and down, plunging toward the ground. A deadfall, an old tree; down and down farther.

Mayfridh laughed.

"What is it?"

"He's stuck in a fallen log near the river. He can't move."

Christine smiled. "He can't hurt me."

"You can bargain with him. Help him free if he gives you the keys."

"But if I free him—?"

"Not free in Ewigkreis. Banish him back to the Real World."

"How? I can't do that. I don't have any magic."

Mayfridh paused, her lips tightly compressed, as she considered. "If you give me your hands and a spell, I can pass to you a limited ability to wield enchantment. Limited. You are only a human after all."

"Sorry," Christine said, her voice touched with sarcasm.

Mayfridh felt a jolt of guilt; her mind skating back to the memories of Jude. "I didn't mean to be—"

"It doesn't matter. Here, do your work. I want to get out of these dungeons." Christine passed her hands through the bars. She glanced around her, agitated. "I feel like I'm choking on the dark."

Mayfridh pressed her palms against Christine's, molding the spell into her skin and willing it down into her bones. "There," she said, "your hands are faery hands now. You can work magic."

"Really? That easily?" Christine withdrew her hands.

"I'm the queen," she replied, knowing she sounded imperious. "I make the rules here."

"Most of the time," Christine said with a wry smile. "There's Hexebart."

"Yes, yes. Most of the time," Mayfridh conceded, embarrassed. "Beware of Mandy, Christine. He's dangerous and he's clever."

"I'm sending him back to Berlin, and then I'm going home to New York and I'll try to forget I ever met him."

An incongruity occurred to Mayfridh. She had been too preoccupied to think of it before. "Christine, how did you get across to this world?"

Christine touched her back, not looking up. "Jude and a sculptor's mallet."

Mayfridh winced. Guilt like nausea. "Oh. Oh, I'm sorry."

"There was no other way. Quickly, explain to me where Mandy is and how to make a spell work."

Mayfridh explained and sent Christine back up the long tunnel toward daylight. Then she sagged against the door, gazing across at Eisengrimm's dark, still, silhouette. All around her, she had caused pain and suffering. She despised herself for it. And despised herself all the more for knowing she couldn't be any other way.

🐦

Christine breathed daylight into her pores, feeling her lungs unfold with relief after the pressing dark of the dungeons. Mayfridh's calm spell had only worked briefly and superficially, like a bandage on a gash, barely holding her together. She took a moment in the garden to collect her thoughts. Mandy was trapped in a log by the river. She had spells in her pockets and faery hands, making her feel a little invincible.

Christine set out toward the river.

The sky had grown dark and the wind had picked up. Rain clouds swirled, heavy with winter. Leaves whipped across the ground, yellow and frantic, as though trying to escape the coming season. Christine found herself hurrying her step too, reacting to some primitive instinct that affected all natural things when inclemency threatened: prepare yourself, collect your things, go inside. How she longed to be home, back in New York, surrounded by familiarity.

The river. She followed Mayfridh's instructions, picking her way along the rocky edge until she saw the outcrop she had been directed to. From here, she scanned the surrounding area. Deadfall. Mandy was under there, lying very still and quiet. He certainly would have heard her footsteps on the dead leaves. She felt in her pocket for the banish spell. Once she had the keys she could send him away.

"Mandy?" she called. "I know you're there."

His silence spooked her. Perhaps Mayfridh had been

wrong, or he had escaped already. She approached the fall of old branches and trailing gray foliage, gingerly lifting it.

"Ha!" A snarl and a flash of pink skin.

Christine jumped back. He was under there all right, and he was angry.

"Mandy, I can get you out of there," she said, "but only if you cooperate."

"Christine Starlight?" His voice sounded no different from the Mandy she knew; friendly, even.

"Yes, it's me." She pushed aside the branches again, throwing them to one side so she could see him properly. He lay half on his side, his legs twisted together inside a trunk. She almost laughed. He looked like a fat, helpless seal.

"Get me out of here," he said.

"I will. If you cooperate."

"Cooperate how? I'm stuck here. I took your ball of twine and ended up here. I didn't know what I was doing, and now look at me! I've been here for days."

So he was lying to her. He hoped she knew nothing.

"Let me clear these leaves away." She cleared the area, staying in a safe arc away from him.

"I think if you pulled me hard enough I'd come free. Or you can try to break away some of the bark. I just want to go home."

"I'll get you home, don't worry." She kicked away the last few branches and sat cross-legged in front of him, just beyond his reach.

"Christine? Are you going to help me?" His eyes were desperate.

"If you hand over the keys."

"What keys? What are you talking about?"

"I know everything, Mandy. I know what you do, I know what you're planning. And I know you have Mayfridh's keys. If you hand them over, I'll send you home."

A twisted expression of anger and hatred stole over his face in that instant, and Christine recoiled with a gasp. All this time she had known him and found him loathsome, as if that expression were barely concealed beneath the congenial surface. Now she was seeing the real Immanuel Zweigler and it horrified her. This was the face that his victims must have seen in their final grisly moments. Suddenly, he was no longer a man, but a monster, an ogre, a child's nightmare.

"Get me out of here!" he hissed.

"Hand over the keys."

His fingers went to his neck, where Christine could see the chain biting into his pallid skin. "What color is that shirt you are wearing?"

The question threw her. "What?"

"Answer me!"

"It's blue."

He sighed. "I wish it were red. I'd like to see red. People speak so highly of it."

"What the hell are you talking about?"

Mandy took an imperious tone. "I will give you the keys on the condition that you fetch me the sack hidden under that rock."

Christine glanced over her shoulder at the place he indicated.

"I want to take it with me."

"What's in it?"

"Never you mind."

Christine rose and walked to the rocky outcrop, leaned over the water, and felt around beneath. Her hand caught on a wet piece of material. She hauled it toward her. It was heavy and it clattered. She pulled it up out of the water, dreading to peer inside. *Bones, there would be bones in here.*

"Bring it to me," Mandy demanded.

Christine pulled the sack to the log and dropped it out of Mandy's reach.

"Give me the keys," she said.

"Give me the bones."

"If you give me the keys, I'll send you home. You won't be stuck anymore."

"I'm not leaving without my bones."

"You'll have to stay, then."

"And Mayfridh and the bird will remain locked up, and we'll all go off to winter together and you'll never get back either."

Christine crouched in front of him. "The keys."

"It seems to me unfair that I should have to comply with my part of the bargain first."

"What do you mean?"

"In exchange for the keys you will give me two things: my bones and my freedom. How can I trust you to give me one if you won't advance me the other?"

Christine slid the sack toward him. She hadn't the energy or patience to quibble. "Here. Now hand over the keys."

He pulled the bones toward him greedily, tucking the sack up under his abdomen with all the relish of a fat boy given a bag of sweets. "Your keys," he said, pulling the chain over his neck and holding it out for her.

"Thank you." She knelt and reached out to take the chain, saw his nose flare. He was sniffing her. She shuddered, snatched the keys, and hung them around her own neck. "Okay, now I'm sending you back and you should know that Jude and I are leaving as soon as we can, and that everybody at the hotel knows what a monster you are."

He twisted his lips into a smile. "And whatever shall you do about it? Report me to the police? Expose me in *Der Tagesspiegel*?"

Flustered and angry, Christine felt in her pocket for a

spell. She allowed it to rest in her palm, felt the almost-hollow weight of it, then blew on her palm and whispered, *"Banish."* She pushed the spell forward as Mayfridh had instructed her, triggering a blur of events.

First, Mandy seized her hand. In the split second she thought he intended to take her with him, he had gathered with unnatural speed a shiny object from among the fallen leaves, then pain bit her wrist and he released her.

Then, he said, "Ah, red."

Last, he disappeared and blood was pouring onto the ground. Her blood.

Confusion. Pain.

Realization: her hand was gone.

Christine screamed and pulled her wrist toward her. Bleeding and bleeding. She screamed again, in pain and shock. From somewhere she collected wits enough to feel in her pocket with her remaining hand for a spell, pressed it down on the wound and cried out, *"Stop bleeding! Stop bleeding!"*

Seconds passed. She was aware of the sound of her breathing, the dull gray of the sky. Slowly, she turned her eyes to her wrist, dreading the sight. The stump was sealed over, a mass of twisted skin and blood. She gasped for breath. Surely this wasn't really happening. Her jeans were stained with blood, her remaining hand streaked and dirty. She sank forward, sobbing. The keys clattered around her neck. The world had taken on a surreal edge. Bare branches seemed sharp against the sky, and the clouds were low enough to touch. For the rest of her life, she would have pain; for the rest of her life, she would be maimed.

❦

Long afternoon sunbeams broke from the clouds, filling the cramped room in Klarlied's cottage with warm light. Now that Mandy was gone, the weather was trying to rebalance. The gray wintry clouds had blown away, but still the cold was sharp, and the fire was roaring in the grate. Mayfridh had brought Eisengrimm and Christine here because she simply didn't know what else to do. Usually Eisengrimm would have advised her, but he was still unconscious. Klarlied was a witch and a healer, and she had taken them in graciously.

Mayfridh watched as Klarlied bandaged Christine's wrist with infinite care. In the next bed Eisengrimm lay on his side—he had woken briefly to change into Wolf—breathing shallowly, his eyes closed. All this pain and suffering on her behalf, because she had been stupidly adventurous, because she had unwittingly lured a faery hunter into her safe, peaceful world. Beyond her two friends' suffering, there was also the horrible knowledge that Mandy had killed a half-dozen of her subjects. She was a bad queen, a bad friend.

"Does it hurt very much, Christine?" Mayfridh asked.

Christine looked up with shadowed eyes. Her face was pale and drawn. "I can deal with pain," she snapped, "but I don't know how I'm supposed to live normally with only one hand."

Mayfridh approached and sat on the bed next to her. "I'm so sorry."

"It isn't your fault. I don't blame you." The strain in Christine's voice told a different story.

"If there's anything I can do . . ."

"Can you make it magically grow back?"

Mayfridh couldn't tell if Christine was serious. "I . . . no. That's not possible."

Klarlied tied off the bandage. "Perhaps Queen Mayfridh can have a smith from the village make you a hand of silver," she said in her melodic voice, "then she could enchant it so it behaved like a real hand."

Christine turned eager eyes on Mayfridh. "Can you do that?"

"It would only work while you were here."

Her shoulders slumped forward again. "Oh." She lay down on the rough blanket, her bandaged wrist across her chest.

Mayfridh shifted to the next bed, touched Eisengrimm's ears gently. "Do you think he will live?"

Klarlied went to a side table, where she washed her hands in a deep basin. "I do. He'll need a lot of rest. Some of his bones are crushed. But he is a shape-shifter, and they are resilient."

Mayfridh gazed at Eisengrimm's face. As with any friend, she had long ago ceased to see his physical features. The fact that he was a wolf rarely crossed her mind. But now, looking at him unconscious, she was acutely aware of the gray fur around his muzzle, slightly darker under his chin, of the whiskers around his nose, the pink of his gums and the white flash of his teeth as he twitched in a dream. She leaned to kiss his bristly head. "I wish he'd wake up."

"The longer he slumbers, the more he heals."

Mayfridh glanced at Christine, then said to Klarlied, "Could you leave us alone a few moments?"

"Of course, your Majesty." Klarlied took the water basin under her arm. "Call me if you need me."

When the hessian curtains swung closed behind Klarlied, Mayfridh leaned over Christine.

"I have to find Hexebart," she said.

"I know," Christine replied. "We should go back."

"You took a serious blow to your back. If you stay here a little longer it will have time to heal before the pain returns. And Klarlied can tend to your wound."

"So could a nice, modern German hospital."

"No, it couldn't. You used a spell on the wound. Klarlied

is a witch, she knows how to treat a wound which has been enchanted."

"You think I should stay here?"

Mayfridh nodded. "A little while. Then somebody would be here when Eisengrimm wakes."

Christine turned her head to look at Eisengrimm. "What if the seasons change? It's getting very cold."

"I'll send one of the royal guard to mind the giant birch. A warning will be dispatched."

"Do I even have a choice about when I go back? I mean, the first time I came, I got home just by waking up."

"We can anchor you here with a spell—then when it's time to go, you can use the passage in the forest as I do." Mayfridh touched her hand. "You are partly faery, the passage will work."

Christine frowned. Mayfridh could tell she didn't want her to be alone with Jude.

"You don't think Hexebart will come back of her own accord?" Christine said.

"I doubt it. Her passage was from the dungeons. A royal guard waits there, but she would expect that. If she doesn't return and the seasons change, we'll be left without any magic. Our race will die off."

"Oh," Christine said, casting her eyes down.

They sat quietly in the warm room for a few moments, listening to Eisengrimm's breathing. The golden sun faded out of the window, and velvety twilight settled over them.

"I'm very sorry, Christine," Mayfridh said. *For everything. For your injuries, for knowing Jude's deception, for loving him so passionately.* "You've done so much for me, and I can't think how I deserve it."

"Perhaps little girls who become blood sisters just grow up to do this for each other," Christine said.

"Maybe you're right," Mayfridh said. *Or, at least, they should.*

"You're the only person left who knew me when I was who I really am. Before the accident."

"And who are you now?"

Christine shrugged. "I'm different. I've been beaten up by the world."

Mayfridh leaned in and kissed her forehead, then rose to leave. "I must go before the sun comes up again. Time is passing too quickly."

"He asked me to marry him."

Mayfridh froze. "Jude?"

"We're getting married as soon as we're home in New York."

Mayfridh forced a smile. "I'm so happy for you. Jude is . . . lovely." The profound inadequacy of the word was clumsy in her mouth.

"Tell him I'll be home soon."

"I will." Mayfridh took a last loving glance at Eisengrimm, and headed out into the twilight.

CHAPTER TWENTY-SIX

*C*urse *those squeaking stairs! In the dead of night they* were as loud as gunshots. Mandy crept slowly, slowly. He didn't want any of the artists to know he had returned. What had Christine said? *Everybody at the hotel knows what a monster you are.* He couldn't risk them interfering with his work. Maybe, in a few days, when he'd spent some time with his Bone Wife, he would call his solicitor and have them all evicted. Not too hastily, though. He still hoped that Mayfridh would return and he could fulfill his plans for her. How it pained him that she had slipped through his grasp.

His own lounge room alarmed him. So bright with color! Hues were bleeding into everything now, not just a bright object here or there. He could see the carpet was the color of grass, the sofa the color of Christine's blouse, and the rug on it a lighter, warmer shade of her blood. He paused for a moment, gazing. Then he noticed the mess. Empty plates and food scraps and pillows where they shouldn't be. Who had been here?

Tiptoeing now, he explored the rest of his flat. He was alone. He couldn't risk being discovered, so he unlocked the door to the dark staircase and headed up to the soundproof boning room. He was a large man, and the bag of bones was heavy and cumbersome. The stairway was so narrow that he had to breathe in tight and yank the sack behind him, but finally he had his booty safely in the attic room. He tipped the bones out on the floor. Gorgeously, a pale blue sheen covered them. He had never seen it before, and spent a few precious moments holding them aloft in the light, tilting each this way and that to enjoy the pale color. Christine's hand was among his stash. He scooped it up and sniffed it. Faery bones. No doubt at all about it. She was a human with the hands of a faery. One could say he had done her a favor by removing it.

He turned the hand over; what a special prize. He already had a plan for the bones inside. He settled on the floor crosslegged, like a child excited about playing, and pulled off the cheap shining ring on the engagement finger. He cast it aside and it rolled into a corner of the room. The work of art he had planned would prove far more precious a jewel. He reached for a blade and started to work.

The black windows allowed him no access to the night outside. Still, it must be growing dark because it was growing cold. He padded downstairs for warm pajamas and returned to his work. Carving, joining, polishing, under the fluorescent lights, solitary and creative in a dark, sleeping world. The early hours of the morning passed. His hands ached, his eyes stung. A tiny sliver of light from a scratch in the window. Dawn approaching.

He held up the product of his hours of labor. A delicate chain of glistening white, every link carved lovingly out of the fine bones of Christine Starlight's fingers.

Mandy turned to the Bone Wife, waiting patiently for him. A pity she had no neck to hang it around, but he approached and slung it over her waist. Her fine hips stopped

the chain from sliding all the way to her feet. It fell in a soft
V between her thighs.

He fingered the chain gently, turning the links over and
over. What a fine sculptor he was. What a brave hunter and
unique artist. And with a pile of bones waiting for him (not
quite the pile he had hoped . . .) it wouldn't be long before
the Bone Wife could wear her new necklace about her
gleaming white throat.

Mandy stood back and admired her. "Come, my love," he
said, "we shall dance."

With that he stepped in and grasped her about the hips.
He stepped back, and she stepped forward; he stepped forward, and she stepped back. Slowly at first, then in a circle.
Mandy began to laugh. She was actually getting the hang of
it. "Yes, my dear Wife, that's good."

Step, step, around in a circle. He hastened his pace; she
kept up. Soon they were whirling around the vat as the city
woke up far below.

Then she misplaced a dainty foot and came crashing
down. Mandy fell down next to her, kissing her pale curves.
"Never mind, never mind, my darling. Soon you will be finished, and there will be so much magic in you that you will
dance like a ballerina." He laughed, sitting up and shaking
his head. His body cried for sleep, to be horizontal in a warm
soft bed, but the bones were just within his reach and his
fingers craved them like a sinner craved absolution. He
crawled over to the bones and began to sort.

❧

As she walked up Vogelwald-Allee through the blustery
November wind, leaves skidding and overtaking her left and
right, Mayfridh made a deal with herself. It was up to Jude:
if he asked about Christine first, then she would let him go.
She would let him continue his deception with Christine

(poor Christine, how that guilt swirled in her stomach like bad cream) and say good-bye. But, if his first concern was for Mayfridh, then she would know that his love for her was more than his pity for Christine. And she would do everything to make him hers.

She steeled herself as she opened the front door to the hotel. Mandy could be around here somewhere; she had to be on her guard. She recalled his face in the half-light of the dungeon, full of hate and longing, and it made her shudder with fear.

Inside the hotel, all was quiet. She hurried up the stairs to the sanctuary of Jude's apartment and knocked on the door. Her heart was hammering fast. He opened the door. His face grew pale. He grabbed her hand and yanked her inside, kicking the door closed and embracing her. "Mayfridh," he gasped, "thank God you're all right."

She knew she had won.

For a few moments there was nothing but the warmth of his arms and the beating of his heart, and then he drew back, took a breath. "Where's Christine?"

"She's still in Ewigkreis."

"Why?"

"To recover." She looked pointedly at the sculptor's mallet on the kitchen table, deciding not to tell yet that Christine had lost her hand. That knowledge would confuse his feelings; Mayfridh liked it better when it was obvious he loved her.

"When will she be back?" he asked.

"Perhaps a day or so."

For nearly a full minute they stood gazing at each other. Mayfridh knew she had so little time for standing and gazing—Hexebart was still loose—but she was frozen. He was frozen.

Then he seized her and kissed her—passionate, violent

kisses—and her body was surrendering and surrendering, with hot blood and lips and eyes; and she was consumed by that blissful feeling of emptiness withdrawing, of loneliness vanishing, of happiness being possible. Sometime.

Afterward, they lay in a tangle of clothes and warm limbs, breathing slowly in the afternoon shadows. Sunlight, dappled and dimmed by branches moving outside, shone on the sill and the carpet but didn't reach the sofa. Mayfridh shivered and pulled her blouse over her shoulders.

"Jude," she said, "would you be my king?"

He opened his eyes. Alarmed. "What?"

"Would you come back to Ewigkreis with me and be my king? Raise heirs with me, grow old with me . . ." The panic in his eyes finished her sentence. "Jude?"

"I can't, Mayfridh."

"You can. You'd become one of us, you'd live four hundred years. It's a beautiful place. You could paint all day and never have to worry about anything."

He fell silent and she sat up, looking down at him.

"What's wrong?" she asked.

"Would you do it?" he countered, his voice touched with anger. "Would you give up everything and join me in my world?"

"But I have so much more to lose," she said. "My magic, my power, hundreds of years of youth and beauty."

"I belong in the Real World," he said. "I belong in a place where there are urban spaces and traffic noises and cynicism and alienation. All the things that drive my art. What would I paint in Ewigkreis? Landscapes?"

"Forget I asked."

His voice dropped to a whisper. "I belong with Christine."

"You don't. You belong with me. You know it, you feel it."

"I don't know what I feel."

She climbed to her feet and straïghtened her clothes. She had expected him to say yes. He loved her, she knew he loved her. If it wasn't for Christine . . . a surge of anger and resentment swept through her. Christine, with her plain face and her infinite ability to make people pity her.

"I'm sorry," he said.

"So am I." All her hope deflated in her chest.

"Mayfridh," he said gently, reaching for his clothes, "you didn't come back here just for me, did you?"

She took a deep breath and shook her head. "No, no. I have to find Hexebart."

"Gerda needs you to remove the spell that Hexebart put on her."

"Of course, I . . . oh no."

"What's the matter?"

"Spells! I didn't bring a single one with me. Christine still has them." How could she have left Ewigkreis without spells? Too many of her thoughts had been spent on fantasies of Jude.

"So you can't fix Gerda?"

Mayfridh shook her head. "Only after I find Hexebart."

"We've searched for her all around the hotel. I don't want her to run into Christine. I don't want her telling about . . . you know."

Mayfridh felt a flush of impatience. He was so selfish, so preoccupied with himself and his stupid deception. "I'll find her. Where has she been so far?"

"I saw her in the park at the end of the street when she came to tease me about knowing my secret," Jude said, "and Gerda saw her in her apartment. And she stayed in Mandy's flat one or two nights."

"So she's been making mischief with my friends."

"Yeah, so she's probably still nearby."

Mayfridh tried to follow the twisted paths of Hexebart's

logic. "Because she's taking out her hatred of me through hurting you and Gerda—"

"And Christine as soon as she finds her."

Mayfridh's heart went cold. "Ohh," she said, "I think I know where she is."

***

Christine woke from the welcome oblivion of sleep to find that she still lay among the rough bedcovers at Klarlied's cottage, and that her left hand was still missing. She groaned involuntarily and rolled over. Eisengrimm was watching her.

"Eisengrimm." She swept her hair out of her eyes. "You're awake."

"I have been for an hour." His golden eyes were deep with measureless compassion, his mellow voice warm and gentle. "Christine, what happened to you?"

She held up her wrist. "Immanuel Zweigler happened to me. Mayfridh enchanted my hands so I could magically banish him. He took one as a souvenir."

He shook his gray head. "You have suffered too much."

"So have you."

"I'm her counselor. I'm employed to suffer for her."

Christine sighed. "I let her go back to the Real World. Alone."

"You were wise to stay and heal."

"You don't understand. I've left her alone with Jude. Jude's in love with her."

"Are you certain?"

"Yeah. Pretty certain." She sat up and gazed across at him. "But she'll be gone soon enough. And Jude and I will get on with our lives and . . ." A sob broke through her words. "Oh, God, who am I kidding? I'm in pain every day. I only have one hand. I'll be such a burden to him."

"If he loves you, you won't be a burden."

"He doesn't love me the way he loves her. How could he? She's so beautiful and rare. I'm so . . . I'm interchangeable with anyone."

"Christine, that isn't true."

"You're in love with her too. You know the power she has."

"Then why did you let her go alone?"

She shrugged. "Because there are some things you can't fight. Because maybe he deserves the thrill of a grand passion before he settles down with me. I don't know."

The hessian curtain at the doorway parted and Klarlied peeked in. "Ah, Counselor Eisengrimm. I thought I heard your voice. How do you feel?"

"Very sore, but lucid."

"Thorsten and Brathr wait for you in the kitchen. They are eager to speak with you."

Eisengrimm glanced at Christine. "The mayor and the reeve," he explained.

"Shall I send them in?" Klarlied asked.

"You should rest some more before you take on official business," Christine said.

"I can't. Winter is very close and matters are very serious." He turned to Klarlied. "Send them in."

Christine stretched and got out of bed. "I'll leave you alone with them."

"Thank you, Christine." He looked so vulnerable lying curled on the bed, bandages around his ribs; a hurt dog rather than a queen's counselor.

Christine slipped out as two men strode in. She hoped they would be kind to Eisengrimm. It wasn't his fault his queen was so flighty.

Klarlied stopped her, with a smile, in the kitchen. "Would you like some soup?"

"No, I'm going to get some fresh air." She felt in her

pocket for the remaining spells. She had deliberately with-held them from Mayfridh, and felt a twinge of guilt over that. For some reason, when Mayfridh was leaving, Chris-tine's desire to own the spells was greater than her concern for Mayfridh's needs. Perhaps it was simple jealousy, or simple curiosity. Or perhaps there was nothing simple at all about her feelings for Mayfridh.

Christine found herself in Klarlied's neat square of gar-den. Hedges were over-spun with spiderwebs that glistened in the morning sunshine, wafting to and fro on the breeze. Christine shivered against the cool, but relished the fresh air. She had been cooped up too long in the cluttered, stuffy cot-tage. Klarlied's home stood at the end of a dirt road. Wheat fields spread out behind it, stubbled and golden. The slanted sunshine dazzled on the fields. Christine pulled a spell from her pocket. As far as she knew, her remaining hand was still enchanted. She had no idea what magic she wanted to per-form—given that *turn back time to before Mandy took my hand* was not an option. She gazed at the spell and a cloud moved over the sun.

"*Butterfly,*" she said, and blew. The spell disappeared and an indigo butterfly flew from her fingers and up into the sky. She laughed. What a curious pleasure it was to make magic happen, like a shiver and a held breath and a liquid tingle. She took another spell and held it out. "*Birdsong.*" As she blew, the spell dissolved and the air around her was filled with the sweet strange song of a bird she didn't recog-nize. It swelled and withdrew, leaving her standing, smiling for the first time in many long hours, in Klarlied's garden.

She checked her pocket. Only four left now. She had best be prudent and save them, give them to Mayfridh when she got back to the Real World.

Voices from nearby. She turned to see the two men—the mayor and the reeve—leaving the cottage, muttering to each other in serious voices. She hurried inside to find Eisengrimm sitting up on his bed. His eyes were thoughtful.

"Is everything all right?" she asked him.

He shook his head. "No. Not at all." His shoulders were hunched forward and his fur was dull.

"Lie down," Christine said. "You look sick and sore."

"I am sick and sore." He did as she directed and closed his eyes.

"Tell me what happened," she said, curling up next to him and gently stroking his ears.

"The officials in the village, and most of the villagers it seems, are unhappy. Very unhappy. Hexebart has disappeared with the royal magic, six faeries have been murdered, winter is coming, and their queen is nowhere in sight."

"Did you explain she's gone to find Hexebart?"

"Yes, but she made no official announcement, took no guards or helpers. It looks suspicious. It looks like she's run away."

A brisk wind gusted overhead, moaning softly over the eaves.

"What will they do?" Christine asked.

"They have already done it. They have officially expressed their lack of confidence in the queen. When she returns, she will have to prove herself fit to rule, and she will have to name an heir."

"Name an heir?"

"They ask it of rulers whose competence is in doubt. She can name anyone she wants, and the villagers vote on whether to agree to it. That's how Liesebet made Mayfridh her heir, even though she was a human changeling."

"Would she name you?"

"She has tried in the past. I won't let her."

"No?"

"I have no desire to be a king."

She smiled and rubbed the back of his neck. "You'd make a fine king."

"She could also prove her intention to produce an heir."

Christine was confused. "How so?"

"She could marry. Then it would be assumed a child would result."

Christine opened her mouth to ask, "Who would she marry?" but no sound came out because she knew precisely who Mayfridh would make her first choice.

"Christine?"

"She can't take him away from me, can she?" she breathed.

Eisengrimm fixed her in his golden gaze. "I don't know, Christine. Can she?"

Mayfridh thrust money into the taxi driver's hands as they pulled up outside Diana's house at Zehlendorf.

"Here, keep the change," she muttered, hurrying to open the door, and emerging onto the quiet street. The last of the sun's rays had disappeared, leaving only the cold gray shadows of twilight. The front of the house was dark and silent. She hoped that she was wrong, that Hexebart hadn't discovered Diana and come to make the same kind of mischief she'd made at Hotel Mandy-Z. She hurried up the front path, stopping when a flash of gold caught her eye.

In the long grass lay a spell. She bent to pick it up. Hexebart had been here and left in a hurry, dropping this behind her. Mayfridh stood and checked the tree branches nearby. She couldn't see the witch anywhere. She tucked the spell inside her blouse and tried the front door. Unlocked.

"Mum?" she called, entering the dark hallway. She

turned on the light. The house looked dusty and shabby, and the smell of old cooking filled the air.

"Mum?" Mayfridh advanced into the house. The lounge room was empty. The kitchen was a chaotic mess of dirty plates and pans; the fridge door gaped open; spilt butter and water lay on the floor. She kicked the fridge door closed and was heading for the hallway when she heard a tiny mewing.

Since when did her mother own a kitten? She turned and cocked her head, trying to locate the sound.

Mew, mew.

It was coming from the cupboard under the sink. Mayfridh approached warily. This could be one of Hexebart's tricks.

Mew, mew.

She reached for the cupboard door, pulling the spell from her blouse and holding it defensively in her right hand. With a quick movement, she flicked the door open and stood back.

No kitten. No witch. Her mother.

"Mum!"

Mew, mew.

Hexebart had enchanted her. Mayfridh's relief that it was only a little spell was quickly replaced by alarm. Diana's feet were bandaged.

"What happened?"

Mew, mew. Tears ran down Diana's face and she reached out with desperate hands for Mayfridh.

Mayfridh helped her out of the cupboard and struggled with her to the lounge room, where Diana gratefully sank into the sofa. Mayfridh balanced the spell on her palm, turned it to Diana, and said, *"Speak."*

"Oh, Mayfridh, I knew you'd come to save me."

"What happened?"

"The witch. She took some of my toes."

Mayfridh slid onto the sofa next to Diana and gently unwrapped the bandages on her mother's right foot. Hexebart had taken two toes. Mayfridh eyed the other foot and shuddered, imagining the pain. Hexebart had done it cleanly, dressed and bandaged it properly; protecting her prey for more enjoyment later. Not like the horrifically crude wound Mandy had inflicted on Christine.

"I'm so sorry," she said, buckling again under guilt. It seemed she was the only person who was unscathed.

"She's gone, though," Diana said. "I heard her leave just before you got here."

"She probably heard me arrive."

"Will she come back?"

Mayfridh looked up into the face of a terrified child. "I don't know, Mum. I hope not. I have to find her and take her back to Ewigkreis."

"You have to go?"

"I have to do what's right for my kingdom before winter comes."

"Please don't leave me alone."

"I won't, I won't," Mayfridh soothed.

"You will. You'll go off to find the witch and then I'll be alone." Diana began to cry, pressing her hands into her face.

"Mum, calm down," Mayfridh said, gathering Diana into her arms. "It's all right, I'll look after you."

"For how long?" Diana said, her voice rising into a hysterical sob.

"You have to calm down." Mayfridh knew it was ridiculous to ask a mutilated woman, who had been locked in a cupboard for days mewing like a kitten, to calm down.

"Take me back with you, then. Don't leave me here alone."

"What do you mean?"

"Take me to faeryland. I have nothing when you go. I don't want to be left here alone to grow old with nothing."

"Mum, please—"

"Don't tell me to calm down!" she shrieked, holding out her hands. "Look at me! I have nothing. *Nothing.* Once you're gone, what have I left to live for? Take me with you. You can take a human with you, can't you? Liesebet took you."

"Yes, I can take a human with me." Just one human. Any more would risk unbalancing the seasons. Mayfridh already knew which human she wanted to take. "But it's more complicated than just deciding—"

Diana threw herself down at her full length on the sofa and sobbed like a child. Mayfridh crouched next to her, rubbing her back and letting her cry. "Shh," she said. "Shh."

At length the sobs began to dissipate and turn into soft hiccups. She sat up and took Mayfridh's hands between her fingers. "I don't want to lose you again, Little May."

Mayfridh didn't know what to say, so she said nothing.

"Please, take me with you."

"It's not so easy to—"

"Just tell me you'll think about it."

"Yes," Mayfridh said, immediately regretful of raising the false hope, "of course I'll think about it."

The queen, the queen, the horrid little queen!

How did she get away from Immanuel? How did she know where to look for Hexebart? Hexebart is not happy, hiding from the changeling piglet in a thorny bush in the cold. Hexebart has been enjoying herself most thoroughly. Now she has to run away again, or the piglet can command the royal magic and make Hexebart go home. Hexebart doesn't want to go home, ever ever ever.

Ooh, how it aches and gripes in Hexebart's belly that

the queen's head is still on the queen's shoulders. Immanuel should have killed her. What use is Immanuel?

Hexebart smiles to herself and clicks her fingers. Immanuel may be home, Immanuel may still want to kill the queen. And Hexebart would like very much to help him. Between the two of them . . .

Off into the night. What a team Hexebart and Immanuel will make! Why, Hexebart can barely stop herself from singing with joy.

CHAPTER TWENTY-SEVEN

Twenty-four hours without a break, and Mandy's hands were sore from the work he had done. His eyes felt as though they had been rubbed with sand, his head ached, and his limbs were heavy, but the Bone Wife now had a fine pair of breasts. He stood back to inspect her. Yes, the latest work was rough, but he was proud of it nonetheless. His Wife had been so long only half a body, a fragment of her finished self, but now she looked more real, more like the obedient spouse she would eventually become. With some time and detailed work, the rough edges could be smoothed, the curves could be evened out, and—

Mandy gasped as he realized. The blue sheen on the bones was no longer visible. He looked up to the light, then back to the sculpture. Had something changed in the room? Had some subtle shadow fallen over the bones?

He lifted his wrist to his nose and sniffed. He had been working for so many uninterrupted hours with the bones that he had forgotten about the awful scent of his own. Unmistakably, it was fading. And if that small physiological change was happening, then . . .

"My colors!" he exclaimed, and immediately fled down

the stairs to his lounge room. The bright colors were fading once more to gray. "No, no!" To have never known colors was a small torture; to have known them and lost them was a grand tragedy. His eyes flew frantically from the sofa to the rug to the paintings on the walls. He switched on the television with the sound down and watched it greedily, but already the reds were fading, the blues were cooling, the yellows had blanched to white. He watched an hour, two hours, then had to admit that it had all become black, white, and gray again. His colors were gone.

His instinct was to bellow with anger, to kick things and tear things to pieces, but he had to be quiet and get back up to his boning room without squeaking a floorboard. The artists couldn't know he was back. With silent rage, he moved back upstairs, his limbs shaking and his eyes twitching with tears. He locked the door behind him, laid himself flat on the floor at the feet of his Wife, and howled. Oh, it was unfair. Faeries tortured him! Mayfridh was responsible! He would kill her so slowly, so painfully. He would cut her throat so she couldn't scream, and dip her in the boiling vat, and cut off her head, and make her eyeballs into buttons for his Sunday jacket! Mandy closed his eyes, soothing himself on fantasies. Within a few minutes, he had drifted into sleep.

He woke with a start an hour later. The bright lights of the boning room dazzled his eyes. Not a trace of color marked the world around him. What had woken him? He had gone for days without sleep; something significant must have troubled his senses to rouse him. He sat up and listened . . . but of course his boning room was soundproof, so it was some subtler sense that had pricked him awake. Warily, he rose and opened the door. Leaned his ear out into the narrow stairwell.

The television! He distinctly remembered muting the sound so that the artists couldn't hear it and know he was home. He stole down the stairs as quietly as he could, through his studio and into the lounge room. Then he stopped cold.

"Hello, Immanuel." It was the hag from the dungeons in faeryland.

"How did you get in?" he whispered, reaching for the remote and turning off the television.

"It wasn't locked."

Mandy shook his head. He was certain he had locked the door. Hadn't he? Or had he been too excited to think of it? "You must be quiet. The others will hear us."

Hexebart grinned and shook her head. "Oh no, for I have enchanted the floor. They will hear nothing." She jumped up and down on the spot for emphasis. Mandy cringed, waiting for doors downstairs to open, for interfering footsteps to approach. They didn't.

"What are you doing here?" Mandy asked. She stood very close now, and her stench enveloped him. Faery bones, a damp moldiness, and garlic. Her white-gray hair was matted and tangled, her teeth rotted with streaks of brown.

"I came to visit you, Immanuel."

He assessed the hunch in her back, the crooked bow of her limbs. Those bones would be of little use to him, especially for the working of arms and hands and fingers. No, he needed Mayfridh's strong, fine skeleton for that. "And for what purpose is this visit?" he asked.

"I know things. I can help you with your plans for Mayfridh."

"You said that once before, and then you disappeared."

"But this time I need your help. I need somewhere safe to stay. If Mayfridh finds me, awful things will happen to me." She dropped her head and pretended to weep. Mandy took a step back, disturbed by the peeping cries and pretended tears. When she realized he hadn't fallen for it, she raised her head and smiled. "Immanuel, you are clever. Are you clever enough to catch the queen?"

Mandy said nothing, waiting for her to continue.

"She is *magic*, you know."

"I know."

"And you want her magic? Am I right?" She smiled and playfully touched his wrist. He jerked his hand away. "You want to kill her and take her magic?"

"Yes."

"She has so much magic. Whoever kills her will get it all. All of it." She swept her arms around in a circle, then leaned in close, her breath hot in his face. "I can help you kill her."

"How?"

"I'm made of the same stuff as her."

"Then why shouldn't I kill you?"

Hexebart took a step back, an angry scowl on her face. "Immanuel, we are friends. Friends don't kill each other."

"You've got magic. I saw you disappear from the dungeons."

Hexebart held her forefinger and thumb a half-inch apart. "Hexebart has only a little crude magic. She's old and sick and no use to you at all. Mayfridh's the queen. Her magic is royal magic. You could do anything with it, anything at all."

"How can you help me kill her?"

"I can tell you when she's nearby. I can help you capture her. I can keep you hidden from the others so they never know you're here." She cackled and shuffled her feet in a little dance, singing, *"Use a little magic to catch the dirty queen, use a little magic to catch the dirty queen."*

"What if she doesn't come back?"

"Oh, she'll come back," Hexebart said knowingly. "She'll come to find me. Won't be long now. Not long at all."

He smiled, his hopes lifting. Perhaps he would get

Mayfridh's skull after all. "All right, I'll let you help me,"
he said. Then he'd boil her. There might be a few useful
bones, a smidge of magic. "I want to cut off her head."

"Hee, hee!" Hexebart squealed, clapping her hands. "Oh,
I should like to see that!"

"You can stay here, but don't disturb me while I'm
working."

"Hexebart will be very quiet," she said solemnly.

"And don't make a mess."

"Hexebart will be very tidy," she replied. "But, Immanuel, Hexebart is hungry."

"Help yourself to what's in the fridge."

"There's very little food left. I already looked."

"I'll go shopping when I can. I don't want anyone to
know I'm here, so for now I'm staying locked up inside.
There are cans of food in the cupboard."

"Cans of food. Yes, yes. Shall I make you food, Immanuel? Shall I bring it to you up the stairs?"

"No. Stay away from me and stay away from my work."
Who knew what she was capable of? He didn't want her
wrecking his sculpture. "I'll come down when I'm tired and
eat something then."

"We are friends, aren't we? Immanuel?"

"Yes, we're friends." He forced a smile.

She turned on her toes and started singing another song;
something about Mayfridh's head rolling down the stairwell
and being friends with "Im-man-u-el." Mandy turned to go
back upstairs and lock the door to his boning room. It would
frighten her to see the vat, though she would see it soon
enough.

Mayfridh spent two hours searching in the trees and bushes
near her mother's house, then finally admitted that Hexebart

had long since disappeared. Back at home, Diana fluttered about nervously, her feet freshly bandaged by a bewildered local doctor.

"Are you sure she's gone?" Diana said. "Are you sure she isn't coming back?"

"I think I know where she is," Mayfridh said, remembering that Mandy had set Hexebart free, "or where she might turn up soon." She collected her coat and headed for the door.

"Don't leave me here alone. What if she comes back?"

Mayfridh turned, impatience beating in her temples. Diana was justified in her worry, and a locked door was no deterrent to Hexebart. "Come on then. I'll drop you off at a hotel in the city."

Diana nodded. "I'll just pack a few things."

Mayfridh phoned for a taxi and waited impatiently in the hallway, wishing she wasn't impatient. Hexebart had to be found and returned to Ewigkreis before the season changed. The witch was so full of magic she could easily create an anchor spell and stay in the Real World, while Mayfridh returned home empty-handed. And then . . . ? Then her people would be caught forever in an endless winter. The responsibility weighed heavily on her.

Finally, Diana hobbled downstairs with a large suitcase.

"You need all that?" Mayfridh said, taking the case from her.

"I don't know how long I'll be gone," Diana said. "Maybe I'll never come back if you decide to take me with you . . ."

The taxi pulled up and Mayfridh pointedly ignored her mother's hint. "Come on. I need to get back to Hotel Mandy-Z quickly. There's a lot at stake."

By the time Mayfridh had dropped Diana off and arrived at Mandy-Z, it was nearly ten P.M. Frozen for a moment, she stood at the front of the building looking up at Mandy's apartment. No lights in the windows. Was he staying away now that everyone knew what a monster he was? Or was he up there, lurking in the dark, with Hexebart by his side? A noise behind her stopped her heart. She spun round. Just a cat slinking off in the gutter. She hurried to the front door, knowing she was vulnerable alone; Mandy wouldn't waste a moment in killing her if he found her again.

With her key in the lock she hesitated. Already Eisengrimm, Christine, Gerda, and Diana had suffered at the hands of her enemies. Shouldn't she just leave them all in peace? But Hexebart had to be found, and she needed their help. She needed Jude.

Mayfridh listened carefully at the threshold of the gallery. Light under Jude's studio door, the radio playing within. There were more pressing matters to worry about than Jude, but she crossed the gallery anyway.

The door was unlocked. He looked up as she closed the door behind her. He was crouching next to a box, stacking it full of paint tubes and brushes.

"Packing?"

"Going home. As soon as Christine comes back." He stood and stretched his back. "Did you find Hexebart?"

"Not yet. I suspect she's with Mandy."

"And where's Mandy?"

"I don't know. He's not here?"

"We haven't seen or heard him. And we would have heard him in this creaky old place."

"Where could he be?"

Jude shrugged. "One of the richest men in Berlin? Anywhere. In any hotel. In any one of his apartments."

Mayfridh ran a hand through her hair in frustration. "Damn him, and damn Hexebart."

"Don't go near him alone, Mayfridh," Jude said, his face serious. "Promise me you'll take one of us with you."

She gazed at him. "I've hurt so many people."

"What do you mean?"

Of course, he didn't know about Christine, nor Eisengrimm, nor her mother. And how could she bear it if Jude was the next victim of Hexebart's magic, or Mandy's violent nature? "I'm so confused," she said, her voice cracking on a helpless sob. "I don't know where to start."

He approached her, put a gentle hand on her elbow. "Hey, it's okay. If Hexebart's with Mandy, we'll find him. We'll start by phoning all the hotels in town. Then we'll try Mandy's solicitor, his secretarial service . . . someone must have heard from him."

His tender voice, his soft eyes, heaped woe upon her woe. "Oh, Jude," she said, folding against his chest. His arms caught her tentatively. "Won't you come back with me? I can't be happy without you."

"You'll forget me."

"I don't want to forget you. I want to look at your face every day for the rest of forever."

"I don't deserve that happiness," he said, "and you won't remember me once winter comes, so you won't suffer."

"I will. Somewhere inside I know I'll suffer. It will be a scar on my soul." She turned her face up to him. "Tell me that you'll think about it."

"I won't think about it. Don't make me think about it. You know it's wrong. You know I don't belong in your world. I belong here, and I have to take care of Christine."

"Just ten seconds . . . for ten seconds tonight, before you sleep, think about it. Ten tiny seconds of your life. Please, Jude, please. Don't leave me with no hope at all."

He smiled. "Ten seconds, then. That's an appropriate

amount of time to think about my plans for a few hundred years."

She leaned into him and encircled his waist with her arms. "Kiss me, my love."

He kissed her, his hands moving to the small of her back, pressing her hard against him. "I love you," he muttered.

Then the door burst open.

Mayfridh and Jude dropped their arms and jumped apart, but it was too late. Gerda glared at them with steely blue eyes.

"Gerda," Jude gasped. "Gerda, don't—"

"Don't what?" Gerda demanded, and Mayfridh was horrified to see a lizard jump from her lips and land on the floor. "Don't interrupt your fun? Don't stop you from cheating on your fiancée? Don't spit fucking locusts and beetles?" She turned on Mayfridh and pushed a finger into her chest. "When were you going to come and fix me? Before or after you betrayed your best friend?" Such a barrage of insects and small reptiles sprang from her mouth that Mayfridh couldn't count them.

"I can't fix you," Mayfridh said. "Not yet. I didn't bring any spells. I have to find Hexebart."

"You're doing a fine job of looking for her, aren't you?" A tiny frog landed in Mayfridh's hair and became entangled. With a shriek, she loosened it and it dropped to the ground.

"Gerda, calm down," Jude said.

"You know what?" Gerda said. "I will calm down, but only because I hate the feeling of these things coming out of my mouth. Though I *will* ask you one question." She held up her index finger for emphasis. "Will you tell Christine about this, or will I?"

When Mandy finally slept, it was on the bare floorboards next to the vat, with the fluorescent lights still on overhead, and his arm hooked around the Bone Wife's ankle. He dreamed about her completed, with strong arms for carrying things, with a mane of bright hair that he could almost see, with Mayfridh's face painted onto the front of her gleaming head. Waking, seeing his Wife standing there unfinished, filled him with a great sadness. If Mayfridh didn't return, it could be years before she was ever whole.

He lay still for a moment, looking up at her, then hunger and discomfort made him lock the boning room carefully behind him, and go downstairs in search of breakfast.

The soft, early morning light in his lounge room was a welcome relief to his eyes, but the mess that Hexebart had made startled him. She lay asleep on the sofa surrounded by empty food tins, by wrappers and scraps and dirty plates and spoons. The sofa had been pulled close to the television—which was blaring an American news broadcast—and in the process the rug had been bunched up. He bent to straighten it, and noticed it was wearing at least half a bottle of spilled tomato ketchup. A glimpse of the kitchen through the doorway told him that the mess wasn't confined to just one room.

"Hexebart!" he bellowed.

She woke with a start, her eyes bleary and blinking. "What? What is it?"

"You promised me you'd be tidy." He swept his arm around him to indicate the mess.

"Yes, yes."

"You've made a terrible mess."

"I'll clean it, I'll clean it. Only don't throw me out, no, don't throw Hexebart out. Hexebart can help you."

Mandy stalked to the kitchen and began searching for

food. All the bread was gone, all the cheese and the cold meats in the fridge had been gnawed on and left unwrapped on the bench, so he threw them out. He switched on the coffee machine. The cupboards were open and all that remained in them were condiments and two tins of beans. He opened the freezer and found a bag of peas. Hexebart, in the space of one night, had almost cleaned him out of food.

He turned to see her in the doorway, trying to charm him with a smile. He shuddered.

"Did you eat everything?" he asked.

"Hexebart only ever eats bread and water in prison."

"You could have left some for me."

"I left the meat and the cheese." She indicated the rubbish bin.

"You'd already chewed on them."

Hexebart approached the bin and reached inside. "I'll fetch them."

"No, no. We don't eat food that's been in the rubbish. Not in the Real World."

She shook her head and clicked her tongue. "What a waste. What a terrible waste." Then she turned, bright-eyed, and said, "Mayfridh came back."

Electricity. "What?"

"She came back last night, but now she's gone again."

"Where has she gone?" Frustration clawed at him. She had been here, in the hotel, and he'd slept through it.

"Hexebart was listening the house, yes she was. Hexebart can hear everything that goes on."

"Where is she?"

"She came and she kissed Christine's lover. Gerda found them and sent her away."

"Where is she now?"

"She went to stay in a hotel."

"Which one?"

"I don't know," Hexebart said, pouting at his ungrateful questions. "She didn't say."

Mayfridh, in a hotel, probably nearby. Could he make discreet inquiries? Find her? Kill her while she was alone? What were the risks involved?

Hexebart was talking again. "But she'll be back. She'll be back very soon, I know, because she's looking for me and she thinks I might come here."

Mandy was suspicious. What could this foolish old woman have that Mayfridh wanted? "Why is she looking for you?"

"Because I'm a poor prisoner and she's a mean little sow and can't bear it that I've esca-aped." A song ensued, about escaping and about the dungeon. There was no way of telling if she was lying, or crazy, or perfectly serious.

Mandy opened a tin of beans and took a spoon from the drawer. "I'm going to my bedroom for a few hours' sleep. Next time you hear her come, wake me up immediately."

"Yes, Immanuel."

"If you're so good at listening to the house, tell me next time they're all out. I'll go shopping for food."

"Ooh, yes, Immanuel. I'll listen very hard."

"Good." He moved through the lounge room on his way to his warm, soft bed. "And clean up your mess."

"Yes, Immanuel. Yes, I will."

He didn't believe that for a moment.

❧

Christine leaned out the window of Mayfridh's bedchamber, trying to imprint upon her memory the view of Ewigkreis laid out before her. Russets and golds and the wind playing on the trees; the river lazy in the east, the Eternal Woods dim and mysterious, stretching into the distance.

"It's so beautiful and I can't take it with me," she sighed.

Eisengrimm spoke from the bed behind her. "Perhaps you should have brought a camera," he said, a smile in his voice.

She turned her back to the window. His ribs were still wrapped in bandages, but his vigor and movement were returning. "A photograph never captures a place. The smell, or the silence, or the way the light moves." She glanced over her shoulder. "Part of me really doesn't want to say good-bye."

"You can stay a little longer if you like."

Christine shook her head. "I have to get back to my own world. I've left them alone together for long enough."

"How's your hand?"

"Comfortable." She held up the velvet-lined silver hand that Klarlied had ordered from the silversmith. It was an exact match for her remaining hand, with intricate carvings, and jointed fingers. A shortage of magic in Ewigkreis meant it remained unenchanted.

"A pity we couldn't make it work for you."

"It wouldn't have worked back home anyway. It doesn't matter. None of it matters."

"It matters to me. I regret your injury very deeply."

She sighed and turned to the window once again. The giant birch was almost bare. Winter was close. "You'll forget it."

"If I could remember, I would. I'd remember you forever."

"How much of autumn is there left, do you think?"

"A week at most. Mandy's work upset the balance. We'll have a long winter, but the seasons will right themselves by spring."

"It must be beautiful here in spring."

"It's always beautiful here."

Christine took a last look around the room. So many

months ago, when this adventure started, she had found the low roof beams and the dank smells uninviting. Now she had grown fond of the Autumn Castle, its dusty corners and its grimy windows and the layers of white linen to sleep in. Perhaps it was simply appealing by association: here she felt no pain. Soon she would be consigned to pain for the rest of her life.

"What's the matter, Christine?" Eisengrimm asked.

"Thinking about how I'll feel when I go back. Thinking about my back. It's really going to hurt. Jude had to hit me hard."

"I wish you the best with it," he said, "and I wish you the best with Jude."

"Yeah, and I wish you the best with your pain and your love." She sank down on the bed next to him. "What's wrong with us, Eisengrimm? Why can't we find somebody who loves us perfectly, wholly, and completely?"

"Very few people do find that somebody, Christine. It's rare."

She lay on her back, enjoying each breath that ventured into her lungs, wishing and wishing and not even sure what she was wishing for.

"It's time to go," she said.

"Good-bye, Christine."

She sat up and leaned over to hug him gently. "I will miss **you** so much."

"I hope your life is full of wonders."

"I hope your life is full of joy." She took one last look out the window, one last look at Eisengrimm. Found tears on her lashes. "Good-bye," she said.

"Good-bye. Maybe someday . . ."

"Maybe. You never know."

Christine made her way down to the passage—a dreamy mirror of afternoon colors standing in the forest. She stepped through into the painful embodiedness of reality. Behind her, the Autumn Castle had disappeared, and Berlin traffic sounded in the distance. She took a moment to catch her breath, then headed toward Hotel Mandy-Z.

Hexebart searches the cupboard again, but all the cans are empty and gone. Oh, woe. Real World food is so tasty and exciting on her tongue, and now it's all gone. All, all gone. She runs her fingers around the edge of an empty can and laps up the tiny dollop of sauce. If only Immanuel would go shopping soon. Hexebart is growing hungry again.

She leans her head out of the kitchen and listens. Immanuel is still sleeping. Hexebart hears his snores. Why, she could sneak in there right now and have a piece of him for lunch. There's certainly enough meat on him. But no; Hexebart grinds her teeth. She needs Immanuel for now. Immanuel can kill the queen before she finds Hexebart, and Hexebart can go free with the royal magic and spend her life looking for Liesebet.

Hmmm . . . but while Immanuel sleeps, Hexebart could get up to other mischief. He often hides himself up in the room behind the door with many locks. . . . Hexebart wonders what's behind that door. A mystery. Maybe he has more food up there. That's it! He's hiding food from Hexebart! Or maybe he has jewels and other pretty Real World things that he doesn't want Hexebart to have. Selfish, selfish. Hexebart begins to creep up the stairs.

Then stops. And listens.

Downstairs, far below, somebody has come home. Is it the pig queen? Is it time to wake Immanuel and tell him to kill her?

No, it's somebody else. It's Christine.

Oh, Christine, oh, Christine,

Where have you come from, where have you been?

Hexebart isn't so interested in Immanuel's secret room of food and treasures now. She would rather go and speak with Christine. Hexebart opens the door and dances lightly down the stairs to Christine's apartment. She can't wait to see Christine's face. Oh, ha ha! Hexebart has so much to tell her.

CHAPTER TWENTY-EIGHT

*M*ayfridh *hadn't expected to find herself sharing a hotel* room with her mother on one of her last nights in the Real World. She woke up disoriented. The colors of the room were unfamiliar, the sheets stiff and tight. It took a moment to remember: Gerda walking in, spitting lizards and insects with rage, insisting that Mayfridh make a quick exit before Gerda took it upon herself to tell Christine everything. Jude had bundled her out the door in less than twenty seconds. "It's better this way," he said. "I'll sort it out with Gerda. You go stay with your mother."

Mayfridh sat up, cradling her head in her hands. Why was she so worried about what Christine would think? Hadn't she been trying to encourage Jude to leave Christine, to tell her that the New York wedding was off and that he was going to become King Jude of Ewigkreis?

"Are you all right, love?" This was Diana, awake in the next bed.

Mayfridh dropped her hands and forced a smile. "Yes, Mum. I'm fine."

Diana reached out and grabbed her fingers. "Thanks for coming to stay with me. I felt much safer."

Mayfridh squeezed Diana's hand fondly. "I'm glad."

"What has the day got in store for you?"

Mayfridh was climbing out of bed and pulling on her clothes. "Same as yesterday. Find Hexebart."

"I'll just stay here, shall I?"

"Stay here and rest your feet. It's safer that way. I'll come to get you if I find her."

"And then you'll leave?"

Mayfridh nodded. "I'll have to leave very soon after."

Diana's head drooped. Mayfridh sat next to her on the bed. "Mum, promise me something."

"What?"

"Promise me that . . . if I can't take you with me . . ."

Diana looked away quickly, a petulant expression crossing her face.

"Mum, I might not be able to take you with me."

"You're the queen."

"There are other considerations. It's very complex." She patted Diana's knee. "Mum, if I can't take you with me, will you promise to get on with your life? Will you go home to England and find old friends?"

"I have no old friends."

"Then make new ones. You can't organize your life around me."

Diana's lips twitched with irritation. "If I hadn't organized my life around you, I wouldn't have been there for you to come home to after twenty-five years. You're my daughter, May. One day, perhaps, you'll have a child and you'll know what true fear is. To lose my daughter, not to know on any day for twenty-five years whether you were alive or dead, sick, in pain, miserable, longing to be home . . ."

Mayfridh let the silence beat out for a long time, and she thought about all the times she had missed with her mother and all the times she was yet to miss. Shopping trips and morning teas and mother's days and first grandchildren. A flicker of imagination teased her: Diana in a few years, learning to trust the world again, smiling or laughing, holding a plump-armed child. The knowledge that it wasn't to be made her heart lurch under her ribs. "I'm so sorry, Mum."

A knock at the door.

"Who would that be?" asked Diana.

"Jude," Mayfridh said, rising and heading toward the door. "He's going to help me with Hexebart."

"Jude? Christine's boyfriend?"

Mayfridh tensed at the appellation. "That's right." She opened the door and Jude came in.

"Hi," he said, leaning forward to kiss her cheek.

Mayfridh pulled back and glanced at Diana. Had she seen?

"Oh, hello, Diana," Jude said, trying to sound smooth and not managing. "I didn't realize you were sharing a room. I thought you might be . . . next door . . . or something."

Mayfridh saw the spark of realization in her mother's eyes.

"Be careful," Diana said quietly. "I hope you find your witch."

"I hope so too," Mayfridh muttered, grabbing her coat. "Come on, Jude."

They turned off Unter-den-Linden and headed down Friedrichstrasse, past gleaming car showrooms and dusty building sites. The sky was pale and streaked with clouds, and early morning sun reflected off the crooked-pin shapes of building cranes. Streetcars, trains, taxis moved in the rhythm and tune of city mornings; other people's overcoats brushed against her as they vied for space on the narrow wooden boardwalk under a construction site. Mayfridh was overwhelmed by it, by the addictive cadence of the Real World, by the proximity of Jude who was the Real World's star citizen and witness. The vast silent spaces of Ewigkreis were empty and bare by comparison. A measureless ache suffused her, and she couldn't identify if it was in her heart, or her head, or her hands. *How could I forget this? It is everything to me, it makes me who I am.*

"So, we need to talk about the Gerda situation," Jude was saying.

For a moment she was bewildered. How was she to discuss something so mundane when such an epiphany of self-knowing was upon her? But of course, it was the very mundanity of the Real World that gave it its addictive flavor.

"Okay," she said. "Have you spoken to her?"

"Yeah, I talked to her last night. I promised I'd tell Christine about you and me, but only after you've gone. Only after we're back home in New York."

"And Gerda agreed not to mention it in the meantime?"

"Gerda was pretty dubious, actually. But she hates talking so much at the moment that she nodded."

"And will you tell Christine?"

"Oh, yeah. I have to, I know that. Gerda will check up on me." He lit a cigarette and blew out a long stream of smoke. "I'll tell Christine before we get married, give her a chance to back out."

"She won't back out."

"I hope not."

They walked in silence a few moments, then Mayfridh had to ask, "So, you've decided not to take up my offer?"

"Mayfridh, I—"

"Did you give it ten seconds' thought? Like you promised?"

"I did. I gave it more than ten seconds. I haven't stopped thinking about it."

"And still you decided not to come with me?"

He swept his arm around him. "I belong here."

"I know." Mayfridh refused to give up hope; she might convince him yet. At least he'd admitted to thinking about it.

"I have to take care of Christine." He shook his head. "I'm not looking forward to seeing her face when I tell her about you and me. Guilt is a terrible feeling, Mayfridh. It's like a kind of nausea that never goes away."

"If you come with me, you'll forget all your guilt. You'll forget Christine, the accident, the betrayal . . ."

"Don't, Mayfridh," he said. "I've thought of that. I've thought of everything."

"Ewigkreis is very beautiful," she said. "It's—"

"No. No. Here, I'm alive. There, I'd be a shadow."

As will I.

He led her down the street behind Vogelwald-Allee, into the park near Hotel Mandy-Z. Jude had seen Hexebart run in there to hide, and Mayfridh hoped she might be there again, waiting for Mandy to return.

"That's where I last saw her," Jude said, indicating a tall elm. "She just seemed to disappear."

"She can climb trees very quickly and hide in them, although not so easily now that all the leaves are falling." Mayfridh thought about the birch outside the great hall. When would the last leaf drop? Would she be pulled back, empty-handed, to Ewigkreis? The thought sickened her with dread. "She also likes to hide in bushes and hedges, so we'll have to check them all."

"What do I do if I find her? I mean, what if she turns me into a frog or something?"

"She can't turn you into a frog. If you find her, grab her as hard as you can."

"But—"

"Whatever she does to you, I can undo. Once she's in my presence, I command her magic again. She has to do as I say."

They began the search. The grass was overgrown and Mayfridh's feet sank into the bed of sodden leaves.

"And what happens if we don't find her?"

Mayfridh shook her head. "We have to find her."

"Would it be very bad?"

"She has the royal magic that our world runs on. Without it, we'll be caught in winter forever. Endless night, frozen ground, nothing will grow. Our race will die out."

Jude stared at her, astonished. "I had no idea it was so serious."

"We still have time."

"She could be anywhere in the world. She could have jumped a train to Frankfurt by now."

"No, she can't go too far. We're bound by the passage until it closes."

For an hour they searched the park with no success. Mayfridh taught Jude to look for the little signs that Hexebart had been present—bent twigs, dropped threads or spells—but there was no sign of her. A headache had started throbbing over her right eye. Perhaps it was worth going back to Ewigkreis briefly to take the remaining spells from Christine. Hexebart could hide from a searching spell, but magic might pick up the signs of her movement in the Real World where their eyes couldn't.

Jude touched her elbow gently. "She's not here. I'm sorry."

"Let's go out to Zehlendorf. She might have returned to my mother's house. We can search the streets out there."

"Sure, if you like."

"And then we'll scour the newspapers for reports of strange events—anything that might be related to Hexebart. We'll get Fabiyan and Gerda to help. Christine might even be back soon." Mayfridh felt a sudden jolt of guilt as she realized she still hadn't told Jude about Christine's injury. Not because she was deliberately withholding it; she had simply forgotten.

❦

Christine let herself into Hotel Mandy-Z and hung her coat on the hook. Her back was throbbing and she needed painkillers and a soft place to lie, but she couldn't walk past Gerda's door without stopping to undo Hexebart's enchantment. Poor Gerda had suffered for days, and must have been frantic when Mayfridh arrived without spells to help her. Christine had the last four spells in the pocket of her jeans and she patted them lightly with her silver hand. She knew she had to give them back, and wondered at her extreme reluctance to do so. Surely she should be happy to put all this faery magic behind her and try to lead a normal life. But then, what was normal about her life? The chronic pain, the missing hand, the fiancé who loved somebody else, the still-unaccessed multimillion-dollar trust fund?

She knocked lightly at Gerda's door, then pushed it open. Gerda sat on the sofa, her knees drawn up, a bucket positioned between them.

"Hi," Christine said. "Don't say a word. I have spells to fix you."

Gerda's eyes rounded in surprise and excitement. Christine closed the door behind her and approached, sitting on the coffee table in front of Gerda. She fished in her pocket for a spell. Gerda reached out to touch the silver hand, her eyebrows shooting up in shock.

"It's a long story. Let's fix you first," Christine said, balancing a spell on her palm. She wasn't exactly sure what to say, and bit her lip as she thought about it. Moments passed and Gerda began to look worried. Christine took a deep breath, and said, *"Speak normally."* She couldn't be more specific than that. She blew on the spell; it dissolved.

Gerda tentatively opened her mouth and said, "Did it work?"

Christine laughed. "I guess it did. No bugs and lizards."

Gerda threw the bucket aside and clasped Christine against her in a hug. "Oh, thank you. Thank you so much." She sat back again and indicated the silver hand. "What happened to your hand?"

"It's gone."

"Gone?"

"Immanuel Zweigler took it." Christine told Gerda the whole story, while Gerda shook her head in anger and disbelief.

"I'm so sorry, Christine." Gerda took the silver hand in her own and traced her fingertips over the carved vines and birds. "This is beautiful."

"It'll probably tarnish."

Gerda smiled. "I'm glad you can joke about it."

"What's the option?"

"Revenge."

"Revenge?"

"On Mandy. He can't get away with this. He deserves to be punished."

Christine leaned forward, puzzled. "What can we do to him in this world? Here, there are police and courts to worry about."

"We've got magic."

"Do we even know where he is? I presume he'd be in hiding now that we all know what a monster he is."

"All the others think he's disappeared, but I don't." Gerda lifted a finger to the ceiling. "I think he's up there."

Christine shuddered. "Here in the hotel?"

"I think he's hiding up there. I read his diary. He needs that boning vat, he needs to be near his sculpture. While they're all frantically searching for the witch, I think she's up there too. She's magic. She can probably cast a silent spell."

"And what did Mayfridh say when you suggested this?"

"I haven't spoken to anyone about it. I hated speaking, and . . ." She shrugged. "I don't know if I like Mayfridh anymore."

Christine was unnerved. "Why? What did she do?"

Gerda tapped Christine's silver hand. "For one thing, she's told nobody that this happened to you."

"What? Not even Jude?"

"Do you think she forgot? That's bad enough. Or maybe she didn't want Jude to know for other reasons."

Christine narrowed her eyes suspiciously. "What reasons?"

"Oh, who knows?" Gerda waved a dismissive hand, clearly fearful that she'd said too much.

Christine sat back on the coffee table, heavyhearted. She understood what Gerda meant: Mayfridh knew that Jude's love for Christine relied on a healthy dose of pity. If Jude's deepest compassion were aroused for Christine, it would dull his feelings for Mayfridh. "I feel like such an idiot sometimes, Gerda."

"She'll be gone soon." Gerda tapped her knee. "But don't trust her."

Christine raised her shoulders helplessly. "I . . . What difference does it make?"

"Forget about her. Let's concentrate on Mandy. We'll have a meeting, all of us, tonight. We'll decide what to do about him. We'll stop him from hurting anyone ever again." Gerda stood up and helped Christine to her feet. "I'll organize it. Meet here at seven o'clock. Tell Jude. We'll go somewhere nearby, somewhere Hexebart and Mandy won't hear us. In the meantime, go upstairs and rest. Your back must be hurting."

"It is."

"Do you need a hand?"

"No, I can manage. Thanks, Gerda."

She left Gerda with her plans to lead a mutiny, and took herself upstairs to her own apartment.

"Jude?" she called as she let herself in. No answer. He was probably out with Mayfridh, looking for Hexebart. She dropped her keys on the kitchen table and went to the sofa. The curtains were drawn against the gray daylight. Christine slumped down among the soft cushions and closed her eyes. Relax. Outside, traffic noise and distant trains, two men with loud voices unloading a van, and a nail gun on a nearby building site. No real quiet. She opened her eyes and gazed at the carved silver hand, choking on a sob.

Unexpectedly, a noise deep inside the apartment.

Christine sat up, ears straining. A floorboard creaked. Footsteps?

"Jude?" Her heart hammered. What if it were Mandy, waiting for her, waiting to take the other hand? She leapt from the couch, unplugged a heavy lamp, hefted it in her good hand, and tiptoed toward the bedroom. The door was ajar a few inches. "Who's there?" she called, forcing a note of bravery into her voice.

"It's me." A little voice, old and husky.

Christine recoiled. "Who is it? Get out of my apartment."

"I have something to tell you."

Hexebart. It was Hexebart. Christine looked at the lamp in her hand. It wasn't proof against magic. "Come out of there. Let me see you."

Four crooked fingers curled around the door and slowly pulled it open. Hexebart peeked out, a wicked glint in her eye. "Hello, Christine."

"What are you doing here?" Christine knew she should detain Hexebart, but was frightened to move any closer.

"I came to say something to you."

"What? What are you talking about?"

"I know something about Jude."

"Jude?" How did she even know who Jude was?

Hexebart clicked her tongue and pointed at Christine. "I think you know. I think you know—deep under deep— what's wrong, why it's wrong."

Christine was bewildered and frightened. Where was Mayfridh? Should she call out for Gerda to come and help? "You have to go back to Ewigkreis," she said. "Mayfridh needs the royal magic."

Hexebart's face crinkled up in anger. "Why should I care what the preening pig needs? I didn't come here to talk about her, I came here to talk about Jude."

"What about Jude?" Was this to do with Jude and Mayfridh?

"He's a liar."

Christine shook her head, baffled. But before she could say a word—

"And a killer."

"A killer?"

The witch revealed her stained and crooked teeth in a smile. "Oh, yes. Yes. You know who he killed, you know."

"I don't know what you're talking about."

Hexebart cackled and her long bony finger pointed to Christine's chest. "Your mother and father are dead."

An awful tide of dread began to rise up inside her. "Yes," she managed to gasp.

"Jude killed them."

Christine felt her lips moving, heard the word "No!" shouted in the dark hallway, but a searing shock of reality— an overwhelming moment when the knowledge of her own existence grasped her and shook her—blunted her senses and sent her pitching to her knees. The lamp crashed from her hand, cracking in two on the floor. When she looked up, Hexebart was gone. And she knew. Hexebart was right: Christine had already known.

Deep under deep.

∽

Mayfridh saw Christine and the artists already assembled around a table under the bright lights of a fast-food restaurant. They had arrived together, and Mayfridh had walked alone from her hotel. Gerda's phone call had been brief and terse: "Meet us there at seven-thirty. Don't even think of coming by Mandy-Z first."

Mayfridh's first surprise was that Christine was back. Her second—and it should have been no surprise—was that Jude wouldn't meet her eye. No doubt he wondered why Mayfridh hadn't told him about Christine's injury.

"Hello, everybody," she said, taking the seat next to Pete. Empty food wrappers were piled in front of him on a plastic tray. "Christine, when did you get back?"

"A few hours ago," she mumbled.

Christine seemed more hunched and skinny than ever before, almost as if she had folded in on herself. Was it the pain? The loss of her hand? Or had Jude already told her their guilty secret? The first glimmer of gladness that she would forget all this stole over her. "And how are things in Ewigkreis?"

"Eisengrimm is recovering well, but winter's very close. Eisengrimm said a week."

Steel fingers constricted around her heart. "How is your hand?"

Christine held up her left wrist. Attached to it was a beautifully carved silver hand. "I have no idea as I don't know where it is."

A tense silence followed as all eyes at the table watched to see what Mayfridh would do. "Of course. I'm very sorry."

Pete slurped on his shake and dropped the empty container on the table with a satisfied sigh. It broke the tension. "Come on, Gerda," he said, "what's your devious plan and why are you revealing it here?"

"We're meeting here because I don't think it's safe to talk back at the hotel," Gerda said.

"What do you mean?" Fabiyan asked.

"Because I think Mandy and Hexebart are there."

"We haven't heard them or seen them," Jude said.

"I've seen Hexebart," Christine said, and every pair of eyes turned on her, shocked.

"What?" Mayfridh gasped. "You've seen her? Since you've been back? Why didn't you tell me? Did you try to catch her?"

"She was in my apartment but she ran when I came in. I didn't try to catch her because I figured I'd lost enough body parts already."

"Did she say anything?" Jude asked.

"Like I said, she ran when I arrived."

"It doesn't matter that we haven't heard them," Gerda added.

"Yes, yes," Mayfridh agreed. "She could have enchanted the apartment. It's easy to do. I should have thought of that."

"We don't know for sure they're up there," Pete said.

"No, not for sure," Gerda conceded, "but if they are, we can't risk them hearing our plans."

"What plans?" Jude shook the ice at the bottom of his drink in a nervous gesture.

"The plans we're going to make tonight," Gerda said, "to stop Mandy from hurting anyone ever again."

"Revenge on Mandy isn't as important as capturing

Hexebart," Mayfridh said. "My world is at stake, the survival of my people."

Gerda shrugged. "My guess is that Hexebart is hiding with Mandy, right? She thinks you won't come near her as long as he's there to protect her. But, if he's out of the picture, she has nowhere else to hide. You can do what you want with her."

"What you mean 'out of the picture,' Gerda?" Fabiyan said, a nervous laugh on his lips. "It sounds like you intend to murder him."

"Murder him? No. I'm not suggesting anything illegal. I'm suggesting something . . . unnatural."

"Like?"

"Mayfridh here can put a spell on him. Think about it. We can turn him into a frog. He can't kill any more faeries, then. He can't cut Christine's other hand off, then."

Mayfridh spread her hands in protest. "I can't turn him into a frog."

"What? Why not?"

"I don't have that kind of magic. Even Hexebart couldn't do it. Only a dedicated sorceress, someone who'd spent her whole life on . . . It's preposterous to suggest it."

"Don't you have a sorceress back home who can come and do it for us?"

"No. Nobody like that lives in Ewigkreis. We're peaceful people. We use magic for little things to bring harmony and balance the seasons, to alter moods and make small enchantments. Hexebart did about the worst she could do to you, Gerda. Besides, I don't have any magic." She turned to Christine. "Unless you brought spells from Ewigkreis?"

Christine reached into her purse and pulled out three spells, which she lined up on the table between the empty wrappers and cups.

"Three?" Mayfridh said. "You only have three?"

"That's right."

"What happened to the others?"

"I used them."

"You *used* them? For what?"

Three spells weren't enough to do anything. She wanted at least two to help her find Hexebart—in case Gerda was wrong and the witch was hiding elsewhere. The other she would prefer to keep spare. What if she met with Mandy and needed a protection spell?

"I used them. I had to fix Gerda—you couldn't help her. I had to anchor myself in Ewigkreis while I recovered."

"What else? I thought you found eleven in the dungeons."

Christine scooped the spells back into her purse. "We'll discuss this later," she said, her lips tightly drawn.

"It's not important," Gerda said. "We have three. We should be able to do something with them."

Mayfridh was about to say that the spells were hers, that she should decide how they were used, that she was the queen. But she sensed that the sympathy at the table was firmly reserved for Christine, poor handless harmless helpless Christine. Annoyance niggled in Mayfridh's chest. How could the girl bear to be so pitiable? "Very well," she said quietly. "What do you suggest we do with them?"

"Is it possible to get into his apartment with a spell? Pick his locks?" Gerda asked.

"Yes."

"Then we'll use one for that."

"And what will we do to him once we're in his apartment?" Pete asked.

"Well, I'm open to suggestions," Gerda said. "Look, we're all agreed, aren't we, that he should be punished for what he did to Christine?"

Everyone nodded.

"And that, if possible, he should be stopped from killing more faeries."

"Of course," Christine said. "But how, without breaking a law which will land one or all of us in prison?"

"We could push him down the stairs," Gerda said.

"Murder," Christine countered.

"We could set fire to his apartment."

"Arson," they all chorused.

"We could use a spell to make him a nice person."

"Not even possible," Mayfridh said. "Think again."

"We could destroy that stupid sculpture."

"Then he'd want to kill more faeries," Pete said. "He'd be even angrier."

"Help me out here," Gerda said, hands spread on the table. "What can we do to him?"

They all fell silent as one minute, two minutes, ticked by. Then Fabiyan opened his mouth and tentatively said, "Electrocution, by accident."

Gerda narrowed her eyes. "What do you mean?"

Fabiyan shrugged. "I do not understand very much of his writing, but I read about his vat. He has two lights above door. One is warning light for overflowing from high temperature. He cannot tell these lights by color, only by position. If I rewire them, he is in danger of accidental electrocution."

Pete snapped his fingers. "Yes, I remember reading that."

"There's no guarantee the vat will overheat and electrocute him, is there?" Gerda asked.

"I can maybe adjust thermostat," Fabiyan offered. "The next time he starts vat, it will overheat and overflow. He'll see the light, think it is ready, go upstairs to use it and . . ." Here he made a zapping sound, like the spit of electricity. Very convincing. Mayfridh wondered if all electricians could make convincing electrocution noises.

Gerda nodded slowly. "Yes, yes. That would work."

"How can we get into the room to do that? Deadlocks, remember?" Christine said.

"The spells," Gerda said.

Mayfridh dug her fingernails into her palms in frustration. Were they really going to use the only magic she had left to open doors? Mayfridh hated Mandy as much as the rest of them, but once her world moved on, he would never cross to Ewigkreis again.

"But there are three locks on the door," Christine said.

"And we'll only have two spells left." Gerda slumped forward on the table. "We're one short."

Mayfridh saw an opportunity. "If you help me catch Hexebart, we'll have all the magic we need."

Gerda shot her a suspicious glance. "Are you sure? It sounds like you don't have any control over her."

"It's my magic," Mayfridh said, aware she sounded petulant but unable to check herself. "When she's in my presence she has to spin me the spells I want."

"You hope," Christine said gruffly.

"Look," Jude said, leaning his elbows on the table, "there's a lot to think about here. I don't know if I want to be responsible—even partly—for Mandy's death."

"Look what he did to your fiancée," Gerda protested, reaching for Christine's silver hand. Christine pulled away and slid her hand under the table. "And he's a mass murderer."

"Of faeries, not people."

"I'm a faery," Mayfridh said quietly, but nobody seemed to hear her.

"I think we should all sleep on it," Jude continued.

"I don't care if he dies," Christine said, not raising her eyes. "He's a monster."

"Come on. Let's go home," Christine said. "Mayfridh, are you staying with us or with Gerda?"

"I . . ." Mayfridh glanced at Gerda, who shook her head in warning. "I'll stay with my mother."

"We'll see you in the morning," Gerda said.

Mayfridh gathered her hotel keys and stood. "I'll come by early." She glanced around. Christine wouldn't meet her eye, Jude wouldn't meet her eye, Gerda gave her a challenging stare. "Fine, I'll see you then." She left the restaurant and headed out into the cold, dark street alone.

Hexebart listens the house.

She is so very hungry and wicked Immanuel won't go out for food in case the people hear him or see him. Then, aha! At last, she hears them getting ready to leave. There is to be a meeting to decide "what to do about Mandy." Hexebart wonders who Mandy is, then realizes they mean Immanuel. Hee hee, a plot! A plot against Immanuel. What fun. Hexebart wishes she could be at the meeting and listen, but now they're all gone Immanuel might chance a trip to a supermarket for more food.

Tiptoes, tiptoes. She goes to Immanuel's bedroom.

"Immanuel," she says. "Immanuel, are you awake?"

"Yes." Immanuel sounds gruff and tired.

"They've all gone out, Immanuel."

He sits up in bed. Hexebart thinks he is an ugly man. "Where have they gone?"

Hexebart nearly says, "To a meeting," but that won't do, no, that won't do at all. Because then he'll guess they're with Mayfridh, and then he'll want to go and find Mayfridh, and then there won't be any more food.

"I don't know," she says.

"Why don't you know? Didn't you tell me you could hear all their conversations?"

"But if they don't say where they're going, I can't know," Hexebart protests, and this is her sad old lady voice. She uses the sad old lady voice sometimes when she's angry, so Immanuel doesn't know just how angry she is. She thinks about a nasty spell she'd like to use right now on Immanuel. But she needs him to protect her from the little queen.

Immanuel throws back the covers and gets out of bed, switching on a lamp. "I expect I should go out for some food while I can," he said.

Hexebart claps her hands. "Oh, yes, oh, yes, oh. Get some of those sausages that come in a tin." How Hexebart loves those salty tasty little morsels.

"I don't see why I should get you anything," Immanuel says in a surly tone. "You've not been very helpful so far. When are you going to find out which hotel Mayfridh is staying in?"

"As soon as they say it," Hexebart replies. "As soon as they say it, I'll know. I listen the house all day and all night, and all I want is a few little sausages in a tin."

Immanuel shakes his head. "All right, all right. Sausages in a tin." He pulls on his coat and Hexebart follows him to the front door. "I'll be back soon," he says. "Don't get up to any mischief."

Hexebart gives him her charming-est smile. "Oh, no. Hexebart will be very good. Hexebart is very grateful, Immanuel."

His face is half-smile, half-grimace. The door closes behind him.

Hexebart spins around in a circle. Hee, hee! She races upstairs and finds the door with all the locks on it. Isn't it funny how Immanuel thinks he's more clever and wise than

Hexebart? But Hexebart can find out all his secrets, easy as this, easy as that. Hexebart's index finger grows long and skinny, and she pokes it in the first lock. Pop! Magic goes in, the lock opens up. Pop! Pop! And now the door swings open and Hexebart laughs. She tries to think of words to rhyme with "Immanuel" and "secrets" to make a song, but she's too busy creeping up the dark, narrow stairs and pushing open the door to a big bright room.

Ouch! The light is too bright. Hexebart blinks.

What's this, what's this? A big bowl of poison. Hexebart has never seen a bowl so big, and she knows instinctively not to touch it. Something feels all wrong in this room. Something feels bad, so very bad, and Hexebart doesn't like it, no. Shivers and shakes and quivers and quakes. Her fingers clutch up against each other, cold and colder. What's wrong, what's wrong?

Hexebart turns in a slow circle. There is a sculpture. It is a woman with no arms and no head. And that's where the bad feeling is coming from.

All Hexebart's breath is pulled out of her on a hook. The woman is made of faery bones! Hundreds and hundreds of faery bones!

Hexebart approaches, touches the sculpture. Oh, how horrid! Oh, how awful! Oh, how dreadful! She runs a trembling finger down the sculpture, and feels years of pain and suffering and fear. Immanuel made this? Is he an ogre?

And then . . . a shock to her fingertip as she nears the bottom of the sculpture. There's magic in here. Somehow Immanuel has saved some faery magic and it's mostly around here near the knees . . .

Hexebart shrieks and jumps backward.

Oh no oh no oh no, oh no no oh oh!

Liesebet!

Hexebart sinks to her knees and cries out. "Liesebet!

Oh, Liesebet!" And Jasper too. They are both here. They are both in this foul sculpture of a woman. Jasper's magic permeates the bones, cold and reluctantly expanding, like the pain in an old man's fingers.

"*Oh, oh,*" Hexebart weeps. "*Oh, and oh.*"

CHAPTER TWENTY-NINE

A *re you coming to bed?"*
Christine turned to see Jude in his pajamas, waiting by the bedroom door.

"Um . . . soon."

"Why are you sitting here in the dark?" He moved to turn the light on.

"No, no. Leave it off." Christine pulled her knees up under her chin, her feet on the sofa. "I'm just thinking."

"Don't think too hard." He touched her hair. She forced herself not to flinch. "What are you thinking about anyway?"

"A million things," she sighed.

"You'll get used to it, Christine," he said softly, and his tenderness jolted her. "When we get back to New York, we can see all the right medical people, get you a proper prosthetic hand—"

"Don't, Jude. I can't bear to be treated like I'm a medical oddity, like some poor pitiful invalid." Although he had always treated her that way.

"But, Christine, I—"

"Jude, please, go to bed. Please just leave me alone here in the dark for a while. I don't want to talk about it."

He backed away, his palms raised. "Okay. Okay, babe. But if you need me, you know where I am."

She heard the bedroom door shut, and leaned her head back on the sofa, eyes closed. God, she was so twisted up inside. She hated him, she loved him. The depth of her fury was beyond measure, and it was not because he had caused the accident that killed her parents and left her constantly in pain. Long ago she had allowed her anger for that juvenile driver to become an abstract, impersonal murmur of if-only, of accidents-happen, of wishing-what-might-have-been. It was fading, it would die. Certainly, she would never have knowingly formed a relationship with that person, but time and fate and acceptance would have led her to forgive him.

What Jude had done was unforgivable. At the very best, he had hidden from her a truth that was significant in every moment of their shared life. At the very worst . . . Christine could hardly bear to think of it. Could it be that Jude had sought her out and stayed with her *because he felt sorry for her?* How could she reclaim any dignity from such a situation? For all these years she had battled with a suspicion that he didn't really love her. Sweet Jesus, what if she were right?

Christine opened her eyes and dropped her feet off the couch, leaning forward with her forehead resting on her knees. She suppressed a groan. Of course she was right. Of course the relationship was based on a deception. She could almost admire him for how far he was prepared to go: he was about to marry her. He was willing to sacrifice his heart for the rest of his life out of the guilt that he felt; but she didn't make the mistake of thinking it was for her sake. No, it was for his. So he could be the noble, compassionate Jude who always did the right thing, rather than the hopeless, careless boy who had killed two people in a moment's inattention.

Did she love him or hate him?

She loved somebody; she could still feel it in her heart. A

deep sweet ache that poets could turn into words, but which remained inexpressible to her. But the somebody she loved didn't exist, and she was like a teenager who died of yearning for an imaginary boy.

"I can't marry him," she whispered into the gloom. Such an emptiness filled her as she imagined returning home to New York without Jude, with a dull, dark space where he should be. Sobs started deep inside her, but she kept them quiet. She didn't want to talk to Jude about it, not yet. Not ever. If only she could simply walk away from all of this and forget, as Mayfridh would. She longed for Ewigkreis. No pain in her back, no pain in her heart. Just endless rural peace and ignorant bliss.

The bedroom door opened softly. "Christine," he said, "are you crying?"

"No," she replied, rising from the sofa. "I'm just coming to bed now."

He held his arms out, but she sidestepped him. "Don't, Jude," she said. "I'm not feeling particularly affectionate at the moment."

"Okay. Come to bed and get some rest. I'm concerned about you."

"I know you are," she said. He was always concerned about her. It was all he could ever offer.

Hexebart listened the house last night."

Mandy looked up from his desk, where he was sketching arms. It was important that his Wife's arms had exactly the right balance of grace (for aesthetics) and musculature (for physical labor). He was irritated by the hag bothering him just as his pencil was tracing the most perfect of curved lines. "What?"

"I listened and listened, when they all got home. Guess what I heard, guess what I heard?"

"What?" he demanded again, his voice becoming nasty.

Hexebart flinched and backed away. "Hexebart is only trying to help you, Immanuel," she said. "I have a plan to help you catch the queen."

Mandy placed his pencil carefully on the desk. He could never be certain if Hexebart were serious or merely amusing herself. "What is your plan?"

"Well, you see, Hexebart has something the queen wants very much."

"What is it?"

"Never you mind. It's a private thing."

Mandy rolled his eyes. "If this is more of your time-wasting—"

"No, no. You have to trust me."

"What is your plan?" he said again.

"I'll tell her to meet me here and that if she meets me here, I'll give her the thing she wants."

Mandy nodded slowly, taking a deep breath. A typically vague explanation. "I see. How are you going to tell her to meet you when we don't know where she is?"

"Oh, I know where she is," Hexebart replied airily.

Mandy's attention snapped into focus. He shot out of his chair. "What?"

"I said I listened the house last night. I heard them talking about a particular hotel that—"

"Which hotel? Where is she?" Why hadn't the old hag told him last night? He stalked over and reached out to shake her.

Hexebart slipped out of his grasp like mercury, and shoved a hard finger deep into the flesh of his chest. "Now you listen to me, Immanuel," she hissed.

Mandy took a step back, surprised and, if he admitted it to

himself, a little frightened. He had never seen her as anything but a pathetic, occasionally mischievous hag. He had to remember she was a faery, and faeries had magical abilities and unpredictable natures. "I'm sorry, I—"

"Do you want to kill the little queen?"

"Yes, you know I do."

"And do you want to do it in your lovely secret room up the stairs?"

"Yes," he said.

"And hasn't Hexebart been helpful so far? Making the silent spell. Listening the house."

"Yes."

"Then stick with Hexebart's plan and don't be grabbing me and threatening me or I won't tell you a thing. I swear I won't."

Mandy bit his tongue. He could relish killing her and boning her later. "I'm sorry, Hexebart. What is your plan?"

"I already told you. I'll bring her here tonight, I'll say I'm alone, we'll trick her upstairs into your room, and then she'll get what she deserves. Sulky little sow. Nasty little changeling."

"All right, all right then," Mandy conceded. He would trust Hexebart to lure Mayfridh into the apartment. If she couldn't, he would torture her tomorrow for Mayfridh's whereabouts.

Hexebart was giggling. "Hee, hee," she said, "I know, I know."

"What do you know?" he asked.

She gave him a coquettish smile. "I know what Immanuel has up in the secret room." She pointed at the ceiling. "Hexebart knows, Hexebart kno-ows."

"How do you know?"

"Hexebart has special fingers." She held her left hand out and, right in front of his eyes, the index finger extended and grew thin, the bone within creaking. "Hexebart can get into any room."

"You've been snooping in my boning room?" She must have seen the Bone Wife. Did she realize it was made of faery bones?

"You have a magic doll," she said. "I saw it."

"It's not a doll, it's a work of art," he replied.

"You want more magic for the doll. That's why you want Mayfridh."

He gazed at her warily. "And what if I do?"

"You boil off everything, just keep the bones."

"That's right."

"There's more magic. There's magic in her eyes and magic in her hair and magic in her skin." Hexebart pinched a fingerful of her own crepey skin to demonstrate.

"I only want her bones."

"You'll waste the magic. I know a way to extract it all."

"How?"

"Hexebart can show you. Hexebart can make you a little spell to help." She pushed her hands together and her fingers tapped each other gently. As Mandy watched, a golden glow began to grow between them. "Ah, ah, spin and spin," Hexebart said. Moments later she presented him with a glowing ball, about the size of an eyeball. "For you, Immanuel."

"What is it? What do I do with it?"

"Make Mayfridh touch the doll, then blow this spell on her and say, *'Extract.'* All the magic will flow into the doll. Then you can kill the queen and not waste a drop of royal magic. Lovely, lovely royal magic." Hexebart leaned close. "She's full of it, you know," she whispered, her breath warm and garlic-scented in his face.

Mandy gazed at the ball on his palm. This was worth all the food Hexebart had eaten, all the mess she had made. He was feeling so fond and generous in that moment, he considered letting her go once Mayfridh was dead. His smile turned to a frown. If she knew what the sculpture was made of, why wasn't she worried that she might be his next victim?

"Why are you helping me?" he asked.

"Because you're hiding me until Mayfridh is dead. Once she's dead, I don't have to hide and I don't have to stay here. Hexebart is running away to Paris."

Mandy weighed her words. He had a spell to extract all of Mayfridh's magic, and he had Mayfridh's bones within his grasp. The Bone Wife would be finished, and she would be perfectly enchanted. She would be able to make him breakfast in bed, wash his sheets, clean his toilet. Oh, it would be bliss, a lifetime's achievement, a boyhood dream made manifest. "Very well, Hexebart. You may run away to Paris," he said. "As long as I finish my sculpture, I don't care what you do."

"Oh, you wait until you see your dolly dance once she has royal magic in her," Hexebart said, lifting her skirts and kicking her legs in a jig. "La, da da. La, da da."

"What time?"

"Midnight," Hexebart said in a portentous voice, raising a crooked finger. "The hour for witches." With a sweep of her arm, she cleared the drawings off his desk.

"Hey!" he protested.

"Shush now, Immanuel," she said, reaching for his hands. "We are too busy for drawings. We have scheming to do."

❧

Mayfridh was returning from the breakfast room of her hotel when she heard the phone ringing. She placed her room key on the table and scooped up the receiver. This would be Jude, she knew it. He would be phoning to tell her he'd made his decision, he was coming to Ewigkreis with her.

"Hello?" she said.

"Hello? Hello?" A female voice, familiar but too strange in this context to pinpoint exactly.

"Who is this?" She could hear Diana in the bathroom, water running, a soft humming.

"It's me."

Mayfridh puzzled a moment longer, then the voice made sense. "Hexebart?" she gasped. Of course, Hexebart. The old witch was too clever to appear in person. "Where are you?"

"Never you mind, never you mind that." Her voice was distant, quiet, as though she hadn't quite got the hang of how to use the phone. "You must do as I say, Queen Mayfridh. I know things, I know awful things."

Hexebart had never called her Queen Mayfridh. "What are you talking about?"

"I know awful things and I was wrong. I want to give your magic back."

"Hexebart, you'll have to explain better than that."

"He's coming," she whispered urgently. "I have to go. Meet me at Immanuel's house at midnight. I'll leave the door open and I'll make sure he isn't home. Bring the others if you like."

"If you're going to give my magic back, why not now? Why not come here in person?"

"Trust me, stubborn girl." Then the phone clicked.

"Hello? Hexebart? Damn!" She slammed the phone down as her mother emerged from the bathroom.

"Is everything all right, May?"

"I don't know. I doubt it." She was already grabbing her coat and scarf. "I have to find Jude and the others and see what they think."

Diana gently took her elbow as she headed for the door. "Jude and the others? Don't you mean Christine and the others?"

Mayfridh shook her off with an involuntary scowl. "They're all my friends now."

"May, I hope you're being careful. With your own heart, and with the hearts of others." Diana's eyes were soft and sincere; Mayfridh felt herself start to crumple inside.

"Mum, I'm . . ." Then a sob caught in her throat. "I'm in a terrible mess, Mum."

Diana folded her into her arms and rubbed her back. "Oh, May. Are you in love with him?"

Mayfridh nodded. "And he's in love with me, but we can't be together."

"Because he belongs to Christine?"

"No, because he belongs to the Real World." Mayfridh brought her tears under control and stood back. "I can't deal with this now, I can't think about it. Hexebart called. She wants me to meet her tonight, she says she'll give back my magic."

Diana's face paled at the mention of the witch. "Tell me you aren't going near her. Tell me you don't trust her."

"Of course I don't trust her, but it may be my only opportunity to catch her. If the others will help." Mayfridh pulled on her coat. "She called me Queen Mayfridh, Mum. It's the first time she's ever done that. She said she'd found out something awful. Maybe she knows about Mandy and his bone-hunting. Maybe it's made her change her mind about me." Mayfridh almost laughed, imagining Eisengrimm's skepticism. "Whatever she has planned for me, though, she has to be at Mandy's at midnight to do it. She's eluded me until now, and time is running out."

Diana gave her a quick squeeze. "Be careful, May. I don't want to lose you a second time."

Mayfridh forced a smile. They both knew that a second loss was inevitable. "I'll be careful." She kissed her mother on the cheek and headed for Hotel Mandy-Z.

She found Jude alone in his studio. He was sitting on the blue sofa surrounded by sealed and labeled boxes. The room seemed bare and empty, cleared of the usual mess. He gazed at a half-finished canvas, a cigarette dangling between his lips.

"Hi," she said.

"Don't close the door," he replied, obviously mindful of their last encounter here, when Gerda had found them. "I'm expecting Christine."

"What are you looking for?"

"I never liked this one, so I'm leaving it. I'm just trying to memorize the parts of it that I can use somewhere else."

She didn't have time to appreciate his painting. "Hexebart has been in touch."

"Yeah?"

Mayfridh explained while Jude responded with a dubious drawing-down of his eyebrows.

"It may be my best chance of capturing Hexebart," she finished. "I have to do it."

"I understand. I think the others will understand too, and we'll come with you, but not Christine. Christine has suffered enough. If we all get turned into frogs—"

"I keep telling you she can't turn us into frogs, and I'll have those last few spells with me in case she tries any mischief."

"Nevertheless, I don't want Christine there. She's not herself, Mayfridh. She's withdrawn; she won't talk to me. I can't imagine what she's going through." He held up his left hand, the cigarette firmly between his two forefingers. "You know she lost her engagement ring along with it."

Mayfridh's skin prickled with irritation. He spoke as though he were really in love with Christine. "Jude, don't pretend there's nothing between us."

"There's nothing between us, Mayfridh," he said, and drew deeply on his cigarette.

"I'll never believe that. You can still change your mind and come with me. If I can catch Hexebart tonight, I'll be leaving tomorrow. You could come with me. You could forget all your guilt, all the awful things that weigh on your heart. We'll have love and laughter and a future. You'll be the king of a magnificent land, you'll live for hundreds of years, young and beautiful."

Jude shook his head. "That's not my future, Mayfridh," he said.

"Why not?" She wanted to stamp her feet and shout. How could he be so stubborn?

"You know why not," he replied gently. "Just as you know why you'd never trade faeryland for the Real World." He lifted himself from the sofa and crushed his cigarette out on the floor. "Come on, we should find Christine and the others."

Mayfridh was frozen to the spot, her mind suddenly aflame with possibilities. Did she know that she would never trade Ewigkreis for the Real World? Did she know for sure?

❧

Midnight. He only had to wait until midnight.

Mandy paced the boning room. Around once, twice, three times. The hag had arranged for Mayfridh to come to him; had given him magic to lure her up here. Dreams were coming true.

He stopped in front of his Bone Wife. So many years had passed since he first conceived of her. Childhood had curved into adolescence, adolescence had wheeled into adulthood with all its attendant mundanities: financial commitments, business agreements, personal responsibilities. Yet he had always clung to this dream, and resolved to call it destiny rather than fancy. The long gestation was nearly over. He was like a pregnant cat, pacing and settling, pacing and settling. A life's work would culminate in the next few hours. He only had to wait until midnight.

He reached up to switch the boiler on. It clunked and swallowed, then slowly the sweet hiss of the elements warming up began to fill the room. The engine was a white-noise backdrop to his musings. He closed his eyes and felt a warm wash of contentment, of *rightness*. Her head from her neck, her flesh from her bones, her essence surrendered to the most sacred of his boyish dreams. He could imagine the colors he would never see, deep crimsons and wet purples; he could imagine the feel of her under his wicked thumbs, the pressure of longing, and a sweet, violent end for the queen of the faeries.

Mayfridh stood at the window of Christine and Jude's apartment, gazing at the world outside. It was eight minutes before midnight, and teeming rain swept the dark street. Beyond Vogelwald-Allee, cars slid past on Friedrichstrasse, muted to silence by the double glazing. Lights from shops, the glitter of streetlights, and the rhythmic change of traffic signals from green to red reflected on the slick road surface. Mayfridh felt at once a part of it, and excluded from it: attached by a deep love for the city and its ceaseless cadence, estranged by the fact of her being made of different stuff. The Real World wasn't her world. She hadn't aged since she reached adulthood and wouldn't for hundreds of years to come; she would live for 'four hundred years; she had the ability to perform magic and distribute goodwill and blessings to her entire land. She was different, she was other.

Behind her, the door to the apartment opened softly and she heard voices, urgent with whispers. Christine approached over her right shoulder and tapped her gently. "Mayfridh, Pete and Fabiyan are here. It's nearly time."

Mayfridh slowly turned from the window. "Thanks, Christine." She touched Christine's shoulder, smoothed hair away from her pokey face. "Thanks for everything."

Christine involuntarily gave her a smile, wary though it was. Suddenly, Mayfridh wished for nothing so much as to have never come to the Real World, to have never met Jude or Mandy or reunited with Christine or Diana. She regretted too deeply the chaos of the heart that had followed her.

"Gather close, everyone," Mayfridh said, keeping her voice low. Christine, Jude, Gerda, Pete, and Fabiyan surrounded her. "Christine, the spells?"

Christine handed over the remaining three spells. Mayfridh could sense her reluctance. She pushed two into the pocket of her overalls and weighed the third on her palm. "I'm going to work a protection spell over all of us. It won't protect us from everything, so you still have to be vigilant and sensible, but if Hexebart tries any mischief it should minimize the effect and duration. Everyone hold still." Mayfridh worked the magic, all the time watching them watch her—especially Jude—and feeling vainly pleased with their awe.

"Okay," said Gerda, when Mayfridh had finished. "Can we go over the plan again?"

"First we check that Hexebart was telling the truth, and that Mandy isn't home," Mayfridh said.

"And if he isn't," Pete responded, "Fabiyan and I will go down to the laundry to the fuse box and switch off the electricity so we can rewire the warning lights."

"But if he's there," Gerda said, "we all close ranks around Mayfridh so he can't get her."

"It's really important for me to catch Hexebart," Mayfridh

said. "The survival of my whole world is dependent on it. I know that I can't expect you to understand fully—"

"Sweetie, we wouldn't be helping if it were anything less dire," Gerda said drily. "I have no desire to be near that witch again."

"We understand," Jude said. "We'll do our best."

"If we see her, we have to keep her hands apart. She can't do any magic with her hands apart," Mayfridh warned.

"I'll grab one hand, Gerda can grab the other," Jude said.

"Good," Mayfridh replied. "So, Pete and Fabiyan will take care of the electricity, and Jude and Gerda will help me with Hexebart."

"Um . . ." This was Christine, leaning on the back of the sofa. "What am I supposed to be doing?"

Jude turned and tapped his index finger gently on her shoulder. "You're not coming."

"What? Why not?"

"Because you've already sacrificed enough of yourself to help me," Mayfridh said.

"Because I won't let you come," Jude added.

Christine looked from Jude to Mayfridh. "Oh, and you two have already discussed this and decided upon it, have you?"

"Shh," Gerda said, "don't raise your voice."

Christine glanced around, dropping her voice to a harsh whisper. "I'm not an invalid, I'm not an idiot. Stop treating me like one. I'm coming with you."

"No," Jude said forcefully. "No, you're not."

"Yes, I am."

Pete intervened, waving his skinny arms. "Guys, guys. This isn't a good time for arguing."

"What if Mandy's up there? What if he decides to take your other hand?" Jude said.

"It's my decision. It's not yours."

"I'm only trying to protect you."

Christine fell silent a moment, shaking her head at him. Then she said slowly, "I never asked you to protect me."

"If she wants to come, let her come," Gerda said irritably. "If Mandy's there, I'll push her down the stairs and out the door myself." She checked her watch. "Come on, it's time to go."

They left the apartment and, as quietly as they could, filed up the stairs to Mandy's apartment. Jude led the way with Mayfridh close behind him. She glanced over her shoulder. Christine's arm was interlocked with Gerda's, behind Pete and Fabiyan. Mandy's door now stood in front of them.

"She said she'd leave it open," Mayfridh told them.

Jude pushed the door. It swung inward. "Reliable so far," he said, then beckoned the others to follow him inside.

The television was on with the sound down, and all the lights were blazing. Half-eaten food on dirty plates cluttered the tables and floor.

"Hexebart?" Mayfridh called timidly.

Pete and Fabiyan broke away from the others and began checking the rooms.

"Nobody down here," Fabiyan said. "We should check upstairs."

They advanced up to Mandy's studio. Again, it was empty.

"Okay, Mandy's not here," Pete said. "Fabiyan and I are on our way to the fuse box. Who's got the flashlights?"

Gerda and Jude held up a flashlight each.

"We'll be back in a few minutes," Pete said, and he and Fabiyan disappeared.

"Mandy's not here," Mayfridh mused, "and neither is Hexebart."

Christine indicated the locked black door that led to Mandy's boning room. "She could be up there."

"Three locks, two spells," Mayfridh replied.

At precisely that moment, the door clicked and swung inward on a narrow, empty stairwell. Mayfridh jumped back with an involuntary shriek.

"Queen Mayfridh?" Hexebart's voice, from up the stairs.

"Hexebart?"

"Come upstairs. I have something for you, but you have to come alone."

Mayfridh peered up the stairwell to the bright yellow line of light. A low rumble came from nearby. Hexebart hadn't yet shown her face.

Jude was shaking his head. "Don't go up there. Mandy's probably up there with her. It's a trap."

"I have to catch her."

"Then we'll come up with you." He moved to stand next to her. "Come on."

The stairwell was too narrow for Gerda to flank her on the other side, but she followed. Christine made to join them, but Gerda turned and said, "We need you down here to tell Pete and Fabiyan what's going on."

"Okay," Christine replied, and took up position by the door.

"Don't let that door close behind us."

"I won't."

Mayfridh's heart hammered as she took the narrow stairs one at a time. The reassuring warmth of Jude's shoulder pressed against hers was not enough to ease her trepidation. *What if, what if, what if?* She wanted to turn and run, but Hexebart was up there and she needed Hexebart. Everyone in Ewigkreis needed Hexebart.

Two steps from the top of the staircase and a black shape loomed out. Mandy.

Mayfridh screamed, Jude tried to move in front of her, but Mandy grabbed his collar and pushed him aside, sending him pitching down the stairs. In an uncannily swift movement he had Mayfridh by the hair, dragging her up toward him. She felt Gerda's hand around her ankles, but then Mandy turned and with a grunt, kicked Gerda in the stomach. He pulled Mayfridh in with him and threw her on the floor. She struggled to her feet, but he kicked her again. Gerda was still trying to enter the room, but Mandy pulled himself up tall and Mayfridh realized with horror that he had a spell sitting on his palm.

"Over and out!" he shouted, and it was Hexebart's voice that emerged from his eel-like lips. Gerda pitched down the stairs after Jude.

Mayfridh heard the door slam. She looked around frantically for Hexebart, but soon realized she was alone in the boning room with Mandy. The roar of the engine that drove the vat drowned out her frantic heartbeat.

"Did you like my use of faery magic?" Mandy said, now speaking in his own voice. "That hag you had in the dungeons has been very supportive of my plans. Though I hope I won't have to cut my own hands off." He sniffed his hand and wrinkled his nose in distaste.

Mayfridh felt her whole body crumble from the inside. So Hexebart had been tricking her. Of course. But she hadn't thought the witch would sink as low as helping Mandy murder her. She tried to sit up, but Mandy kicked her hard in the side. Her breath flew out of her.

"Don't try to escape. I'm not going to let you escape."

With shaking fingers, she attempted to reach the pocket that held the spells, but he saw her move and in an instant was on the floor, kneeling on her ribs and pinning her hands up above her head. "I'm not a fool," he spat. "I can't stand to think for a moment that you believed you might get away. I'm inexorable and unstoppable. Tonight, I will finish my sculpture." He reached for a rope that lay coiled near the feet of his awful sculpture, tied her hands together, and then tied them to the gleaming ankles of his Bone Wife so that her fingers curved onto the smooth white surface.

Under the yellow-bright light, with the rumble of the motor and the hiss and spit of the vat nearby, Mayfridh's perception shifted into the tunnel vision of panic. Details leapt out at her: the tiny hairs of wool on Mandy's pullover; the stubble on his ruddy chin; a rough knot in the floorboards she lay on. She tried to calm her breathing so the details wouldn't overwhelm her and make her black out, but suddenly everything did black out, although not in her mind. Fabiyan and Pete had found the fuse box.

"What the—?" Mandy bellowed. His voice was excruciatingly loud in the sudden quiet that followed the vat turning off. The liquid still spat softly inside it.

Mayfridh allowed herself a moment of hope, that somehow Mandy's plans would be thwarted by the blackout. Then he turned and Mayfridh noticed something glowing in his hand. Another spell. The only light in the room, it threw his face into evil shadows.

"I can see well enough by this light," he said, "until I can find a candle. The vat is hot enough, and I'll have you in it soon." He held up the spell for her to see. "Hexebart wove this for me."

"What is it?"

"It's a way for me to get everything I need from you before I kill you."

Mayfridh tortured her mind trying to imagine what the spell would do. "Hexebart isn't to be trusted."

"Not by you, she's not." Mandy laughed. "As to whether I can trust her, well, it seems I've done all right so far. Let's get on with it, shall we?" He leaned close and held the spell on his palm, ready to work Hexebart's traitorous magic.

CHAPTER THIRTY

C*hristine waited, her back pinning the door open, when* shrieks and thumps above alerted her that everything had gone wrong. As she moved to peer up the stairwell, Jude tumbled into her, knocking her against the threshold. An agonizing bolt of pain shuddered down her spine.

"Mandy!" he gasped, struggling to his feet, just as Gerda thudded into him, knocking him to the floor.

At the mention of Mandy's name, Christine instinctively recoiled. Too late she saw the door begin to move. She tried to jam her shoulder against it, but it slammed shut, shaking her whole body with a violence that echoed in her bones.

Jude climbed to his feet and pounded on the door. "Open this up, Mandy. Open it immediately or I'll call the police."

"I doubt he can hear you," Gerda said, standing with a theatrical wince. "It's all soundproofed."

Christine tried the door. All the locks had snapped back into place. "Maybe we should call the police," she said. "They might be able to stop him before he kills her."

"He won't kill her just yet." A voice from behind them.

Gerda and Jude gasped. Christine turned gingerly. Hexebart stood two paces away with a satisfied smile on her face.

"I thought—" Christine started.

"Hexebart gave Immanuel her voice for a little while," the witch said. "Clever? You all thought it was me."

"What have you done?" Jude demanded. "He's going to kill her."

"Oh, pish!" said Hexebart with a dismissive wave. "I have a scheme. Let me at the door." She moved toward the door, but Jude stood in her way.

"What are you up to?" he said.

"Out of my way."

Jude grabbed her arm roughly. "Gerda, get her other arm."

"I don't like you, boy," Hexebart said, trying to twist out of his grasp. "Get out of my way."

At that moment, the lights went out and they were all plunged into darkness. Then three lights came on in the room. Gerda's and Jude's flashlights, and a ball of light between Hexebart's hands. She had escaped Jude's grasp.

"Now stay away from me," Hexebart said. Her haggard face was thrown into shadowy relief by the dim lights. "Let me open the door. The queen needs our help, you know, and you can't do anything without me."

Jude advanced on the witch again, and she flung out her arm and cast the spell. He staggered back, his arm in front of his eyes, a cry of pain on his lips.

"Jude?" Christine shrieked.

"I can't see a thing. She's sent me blind."

Gerda backed away.

"Now, let Hexebart do her work. Stupid Real World people."

Christine had an arm around Jude, grabbed his flashlight, and tried to peer into his eyes. "Can you see anything? Anything at all?"

"I . . . maybe. I think I can see the light. Actually, I think it's coming back already. There you are." He touched her face tenderly, and for a moment all her anger toward him dissolved.

"Mayfridh's protection spell must have helped."

Gerda's gasp of horror made her turn back to Hexebart. The witch's index finger had become as long and thin as a knitting needle. She inserted the end into each lock individually and they all snapped open.

"Come," the witch said, standing back, "Hexebart should very much like you all to see what she has planned for the man who killed the queen."

❧

It was a scene from a nightmare. In the almost-black space of the boning room, while her hands were tied and the vat waited hot and poisonous nearby, Mayfridh watched Mandy loom over her with a sneer. Gently he dropped the spell onto her wrists and said, *"Extract,"* then sat back on his haunches to watch.

Extract? What diabolical enchantment had Hexebart made for him? Was it the kind of extraction spell that took a faery's soul and essence for use in black magic? She had heard of such spells, but had no idea that Hexebart's ability extended so far or her hatred extended so deep. Frantically, she fought against the ropes, kicked out at Mandy. He easily grabbed her ankles and pinned them down.

"Frightened?" he asked.

"What have you done to me?" Then, she felt it. A slow, sweet energy moving into her fingers and hands, coursing down her wrists and into her torso. Something familiar and comforting about it, a feeling of being safe and protected and—

Jasper! She gasped as two realizations fought for her attention. The first: royal magic was pouring into her, Jasper's royal magic. She finally knew what had happened to her parents. Mandy had killed them for his sculpture. And this explained the second realization: Hexebart was helping her. At last the hag believed Mayfridh had nothing to do with her parents' disappearance.

Mandy laughed when she gasped. "Does it hurt to lose your magic?"

The spell extinguished, the room was now pitch-black. Mayfridh was grateful that Mandy couldn't read the relief on her face. She didn't answer, but began to twitch her fingers together to make the magic work and untie the ropes. They slid off her hands and onto the floor. Still she kept her fingers on the ankles of the statue, reclaiming every last drop of her father's magic.

"I'll light a few candles," Mandy said, and his voice came from across the room. She hadn't sensed him move. "I'll need to see where your throat is if I'm going to slit it accurately."

The flow of magic slowed. Mayfridh could feel it in her heart now, pumping around with the blood. It left her temporarily breathless. Jasper's magic was only a tributary of Liesebet's, less than a tenth as powerful, but it weighed in her heart and her chest like the burden of a nation. A light flickered on the other side of the room and Mandy's figure appeared in the dark, silhouetted by a candle. She maintained her position, pretending she was still tied and helpless. What to do now? She was a novice at this. She had only ever used spells spun by Hexebart or used leftover magic in her fingers. Where to start in trying to overcome Mandy? He had the speed and strength of a beast, and a boiling vat of poison and acid stood only a few feet away.

While she was deliberating, the sound of locks popping echoed up the stairs. Mandy's eyebrows drew down and his head turned in that direction. In the dark, Hexebart appeared at the top of the stairs, with Jude, Gerda, and Christine hovering behind her.

"What's this, Hexebart?" Mandy said.

"Immanuel, you have been very wicked."

Instinctively, Mayfridh drew away from the statue and curled up in a corner of the room. Mandy didn't see her move; he was preoccupied with Hexebart.

"Wicked?" he said. "What do you call breaking into my private space just as I'm about to kill . . ." He turned to where he'd left Mayfridh, saw she wasn't there, and turned back to Hexebart, understanding coloring his gaze.

For a few long seconds Mandy and Hexebart locked eyes across the dimly lit room. Mayfridh held her breath, wondering which of them would pounce first. In the candlelight, she saw Mandy's shoulders and back tense. She was about to call out, but Hexebart's left hand shot up, releasing a bright spell from her fingers. It was too far off target. Its trajectory was nowhere near Mandy, and Mayfridh wondered how Hexebart could have aimed so poorly.

Then the spell landed on the Bone Wife. The gleaming sculpture erupted with bright light and Mandy's eyes bulged with horror.

"What have you done? What have you done?"

The light blazed once and then sucked into the bones. The sculpture's feet began to twitch.

"She wants to dance with you, Immanuel," Hexebart said.

Mandy approached the sculpture with frantic hands reaching for her curves. "What have you done to her?"

The twitching turned into shuddering. The left leg went up, then down. The right leg went up, then down. The left leg kicked, the right leg kicked. Mandy backed away.

"Come, Immanuel, dance with your beautiful wife," Hexebart said, cackling heartily.

The Bone Wife jumped—once, twice—then began to spin, dance, kick, jump, more and more frantically, advancing on Mandy.

"Stop it!" he shouted. "Stop it! I command you to stop it!"

This only made Hexebart laugh louder. Mandy turned and stalked toward her. Christine, Jude, and Gerda scurried out from behind the witch and took refuge in the corners. Hexebart was doubled over with laughter and hadn't seen Mandy's sudden approach.

"Hexebart!" Mayfridh shouted, scrambling to her feet. "Look out!"

The Bone Wife's feet clattered on the floor, spinning madly. Hexebart looked up in time to see Mandy's hands closing in on her. She tried to duck sideways; Mandy hunted her, the Bone Wife trailing them.

"Ha, ha, this way, this way!" Hexebart cried with glee.

Mayfridh realized in horror that she was leading Mandy toward the vat. "Be careful," she called.

Hexebart paused; Mandy stopped in front of her, his shoulders tensed to pounce.

"Dance, dolly, dance!" Hexebart cried.

The Bone Wife jumped and spun at Hexebart's words, then curled her left leg, and released it in a devastatingly powerful kick. It thudded into Mandy's fleshy behind, knocking him sideways and up, into the side of the vat. He turned, enraged. Kick, kick. The Bone Wife's feet contacted with his jaw, knocking him over, balancing him on the edge of the vat. A look of horror crossed his face and his arms flailed out frantically. Kick, kick. This time she got him in the chest, knocking breath from his lungs. He began to overbalance, to fall backward. He screamed once, his hand shot out and caught Hexebart by the neck.

"No," Mayfridh shrieked, running toward them.

Hexebart had the royal magic. Mayfridh had to get her home safely. "No. Hexebart!"

Splash! They both disappeared into the vat.

"No!" Mayfridh shrieked again, narrowly avoiding the wash of hot toxins. She could see nothing in the semidark but the boiling surface of the water. The Bone Wife still clattered and danced behind her, its frantic pace intensifying.

Suddenly, a hand thrust up out of the fluid. Hexebart's gnarled fingers, half eaten by the acid bath, reached out to her. Mayfridh braced herself against the vat and grabbed the witch's hand. A sweet rush of feeling began to flow from Hexebart's fingers to Mayfridh's own. The royal magic, Liesebet's magic, at last being passed to her. Hexebart knew there was little time and was pumping out the magic too fast. Mayfridh felt her veins might explode as the weight and pressure began to intensify, to crowd her organs and her mind. The responsibility was overwhelming. A groaning began in her ears; her own voice. Then she realized the hand she was holding was no longer attached to a body, that Hexebart was gone and the magic was transferred. A loud bang sounded behind her. Something sharp hit her in the back of the head, but she barely felt it. The devastating weight of the magic was already pulling her down. She dropped Hexebart's hand and collapsed, the floor slamming into her body.

❧

Christine barely had time to register what Mayfridh was doing—she seemed dangerously close to the vat and was clearly losing consciousness—when the mad clatter of the Bone Wife's feet reached a crescendo and she began to shake into pieces. First one foot flew off, then the other. Chips of bone missiled through the air, and a violent shuddering signaled her imminent detonation. From across the room she heard Jude call, "Get down!" Christine covered her head with her arms and skidded to the floor, cowering against the wall as the sculpture blew into fragments, sending bone shards in all directions.

A quiet descended, and Christine realized she was sitting on something sharp. She supposed it to be a chip of the sculpture. She pulled it out from underneath her and held it in front of the flashlight beam.

Not a chip of bone, a ring. Her engagement ring. Mandy must have cast it in the corner when he'd brought her hand here. She gazed at it in the beam of the flashlight, then remembered Mayfridh near the vat and looked up to see what had become of her.

Mayfridh lay on the floor, breathing shallowly, but conscious, her eyes open. Gazing into Jude's eyes. He crouched over her, smoothing her hair away from her face.

Christine felt her bottom jaw tremble. She clutched the ring so hard it cut into her palm. A sob stabbed at her throat. Her hair spilled over her fingers as her head dropped into her hands, and she cried quietly in her corner, alone.

❧

The rain was easing outside as Christine, Mayfridh, Jude, Gerda, and Pete waited in Jude's apartment for the lights to come back on. Gerda hunched over Mandy's memoir by candlelight, flicking through the last pages, while Mayfridh explained to Jude and Pete how Hexebart had finally given back the royal magic. Christine sat, numb, on the sofa. With a weary sigh, Mayfridh sat next to her. An uneasy stiffness filled the space between their bodies. There was a hum and the lights blazed back to life. A few moments later, Fabiyan bounded up the stairs and into the apartment.

"I will go upstairs in little while and switch off boiler," he said, closing the door behind him.

"No hurry," Gerda said. "We'd better make sure Mandy's good and dead." She held up the notebook. "I don't know if they'll ever find his remains, but I think we're safe if they do."

"Why's that?" Pete asked.

"The last line he wrote: '*Farewell. I go to a better place.*' It sounds like a suicide line. That, along with all the ramble about faeries, should well and truly divert suspicion away from a cabal of witless artists like us." She placed the book carefully on the coffee table. "I feel completely over-whelmed."

"Is there any other way to feel after you've watched a witch and a faery hunter boiled alive in a vat?" Pete said. "Mayfridh, will your *believe* spell wear off and make us all go nuts?"

"I don't think so. I think once you've believed, you'll always believe."

"Are you going to go home?" Jude asked Gerda.

"To Stockholm? Indeed. As soon as I can get a flight. What about the rest of you?"

"I have already booked train for day after tomorrow," Fabiyan said.

"I'm going to hang out at the airport until they find me a seat," Pete said. "Jude? You and Christine missed your flight on Sunday, will you still . . ."

Jude shrugged. "I'm not hanging around here."

They all turned to Mayfridh.

"And you, Mayfridh?" Christine asked. "When do you have to leave?"

"Tomorrow," she said. "I'm leaving tomorrow. I want to fetch my mother from the hotel and take her back to her place tonight, get her settled in, and say good-bye. And then . . ."

"You'll forget all this, won't you?" Jude asked.

Mayfridh nodded.

"I wish I could forget," he said wistfully.

Mayfridh looked as though she were about to say something, then thought better of it. "I'd better go," she said. "I don't have much time."

"Stop by tomorrow on your way to the passage," Pete said. "Say good-bye properly."

She smiled tightly. "I'll see."

As she left, Gerda yawned widely and picked up the memoir again. "Come on, Fabiyan. Let's go turn off the vat and put this notebook back."

"I'll come," said Pete.

"Do you need any help?" Jude asked.

"No, you two stay here and . . ." Gerda shrugged, didn't finish the sentence.

Within minutes they had all left, the apartment door had closed, and Christine was alone with Jude. She felt trapped inside herself with anger and pain. Jude slid onto the sofa next to her. It seemed he didn't know what to say either.

Finally, she turned to him. "Do you still intend to marry me?"

He looked startled. "Yes. Of course." But he didn't sound sure, not anymore.

"Okay, then. Before we get married, is there anything you want to tell me?"

"What do you mean?"

"Is there something you need to get off your chest? Something you haven't told me?"

His dark eyes narrowed suspiciously. "Why do you think that? Has somebody said something to you?"

"Jude, just tell me. If there is something you've concealed from me, tell me now. I want to hear it from your lips. I don't know what I can forgive if it goes too long unspoken."

His eyebrows curved up and a look of guilty pain crossed his face. "Oh, Christine. I'm so sorry. I'm so sorry, it just happened."

Seeing him in distress softened the edge of the anger. "Didn't you know? Didn't you know I'd understand an accident?" she said.

"I fell in love with her, Christine," he said. "And when you weren't here and she was, I just—"

Christine bolted upright, startled. "What? What are you talking about?"

Jude's face took on a bewildered expression. "What are you talking about?"

"You and Mayfridh . . ." she sputtered. "You . . ."

He was nodding. "Yes. Isn't that what Gerda told you?"

"Gerda didn't tell me anything." So not only had Jude betrayed her and lied to her, Mayfridh had too. "Did this happen before I sacrificed my hand to help her, or after?"

"Before," Jude said softly. "And after. But don't be angry with her, be angry with me. I've let you down, I've—"

"Oh, shut up, Jude. Just shut up." She stood, fished the engagement ring out of her pocket and handed it to him. "I'm sick of your self-pity. I'm sick of your egotistical nobility."

"Christine, don't do this. We'll get over it. I want to marry you. Mayfridh's gone, I belong with you."

"The worst thing, Jude, is that you don't even know why I'm angry."

"You're angry because—"

"Don't!" she shrieked. "Don't even pretend for a moment to understand me. I *know* what you did, Jude. I *know.* So you slept with Mayfridh? What's one small betrayal like that? Really?"

Jude shook his head. "Christine, I don't follow."

Seconds ticked past. Christine felt her heart thumping

in her throat, her face felt hot. Despair and resentment choked her.

"I could have forgiven you for killing them," she said at last. "I can never forgive you for making me your charity project. You took my dignity from me."

The blood drained from his face. His mouth moved but no sound came out.

She stalked toward the door.

"Where are you going?" he squeaked.

"I need to talk to Mayfridh."

"Christine—"

She turned, held out her silver hand in a "stop" gesture. "Don't come near, don't follow me. I can look after myself."

She slammed the door behind her and raced down the stairs. The pain in her back pulled her up on the front step. Rain cooled the hot blood flushing her face as she walked down to Friedrichstrasse to find a taxi.

❦

Diana sighed as Mayfridh helped her through the front door of the house at Zehlendorf.

"I honestly thought I might never be coming back," she said.

Mayfridh slid Diana's suitcase inside and closed the door behind her. "We need to talk about that, Mum."

"Have you reconsidered? Can you take me with you?"

Mayfridh felt the familiar rush of guilt. "I still don't know."

"It's Jude, isn't it?"

"I've asked him to come with me. He's said no, but—"

"But you hope he'll change his mind."

"Tonight, he said something that gave me hope." *I wish I could forget.* Until he had spoken those words, Mayfridh had accepted that she had to let him go and take Diana with her back to Ewigkreis. Now the decision was not so clear. "It's not that I don't love you, Mum. It's not even that I don't love you as much as Jude. But I have to think about my kingdom. About heirs, about the future." This was only partially true, but she saw no reason to bruise Diana with the whole truth: that everyone ran second to Jude in her heart. Deep down, she hoped at any moment to hear the phone ring, for him to contact her to tell her he'd changed his mind.

Diana shook her head sadly. "I'm tired. I was having such a nice dream when you came by and woke me." She smiled. "I'm glad you're back safely. Will you be leaving in the morning?"

"Yes."

"I'll get a good night's sleep."

"Me too." Her body was heavy with magic, with the responsibility that it brought. It terrified her to return to Ewigkreis with it, to be the sole guardian of such a burden. All the years that Hexebart had hoarded it, Mayfridh had been left to cultivate a carefree heart. Now the thought of the empty castle, the quiet fields, became nightmarish: a hollow place to fill with years of duties and obligations. Her mother's house here in Zehlendorf was so warm, so loving and free by comparison. "I'll miss you so much."

"Shh, now. Save all that for the morning," Diana said, extending a gentle finger to Mayfridh's lips.

A knock on the door made them both jump.

"Don't answer," Diana whispered urgently.

"It's all right, Mum. Hexebart is gone. Mandy is gone." It was Jude, it had to be Jude.

Diana shrank back in the hallway as Mayfridh went to the door and opened it.

"Christine?"

"I need to talk to you." Her hair and clothes were wet, and she wore an expression of rancor and resolve.

Mayfridh turned. "Go on, Mum. Go up to bed. I'll wake you in the morning."

Diana tried a smile and headed upstairs, still slow on her bandaged feet. Mayfridh held the door open for Christine. "Come in, then."

"No. You come out. I want to walk."

"It's cold and it's wet."

"It matches my mood," Christine said. "Come on."

Mayfridh shrugged and stepped out of the warm pool of yellow light into the dark, drizzly outside. They walked in silence down the path and up the empty, cobbled street. Rain caught in her hair and pasted her clothes to her skin.

"Christine?" Mayfridh said, after five minutes had passed and Christine still hadn't said anything.

"Over there," Christine said, pointing to a little stone church.

"All right." Mayfridh followed her across the road and through the iron gates. Christine ascended the steps and sat down on the stoop, just behind the dripping eaves. Mayfridh joined her. A gust of wind shook raindrops from nearby branches. A car sped past, a brief light in the darkness.

"Okay, listen to me," Christine said, turning to Mayfridh with an urgent gaze. "I know everything, okay? I know everything about Jude, and about you."

Mayfridh hung her head. "I'm so sorry."

"Do you love him?"

Mayfridh started to mumble something about passing attractions and the heat of the moment, then decided that Christine deserved better. She deserved for someone to tell her the brutal truth. She lifted her head to meet Christine's gaze. "Christine, I love him with a passion so primal that I can't give words to it."

"He's in love with you," Christine said. "He told me so."

"Oh."

"I love him too, Mayfridh. I love . . . I love his eyes, and his hands and how sometimes they're dirty with paint." Christine's eyes filled with tears. She blinked them back. "But he doesn't love me." Her voice trailed to a whisper.

"I think he does, but in a different way from—"

"He doesn't love me," Christine said forcefully. "He feels sorry for me, he feels *responsible* for me. He feels no passion or desire for me."

Mayfridh didn't answer. They sat on the church step for a long time while the drizzle fell around them, their shoulders huddled against each other for warmth.

At length, Christine drew a deep breath. "Mayfridh, I came to ask you to take me with you."

Mayfridh pressed her hands to her eyes. "Oh, no."

"Is it a possibility? I could be without pain. I could forget Jude and all he's done to me."

Mayfridh could have laughed. She had two people in the queue for passage back to Ewigkreis, neither of them the one she wanted to take. Then a new thought—or perhaps a thought she had entertained before and dismissed—began to circle around her mind. A way for her to be with Jude, with her mother. A way for Christine to be released from her grief and pain. A way for Mayfridh to be relieved of the terrifying burden of her sovereignty. The cost was dear, very dear. But all around her people had sacrificed themselves for her life and her happiness. A restitution was due.

"Mayfridh?" Christine was asking. "Is it possible?"

Mayfridh took Christine's good hand in her own. "Christine, how would you like to be the queen?"

Mayfridh paced up and down her white chamber, window to door, waiting for Eisengrimm's return. Ordinarily, she would be thrilled to be excluded from a meeting of officials, but today she wished she could be there as they discussed her future. She stopped at the window; the birch was almost naked. How could she stand it if they said no? How could she stay in this bare, empty place forever? How could she forget about Jude?

Pace, pace.

Her bag was already packed in the event that they agreed. Just a few souvenirs of Ewigkreis. A miniature of herself and Eisengrimm, two dresses she couldn't bear to leave behind, a carved puppet she had loved as a child. Apart from that, she was ready to go, ready to start a new life in the Real World as Jude's wife. Christine and Jude were waiting on the other side of the passage for the verdict. Christine by now had organized money and a place for them to live in New York. New York! It sounded like the most heavenly place in the universe. But if her plans fell through, if the village had voted against her choice of replacement . . . *Just keep pacing. Eisengrimm will be here soon.*

Right on cue, the door swung inward and Eisengrimm slunk in. As usual, his face didn't give much away, but his shoulders were slumped forward, a defeated gesture.

"Oh, no," she said. "They said no, didn't they?"

Eisengrimm shook his head. "Mayfridh, they said yes. Christine is well liked by all who have met her on her visits."

"Yes? They said yes?" She felt her heart lift. "Then why do you look so . . . sad?"

He approached, leaned his head against her hip. "Because you're leaving, dear girl. I'm sad because you're leaving."

Tears pricked her eyes. "Don't, Eisengrimm. Don't you make me cry."

"Come, let's walk down to the passage. Have you got everything you need?"

She lifted her bag off the bed and took a last look around her white chamber. "I think so, yes."

He led her to the autumn forest in silence. Once they arrived at the passage, she felt a sudden nausea grip her. This would be the last time she ever saw Eisengrimm. Even though Jude and her new life in the Real World waited on the other side, she barely had the courage to take one step toward the passage.

"I'm glad that you have found happiness, Little May," he said. His voice strained around the words "and I'm glad that Christine will be our new queen."

"You could have been king, you know. If you weren't so reluctant."

"A wolf king? Perhaps I could have ruled if I had a queen by my side. But not alone."

Mayfridh laughed. "Well, if you weren't a wolf I'm sure I could have married you," she said lightly, "but we are what we are and must act in faith with it."

His head hung forward, and she knelt to embrace him.

"Good-bye, old friend," she said.

"Good-bye, Little May."

She glanced at the passage. "I want to go, but leaving you feels like—"

"Feels like losing a piece of my heart." His voice cracked. Mayfridh was taken aback by the uncharacteristic display of emotion.

"Yes."

"I won't forget you," Eisengrimm said, collecting himself.

"I'll never forget you either. We won't forget each other. The forgetfulness is Christine's balm, not ours. Be as good to her as you've been to me."

"I will."

She stood and deliberately turned away from him. "Good-bye," she said softly. He didn't say another word as she stepped through into the Real World.

It was early evening in the Tiergarten. Christine's face was pale and fearful in the dark. Jude smoked and paced. Mayfridh stepped out and they both looked up.

"Well?" Christine asked.

"It's been approved. They're waiting for you."

This news didn't appear to bring Christine any relief, and Mayfridh gave her shoulder a squeeze. "You are sure you still want this?"

"Of course."

Jude stood uncomfortably nearby, not sure whether to embrace his old lover or his new lover.

"Then," Mayfridh said, "I declare you queen."

"Queen Starlight." Christine laughed.

"Hold perfectly still while I transfer the royal magic to you." Mayfridh enclosed Christine in a warm hug, felt her skinny body tremble. The magic began to pass between them. In every second Mayfridh felt lighter, more carefree, the weight lifting and lifting, the muscles around her heart loosening and her lungs filling to their full depth. Finally, the transfer completed, she stood back.

And saw that Christine was beautiful.

Nothing about her face or hair had changed. She still had the same eyes, nose, cheeks. Something from within illuminated them, made her seem intense and noble. Mayfridh glanced at Jude. He had noticed too. His bewildered eyes were fixed on Christine's face. Anxiety pulled in Mayfridh's stomach: now she had relinquished her role as queen of the faeries to become an ordinary human, would she lose as much beauty as Christine had just gained?

Mayfridh took her place at Jude's side.

"It's time to go," she told Christine.

"Gladly," Christine said with a wry smile. She turned to

Jude. "I won't remember you. Good-bye." It was said kindly, with relief rather than bitterness.

"Uh . . . good-bye," he said.

"I'll remember you, won't I?" she said to Mayfridh.

"Yes. You'll remember everything that happened in Ewigkreis, though some of it may not make sense once the Real World memories are gone. But you won't remember . . . the bad things about me. The things that happened here."

"Good." She glanced all around her. "Good."

"Eisengrimm will take care of you," Mayfridh said. "Now you must go. They're waiting for you. They'll want to perform the coronation before the season turns."

Christine's hands trembled as she pushed her hair out of her eyes. "Okay, then."

Mayfridh took her friend's fingers in her own. "Long may you live, Queen Starlight."

Christine squeezed back. "Yeah," she said, turning away now, moving toward the passage. "Long may I live."

Mayfridh glanced at Jude. Uncertainty all over his face. She took his hand in hers, realized she was clutching it too desperately.

Christine stepped through the passage and disappeared.

❧

The coronation had been organized in less than a day. Newly minted Queen Starlight, Christine sat at the head of the table in the Autumn Castle, a huge and noisy banquet whirling around her. Outside the great hall, a wicked wind stalked the castle grounds, the forests, and the village. Huge fires in all the grates kept its cold fingers at bay. Eisengrimm sat close by, keeping watch on her.

"How are you feeling, Christine?" he asked.

"You keep asking me that," Christine laughed.

"You look pale."

"I'm always pale."

"You look frightened."

She sighed. "I'm often frightened."

"Don't worry. At any time we could all wake up at the Winter Castle, and you'll forget your fears. And you have me to guide you through the duties and obligations."

"I look forward to it." She rubbed his ears and glanced around the hall. Many of the villagers had been invited, and a few of them gazed at her fondly, raising their glasses and shouting blessings as she caught their eyes. Klarlied, the new royal witch, gave her a warm smile from across the room. A comforting welcome. A new life of simple pleasures and people, of learning her magic with Klarlied and becoming a good ruler with Eisengrimm, of peaceful spaces and freedom from pain. Why the misgivings?

"Everyone feels a little anxious at the turn of the seasons," Eisengrimm said, as though reading her mind.

She leaned her head on his shoulder. "I have no right to be melancholy. You've lost your love forever."

"Perhaps that's true. But perhaps it's for the best. While she was here, I had no chance of ever recovering from that love. Now she's gone . . ."

"She won't be there to fall in love with every morning. I understand." Christine thought about Jude, and a big bubble of panic rose up. To forget him forever? Awful, impossible. She'd made the wrong decision, she had to go back.

Deep breaths. Let him go. Let it all go. He wasn't the Jude she thought she knew, he was somebody else, somebody with lies in his heart and vanity on his brow.

A noisy commotion from near the door. A royal guard raced in, excitement and panic coloring his cheeks. "The last leaf, the last leaf!" he cried. "There's only one left."

Voices, gasps, cheers all around her. Christine's heart picked up its rhythm.

Eisengrimm leapt from his chair. "Queen Starlight? It's customary for the queen to watch the last leaf fall. Would you like me to accompany you?"

"I . . . yes. Yes, I don't want to be alone."

He led her along the corridor away from the banquet, and up the stairs to the white chamber. He pushed open the window with his nose and stood, paws on the sill, overlooking the giant birch. Christine joined him, clutched her fingers around his foreleg.

"Gentle now," he admonished with a smile in his voice. "I'm still recovering from an injury."

She searched the tree with her eyes, found the last leaf. Slanted evening sunlight stained the branches, the wind howled. The leaf hung as if by a thread. It reminded her of a loose tooth she'd had as a child. It had hung there day after day, spinning under the impetus of her tongue or her curious fingers, but not coming free. Then her father, under pretense of inspecting it, had suddenly and violently pulled it out. She had started to cry, but her father's warm laughter at her startled expression had made her laugh too. Before long they had been rolling on the sofa in fits of laughter as he clutched the tiny tooth and she explored the smooth gap with her tongue.

With a rush of fear and longing, Christine realized what it meant to forget. Everything.

She moved closer to Eisengrimm, her arm curling around his ribs. "I wish you could hold me," she whispered. "I'm so afraid."

"The seasons *will* change, Christine. Nothing can stop them."

A violent gust of wind tore up from the valley. The leaf spun, struggled, broke free.

And . . .

at last . . .

fell . . .

The Tale of Silverhand Starlight

❧❦❧

I n days of old, there was a great and beautiful queen named Silverhand Starlight. One of her hands was made of silver, but it moved as gracefully as any person's real hand. Queen Starlight's dearest companion and counselor was a wolf named Eisengrimm. They spent all of their waking hours together, working by day on making her kingdom bountiful and happy, and spending their evenings sharing memories and thoughts, until they were so close they were almost of one heart and one mind.

Some years after her rule began, the people of Queen Starlight's realm began to ask if she would ever marry and give them a king and an heir. Now, this troubled Queen Starlight greatly, as she had not yet met any man for whom she felt a great love. Her dearest love and affection were reserved for Counselor Eisengrimm, but he was a wolf and a marriage between them was forbidden.

"If I could but marry you, Eisengrimm," she said, "we could be good companions for each other. I trust your judgment and I love you dearly."

"Queen Starlight," he said, "you know that there is a way you could marry me, but it's dangerous and difficult and I advise against it."

Now, Eisengrimm hadn't always been a wolf and Queen Starlight knew this. He was once a man, but had been put under an enchantment by a sorceress named Zosia. The only way for him to be restored to his true form was for a true love to seek out Zosia and demand to know his real name, which she had stolen from him. But Zosia lived many, many miles from Queen Starlight's castle, and was known to be an evil sorceress who stole souls and hoarded treasure.

Queen Starlight tossed and turned every night for a month and a day as she thought about Eisengrimm and Zosia. Finally, she decided that she loved Eisengrimm truly, and that he surely felt the same way. He was the only king she would ever desire to have by her side, and so the journey was worth the risk. The next morning, without telling a soul, she set out alone.

Now, many surprising things befell Queen Starlight on her journey to Zosia's woods, so that by the time she arrived, she looked little like a queen. Her hair was dirty, her clothes were torn, and she had become thin from lack of food. What she still possessed were her fine silk gloves that she wore to protect her beautiful silver hand, à jewel on a gold chain, and a ring made of diamonds.

Zosia's woods were dark and treacherous, and as night fell Queen Starlight thought she would be safer sleeping in the hollow of a tree until daylight came again. She nestled herself into the hollow, then heard a loud voice saying, "Ouch!"

"Who's there?" she asked.

An owl wriggled out from behind her. "I sleep in this tree," he said. "There's no room for you."

Queen Starlight quickly explained who she was and what she was here for.

"Well, you can't sleep here," the owl said, "but I can give

you some advice. Zosia is greedy for jewelry for her hoard. Maybe that can be of help to you."

Queen Starlight bade farewell to the owl and went on her way. She found a bed of lichen and decided to settle there for the night.

"Ouch!"

"Who's there?" she asked.

A lizard wriggled out from under her. "I sleep under this bed of lichen," he said. "There's no room for you."

Queen Starlight quickly explained who she was and what she was here for.

"Well, you can't sleep here," the lizard said, "but I can give you some advice. Zosia collects souls for her sorcery. Maybe that can be of help to you."

Queen Starlight bade farewell to the lizard and went on her way. She found a pond of warm mud and decided to settle there for the night.

"Ouch!"

"Who's there?" she asked.

A frog hopped out. "I sleep in this pond of warm mud," he said. "There's no room for you."

Queen Starlight quickly explained who she was and what she was here for.

"Well, you can't sleep here," the frog said, "but I can give you some advice. Zosia loves to win at games and is fiercely competitive. Maybe that can be of help to you."

Queen Starlight bade farewell to the frog and went on her way. By this time it was nearly morning, so she decided not to sleep but to find Zosia's cottage. She mused over everything the woodland animals had told her, and decided on a plan.

Zosia's cottage had tiny windows, and nestled among a copse of black trees. As the sun rose, Queen Starlight knocked on the door.

"Who is it?" Zosia asked.

"A traveler," Queen Starlight replied.

Zosia opened the door and peered out. "What do you want, traveler?"

"I want to play a game with you."

"A game? What do I get if I win?"

"I have jewels."

"How many jewels?"

"Two."

"And when you run out of jewels? For I shall surely win."

"When I run out of jewels, I have my soul to play for."

"Your soul? Well, that sounds like good enough stakes for me. Come in and let's play." Zosia opened the door wide. She pulled up two chairs by the hearth and Queen Starlight sat down.

"Now, Zosia," Queen Starlight said, "if I should win the game, I want only one thing."

"What is it?"

"A word."

"Ha! Is that all? Well, I know you won't win because I always win at games. But a word is nothing to me, and I'll happily give it to you if you should beat me." Zosia sat down and nodded. "Let us begin then."

Queen Starlight held out the jewel on the gold chain. "Here is the first prize," she said, "and you may win it if you can tell me how many eyes I have."

"Why, that's easy," said Zosia. "You have two eyes."

Queen Starlight nodded and handed over the jewel. "You are right. How clever you are!"

Zosia grabbed at the jewel greedily. "Let us play again."

Queen Starlight held out the ring made of diamonds. "Here is the next prize," she said, "and you may win it if you can tell me how many ears I have."

"Why, that's easy," said Zosia. "You have two ears."

"Once again you are right," Queen Starlight said, handing over the ring. "Zosia, you are too clever for me. I can't play anymore."

"No, no, you promised a game."

"I've no more jewels."

"You said that once you ran out of jewels you'd play for your soul."

"I may need it, and you are sure to win. I can't play anymore."

"No, no, no! You made a promise and you have to stick to it." Zosia was growing angry now, her face dark with rage, her hair sticking up. "You are bound by the rules of the game."

"Very well," said Queen Starlight. "The next prize is my soul. And you may win it if you can tell me how many fingers I have." She held up her hands in their fine silk gloves.

"Why, that's easy," said Zosia. "You have ten fingers."

Queen Starlight shook her head. "Oh, no. No, Zosia, you are wrong." She pulled off her gloves to reveal one hand of flesh and blood, and one made of silver. "For I only have five fingers. The others are jewels made of silver."

Zosia looked shocked. "It can't be. I've never lost a game."

"And now," Queen Starlight said, "I want my prize. I want the word I came here to collect."

"Which word do you want?"

"I am Eisengrimm's true love, and I want to know his real name so that I may reverse the enchantment you cast on him many years past."

Zosia ground her teeth and stamped. "No, no, no!" she cried.

"You must," Queen Starlight said, "for you are bound by the rules of the game as much as I am."

Zosia raged and spat, but finally she had to admit she had lost the game and she declared Eisengrimm's true name out loud. Queen Starlight took it with her all the way back to her own realm.

Now, many months had passed since she had set on her way, and though Eisengrimm had done his best to rule in the meantime, her subjects were overjoyed to see her, ragged and dirty as she had become, and cheered as she passed through the village on the way to her castle.

"I shall marry very soon," she declared, waving to them. "I promise you I shall marry very soon."

Eisengrimm heard her saying this and his heart felt heavy. Queen Starlight, he thought, must have met a fine prince on her travels. He could expect little more than to remain a counselor, because a wolf and a queen could never marry.

"I am glad you are returned, Queen Starlight," he said, greeting her at the door to her chamber. "You have been gone a long time."

"Do you know where I went?" she asked.

"To find a suitable husband, I suppose."

"That's right. And I have found him. He is loyal and patient, kind and brave."

"He will be a lucky man to be your king. May I ask, Queen Starlight, what is his name?"

And then Queen Starlight said Eisengrimm's true name out loud. In a second, his wolfish snout and ears shrank back and his fur fell out, and he stood in front of her, transformed at last into his true self. When Queen Starlight saw how handsome and noble he was, she fell in love with him even more deeply than before.

They were married the next day, and lived happily and contentedly for a long time thereafter.

ACKNOWLEDGMENTS

As always, there are many people to thank:

My agent and beloved friend Selwa Anthony.

Stephanie Smith, Karen-Maree Griffiths, and Vanessa Hobbs.

Kate Forsyth, for her wonderful poetry.

My informal support group of writers and thinkers, especially Kate Morton, Louise Cusack, Mary-Rose MacColl, Axel Bruns, Drew Whitehead, the QUT girls, and the sf-sassies.

Luka, for sleeping through the night so early.

My cats, who can't read this and don't care.

Mirko. Did you like it?

ABOUT THE AUTHOR

KIM WILKINS was born in London and grew up on the sunny east coast of Australia. She has degrees in literature and creative writing, and has won the Australian Aurealis Award for fiction four times. She writes for both adults and children, and her books have been published all over the world. Kim is interested in mythology and history, in story-telling and society. She lives in Brisbane with her opera singer partner and her toddler son. You can visit her web site at www.kimwilkins.com.

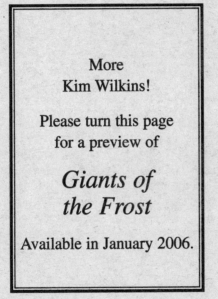

More
Kim Wilkins!

Please turn this page
for a preview of

*Giants of
the Frost*

Available in January 2006.

CHAPTER ONE

[MIDGARD]

This is my story and it's a love story. Mad, really, as I'm a woman who at the slightest provocation has always cursed lovers for fools. I remember one evening, drunk out of my skull after splitting up with Adam, declaring loudly to all assembled at Embankment station that "Victoria Scott does not believe in love." And yet, not long after this declaration, not long after the messiest broken engagement in the history of messy broken engagements, this story commences.

This is my story. It's a love story, and it goes like this.

I found myself on the supply boat *Jonsok* out of Ålesund, heading for Othinsey, an island at zero degrees forty minutes east, sixty-three degrees ten minutes north, or about two-hundred nautical miles off the Norwegian coast. I was sick, sick, sick. The crew kept telling me to get up on deck for fresh air, but the fresh air was awash with rain and salt spray. Instead, I lay down, feeling nauseous, on a threadbare sofa in the aft cabin, listening to the hissing of a radio which baffled my every attempt to turn it off.

The ten-hour journey was made worse by the deep pit of misgivings that I mined while I should have been sleeping. Had I done the right thing breaking up with Adam? Should I have accepted so readily this traineeship at an isolated meteorological research station? Was it good sense to continue with my doctorate when academia had long since become dreary and stale for me? My mother had squawked a horrified "No!" on each count. But my mother, bless her heart, was still waiting on the big lottery win she insisted would solve all our problems. In the meantime, I had to try out some solutions of my own.

Eventually the waves gentled, the boat slowed, and I knew we must be entering coastal waters. I ventured up the narrow metal stairs to the cold deck for my first glimpse of Othinsey.

We cruised through a passage between two enormous cliff faces into the still waters of Hvítahofud Fjord. I saw grey water and grey rock, dark green grass and trees, and painted red buildings with white windowsills. Those buildings made up Kirkja Station. Here, at the age of twenty-seven, I was about to commence my first job which didn't involve burning my fingers on a temperamental coffee machine. I was excited and terrified all at once, and felt a strong sense of . . . destiny is probably too loaded a word. Perhaps what I felt was a strong sense of being in the right place at the right time.

A tall, neat man with a close grey beard greeted me off the boat. "Good afternoon," he said, hand extended to help me on to the jetty. "I'm Magnus Olsen, the station commander. We spoke on the phone."

"Victoria Scott," I said. "Nice to meet you." I picked up my suitcase and turned, nearly running into a young man hurrying down the jetty. Magnus steadied me with his arm around my waist.

"Sorry," the young man said, indicating the *Jonsok*. "I'm eager to have something from the boat." He was about my age, rangy and sandy-haired, and attractive in a boyish way, and he spoke in the same faintly accented English as Magnus.

Magnus presented me for inspection. "Gunnar Holm, meet Victoria Scott. Gunnar's our IT man, and he's also in charge of your induction. He'll show you around the station tomorrow."

"Remind me to tell you about the ghosts," Gunnar said with a mischievous grin, hurrying on to the boat.

I smiled politely, supposing this was some kind of frighten-the-new-girl joke and wondering why Magnus still had his hand resting in the small of my back. We approached the assembled buildings of Kirkja Station, which all sat on a concrete slab abutting a dense pine forest on two sides. The fjord curved around the other two. The impression was one of civilisation vainly making a stand against the deep waters and the ancient trees.

"Come on, Victoria. I'll introduce you to the others," Magnus said. "They're all at the mess hall having Wednesday afternoon drinks. It's one of our traditions."

I met all eight people at Kirkja that afternoon, and— sleep-deprived, bewildered—forgot their names as soon as they were spoken. I know them all now, of course, and it was Frida Blegen who made the biggest impression on me. Like me and Gunnar, she was in her twenties (everyone else was well past forty), and she had spiky hair, a swarthy complexion and eel-like lips. As Magnus stood there pointing out faces and assigning them names, I determined to try out some of my beginner's Norwegian. I said, "Hyggelig å treffe deg," which means something like "Nice to meet you." Frida snorted with laughter and I never spoke another word of Norwegian in my whole time on the island.

Finally, Magnus showed me to my cabin, one of nine laid out three-by-three behind the station. Mine was in the furthest corner to the north-east, crowded on two sides by the dark forest. I put down my suitcase at the front door.

"I assigned you this cabin as it's quieter here," Magnus

explained, extracting the key from his pocket and unlocking the door. "In light of the sleeping problem you mentioned on your employee information form."

"Oh. Thanks for that." I'd had to fill out a four-page document about myself, and had listed my chronic insomnia in the box headed "psychological disorders for which you have received treatment."

"The rec hall can get very rowdy at night." He opened the door and stood back to let me through, giving me six inches of distance from him for the first time since I'd arrived. "I'll leave you to it. You probably want to unpack and settle in."

I peered into the cabin. The words "chilly" and "dingy" sprang to mind. "Um . . . yes."

"I'll see you in the office at eight A.M. sharp. It's downstairs in the admin building." He gave me a charming smile along with the key to the cabin. "I hope you'll like it here at Kirkja. Sleep well." With a wave of his hand, he left me alone.

The cabin had clearly been designed with scientists, not artists, in mind. Four perfectly square rooms, all of precisely equal size, stood left and right off a narrow hallway. Left, kitchen; right, lounge; left, bathroom; right, bedroom. There was a pleasing regularity about it. At least I wouldn't be awake at night shaving off imaginary percentages to make it even in my head. I dropped my suitcase on the dusty gingham bedspread.

The back door stood directly in line with the front door at the end of the hall. Outside, two mouldy deckchairs sat on the slab.

Then the forest.

Spring rain fell lightly. I still wore my anorak, so I pulled up the hood and headed a little way into the trees. The smell was wonderful after the diesel and fish smells on the boat (just thinking of that brought back an echo of the nausea). I was about a hundred feet in when I realised I was counting footsteps. I stopped myself, took a breath and banished sums from my head. There was something familiar about this place and I wondered why. Had I been somewhere similar? In my head, I tracked back over places I'd visited and couldn't recall. The sense of familiarity was very deep, very strong, like a memory from childhood which won't be pinned down. Mum would know. Had we been on holiday near a forest? Given we were so poor we hardly ever left Lewisham, I couldn't imagine we had.

Two hundred and forty-eight, two hundred and forty-nine . . .

Damn it, I was still counting. I turned and made my way back to the cabin, subtracting a footstep each time from my total. I used fewer footsteps going back, probably because I was more confident about where I was going. I had eight left over.

Evening shadows crowded in and by the time I had unpacked and eaten the plastic-wrapped sandwich I had bought at Ålesund, I was exhausted: the result of four days of sleep troubled by new-life trepidation. I showered and snuggled under the tie-dyed bedspread.

It was nine o'clock. If I wanted to be at work at eight A.M., I would have to wake up at seven, so I set the alarm on my watch. But maybe I needed to rise earlier, as I had to find the galley. Why hadn't I asked Magnus what time breakfast was available? Was there food in the cupboards in the kitchen here? Would I have to make my own breakfast? I obsessed about this for a while, realised it was now eleven o'clock and if I wanted eight hours sleep I'd have to nod off *precisely then,* and of course that chased sleep away. So I calculated some more: most people really only needed seven hours sleep so I had an hour to nod off, unless I decided to get up earlier. No, I wouldn't get up earlier, the galley couldn't be hard to find. And now it was after midnight, and I was still doing sums and trying to convince myself that six hours sleep is all one really needs to feel refreshed and finally I gave up and got out of bed.

I set up my laptop on the coffee table in the lounge room and worked on writing up my thesis. Inside, the light was yellow and the bar heater warmed my toes. Outside, the forest waited, peaceful and cold in the rain; dense and dark and vaguely, vaguely familiar.

⁓

Any insomniac will tell you that they can nearly always sleep between five and seven A.M., which is a pity as this is when most alarm clocks in the world go off. I'd been sleeping for just over an hour when a knock at the door of my cabin woke me. I resisted coming up; I willed the knock to go away. But my visitor knocked again and, with a groan, I pulled myself all the way to wakefulness. Checked my watch. Five minutes to seven.

Gunnar waited on the other side of the door. "Sorry," he said, when he saw how bleary I looked. "Magnus sent me. He forgot to tell you about breakfast."

It occurred to me that both my exchanges with Gunnar had commenced with him apologising to me. "I had some trouble sleeping last night," I explained.

"Ah. Magnus told us you have insomnia."

"Not every night. Just when I'm tense. Would you like to come in?"

He slouched in, eyes averted from my blue-hippo pyjamas. "Take your time. Get dressed and I'll show you around the station this morning."

I had a quick wash, threw on a skivvy and a pinafore, and applied some mascara and some lipstick. I had a phobia about my very pale hair, skin and eyes making me look washed-out. Silly, really, as Gunnar was by far the most eligible man on the island and he had already seen me in my pyjamas after a bad night. My mother's fault: I'd been far lower maintenance if her most-uttered phrase hadn't been, "Dress up nice in case there are boys there."

We stopped for breakfast in the galley, which was at the front of the rec hall, across a narrow walkway from the admin building. Toast and tea for me; disgusting pickled fish thingies for Gunnar. I almost couldn't eat watching him wolf them down. Maryanne, the cook-cum-cleaner, was flirting shamelessly with Magnus in an outrageous Manchester accent as they smoked together in the rec hall. We said hello, and then Gunnar led me to the front of the admin building.

"Isn't Magnus married?" I said to Gunnar. "I saw a ring on his finger."

"Separated. He's on the prowl."

"Maryanne?"

"Anyone—but Maryanne is easy prey. I don't think he's really interested. I think he just likes to see the naked adoration in her eyes."

"How come your English is so good?"

"My father is English, and I lived with his family in Cambridge for two years." He indicated a large stone set into the ground. "Did you know that Kirkja is Old Norse for church?"

"No."

"This is the foundation stone for an early eleventh-century church which once stood on this site. It was discovered when the plans were being drawn up for the station. Historians excavated the area while the main building was being constructed behind it. There was a television program about it."

I indicated the three-metre-wide satellite dish mounted on the roof. "Tell me about the communications system."

Gunnar was just as happy to talk about technology as he was to talk about history. He took me around the whole station, showing me the water tank and desalination machine which sat at the back of the station next to the water, and the generator shed and hydrogen chamber on the northern fence. An instrument enclosure, full of pluviographs and anonometers and celometers and a score of other gadgets, lay between the admin building and the cabins.

We entered the admin building via the back door, through a lino-floored storeroom and into a remarkably neat office. Magnus was at his desk, as was Carsten (Danish), the registered nurse who doubled as administration manager. Up a flight of spiralling metal stairs was the control room, where we found Frida, who was a maintenance engineer, and Alex (American) and Josef (Icelandic), who were both meteorologists. The other meteorologist, Gordon (English), had been on the night shift and was wisely in bed. The room was lined on all sides by desks, littered with stained coffee cups and half-finished paperwork, computers and other electronic devices. Both Alex and Josef were glued to a computer screen, complaining about a permanent echo on the radar. Gunnar took me out on to the observation deck. Rainy mist swallowed the forest and the other side of the island.

"There are raincoats in the storeroom," Gunnar said, noting my efforts to shrink back towards shelter.

"It's all right. It's only drizzle."

He raised his arm and I caught a whiff of his musty jumper. "It pays to take a walk out east through the forest. It's very quiet and beautiful and brings you to the beach on the other side in about forty-five minutes. The beach can be really cold if the winds change; sometimes they come straight off the Arctic, but the prevailing winds are westerlies and the cliffs protect us from them. The lake is nice too, though that's where the ghosts live."

"I'm not bothered by ghosts," I said, annoyed that he was continuing with the prank.

He smiled at me. "No? You don't believe in ghosts?"

"I don't believe in anything. And I don't scare easy. Save it for the next trainee."

The door opened behind us and Magnus stepped out. "Awful weather, isn't it?" he said.

"Sure is," I replied.

"We don't make it, we just forecast it," he said. "It's eight A.M. Time to start work."

Gunnar backed away, apologetic hands in the air. "I'll leave you with Magnus. If you need anything, just let me know. I'm in the cabin directly in front of yours."

I spent the day doing little more than filling out forms. Magnus was obsessive about administration. The last form he gave me was a questionnaire about meteorological instruments . . . well, he called it a questionnaire. To me it looked like one of those multiple choice exams I'd left behind in my undergraduate years. It asked me to list the daily jobs in a weather station in their correct order.

"I don't know anything about the daily work," I said. "My degrees are in maths and geophysics. I've never used any of the instruments. I have no idea what kind of reporting relationships are set up here."

Magnus smiled his charming smile. "Go on, just fill it out. See how you go. You might surprise yourself."

I got two items out of ten right. Magnus thought this was funny. I thought it was a unique way to embarrass me. By the end of the day, I'd had enough of him and everybody else. I stopped by the galley and asked Maryanne if I could take dinner back to my cabin, and I holed up there in my pyjamas and got really, really homesick.

Someone knocked on the door around seven. I resisted the urge to shout, "Go away."

Gunnar again.

"Sorry," he said.

"Stop saying sorry every time you see me."

He held out a bottle of red wine. "I'm really sorry. I need to explain something."

"Come in." I led him into the lounge room, a faded brown and grey room where I had the bar heater on high.

He sat in one of the armchairs while I found two glasses which looked like they had been jam jars in a previous life.

"So what do you need to explain?" I asked, sipping the wine.

"I wasn't trying to make fun of you with all the talk about the ghosts."

"No?"

"No. Seriously, no. You thought I was playing a trick on you? Like an initiation?"

"That's what I thought, yes."

"I'm so sorry, Victoria. I want you to feel welcome here. Magnus is the expert on embarrassing people."

"He's very good at it. And you can call me Vicky."

Gunnar laughed. "Really, Vicky, my intention wasn't to make you feel stupid or afraid."

"I'm neither," I said, too tersely.

"I know that."

"Then why mention the ghosts?"

"I'm really interested in history. Othinsey has a fascinating history and the ghosts are part of it. It's part of the story of the island."

"Do you believe in ghosts?"

He shrugged. "Who knows?"

I pulled my legs up on to the couch and made myself comfortable. "Go on, then. Tell me."

"This island was settled by Christians in the eleventh century. They built the church. One day a boatful of new settlers arrived to find everyone on the island dead. Slaughtered. Hanged with the intestines of the calves they'd brought, or burned, or pinned to trees with spears. As there was no sign of anyone having landed or left the island by boat, the story began that they were killed by vengeful spirits, sent by the old gods."

"And nobody tried to settle it again?"

"A few attempts were made. Nothing lasted. It's a long way from the mainland and too small to be self-sufficient. Rumours persist of ghosts—strange noises, sightings down near the lake—which frighten the less rational away. The handful of scientists we have here don't care about those rumours. You don't believe in ghosts."

"I'm about the most sceptical person you'll ever meet. My mother is another story. Every week she visits a new psychic, who tells her she's going to win the lottery. She uses the same numbers every week—I know them by heart—and even though her psychic says they're the right numbers, they never come up. But . . ."

"She still goes back. I know. People need something to hope for."

"If she'd invested the psychics' fees and lottery ticket money into a mutual trust, she wouldn't be living upstairs at Mrs. Armitage's in Lewisham."

"What does your father think?"

"I don't have one. I mean, I suppose he's out there somewhere. My mum raised me alone, unless you count the three husbands who each left in under a year."

"It must have been very hard for her. No wonder she needs to believe she'll win the lottery." He refilled my glass.

"That's very generous of you." I smiled across at him, then wondered if the reason he was being so nice was because he thought he had a chance with me. I nearly groaned. A girl doesn't make the decision to move to a remote sea-bitten island lightly, and coming to Kirkja had seemed an excellent opportunity to avoid entanglements of the heart.

"Do you have a boyfriend back home?" he asked, confirming my suspicions.

"Um . . . I just broke off an engagement. It was messy."

"How messy?"

I sipped my wine: combined with extreme weariness, it was sending my brain in circles. "He got another girl pregnant." Proud of myself for not saying, "He knocked up some tart."

"That's very messy."

"Yes, so I'm going to enjoy a few years of single life. Love is highly overrated."

"Do you think so? I think it's wonderful."

"It looks good in books and movies, I'll grant you that. But in real life it's just . . ." *Never quite enough, never really there, never living up to its promise.* "Let's change the topic."

Gunnar left at nine. I liked him, it would be good to have someone my own age around. I had the distinct feeling that after the wine and the conversation I would be able to sleep, and I was right. I drifted off soon after slipping into bed. Half-sleeping, half-awake, I heard noises outside in the forest. I thought about Gunnar's ghosts and smiled. Some people will believe anything.

[ASGARD]

She had returned, and Vidar knew this before he opened his eyes. Sleep swam away and the morning cold sucked at his nose and cheeks. His senses prickled. Halldisa was nearby. *Twice-born.* Most mortals came upon the earth, spent their lives, and ceased to exist forever after. But Vidar had been made a promise: Halla would be twice-born. All he had to do was wait.

Centuries of waiting.

And then this morning.

He rose and pulled on his cloak, cracked open the door and peered out. The deep slope of Gammaldal to the northeast hid the expanse of Sjáfjord. Mist hung low in the valley and the grass was jewelled with frost. Nobody in sight. No watching eyes to report back to his father, no waiting tongues to say, "I saw Vidar drawing runes in the seeingwater." The fjord would be cold, but the thought of Halla warmed his blood.

He stripped to the waist, waded into the shallows and waited—the water icy around his ribs—for the surface to still. He crossed his hands over his chest. Not a movement now, not a breath. He feared that the excited beat of his heart would make the water pulse and jump in harmony. But soon the surface became motionless.

Vidar lifted his hand. With a graceful movement, he traced a circle in the water. Steam rose where he drew. He waited, glancing all around him for watchful eyes, then focussed and drew four runes in the circle. His breath crystallised on the morning air as he said her name: "Halldisa."

At first he could only see his own reflection, dark hair and dark eyes and the pale morning sky behind him. But then another face formed in the water and he recognised her instantly. Storm-eyed, snow-haired. Seeing her face robbed him of his breath. He drew another rune and whispered, "Where are you?"

Danger, extreme danger. His heart chilled colder than the fjord. *Odin's Island.* He glanced to the east, towards the silver roof of his father's hall which was hidden behind the miles of misty hills and wooded valleys Vidar had put between him and his family. Memories streamed through him: blood and fire and the helpless shrieks of mortal suffering. "There is no love, Vidar," his father had said. "There is only fate."

"Vidar!"

A woman's voice. His young bondmaid, Aud, had woken and found him missing. With a skilled hand he banished his seeing magic and turned to her, deliberately relaxed. "Good morning, Aud."

"What are you doing?" she asked, coming to the edge of the water.

"Catching fish."

Her smile said she didn't believe him.

He waded from the fjord, dripping and cold. "Come, Aud. You may draw me a hot bath and forget you saw me catching fish in Sjáfjord."

"I won't forget," she said, "but neither will I tell." She clearly relished being part of his secret.

He spoke no further and she walked beside him in her usual besotted silence. His mind turned the image of Halla over and over; desire warmed his veins, filled his fingers and swelled his heart. This time he would make her his.

This time he would protect her from the brutal rage of his father.